# Veils of Verdant

Judy Smith

Celeste Plumadore

ISBN: 9798991852500

Library of Congress Control Number: 2024926568

Book Cover by Kari Brownlie

To my husband and children. This book is a testament to all the moments we've shared and the dreams we continue to chase together.

# Part 1 Bonding

# 1 Attraction

Tabby picked up the final book from the library cart: *A Million Little Pieces* by James Frey. The spine bore the label "BIO FRE," prompting her to start toward the biography section. However, she paused, turned back to the desk and created a new label reading "FIC FRE." With a decisive nod, she made her way to the fiction section. Yet, just before reaching her destination, she hesitated once more, changing the label to "362.29." This time, she carefully shelved the book in the non-fiction section, specifically under mental health and substance abuse. She stepped back with satisfaction, relishing the familiar pleasure of knowing that every book was in its rightful place.

As Tabby stepped out of the library, she noticed the sun beginning to set, casting long shadows across the area. Summer was winding down, and it would soon be over.

Her gaze settled on a familiar figure lounging on a nearby bench. It was Jason, a handsome man in his twenties with tousled blond hair and striking blue eyes that sparkled with boyish charm. His collared shirt was unbuttoned and he wore a loosened tie, giving him an effortlessly relaxed appearance. He smiled as he caught her eye.

"Hey, you. Done work?" he called out, his voice friendly.

"Just finished my shift," Tabby said, smiling with amusement at their predictable routine.

"Wanna grab a drink?" Jason was already turning in the direction of their favorite local pub, a few blocks away.

Tabby simply nodded, falling into step beside him as they made their way down the street.

Fitzgerald's Pub exuded a welcoming charm with its cozy ambiance. The décor seamlessly combined rustic elements with comfort, highlighted by a sleek wooden bar that spanned one side of the room. Tables were scattered throughout the space, while booths lined the windows opposite the bar. The lighting was subdued, creating a relaxed ambiance.

Jason slid into the booth opposite Tabby, ordering beers for them both. As the server departed, he sighed. "Mmm ... this is a perfect way to end the day," he said, sensing the stress of the day melt away.

Observing Tabby, Jason realized how much he had been looking forward to seeing her. Tabby, in her late twenties, exuded a mature beauty. Her dark blond hair framed her face, and her hazel eyes, accentuated by stylish glasses, sparkled with intelligence and warmth. She was dressed in a way both practical and stylish, projecting a "girl next door" vibe that was approachable and intriguing. Her gentle confidence had a calming effect on Jason.

The server returned with their drinks. With glasses in hand, Jason raised his and declared, "Here's to the weekend!" They clinked their glasses together, and he continued, "We should plan something fun to do together, since we both have the weekend off."

"You're the fun one—you should come up with something," Tabby said.

Jason thought for a moment. "How do you feel about mini golf?"

"Ugh," Tabby said.

"Aw, what's the matter? Afraid you're gonna lose?"

"Did I say you were the fun one? I made a mistake. Competition isn't fun. I want to do something *together*."

Still grinning, Jason offered another idea. "You don't like friendly competition? Alright then. How about we go to this gallery opening I saw an ad for? I know you like art."

"That's more like it," Tabby said.

Jason smiled. "Can't say I'm surprised ... I should have known you'd prefer something a little more cultured."

"I am a sophisticated woman," Tabby declared proudly.

"Of course you are. What was I thinking, suggesting mini golf? That certainly wouldn't have been refined enough," Jason agreed.

"So, tell me about this art exhibit or whatever," Tabby prompted.

"Well, it's a new exhibition by this up-and-coming artist. From what I know, she uses a lot of unconventional materials in her work—things like feathers and twigs and stuff. I hear her sculptures are pretty cool," Jason explained, his enthusiasm clear.

"Wow. Twigs and feathers. Interesting," Tabby mused, a playful edge to her voice.

Jason took another sip of beer. "You're extra snarky today," he said.

"That's right. You bring out my special bratty side."

Jason let out a dramatic sigh. "You're insufferable."

"Okay, pay the bill and let's check out this art exhibit," Tabby said, prompting them to move on from their playful banter to the evening's main event.

Jason shook his head, reaching for his wallet. "Whatever you say, princess."

As they walked out of the pub, Jason gave Tabby's hand a gentle squeeze. They stepped into the evening air, Jason's spirits high and his heart light, ready to immerse himself in the world of art and Tabby's company.

"Let's get going. It's getting cold," Tabby said.

As they walked, Jason wrapped his arm around her shoulders, pulling her close to share his warmth. "You're cold already?" he teased.

"Aren't you?" Tabby asked, which only made him want to tease her more.

"Nah, I'm alright." Jason ran his hands back and forth across her shoulders to generate heat. "You're just a little baby when it comes to the cold."

"Just keep your arm around me then," Tabby said, nestling closer to his side.

He felt a swell of affection, and Jason tightened his arm around her, enjoying her closeness. "If you insist."

They continued their walk, rounding a corner and passing a few more dimly lit buildings. Jason's gaze swept across the familiar surroundings until he spotted something that made him smile. With a nod of recognition, he announced, "Ah, there it is."

Jason led Tabby up the steps to the gallery, a modern, minimalist space framed by large glass doors. Through them, a few patrons could be seen meandering among the artworks. The gallery's interior was sleek and understated, with each art piece tastefully arranged against the stark white walls.

Once inside, Tabby drifted past the sculptures, her gaze flitting across the artworks on the wall, until she paused in front of a painting of a sun setting over gentle waves, titled *Echoes of Serenity*. Jason, amused by her intent focus, shadowed her closely. Bending slightly, he whispered into her ear, "See anything you like?"

"This one," she answered at once, her eyes fixed.

Jason glanced at the painting, then turned his attention to Tabby. "I have to admit, it is pretty nice."

"I love seascapes," Tabby confessed, her voice growing softer.

"I should have guessed," Jason remarked, his voice warm with affection. "You always seem so calm and peaceful; it makes sense that you'd be drawn to an artwork that reflects those qualities."

"And what about you?" Tabby asked, turning to face him.

Jason pondered briefly, then said, "I'm sort of drawn to the ones that are a little more abstract. The ones that make you think about and question what you're looking at."

"That's your thing?"

"I guess it is. I like the ones that make me pause and attempt to figure out what the artist is trying to express. There's something about the ambiguity that I find fascinating."

"Maybe the artist meant for you to interpret it yourself," Tabby suggested, her gaze shifting back to the painting.

Jason nodded. "Exactly. I like the idea that the meaning is open to interpretation, that each person who looks at it can take something different away from it."

"And what does this painting mean to you?" She asked, gesturing toward another piece, titled *Veils of Verdant.*

Jason studied the painting. "To me, this painting represents the journey of life. The winding path through the forest is the journey we all take as we move through life, full of twists and turns and unexpected obstacles. The trees represent the challenges we face along the way, and the beauty of the forest is the beauty that we can find in life's journey, even amidst the struggles."

Tabby smiled at him. "So introspective."

"That's me," Jason declared. "Always pondering the deep, meaningful stuff."

Tabby gave him a playful look. "Careful, you might tarnish your happy-go-lucky reputation."

Jason shook his head dismissively. "Oh, no one could ever mistake me for a deep thinker. I'm just a carefree guy, remember?"

"I like the way you think," Tabby admitted, her eyes shining with sincerity.

Jason flashed her a grin. "Wait—so, is it my happy-go-lucky attitude or my deep and meaningful thoughts that you like?"

"I love your attitude *and* your depth," Tabby responded, her voice warm.

"Really?" Jason was touched. "You actually like my deep and meaningful thoughts? Even when I get all philosophical?"

"Mmhmm," Tabby nodded, her affirmation genuine.

"Even when I get all existential and question reality?" he asked.

"Yes, even when you barrage me with never-ending questions," Tabby said, exasperation in her tone.

"Oh, you *love* it when I barrage you with my endless questions. Admit it, you secretly enjoy our little philosophical debates."

"Of course, I do. Do you think I hang out with you for your irresistible good looks?" Tabby teased.

Jason placed a hand over his heart, feigning offense. "Wait, are you telling me you're only using me for my intellectual stimulation?"

"Yeah, sorry," Tabby played along, with a grin.

Pretending to pout, Jason said, "I'm hurt. All this time, I thought you liked me for my handsome face and charming personality."

"That's what you want people to like you for?" Tabby asked.

"Of course not. I'm just messing with you. I know you love my intellectual stimulation *and* my irresistibly good looks."

As they reached the end of the exhibit, Tabby turned to him. "Walk me home?"

"Lead the way, princess," Jason grinned, casually wrapping his arm around her shoulder.

As they stepped out of the gallery and onto the street, the cool night air wrapped around them. He kept his arm around her, experiencing the warmth of her presence beside him. "So, did you enjoy your little art outing?" he asked, his tone light, hoping to keep the mood easy and playful.

"Very much. Thank you."

He smiled, genuinely pleased. "You're welcome. I have to admit, I enjoyed myself too. Seeing you all focused on the artwork was kind of cute."

"Then you'll have to take me to another exhibit sometime," she suggested, her voice tinged with hope.

"Of course I will. I'll take you to as many art galleries as you want, as long as you keep giving me that adorable, intensely concentrated look."

"I'll do my best."

"Good—I'm counting on it. But only if you promise not to get all snarky with me," he said, enjoying their banter.

"I can't promise that," she said.

He gave an exasperated look. "Why do I put up with you?"

"Because I'm your bestie. Besties put up with anything," Tabby said, her voice full of affection as they continued their walk home under the starlit sky.

"I guess you're right. I do put up with a lot from you, don't I?"

Tabby flashed him a playful grin. "The snark comes with the sparkling personality. It's a package deal."

He considered her words. "Hmm, so you're saying I just have to take the good with the bad?"

"Think of it like a two-for-one deal," she said, her laughter light and infectious.

"A two-for-one deal, huh? Well, I suppose I can deal with your sarcasm if I get your fabulous personality along with it," he said.

"Home sweet home," Tabby announced, gesturing toward the entrance of her apartment building, one of several multifamily residences in the neighborhood. "Want to come up for a coffee?"

"Sure, I'd love to come up for a bit," he said, following her up the stairs.

Tabby unlocked the door and stepped inside, motioning to the couch. "Have a seat. I'll make the coffee."

"Thanks," he said, stepping into the cozy living room. He took a moment to scan the space, noting the personal touches that made it warm and inviting before settling onto the couch.

As Tabby busied herself in the kitchen, Jason stretched his legs on the coffee table. "Your place is nice. Very cozy," he remarked, appreciating the environment she had created.

"Make yourself at home," she called from the kitchen, her cheerful voice echoing through the room.

"Don't mind if I do," he said, took a closer look around the room. His eyes landed on a bookshelf crammed with a selection of fantasy and romance novels. "Hmm ... I take it you're a fan of romance novels?"

Tabby laughed, entering the room. "Well, to be honest, I love a good romance, but those are just some trashy novels someone gave me."

Jason shot her a sidelong glance, a look of playful skepticism. "Uh huh. 'Trashy novels.' I see. So, you're not a secret romance novel fanatic, after all?"

"If it's a classic romance like *The Thorn Birds*, then yeah, I'm all in. But those are few and far between," she admitted.

"So, you're saying you have a weakness for tragic, star-crossed love affairs?" he teased.

"Absolutely," she responded, a grin spreading across her face.

He laughed, shaking his head. "I should have guessed you had a soft spot for cheesy romantic tragedies."

"Cheesy? How dare you!" she said, handing him a mug of coffee. "Only deep, meaningful tragedies for me."

Jason took the mug. "My apologies. I wouldn't dream of implying your books are anything less than profound. I'm sure they're full of heart-wrenching moments and deep, meaningful insights."

"That's right. More respect in the future, please," she said.

He nodded. "Fair enough, fair enough. I will give your cheesy—excuse me, I mean *deep and meaningful*—stories the respect they deserve."

Tabby eyed him suspiciously, as if trying to gauge his sincerity.

"I swear," he continued, placing a hand over his heart for dramatic effect, "you have my word. I won't insult the quality of your reading material ever again."

"Thank you," she said, a satisfied smile breaking through.

Jason grinned at Tabby, who had settled into the chair beside him. "No problem," he said, his voice smooth and teasing. "I wouldn't want to incur the wrath of a romantic tragedy connoisseur."

Tabby took a sip of her coffee. Jason leaned in slightly, his expression one of genuine interest. "So, speaking of romance, have you ever been in a real, star-crossed love affair like the ones in your favorite romantic tragedies?"

"No, I've been spending most of my free time with you. When would I get the chance to meet a star-crossed lover?"

"Touché. Your time is mostly taken up by our little adventures and shenanigans. But come on, there must have been at least one romantic interest in your life."

"All the dates I've been on have been of the vanilla variety," Tabby confessed. "Not romance novel material."

Jason's grin turned teasing. "Vanilla, huh? So, you're saying your dates have all been nice and tame, never any fireworks or sparks?"

"More or less, yeah. How about you?" Tabby asked, seemingly curious about his own romantic escapades.

Jason answered nonchalantly. "I've had a few flings here and there, but nothing too serious. I'm not really the commitment type."

"Flings?" Tabby asked.

"Yeah, flings," he said. "It seems I'm attracted to fun, casual relationships rather than anything serious. What can I say? I like my freedom."

Tabby's expression turned wistful. "I'm the opposite. I want to be swept off my feet. I want the love, commitment, passion, adoration, devotion, faithfulness, chivalry. The whole deal."

"Oh really? You want the whole fairy tale romance, huh? The Prince Charming, the happily ever after, the picture-perfect love life?" Jason asked.

"That's right," Tabby affirmed, with a nod.

Jason smiled, shaking his head. "And I suppose you expect all those things from your future partner, right? Commitment, passion, devotion, chivalry, and all the rest?"

"Of course," Tabby said, her voice firm yet dreamy.

"Of course you do. You're a hopeless romantic at heart," Jason said.

Tabby grinned. "Yes. So, if you're aware of any single princes, let me know. Especially if they're cute and charming like you, but, you know, relationship material."

"You want me to play matchmaker for you?"

"Isn't that what besties do?" Tabby asked.

Jason said, "I suppose I'm obligated as your bestie to help you find your perfect prince. I can't have my best friend forever single, now, can I?"

"I'd reciprocate, of course, but I don't know any shallow bimbos."

Her laughter mingled with his, and it was good to share this light moment. "Of course not. I bet you don't know a single girl who fits that description. Not like me and my flings."

"Sorry, my girlfriends are all intellectuals, and none are easy."

Jason appreciated her loyalty to her friends. "Oh, I would never dream of insulting your friends like that. They're all sweet, intelligent, respectable ladies, unlike those hussies I'm so drawn to."

Tabby nodded, snickering.

He took a sip of his coffee, shifting gears. "So, let's get down to business. I'm your wingman now, tasked with finding you the perfect Prince Charming. We need to discuss your type, so I know what I'm looking for."

"Okay, ask your questions," Tabby said, leaning in with interest.

His grin spread wide, fueled by his enthusiasm. "Alright, first question: What are your physical preferences? Do you like tall and muscular, or do you prefer slim and artistic?"

"Cute," Tabby said simply.

He burst out laughing. "Cute? That's all you've got? Just cute? You don't care how tall he is or if he's muscular?"

"Personality is way more important," she stated.

He nodded, acknowledging her point. "Of course it is. But what about initial attraction? Don't you care if he's physically attractive, or is personality the only factor?"

"An easy smile, dazzling eyes, windswept hair, sharp dresser, and he should smell good," Tabby elaborated, her expression thoughtful.

Jason was amused by her specifics. "You've got quite the list there! So, this Prince Charming needs to be cute, with a great smile, dazzling eyes, stylish hair, dress well and smell nice. Anything else?"

"And the personality to go with it," she added.

Grinning, Jason continued, "Right, of course. How could I forget? Along with being cute and well presented, he's also got to have a stellar personality. Any particular traits?"

"He should be a gentleman, protective, loyal, kind, witty and passionate," she listed.

Jason nodded, mentally ticking off each attribute. "So, to summarize: cute, charming smile, dazzling eyes, windswept hair, well dressed, smells good and has a great personality. He needs to be protective, loyal, kind, passionate and a gentleman. Did I get everything?"

"Yes, that's about it. Know anyone like that?" she asked.

He laughed, shaking his head. "Of course I don't know anyone like that. With standards like yours, it'll be impossible to find someone who meets all those criteria. I think you're going to be alone forever, princess."

"What kind of bestie are you?" she retorted, with feigned indignation.

He grinned, unabashed. "The honest kind, apparently. Hey, I'm just trying to set realistic expectations for you here. The guy you're looking for is perfect, and he doesn't exist. You'll have to lower your standards a bit."

"No way," Tabby said, her determination clear.

He sighed dramatically. "So, you're saying your standards are non-negotiable? You'd never consider lowering them, not even a little?"

"If the right man came along, I might 'adjust' them a bit. But this gives you an idea of my type," she clarified.

"'Adjust' them a bit? I see. Well, at least you're willing to compromise a little. And this does give me an idea of your type. You want a perfect Prince Charming. Tall order."

"Tall order? C'mon. Even you have some of those qualities," she said.

"Oh really? Which ones do I have?" he said, curious and eager to engage in their lighthearted exchange.

"You smell good."

Jason pretended to be shocked. "Just sniffing me, are you?"

"Well, you've always got your arm around me. You think I can't smell you?" she asked, her tone teasing yet affectionate.

"Oh, so my manly smell has infiltrated your senses? I *have* been holding you close a lot, haven't I?"

"Don't flatter yourself. It's your musky cologne. Not your 'manly' aroma," she said.

He grinned at her, leaning back in. "Ah, so it's just my cologne you smell, then? It's not my natural, masculine fragrance that's driving you wild?"

"Yeah, so that's not a tall order, then, is it? Spritz your friend with your cologne and voilà! One box checked," she declared.

He nodded his head. "So, I should just lend out my cologne to all your future dates to make sure they pass the smell test. Is that what you're saying?"

"If you have an otherwise suitable candidate, sure, why not?" she said.

Jason grinned. "Alright, I'll add 'lend out my cologne' to the list of best friend duties. Anything else you need me to do for you while I'm at it?"

"Let's set each other up, and we'll double-date. Could you manage to be a gentleman if I set you up with one of my friends?"

The thought amused him, and a grin spread across his face. "Me? A gentleman? Well, I could certainly try, princess," he said, the words playful yet sincere. "I'll dust off my manners and treat your friend with the utmost respect. But you know me—I can't promise I won't use a bit of charm to win her over."

"You need to keep your hands off her," Tabby warned.

He leaned back with bravado. "Oh, come on. You know I can't make any promises. I have a weakness for beautiful women, and I can't help if they're attracted to me. Just admit it, you're secretly hoping I'll sweep your friend off her feet."

"No, I'm hoping *your* friend sweeps *me* off my feet. I just need you to be there in case he turns out to be a creep," she said.

"Fair enough. I'll be there as your backup, ready to defend your honor if necessary. And don't worry, I'll make sure my friend is on his best behavior. He'll be a perfect gentleman."

"Good. I've already got someone in mind. I'll call her right now," she said, reaching for her phone.

Jason grinned at her enthusiasm. "Great! I'd love to spend the evening with two beautiful ladies," he said.

"And your friend?"

Jason nodded in agreement. "Yes, of course. I'll think of someone!"

Tabby glanced at the clock. "It's only ten. Not too late. Should I ask if she's free for drinks right now?"

He checked his watch, nodding in agreement. "You're right, it's still early. Go ahead, why don't you call her and ask if she's up to join us. I won't mind tagging along."

"Call your friend too," she reminded.

"Oh, don't worry, I'm on it," Jason assured her, though his hesitation was telling him that he might be more focused on his own anticipation than making the call.

Tabby called her friend. "Hey Ruby, are you free?" She paused, listening intently. "Wanna grab a drink at Fitzgerald's Pub? I'm heading out there."

Jason listened to the conversation unfold with a surge of excitement as he heard the confirmation. "So, she's up for it? Fantastic," he said.

Tabby turned to him with a stern gaze. "You have to behave yourself," she warned.

With a charming grin, Jason raised his hands. "Don't worry, I'll be a complete gentleman. No inappropriate touching or flirting."

As they prepared to leave, Tabby grabbed her coat.

"Smart move," Jason said, but couldn't resist teasing her. "Wouldn't want you freezing your pretty little head off. Can't have my best friend catching a cold, now, can I?"

# 2 Chemistry

As they walked down the stairs to the sidewalk, Jason inquired about Tabby's friend.

"She's cute and peppy ... and sassy," Tabby said.

Jason felt a flicker of intrigue. "Oh, she's sassy? Sounds like you two get along really well then. I like a little sass."

This earned him a playful jab from Tabby. "Then why do you always complain about *my* sass?"

He chuckled, the sound echoing in the cool evening air. "Well, your sass is in a whole different league. You've got the sassiest of sass. No one can match your level."

"Let's see if you still think so after you meet Ruby," Tabby said.

"Now, tell me about *your* friend," Tabby prompted, making her curiosity clear.

Jason's face brightened. "Oh right, he's a good guy. Smart, charming, funny. He's a bit of a player, though."

Tabby sounded skeptical. "Really? A smart, charming jokester who's a bit of a player? You sure you're not describing yourself?"

"Of course not," he quickly responded, trying to sound casual.

Tabby's chuckle echoed in his ears, and he could sense her delight in his attempt to deflect.

Their playful banter continued until they reached their destination. Upon entering, Tabby hung up her coat and Jason scanned the crowd. "So, where's Ruby?" he asked.

"Here she comes," Tabby said. A young woman entered and approached them. Her platinum-blond hair bounced with each step she took, catching the light and turning heads. Her eyes, a striking shade of light blue, sparkled with mischief. She was dressed simply, but with an undeniable sense of style—a white T-shirt paired with baggy jeans and fashionable sneakers. Tabby greeted her with a warm hug.

Jason extended his hand, offering a charming smile. "Well, this must be Ruby. Pleased to meet you. I'm Jason."

Ruby shook his hand. "Ah, yes. The 'best friend.' We meet at last."

Amused, Jason grinned back. "Indeed, we finally meet. I've heard quite a bit about you from Tabby. She says you're quite the sassy one, huh?"

"Me? Heavens no. I'm an angel," Ruby played along.

"An angel, eh? Hmm, I'm not so sure I believe that. You strike me as a little devil in disguise."

Tabby playfully punched Jason in the arm, a reminder to keep the evening friendly. "Behave," she scolded.

Jason rubbed his arm. "I'm just joking! Can't a guy have a little fun?"

"Where's your friend?" Tabby asked.

"He should be here any minute, I'm sure. He can be a bit ... punctually unpredictable," Jason said.

Tabby rolled her eyes. "Charming," she said. "Grab a table. I'll order us some drinks." While Tabby headed to the bar, Jason secured a spot for them, his gaze drifting around the lively bar, absorbing the laughter and chatter.

Tabby soon returned. "Drinks will be right over," she announced. "Two beers and two margaritas."

Jason nodded, smiling as the server approached with their drinks and a basket of pub fries. "Oh, nice choice. You know how to order a proper round. I like your style."

Ruby, sipping her margarita, turned to Jason. "So, Jason, Tabby's bestie, why aren't you and Tabby dating?"

Jason took a sip of his beer before answering. "Ah, the age-old question, isn't it? Why aren't the best friend and the princess dating? It's a mystery to many, I assure you."

Ruby leaned in, intrigued. "You must have some fatal flaw, huh?"

Feigning shock, Jason laughed. "Fatal flaw? Oh, most definitely. I have a plethora of flaws. It's a wonder I can get out of bed each morning with all my shortcomings. But, honestly, dating Tabby would be like dating family! We've been through so much together—it would feel a little strange to take it to the next level." He grinned, taking another swig of his beer, ignoring Tabby's incredulous look.

"Wow, you guys must have known each other for a long time, then, huh?" Ruby asked.

Jason nodded, swirling his beer in the glass. "Yeah, a really long time. Through thick and thin, ups and downs, we've been there for each other. It's a bond that goes beyond dating, you know? We're practically siblings."

Tabby looked surprised. "Interesting tale," she remarked, her tone light but her gaze piercing. "You're quite the storyteller."

Jason laughed. "All part of my charm."

Ruby smiled. "Well, my big brother and I are like best friends, too."

Jason's grin widened, enjoying the conversation. "Ah, I see. You've got a close relationship with your brother, huh? That's awesome. I bet you two go through everything together. Trust me, having a best friend like Tabby is priceless. She's always there to listen, offer advice and kick my sorry butt when I need it."

"Yeah. My brother thinks he's my protector. For some reason, he thinks I'm a troublemaker," Ruby said, a playful gleam in her eye.

"Ah, the protective older sibling, huh? Sounds like your brother's got his work cut out for him. I can imagine you being quite the instigator."

"Like I said, I'm an angel," Ruby said, feigning innocence.

Jason burst into laughter. "Ah, there it is again. The angelic act! Like I said, I'm not sure I believe you. You've got a hint of devilish charm peeking out."

Ruby's phone shook, and she glanced at the screen. "Surprise, surprise. It's my protector," she said. "Excuse me." With that, she stood and stepped away from the table, leaving Jason and Tabby to their conversation.

As Jason watched Ruby move to a quieter corner to take the call, he turned back to Tabby, grinning. "Looks like the protective brother's checking up on his little angel."

Tabby said, "It's probably for the best. Ruby can be ... a bit reckless."

"Oh, really? A reckless angel, huh?" Jason mused. "She sure had me fooled with her innocent act. So, spill. What kind of trouble has she gotten into before?"

Before Tabby could respond, Ruby returned to the table, her phone conversation with her brother wrapping up. " ... no, not at home. I'm at Fitzgerald's Pub. Um ... yeah. Sure. Yup. Bye-bye," she concluded, hanging up.

Jason watched her, still grinning, "So, how's the overprotective big brother doing? Is he keeping track of your every move?"

"Yeah, actually—he's on his way here," she said with a touch of amusement. "He wants to meet you two."

"Oh really? Well, isn't that something? Your brother's coming to join the party, huh? I guess we're in for a visit from the protective lion," Jason said.

Tabby chimed in, "That's so sweet."

Jason took one more swig from his beer. "Sure, if you're into being overprotected. But, honestly, I think I can handle meeting the big bad brother. Let's just hope he doesn't go into full-on protective mode and try to scare me off."

"Don't worry about Jack. He's actually really nice," Ruby reassured him.

Jason relaxed. "Is that so? Well, that's good to know. This Jack fella sounds like a good guy. I bet he's just looking out for his precious little sister."

Tabby teased, "Kinda like I have to protect you because you're like a little brother to me."

Jason feigned offense. "Watch it there, princess. Who's the older one here? I should be the one protecting you."

"Me—I'm older. I'm twenty-seven and you're twenty-six. How can someone not remember their own age?"

"Hey now, I was just teasing. Of course, I know my own age. You're one year older, big deal. It's not like you've got decades on me. I can still protect you, my older but oh-so-fragile princess."

"What would I do without you?" she asked, her response dripping with sarcasm.

Jason grinned. "Oh, you'd be absolutely lost without me. I'm your knight in shining armor, your defender in the land of trouble. Without me by your side, you'd be defenseless against the horrors of the world!"

Ruby smiled as she watched this exchange. "I don't know, Jason, from where I sit it definitely seems like Tabby's the one who keeps you in line. But don't be embarrassed—we're lucky. It seems we're both in excellent hands."

Jason nodded at Ruby, raising his glass in a toast.

"You're right—I guess we both lucked out, huh? Having someone to watch over us is a good thing. Even though some of us might be a bit more overprotective than necessary," he said, shooting a jokingly pointed glance at Ruby.

At that moment the door swung open, and Jason's eyes caught a tall, striking man confidently striding in. Dressed in stylishly casual attire, with black hair and dark eyes, the man exuded an intriguing aura. As he scanned the room, his gaze eventually settled on Ruby.

Jason straightened up as the man approached. "Well, well, you must be the infamous Jack," he remarked, his tone a blend of curiosity and subtle challenge.

The newcomer extended his hand to Jason with a friendly smile. "Well met," he greeted, his eyes appraising Jason. Rising to his feet, Jason shook Jack's hand firmly.

"Pleased to meet you, Jack. You're Ruby's older brother, huh? You definitely look the part of the protective sibling."

Tabby introduced herself and Jason. "Nice to meet you, Jack. I'm Tabby, and this is Jason."

"It's nice to meet you too, Tabby. Ruby's told me a lot about you." He turned to Jason. "I've heard your name mentioned as well."

"Have a seat," Tabby invited, gesturing to the empty chair across from them.

"Yeah, have a seat," Jason echoed. "We were just talking about you."

Ruby joined in with a grin. "Yeah, talking about what an overprotective big brother you are."

Jason nodded. "That's right. Your sister was filling us in on your protective nature. Apparently, you have a knack for keeping tabs on her every move."

Jack shrugged, his smile unwavering as he settled into the chair. "She's very important to me."

Jason acknowledged the sentiment with a nod. "I can see why you'd want to look out for her. She's a fireball, that one. I can imagine she gets up to plenty of trouble."

With a wave, Jack summoned the server and ordered a bottle of cabernet sauvignon for the table.

Jason watched, impressed by the choice. "Cabernet sauvignon? You have good taste, my friend."

"Thanks, I'm not much for tequila, unlike my sister here," Jack said.

Jason glanced at Ruby. "Oh, so tequila's her poison of choice? Can't say I'm surprised. I can definitely see her being quite the margarita connoisseur."

Tabby asked, "What do you guys have against lime?"

Jason let out a laugh at her question. "Don't get me started on the whole lime debate. I'm pro-lime all the way. It adds a certain zest to life. And margaritas aren't margaritas without lime."

"Or tequila," Tabby added.

Jason nodded in agreement, his voice spirited. "Oh, absolutely. It's not a proper margarita without the tequila. That's the essential ingredient. Without it, it's just a limey, watery mess. Trust me, I know my margaritas."

"Yet you always order beer," Tabby pointed out.

Jason held up his hands. "Hey now, don't judge my beer loving. I just enjoy a good pint, especially if it's an IPA. There's room for both beer and margaritas in my life. Variety is the spice of life, after all."

Ruby took a slice of lime from her margarita and dropped it into Jason's beer. "There ya go. A little spice of life for you."

Jason noticed her antics, surprise and amusement crossing his face. "Think you're funny, don't you," he asked, unable to hide his smile.

Ruby chuckled, licking margarita salt from her fingers.

Jason watched her with an amused shake of his head. "You're quite a handful, aren't you?" he asked, his voice warm with affection. "Dropping limes in other people's beers, licking salt off your fingers like a cat."

Ruby, feigning shock, asked, "Did he not ask for that?" She sought backup from Tabby and Jack, who were watching the exchange with grins.

Jason said, "I did not ask for the lime in my beer. That was entirely your mischievous doing. I'll give you credit for thinking outside the box, though. I never would have thought to combine beer and lime together."

Ruby turned to Tabby, her eyes filled with mischief. "A bit innocent, this one, huh?"

Jason, not missing a beat, gave Ruby a playful glare. "I am not innocent, thank you very much. I just prefer my beer without fruit juice in it. And as for being innocent"—he glanced around the group—"well, I'm sure Ruby has her fair share of secrets and mischief."

"Ruby, care to share with the class?"Jack asked, nudging the conversation deeper.

Jason said, "Oh, this I gotta hear. Let's hear some of those secrets. I bet you've got a few juicy ones up your sleeve."

"Not particularly,"Ruby said.

Jason grinned, sensing she was holding back. "Oh, come on, now. You don't have any secrets? No mischievous escapades? No tales of youthful rebellion?"

Jack encouraged her, his tone teasing yet protective. "C'mon Ruby. Tell your friends why I'm so protective of you."

Jason leaned closer, his curiosity now fully engaged. "Yeah, Ruby, why does your brother feel the need to be so protective of you? You've piqued my curiosity now."

Ruby sighed, resignation in her voice. "Alright, fine. One time, he had to bail me out of jail. It wasn't that big a deal."

Jason's eyes widened in surprise "Wait, wait, wait. You got arrested? And your brother had to bail you out? This is juicy stuff. What on earth did you do to end up in jail?"

Ruby muttered under her breath, barely audible. "Indecent exposure."

Jason's eyes widened even further, shock and amusement playing across his face as he turned to Jack for confirmation. "Wait, did she just say, 'indecent exposure'? You got arrested for that? Seriously?"

Jack said, "Ruby has a slight problem with ... impulse control, I guess you could say."

Jason shook his head, impressed. "Well, angel, I gotta say, you certainly know how to cause trouble. Getting arrested for indecency? That takes some serious impulsivity."

Ruby said, defiance in her voice, "It's a stupid law. And sexist. You don't see men getting arrested for being shirtless in public."

Jason laughed, acknowledging the double standard. "You've got a point there. It's unfair that men can walk around without shirts and get away with it while you get arrested for the same thing. It does seem sexist, now that I think about it."

Ruby then turned her attention to him and Tabby. "Alright, now you two spill. I already know he doesn't have any secrets," she said, gesturing toward Jack.

Jason smiled at Ruby's eagerness. Her enthusiasm was infectious. "Well, aren't you eager to uncover secrets? You really want to hear some gossip about me and Tabby?"

"I shared with the class. Now it's your turn. Fair's fair," Ruby countered, her gaze now fixed on him.

Jason smiled as he acknowledged Ruby's valid point. His gaze shifted to Tabby, who seemed captivated by the conversation, and then returned to Ruby. He sighed in resignation. "Alright, alright. You got me there. Only seems fair after your secret was spilled. But honestly, I'm not sure mine is as spicy as yours."

Ruby's eyes were wide with curiosity. "Do tell. I'm all ears."

With a deep breath, Jason steadied himself for his confession. "Alright, fine. So, there was this one time, when I was younger, and much more ... rash, let's say. I was at a party, had a few too many drinks and a dare was issued. A silly, childish dare, but nonetheless, a dare. And me, being young and stupid, decided to accept it."

Ruby's expression showed heightened interest as she urged him on with a simple, "And ..."

With embarrassment and amusement-tinged nostalgia, Jason recounted, "So, the dare was ... well, let's just say it involved something rather embarrassing. To this day, I can't believe I went along with it. But, influenced by the alcohol and the desire to impress my friends, I did the unthinkable."

"Enough with the build-up already. What did you do?" Ruby asked, clearly eager for the details.

Jason took another deep breath, steeling himself for the big reveal. "Alright, alright. I'll just rip off the Band-Aid and tell you. But you're not gonna laugh at me, right? Because this is pretty damn embarrassing."

Ruby placed her hand on Jason's arm, her expression earnest. "We would never laugh at you. Go on, dear, spill your dirty secret." In the background, Tabby snickered, clearly amused.

With a sense of reassurance from Ruby's supportive gesture, Jason summoned his courage. "Alright, here goes. So, during this party, someone dared me to ... well, long story short, I ended up ... streaking through the party, in front of everyone."

A smile crept across Ruby's face. "Well, well, well. Seems you have a bit of a naughty side, after all."

Jason rubbed the back of his neck. "Yeah, yeah, you could say that. I admit, it wasn't my finest hour. But I was young and dumb, influenced by alcohol and peer pressure. I can't say I'm proud of that particular decision in my life."

Jack, who appeared amused throughout the tale, said, "At least Tabby didn't have to bail you out of jail."

"Yeah, you got me there," Jason said, nodding in agreement. "Unlike Ruby here, I may have made some questionable decisions in the past, but at least I've never been arrested. That's a point in my favor, right?"

"Yet," Ruby interjected. "You haven't been arrested *yet*. You're still young."

"You're right, I'm still young. There's still plenty of time for me to get into trouble and end up in handcuffs, I suppose. But I like to think I've learned from my past mistakes and become wiser and more mature."

"Maybe you could impart some of that wisdom and maturity to Ruby here," Jack suggested. "I haven't had much luck with that so far."

Jason nodded, sympathetic to Jack's struggles. "Sounds like I've got my work cut out for me, huh? Imparting wisdom and maturity to an impulsive, free-spirited soul like Ruby. That can't be an easy task."

Ruby asked, "So, do my friends meet your approval, big brother?"

Jack glanced at Tabby and Jason. "Indeed, they do. I'm pleased to say that your choice of friends isn't entirely awful. I suppose you could be fraternizing with worse people."

Ruby beamed at the compliment. "That's high praise, by the way. Jack doesn't approve of any of my friends."

"I can imagine you don't bring home the most well-behaved friends," Jason said. "I bet they give your brother some serious heartburn."

Jack joined in, his tone one of fondness and concern. "You could say she's a magnet for trouble. But with a good heart. As you can imagine, there are plenty of people who would take advantage of someone like that."

Jason nodded. "Yeah, I get that. Her impulsive tendencies could attract the wrong crowd."

"Let's just say some of her friends are of questionable moral character," Jack added.

"Oh? So, you're talking about the kind of friends who have a, shall we say, colorful past? The kind who might not have the best intentions, huh?"

Ruby jumped to her friends' defense. "They're not all bad!"

Laughing, not convinced, Jason retorted, "Right. I'm sure they're all Boy Scouts and Girl Guides, huh?"

Ruby pointed at Jack. "Well, not like him. He's pristine."

Jason glanced at Jack, his voice dripping with sarcasm. "Oh, yes. He certainly has a saintly aura about him, doesn't he? The very model of purity and cleanliness."

Jack turned to Ruby, his tone teasing yet sincere. "Well, if I got in trouble, who would keep *you* out of trouble?"

"Ah, so you're the voice of reason and responsibility in this sibling duo, then?" Jason asked.

Tabby chimed in, directing her words to Jason. "Just like I am for you, Jason."

Jason smiled at Tabby, appreciating her perspective. "Right, you're the voice of reason in my life, too, aren't you? Keeping me grounded and saving me from my own impulsive tendencies."

Jack nodded at Tabby, his expression grateful. "You're a good person, Tabby. I'm glad you and Ruby are friends."

"Yes, I must say," said Jason, "I'm also glad Ruby has such a caring, sensible friend in you, Tabby. It seems you keep her grounded and balanced."

Ruby rolled her eyes. "So, you guys are on his side all of a sudden? He's the overprotective one, remember?"

"Oh, come on, angel. We're not on his side. We're just acknowledging the fact that you can be a bit careless at times. And having a responsible friend like Tabby around to balance you out isn't necessarily a bad thing."

"This is interesting, Jason. You used to call me a pain in the ass, and now I'm the responsible friend. Not complaining, though," Tabby said, reaching for a french fry.

Jason smiled at the memory of his past remark. "Yeah, well, I have to admit, my perspective on you has evolved over time. You've proven yourself to be not just a pain in the ass but a reliable, sensible friend. I've learned to appreciate your company, pain-in-the-ass moments included."

Tabby faced Jack with a grin. "I'm not really a pain in the ass. I'm actually very nice."

"It's true," Ruby said to Jack. "Tabby is super sweet. You two should get together."

Jason's face lit up with amusement. He turned his gaze toward Jack, curious about how he would handle Ruby's bold matchmaking.

"I can clearly see that Tabby is super sweet," Jack responded. "And I'd be delighted to take her out. But maybe I should ask her if that's what she'd like."

Jason noted the exchange, appreciating Jack's demeanor. "Oh, the gentlemanly approach. Very refreshing, Jack. Good idea to ask for consent before making any moves. That's the polite thing to do."

From across the table, Tabby joined in, her smile bright and inviting. "I would like to be asked out."

Jason felt a surge of happiness as he watched the potential romance bloom. "Well, there you have it, Jack. Tabby would like to be asked out. It's your move."

Jack turned to Tabby, his expression earnest. "Tabby, would you do me the honor of accompanying me to dinner tomorrow evening?"

Leaning forward, Jason's interest piqued as he observed Jack pose the question, feeling almost as if he had a stake in their budding relationship.

"I'd love to," Tabby said.

Jason grinned, pleased by Tabby's straightforward and positive response. "There you go, Jack. Looks like you've got yourself a date. Congratulations!"

"Thank you. Always nice to have an appreciative audience when asking for a date," Jack remarked, a slight edge of sarcasm in his voice.

Chuckling, Jason nodded, enjoying the playful interaction. "Oh, it's our pleasure to be your applauding audience, my dear Jack. Please feel free to entertain us with more charming proposals anytime you like."

Ruby shifted her gaze to Jason, her eyes locking onto his. "Seems like our respective chaperones will be otherwise occupied tomorrow night."

Jason grinned, catching her meaning. "Indeed, it seems we'll be left to our own devices for the evening. Whatever shall we do without our chaperones to keep us out of trouble?"

"Maybe we should chaperone each other," Ruby suggested.

"Ah, yes. Sounds like the perfect recipe for a night of chaos and adventure. Count me in."

Tabby turned to Jack, amusement lighting up her face. "Is this what it's like leaving children home alone without a babysitter for the first time?"

Jason burst out laughing at the analogy, finding it quite fitting. "Ha! Yes, exactly. I suppose this is Jack's first taste of parental independence, leaving two slightly reckless young adults on their own for the evening. Hopefully, we don't burn down the house or accidentally summon a demon."

"I'm sure they'll be fine," Jack said, looking at Tabby. "We've raised them well."

Jason appreciated Jack's parent-like tone. "Yes, yes, we've been raised well and are responsible young adults, I assure you. No need to worry about us, Jack. We'll behave ourselves, promise."

As Jack turned to Tabby to ask for her phone number, Jason watched with approval. The scene was unfolding like a well-rehearsed play, and he felt a thrill knowing that a potentially great date was in the works.

"Aw, you two make such a cute couple," Ruby beamed, satisfaction radiating from her.

Jason nodded in agreement. "Indeed, they do have a certain chemistry, don't they? And I must say, Ruby, you've got a real knack for playing matchmaker."

Jack turned to Ruby and said, "C'mon, Cupid. I'll walk you home."

Jason felt the warmth of brotherly love in the air. "Ah, the protective big brother is ready to escort the matchmaking sister home. Quite heartwarming."

As they prepared to part ways, Jack extended his hand to Jason. "Jason, nice meeting you."

Jason shook Jack's hand firmly. "The pleasure is all mine, Jack. It was a genuine joy meeting you, and I have a feeling we'll be seeing each other again soon."

Jack then turned to Tabby, who had been quietly watching the interactions. "Tabby, it's been an absolute pleasure. I'll call you tomorrow."

Jason watched them leave, pondering what the future might hold. Once they were out of sight, he turned to Tabby.

"What are you smirking about?" Tabby asked.

Jason tried to contain his excitement. "Oh, nothing. I was just thinking that with our chaperones occupied and us left to our own devices, Ruby and I have a golden opportunity to let loose a bit. Have some fun, act a little reckless, maybe even break some rules."

"Don't get Ruby into any trouble. I doubt very much if Jack would appreciate that," Tabby warned.

Jason, aware of the need for restraint, said, "Oh, don't worry. I won't do anything reckless enough to get Ruby in trouble. I have some self-control. But that doesn't mean we can't have a bit of harmless fun, right?"

"As long as your harmless fun doesn't provoke her protective older brother to kick your ass," Tabby said, narrowing her eyes.

"Trust me, I'm aware of Jack's capacity to kick ass if needed. And believe me, I have no intention of crossing any lines that would provoke him. Our harmless fun will stay within the bounds of friendly and non-violent."

"Good," Tabby said. "And what happened to your friend who was supposed to meet us here?" she asked, suspicion creeping into her tone.

"Oh right, my friend ..." Jason said, as he rubbed his neck, trying to maintain a casual demeanor. "I guess he ended up having to work late and couldn't make it." Attempting to sound nonchalant, he continued, "Just as well, I suppose, since the evening took an unexpected turn."

"Uh huh. Anyway, I'm going to head home too. Big date tomorrow," Tabby said, gathering her things. As she grabbed her coat and headed for the door, Jason watched her leave.

"Have a good night, Tabby. Enjoy your date tomorrow. And remember, no late-night partying or shenanigans. The fate of your romantic future rests on it."

# 3 Romance

Jack paced his living room, phone to his ear, his mind ticking over the evening's possibilities. "Are you ready for dinner tonight?" he asked, anticipation in his voice.

"Yes! Our first official date," came Tabby's enthusiastic response. "Very exciting."

"Indeed," Jack agreed, smiling. "Where would you like to eat?"

"Let's go to the Bistro," she suggested.

"The Bistro? You must like fine French dining," Jack remarked.

"Too romantic?" Tabby asked, a trace of concern in her voice.

"Not at all," Jack assured her. "I was only surprised it was your choice. I thought maybe you were the burger and fries type."

Tabby's laughter floated through the phone. "I'm a woman of varied tastes."

"Good to know," Jack said, his interest deepening. "So, I'll pick you up at seven?"

"Until then," she said, and they ended the call.

Later that evening, Jack parked his car in front of Tabby's building. He climbed the stairs to her apartment and knocked on the door. When Tabby appeared, she was stunning in a simple blue dress that made Jack's heart skip a beat, her hazel eyes sparkling with warmth.

"Hello, Jack," she greeted him, her voice warm and inviting. "You look incredible."

"Thank you, Tabby," he responded, his eyes not missing the appreciative glance she gave him. "You look absolutely beautiful. Ready to go?"

"Ready," she confirmed, grabbing her coat and walking downstairs to the car. Jack held the door open for her, and she climbed in with a smile.

After gently closing the door, Jack walked around to the driver's side, sliding into his seat. As he started the engine, the anticipation of the night ahead filled the car.

"So, how was your day?" he asked, glancing over at her as they drove toward the Bistro.

"Great, very relaxing," Tabby said. "I mostly texted all day with Ruby and Jason."

"Did they have any new gossip?" Jack asked.

"They confirmed they're going to hang out together tonight. Apparently, Jason is eager to trounce your sister at *Mario Kart*," she said.

Jack shook his head. "He better be careful. Ruby is a *Mario Kart* virtuoso. She'll destroy him."

Tabby said, "I'll have to remember to tease him about that."

"Please do," Jack said with a grin. "He seems like he could use an ego check."

Jack shared details of his day—chores, a jog, the mundane yet comforting routines of his life—as Tabby listened.

"A jogger?" Tabby noted. "I heard jogging is bad for the knees, so that's my excuse to never jog, although I admire those of you who have the motivation."

"Trust me, I didn't always have the motivation. But the key is to have a good playlist. The right music can turn a boring jog into a whole new experience."

Tabby nodded thoughtfully. "Sometimes when I can't sleep, I go for a walk through the park and listen to John Grisham audiobooks."

Jack looked at her in surprise. "Grisham? I would've thought you'd be more of a romance novel type."

"Do you read romance?" Tabby asked.

He responded with a smile, shaking his head slightly. "No, not exactly. I lean more toward non-fiction, particularly subjects like astronomy and the like. What about you? Are you a fan of romance, or do you stick to thrillers?"

Tabby nodded, her eyes lighting up. "Yeah, I'm a sucker for a good, forbidden love story, if it's well written. I actually love anything that's packed with emotional drama. I want to be sobbing by the end of a good book."

Jack appreciated her enthusiasm. "There's nothing quite like the thrill of rooting for a couple who shouldn't be together," he agreed.

"Speaking of hobbies, what do you do besides jogging and being charming?" Tabby asked.

Jack, pleased by her compliment, said, "Well, aside from jogging and charming, I enjoy some target practice. I go to a shooting range now and then to hone my skills. It's a good stress reliever." He paused, his pride clear. "I also tinker with old cars. I'm currently restoring a classic. It was my father's, and it's in pretty rough shape, but I'm determined to bring it back to life."

"What car?" Tabby asked.

"A '67 Mustang Fastback. I've had to replace the engine, repair the body and fix up the interior. I remember riding around in it as a kid."

Her grin was playful. "I was hoping you were going to say a '58 Plymouth Fury."

Jack, intrigued by her specific choice, asked, "A '58 Plymouth Fury? Why that car?"

"I've always wanted to ride in one. I read a lot of Stephen King as a kid."

"So, you want to ride in a '58 Plymouth Fury because of Stephen King?" Jack asked. "That's as good a reason as any. It's definitely a cool car."

"I'm not much of a car enthusiast," Tabby confessed, "but I am absolutely interested in a car that's famous for being possessed."

"Oh, so you're not a car person, more of a demonic possession kind of girl?"

"Exactly!"

"Well, if I ever come across a '58 Plymouth Fury with a demon inside, I'll give you a call. Sounds like quite the ride."

"I'll be looking forward to that call," Tabby said.

As they continued their exchange, they arrived at the restaurant. Jack parallel parked in front of the quaint restaurant before cutting the engine. He walked around to the passenger side, holding the door open for Tabby.

As she stepped out, Jack took her hand, helping her onto the sidewalk. "Ready for some fine French dining?" he asked with anticipation.

"I am," she said.

Jack held the door open for her, gesturing inside. "After you, my dear."

They were enveloped by the warm, intimate ambiance of the restaurant. Seated at a window table, Jack glanced occasionally at Tabby as they perused the menu.

Setting his aside, Jack said, "I think I'm going to order a bottle of wine. Any preference—red or white?"

"Red," Tabby said.

Jack nodded in approval. "Red it is. I like a woman who appreciates a good red." Jack flagged down a server to place their order.

"So, Jack, tell me about your aspirations," Tabby asked.

Jack pondered for a moment before replying. "My aspirations? Well, I aspire to be a great arborist and help keep our environment healthy and beautiful. I also hope to see my car fully restored. And, personally, I'd like to find a partner to share my life with and maybe start a family someday. What about you? Any aspirations you care to share?"

"Similar," Tabby shared. "I want a house in the woods, a loving husband, kids, a dog and a peaceful life."

Jack was charmed by her answer. "Sounds like a pretty idyllic picture of the future you've got there. Can't say I blame you. I think we could all use a little more peace in our lives."

The conversation took a playful turn when Tabby asked, "So, you're into marksmanship. What type of firearm? Or are we talking archery?"

Impressed by her question, Jack said, "Well, I'm partial to handguns myself. I've got a SIG Sauer that's a real beauty. It's got a great feel to it, and I like the stopping power of a good 9 mm. You know anything about firearms?" he asked.

"Absolutely nothing," Tabby admitted.

Jack found her frankness refreshing. "Nothing? Well, maybe I'll have to take you to the shooting range sometime and give you a lesson. I have to warn you, though, guns can be addictive. Once you feel the power of a good weapon in your hands, you're going to want to come back for more."

"Sure, I'll take a lesson. I want to be prepared in case of a zombie apocalypse," Tabby said.

Jack was delighted by her playful spirit. "Well, I can certainly respect a woman who's prepared. We'll make sure you're well versed in zombie-killing tactics. Can't have you becoming zombie fodder in the event of a flesh-eating outbreak."

Jack enjoyed the lighthearted turn their conversation had taken. Tabby seemed equally pleased.

"Thank you. I appreciate it," she said.

"No problem. I'm always happy to share my knowledge, especially with a lovely lady like yourself. But don't go becoming a gun-toting badass too quickly. I don't want you showing me up when we hit the range," Jack said.

"I'll be sure to pace my badass training appropriately," Tabby said.

"Good idea. We don't want you turning into a badass overnight. We'll ease you into it, slowly but surely. Start with the basics and then work our way up to the more advanced stuff. Like how to shoot a .44 Magnum without getting blown back a few feet by the kickback," Jack concluded, his tone playful.

As the server set down their wine and food, Jack's smile widened with anticipation. Once the server left, he raised his glass. "Here's to enjoying the finer things in life: good food, excellent wine and delightful conversation." He watched Tabby clink her glass against his.

"I'll drink to that," she said, taking a sip and savoring the taste. "How's your food?"

Jack looked down with a contented grin. "Oh, it's great. This *bouillabaisse* is superb. I always forget how good French cuisine can be. How about yours? Is the *coq au vin* living up to your expectations?"

"Yes, it's very good."

"I'm glad to hear it," Jack said. "It's always nice to find a place that serves decent French food. I've had my fair share of bad *coq au vin*, trust me. There's nothing worse than a disappointing French meal."

"You do a lot of fine dining, do you?" Tabby asked, amusement coloring her voice.

"I wouldn't say I'm all about fine dining," he said. "But a good meal is something I definitely appreciate. There's nothing quite like a sit-down dinner with fine wine and great company. Though, I must admit, a greasy burger and fries can be very satisfying."

Tabby nodded, her eyes gleaming. "It's important to sweep someone off their feet with that first impression. Then maybe follow it up with a comfort meal, right?"

"Exactly, balance is key. Not every date has to be about candlelit dinners and gourmet dishes. Sometimes, a simple picnic in the park with a homemade sandwich can be equally romantic."

"Yeah, maybe under a cherry tree. Blossoms falling into our hair and food," Tabby suggested.

Jack was charmed by the picture she painted. "Sounds like something from a French film, doesn't it? Perhaps with a few butterflies fluttering around us for good measure."

As Tabby poured herself another glass of wine, Jack's smile turned teasing. "Feeling adventurous with that second glass, are we? Be careful, or you might start getting flirty with me."

"Maybe you should join me with a second glass," Tabby suggested. "We can be flirty together."

"Why not?" Jack agreed, raising his glass. "But beware, I might turn on the charm even more with a bit more wine in me."

"You don't need wine to be charming," Tabby countered, her gaze lingering a moment. "That piercing dark gaze of yours does all the work."

Jack was flattered. "Is that so? I've been told I have a brooding look, but I didn't realize it was that appealing."

Tabby nodded. "It's almost like you can look right into someone's soul. It would be eerie if you weren't so charismatic."

With a grin, Jack leaned in slightly. "Charismatic? I'll take that. And as for peering into souls, maybe I'll have to take a closer look at yours, see what secrets hide behind those pretty eyes."

"It's impolite to peer into someone's soul on the first date," Tabby said, a playful note in her voice.

"Fair point. Maybe I should save the soul-searching for the third or fourth date. How does that sound?"

"And what would those dates entail? The shooting range or a picnic under the cherry blossoms?" Tabby asked, her voice laced with curiosity.

Jack's grin didn't wane. "Why not both? A bit of target practice to get the blood flowing, then a relaxing picnic under the cherry blossoms. It sounds like a perfect plan to me."

"And for the second date?" she probed.

Jack took a moment to think, then suggested, "How about a hike in the woods? We could enjoy some fresh air, beautiful scenery and maybe find a quiet stream to sit by and chat."

Jack noticed Tabby settling back in her chair, her expression contemplative.

"How about geocaching?" she proposed. "I don't like to hike unless there's swag involved."

"Geocaching? That sounds like a fun idea. You a fan of treasure hunts?" He was intrigued by the prospect. "I have to admit, I've never tried geocaching before, but I could be persuaded to give it a shot. Maybe we could even make a bet over who can find the most caches. Loser has to pay for the next date."

Tabby asked, "Are you sure? I mean, that's hardly fair. Me being an experienced treasure hunter and you being a total noob."

"Oh, you're confident in your treasure-hunting skills, are you? Don't worry, I'm a fast learner. I bet I could give you a run for your money. And besides, some friendly competition can be fun, don't you think?"

"Okay, it's a bet," she declared, her excitement lighting up the space between them.

"Excellent! It's settled then," he said. "A bet on who can find the most geocaches. Loser pays for the next date."

As their playful banter continued, Tabby asked with a look of concern, "Wait a minute. Being a tree warden, you don't have some secret forestry insider information, do you?"

Jack burst into laughter, shaking his head. "Secret forestry insider information? What, like a map of all the secret caches hidden in the woods? I wish. Trust me, my job as tree warden doesn't come with any special perks like that. So, you've got nothing to worry about—I won't be using my insider information to win this bet. Besides, where's the fun in cheating, right?"

"Okay," Tabby said, finishing the last bite of her food.

"So, ready for dessert? This place has a killer *crème brûlée*."

"*Crème brûlée*? That sounds rather decadent. I'll have a fruit tart instead," she answered.

"A fruit tart? You don't like to live on the wild side, do you? Well, to each their own. I'll have the *crème brûlée*; you can have your healthy tart," Jack said.

Tabby said, "No, I don't like to live on the wild side—but I'll dip a toe into it and have a bite of your *crème brûlée*. How's that?"

When their desserts arrived, Jack broke the delicate crust of his *crème brûlée* with his spoon, the caramelized sugar shattering. He watched as Tabby dipped her spoon into the creamy custard, taking a bite. "Pretty good," she admitted, "but I still prefer my fruit tart."

"Well, yes, fruit is sweet. But it's not quite as sweet as *crème brûlée*, now is it? Come on, admit it. You know the *crème brûlée* is better."

Tabby paused, a thoughtful look crossing her face. "There's a guilt-to-taste ratio that must be taken into consideration when choosing a dessert. If the ratio is off-balance, it affects the satisfaction level."

"Hmm, a guilt-to-taste ratio. I see you've given this a lot of thought. So, let me get this straight. The *crème brûlée* might taste better, but the fruit tart comes with less guilt and higher satisfaction. Is that it?"

"Exactly," she confirmed, her eyes shining with conviction.

"Well, I must say, your logic is sound. I can't argue with that. The fruit tart might be healthier and less guilt-inducing, but that doesn't change the fact that *crème brûlée* is absolutely delicious."Jack couldn't hide his grin, relishing their lighthearted debate. "Life's too short to not indulge a little once in a while, right?"

Tabby nodded. "Yes, but I choose my indulgent moments carefully. After all, every day can be a special occasion if you're creative enough with your excuses."

"You make a good point there." Jack appreciated her clever outlook on life. "And if there's one thing I've learned in life, it's that you can always find a good excuse to eat dessert if you try hard enough."

As the evening drew to a close, the server approached their table, clearing away the remnants of their meal and placing the check before them. Jack's eyes sparkled with amusement as he glanced at the bill.

"Ah, the bill," he said with a grin. "The moment when reality sets in and we have to pay for all that good food we enjoyed."

"You initiated the date, but I chose the expensive restaurant. Maybe we should split it," Tabby said.

Jack shook his head. "Nonsense. I asked you out on the date, so I'm paying for it. It's the least I can do. I insist."

Tabby smiled at his courteous demeanor. "Well, thank you. That's very charming of you."

"What can I say? My father raised me to be a gentleman." Jack beamed, pleased that she appreciated his old-fashioned manners. "He always said that a man should never let a lady pay for a date."

Tabby said, "Unless she loses at their geocaching bet."

"Oh, right! The geocaching bet. If you lose, then you can definitely pay the bill. But I have a feeling you've got the upper hand there. You seem like a serious competitor."

"Thank you for dinner, Jack. It was wonderful."

"You're welcome," he said, feeling his heart swell with satisfaction. As he helped her slip into her coat, his fingers brushed against the soft fabric, a bittersweet moment marking the end of a delightful evening. He glanced at her, hesitation in his voice. "I guess it's time to call it a night."

"Yeah," she said, walking alongside him to his car.

He unlocked the door and opened it for her, his voice warm. "Here we are, my dear."

Tabby climbed into the car, and he gently closed the door behind her before sliding into the driver's seat. "Buckle up. I'll get you home safe and sound."

As she settled in, she reached to switch on the radio, and Jack noticed her surprise when NPR filled the car. "National Public Radio? Why was I expecting classic rock?" she asked.

"What, you don't like public radio?" He was entertained by her reaction. "I find the news and culture programs more interesting than listening to the same old classic rock songs over and over again."

Tabby nodded in agreement. "No, you're right. I should have known."

"You know me too well already. I enjoy intellectual pursuits, and what better way to feed my brain than listening to the news and current events on NPR?"

"Yeah, who needs catchy tunes?" she asked, her voice dripping with sarcasm. "This program about snake hunters in the Everglades is much more ... riveting."

His laughter echoed through the car. "I know, right? What could be more exciting than listening to people talk about catching snakes in a swamp? It's truly the epitome of high culture."

The radio host chimed in, "The species also has a high reproductive potential, with female Burmese pythons able to lay between fifty to one hundred eggs annually."

Tabby turned to Jack. "How ... romantic."

"Ah, yes. The romantic life of the Burmese python. Truly the stuff of fairy tales."

Tabby's eyes gleamed with happiness. "Ruby never told me you were fun."

His grin widened, enjoying the compliment. "You think I'm fun? I'll have to thank Ruby for that. But seriously, I have my moments. I'm not always all doom and gloom."

"Although Ruby and I have different ideas of what constitutes a fun time," she said as they drove into the night.

Jack sighed, shaking his head. "Ah yes, Ruby and her adventures." He studied Tabby with curiosity. "Let me guess, you're more of an indoor type, preferring the quiet comfort of home to Ruby's wild exploits?"

"A homebody, yes. But life is getting more exciting. You're taking me target shooting. I've never fired a weapon on a date before," she admitted, apprehension and excitement in her voice.

"Well, there's a first time for everything, right? And who knows, maybe you'll discover a hidden talent for marksmanship. I have a feeling you'll be a natural."

As their evening wound down, Jack pulled up to the curb outside Tabby's apartment building and put the car in park. "Here we are. Back home safe and sound."

"Thank you for a lovely evening."

"The pleasure was all mine. I enjoyed spending time with you. You're good company. I hope we can do it again sometime," he said.

As Tabby opened the car door, Jack didn't hesitate—he got out and walked with her to the entrance of her building. At the doorway, Tabby took his hands in hers, leaning in slightly, her eyes searching his.

Jack held her hands tenderly, his gaze affectionate and inviting. After a moment of silence filled with anticipation, he spoke. "I had a great time tonight, Tabby. I mean that. Even though this was our first date, I feel like there's a genuine connection between us. I don't think of you as only a friend. I like you. A lot."

"I like you too," she whispered, inching closer.

His heart raced at her response, and he stepped closer, gently placing a hand on her cheek. Tabby closed her eyes, and Jack tilted her head upward, his breath warm against her skin. He leaned down, his lips hovering inches from hers.

"Are you going to kiss me?" Tabby's voice was soft, expectant.

"Do you want me to kiss you?" Jack murmured, his eyes gleaming with tenderness and desire.

Tabby nodded, and he grinned. He caressed her cheek with his thumb, then leaned in to capture her lips in a tender kiss.

After the kiss, Tabby opened her eyes, a smile blooming across her face.

"That was nice. I've been wanting to do that all night," he said, sensing a warmth enveloping him.

"Call me tomorrow?" she asked.

"Of course. I'll call you tomorrow. Sweet dreams, Tabby," he said, his voice gentle.

"Sweet dreams," she echoed as she headed upstairs.

As Jack drove home, his thoughts lingered on Tabby. He smiled to himself, replaying their conversations, the laughter, the look in her eyes and the softness of her kiss. The night had been perfect.

# 4 Seduction

Ruby sat on her couch, the faint sound of her phone beeping pulling her from her thoughts. She smiled at Jason's number.

"How's it going?" Jason messaged.

"Are you coming over to hang out?" Ruby replied, shifting her position, eager for his company.

"Yup! I'll order the pizza and head over."

Ruby answered with a thumbs-up emoji, unable to suppress her enthusiasm.

After placing down her phone, Ruby felt a flutter of anticipation. She tidied up her space, but soon the task became overwhelming. With a sigh, she plopped down on the couch. She picked up her phone and started scrolling, until she heard a knock on the door. Rushing to open it, her heart raced with excitement.

"Oh, you brought the pizza. Nice!" she said, her eyes lighting up at the sight of the box he held.

"Yeah, they had it ready when I got there," he said, stepping inside and setting the down the pizza. Ruby's apartment exuded a warm atmosphere, overflowing with lush plants and an array of creative projects that added a personal touch to every corner.

Ruby went to the fridge, her mind already on the fun ahead. She retrieved two sodas and passed one to Jason. The pizza sat enticingly on the counter, and Ruby could sense the enthusiasm between them. "So, you want to play *Mario Kart*?" she asked.

"Definitely."

With playful determination, Ruby grabbed the pizza box, carried it into the living room and set it down on the coffee table.

Jason plopped onto one end of the couch, his voice filled with bravado. "I hope you're ready to lose."

"Tabby warned me about your competitiveness," Ruby said, a teasing smile on her lips.

"Yeah, I take my video games seriously. But I can't help that I'm great at them too."

Ruby set up the gaming console, passing a controller to Jason as they settled in for an exciting evening of virtual racing. They dove into the digital world, maneuvering through a variety of colored and dynamic tracks. Again and again, Ruby displayed her superior skill, finishing first in every race with ease.

"Wh—how the hell? How are you this good at this game? I never lose!" Jason said with disbelief.

"You came in second. That's not losing."

Jason said, "Yes, it is losing! I don't take second place; I take first!"

"Want me to let you win the next one?" Ruby offered, suppressing a laugh.

"What kind of question is that? If you let me win, it doesn't count! I want an actual victory, but you're making that nearly impossible right now," he said, crossing his arms.

"Maybe we should watch a movie instead," she suggested, sensing his frustration. "What would you like to watch?"

Jason said, "You're going to judge me, but you said I could pick ... So, we're watching *Joker*."

Ruby tried to mask her disappointment. "Great," she muttered, not quite sounding convincing. "That's a great pick," Ruby lied, trying her best to feign enthusiasm. "I certainly never saw it before."

"Jesus, you're a terrible liar. You are not amused at my pick, I can tell."

"Hey, Joaquin Phoenix is not my type, but if you've got a thing for him, I'm willing to go along. Is it on Prime Video? Because that's my only streaming service," Ruby asked, hoping it might not be available.

"Yeah, it's on there. But let me guess, you think it's shallow and unoriginal," Jason said.

Giggling, Ruby conceded, "Normally I can't stand it when people talk during the movie, but I think you might have to with this one to keep me awake."

"Wow, I'm never going to win with you, am I? You're just going to continue to take shots until it's done, aren't you?" Jason asked.

"No more shots."

Jason gave her a skeptical look. "Uh huh, sure. I trust you. I'll trust you're going to be nice about this and that you're not going to criticize my choice, no matter how much you may dislike it."

"Why are men so fussy about their movie picks? They always act like they wrote, directed and starred in whatever they choose and expect appropriate accolades," Ruby said, poking fun at his defensiveness.

"I don't expect 'appropriate accolades.' I just want you to not act like my choice is a horrible decision. I like the movie, okay?"

"I can either lie or be honest. It's up to you."

"Be honest, please. I don't want you to act enthused just to make me happy," Jason said, rolling his eyes.

She could sense his eyes on her, the corners of his mouth turned up in a gentle tease. "Now just remember, no falling asleep, alright?" he said, a playful challenge in his voice.

"No falling asleep. Got it," Ruby said, her words carrying doubt about her own promise.

"I'll hold you to that," he said as the movie began.

Ruby excused herself, slipping out to the kitchen to grab a bag of chips before returning to the living room. Offering the bag to Jason, she rejoined him on the couch.

"Don't mind if I do," Jason said, opening the bag. As they munched, he glanced over at Ruby. She could tell he was watching her to make sure she was paying attention to the movie. But she wasn't. She was looking at him.

"Do you have something to say?" he asked, his voice carrying a playful note.

"Me?" Ruby pointed to herself, feigning innocence as she popped a chip into her mouth. "I'm watching the movie."

"You are definitely not. You're watching me watch the movie." Jason eyed her with a grin, obviously sensing her lack of engagement. "If you're getting bored, you could always just say so. We can change to something else," he offered.

Ruby was amused by the situation. "You know, I can't recall a time when I've had a guy over and he truly had the intention of watching a movie."

"Are you being serious? Every time you invite someone over, they try to make a move?"

"For the most part, yeah," she confirmed, as if it were nothing new. In truth, she preferred hanging out with her brother, Jack. Despite her complaints, she wished more guys could be as sweet and caring as him.

"How do you put up with that?" Jason pressed, curious. "It's got to be frustrating, having every guy you invite over wanting only one thing."

"What can I say? I guess I'm irresistible."

Jason chuckled. "Okay, okay. I think you know you are. But why are you still single?"

"Honestly? Don't tell Jack this, but I want somebody who's as good as him. Someone he'd approve of."

Jason nodded. "So, you want someone who's as protective, and caring as your brother ... and someone Jack will like? I can't blame you. Jack seems like a good big brother."

"I know," Ruby said, her respect for him shining through. "I actually admire him, but I could never be so straightlaced. I don't have it in me. I can't help it," Ruby admitted. "I'm more like my mom. Jack is like Dad. They even look alike."

Jason glanced back at the movie playing in the background. "That makes sense. If you're laid-back and your brother is uptight, I'm guessing your parents are similar, right?"

"Yeah, and if my dad can fall in love with my impetuous mom, then some responsible, mature gentleman could fall for me. At least that's my theory," Ruby said, a hopeful glimmer lighting up her eyes.

"The responsible, mature gentleman who's good enough for the stamp of approval from your brother? That's a lot of qualifications for your dream guy," Jason said. "Your dream is a diamond in the rough. That's going to be difficult to find. Does Jack know this is what you're looking for in a guy?"

"Heck no," Ruby said. "If he knew, he'd be trying to turn me into a proper lady."

"Alright, you've got my full attention now. What do you mean by Jack trying to turn you into a 'proper lady'? What kinds of things do you do that would horrify your brother?"

"Nothing bad. Maybe partying a little bit."

"A little bit? What does partying 'a little bit' look like in your world? Give me an example."

"Come on, don't tell me you've never partied," Ruby said.

"Of course I've partied. But I've only done harmless things. I'm willing to bet whatever you've done is a lot more than harmless. So, what do you consider partying a little bit?"

Ruby's voice was light and teasing as she said, "You know, cutting loose, being spontaneous, fooling around."

She witnessed Jason's laughter, a slight flush creeping up his cheeks.

"Fooling around? That's your idea of harmless partying? Do you believe that's only 'a little bit'?"

Ruby asked, "You've never fooled around before?"

She became aware of Jason's shift in his seat, a light blush creeping up his neck. He seemed flustered. "Of course I have. But we're not talking about me. We're talking about you and your definition of 'partying a little bit.' Fooling around sounds like it involves a lot more than just some lighthearted fun, don't you think?"

Ruby laughed, enjoying the moment. "Relax. I'm not talking orgies if that's what you're thinking."

The laughter that erupted from Jason was infectious. "No, I wasn't getting that impression! I just want to know how far you're willing to go on a typical night of 'partying a little bit.'"

Ruby reveled in the teasing atmosphere. "Are you asking for graphic details? Or do you want a demonstration?"

She noticed the shift in Jason's demeanor as his laughter faded, discomfort creeping in. "A demonstration, huh? You're serious? Or are you joking?"

"I'm joking," Ruby answered.

She could sense Jason's relief, though disappointment lingered in his voice. "Oh, right. You're joking. Of course you are." As he turned back to the movie, Ruby could see his mind wandering, and she wondered if his thoughts were on that 'demonstration' she had teased.

While the film continued, Ruby was caught paying attention to him instead of the screen. "You're staring at me again," he said with a teasing smile.

"I'm watching the movie!" Ruby protested, stuffing a chip into her mouth. "The dude is like a comedian or something, right?"

"Wow, impressive! You truly grasped the essence of the movie. It's kind of cute yet unsettling how you continuously stare at me watching the movie," Jason said. "I can feel your eyes on me."

"It enhances my experience to see your reaction to it. You're so intently focused. It's adorable."

Ruby sat back on the couch, her attention wavering between the flickering images of the movie and Jason, who clearly noticed her gaze again shifting toward him instead of the screen.

"You think it's adorable that I'm actually paying attention to this?" he asked her. "You should try doing the same."

As the movie continued, Ruby grabbed a handful of chips, their crunching breaking the surrounding silence. "I need to turn on the subtitles," she muttered with a frown. "I can't hear a word they're saying."

Jason, seemingly unbothered by the audio, shook his head. "I can hear them fine." He scooted closer to her and reached for the remote. "Here, I'll turn up the volume. Will that help?"

She shook her head, the characters' mumbling voices only growing louder, not clearer. "How can you even follow what's going on?" she questioned, her frustration growing.

He rolled his eyes, but his smile never waned. "Because if you pay attention, you can understand everything they're saying."

Ruby continued to munch on her chips, the sound obviously bothering Jason. "Can you please stop crunching on those damn chips? It's distracting," he blurted out.

Sheepishly, Ruby tried to quiet her crunching, but the noise persisted.

"A little less loud, please," Jason said. "You'd make a horrible audience member at a movie theater. You're the type who would chat and rustle snacks the whole time."

"I can't chew any more quietly!" Ruby protested, exasperated. "They're chips, for god's sake!"

"Then stop eating them every five seconds. It's annoying and making it even harder to hear."

Pouting, Ruby put down the chips, her lips forming a perfect little frown.

"Oh, don't give me that puppy dog look. It won't work," he said, barely concealing his amusement.

With the chips now set aside, Ruby tried once more to focus on the movie, but her attention soon shifted back to Jason. He caught her looking and scoffed. "You're gonna keep watching me instead of paying attention yourself, aren't you?"

"Maybe," Ruby said.

He was unable to hide his amusement. "Why do you enjoy staring at me instead of the movie so much, anyway?"

"Because I like pushing your buttons," she said, her grin widening as she reveled in their playful back and forth.

"If you think watching me is going to push my buttons, you're wrong. You're going to have to try a little harder than that to get under my skin," Jason said.

For a moment, her confidence wavered, but then she said, "I'm not so sure. You're a pretty easy mark. And apparently I've got all night to push your buttons because this movie is never-ending," Ruby declared.

"It's not 'never-ending.' It's barely two hours long."

"How long has it been on?" Ruby asked, confused.

He glanced at his phone, amusement in his expression as he relayed, "Not even an hour. We're not even halfway through."

Her eyes widened in disbelief. "Is that all? I guess time is relative," Ruby said, trying to play it cool.

Jason snickered, "Like your attention span. You can't even sit through a two-hour movie."

"Not true," she said. "*Sleepers* is one of my favorite movies."

"Is that because you have a thing for Brad Pitt?"

"I've never even met Brad Pitt," Ruby protested, defensiveness creeping into her voice.

"So, you don't have a crush on him because you find him attractive? Are you being serious right now?" Jason asked.

Ruby crossed her arms again, offended. "You think I'm shallow?"

"It doesn't make you shallow to admit that you have a crush on a hot actor. It's not a bad thing to admit."

"Hot guys aren't my type," Ruby declared, her voice defiant.

"Seriously?" Jason said, disbelief etched on his face. "You're going to try to convince me that hot guys are not your type? That doesn't really seem believable."

"Well, look at you, for example," she said, gesturing toward him. "You're all fit and attractive, and I'm not the least bit interested in you," she said, trying her best to sound dismissive.

Jason pretended to be wounded, his hand over his heart as if she had struck him deeply. "Is that so? You're saying you don't find me attractive at all, huh?"

"Why? Do you find me attractive?" she asked.

Jason's expression turned serious as he looked her directly in the eyes. "I think you are the most beautiful woman I've ever met."

Ruby was stunned by his words. "You do?" She hesitated, looking away. "I didn't think you thought of me that way," Ruby said, her gaze settling on the floor as she spoke.

Jason's laughter filled the space. "Why is that?" he asked.

Ruby frowned, confusion coloring her expression. "Well, you never hit on me," she admitted, finding herself a bit puzzled by the entire situation.

He shook his head, still smiling. "So, you think if a guy doesn't hit on you, it means he's not attracted to you?" Jason folded his arms. "I hate to break it to you, but not hitting on someone doesn't indicate whether a guy is attracted to you. Not at all."

"So, what does?" Ruby asked.

"In some cases, like yours, not hitting on you might actually mean that a man is holding his feelings in. He's not expressing interest out in the open because he doesn't want you to know he likes you," Jason said.

Ruby pondered his words, trying to process this new information. "So, telling me to be quiet is your way of showing me you like me?" Ruby asked.

As the movie continued in the background, Jason glanced at her. "I don't have to hit on you constantly to show you I'm attracted to you," he explained. "And when I tell you to chill out and be quiet, it's my way of getting you to actually pay attention."

"I thought you didn't want me flirting with you," Ruby said, trying to decipher his intentions.

"Why would I not want you to flirt with me? That doesn't make any sense," he asked, with a look of amusement. "Just because I didn't respond to your flirty come-ons doesn't mean I didn't enjoy them. In fact, it's quite the opposite. I was trying to be a nice guy, not taking your flirting too seriously." Jason said.

"Oh," Ruby said, a smile forming as she considered his explanation. "That's actually sweet."

Disbelief crossed Jason's features. "Yes, and that's exactly why I don't want to respond when you flirt with me. I don't want to be sweet and gentlemanly all the time. Sometimes I just want to be honest and say what's on my mind. Like, I've been extremely attracted to you since the second I met you."

Happiness lit up Ruby's face as she turned her attention back to the movie, finally enjoying it for what it was. She leaned against him. "You can put your arm around me. I promise not to take advantage of you."

Jason eyed her warily. "You won't take advantage of me? Why should I trust you? You'd probably take advantage in a heartbeat."

"Honestly," she met his gaze. "You're my first 'nice guy.' I don't want to scare you away. I'm kinda enjoying this 'being treated like a lady' thing," Ruby admitted.

Jason grinned, tightening his grip around her. "Oh, you like it when I treat you like a lady?"

"Well, yeah, now that I know you want me desperately," she teased. "The 'wanting' is the best part. Didn't you ever play tag as a kid?"

Jason looked at her, confused. "What does tag have to do with this conversation?"

"Think about it," she said, grinning. "What's more fun? Being chased or being 'it'?"

He burst into laughter, finally grasping her analogy. "Oh, I see what you're getting at now. You like knowing that a man wants you and is chasing you, huh?"

Ruby smiled. "I like attention. Is that a crime?" she asked.

"Nope, liking attention is not a crime. But you seem to crave it even more than most girls. You always have to be the center of attention, don't you? You're the loudest one in the room, the most talkative. It's like you want everyone's gaze on you all the time."

She gave an exasperated look but couldn't suppress a grin. "Okay, you've discovered my fatal flaw."

Jason regarded her. "I wouldn't call it a fatal flaw so much as a quirk of your personality. But you definitely have a major attention-whore complex."

"And you're super judgy," Ruby said.

"Yeah, okay. I'm a bit judgy," he admitted, "but it's accurate to say you're an attention whore. I don't see why you're so mad about it."

Ruby crossed her arms. "If you check your 'nice guy' handbook, you'll see that the word 'whore' should be stricken from your vocabulary."

"Oh, I apologize! The proper term for you would be ... attention junkie, right?"

"More acceptable," Ruby said. She sensed the impact of Jason's gaze, curiosity visible on his face.

"So, tell me," he prompted, genuine curiosity in his voice. "How did you end up this way? Why are you so addicted to attention?"

A hint of vulnerability crept into her tone. "I don't know. Probably because I'm the baby of the family. Kinda like the oldest is the judgy one.

Would you happen to be the oldest, Jason?" A teasing glimmer sparked in her eyes.

"Yes, I would," he said. "How did you know? Can you tell by my judgy nature?"

"You have 'older brother' written all over you. You've got that parental attitude that older brothers usually have. At least in my experience," she said.

"Well, you can't blame me. I had to watch out for my little sister growing up. I guess I ended up with that parental attitude because of how I was raised. But you, being the baby of your family, that would explain why you're so damn needy."

Ruby glared at him. "I'm gonna let that one slide."

Jason leaned back on the couch as he continued their banter. "So, you're letting that one slide because you don't want to admit I'm right?"

She shot him a glare. "No, because I don't want to have to beat your ass like I did in *Mario Kart*."

"You beat me one time at *Mario Kart*, and now you act like you're the greatest video game player of all time. Don't get ahead of yourself. You had a lucky day."

Ruby crossed her arms. "Oh yeah, 'One time.' Sure."

As the credits began to roll on the television screen, she glanced over at him, amusement in her eyes. "Looks like it's done," she remarked, with a mixture of satisfaction and reluctance.

Jason crossed his arms with confidence. "I'd say I deserve extra credit for keeping you focused on the movie long enough to see the whole thing," he said.

"Thank you for introducing me to that absolutely charming film."

Jason nodded, catching the nuance. "Oh, I get it. You're being sarcastic. You didn't believe the movie was even half as good as I described it, did you?"

"The ten minutes that I saw were not bad," she said, unwilling to concede. "But I have to say, I enjoyed our conversation a lot more. You've actually impressed me," she added.

He beamed. "So, you're impressed that I kept you focused?"

Ruby laughed. "I meant the part where you treated me with respect."

The warmth in Jason's voice was unmistakable. "Oh right, you liked the part where I treated you like a lady. I didn't lose too many points for telling you to be quiet and focus on the movie?"

"Well, you only enticed me to distract you more," she countered. "So, I guess it backfired." Ruby leaned in, mischief in her eyes. "When I said I enjoyed pushing your buttons, I meant it. But then you disarmed me by being sweet," she admitted. "You won that tilt, I suppose. I honestly wasn't sure if you would storm off in a huff or pin me down and ravish me. You telling me that you respect me was not even on my radar."

His warm and inviting laughter caused Ruby's heart to race. "Why do I get the feeling that even if I had stormed off or gotten physical, you would have enjoyed it?"

Ruby feigned innocence. "We'll never know."

"You're something else," Jason said, leaning closer. "I think I'm already developing a problem with you, Ruby."

"What problem is that?" she asked, intrigued.

He shook his head. "Well, for starters, I can't seem to get you out of my head. It's like you've burrowed in there, and no matter how irritating you can be, I can't shake you off. Your little attention complex has become an addiction for me."

Ruby shook her head. "Doesn't sound like a problem to me."

"Not for you, but it's definitely an issue for me. I don't like the thoughts I'm having about you. I shouldn't be thinking about you this much after just a couple hours together."

"Oh, come on," she said, her voice dipping into a seductive tone. "You make me sound like a temptress." Ruby reveled in the playful banter, her laughter genuine and infectious as it filled the space between them. She knew she was pushing the boundaries of flirtation, yet she couldn't resist the allure of the game. "I should be ashamed of myself for teasing you, but I can't help it. I really do like you. I mean, I seriously like you, and I'm going to try to behave myself."

Jason was clearly touched by her words, though he teased her in return. "Oh, you're going to try to behave? That's adorable. And I like you too, by the way. A lot more than I should. But I kind of enjoy your feisty attitude. So don't go losing it all of a sudden on me, okay?"

Ruby shook her head. "Who are we kidding?" she responded, her voice tinged with humor. "I'm not going to be able to behave myself."

His laughter echoed around them, a sound of genuine amusement at her boldness. "Yeah, we both know that's a lie. You don't understand what the word 'behave' means, and you know it. Maybe I should try to find a nice, quiet and respectful girl to date instead of you, huh?"

"Or," she countered, leaning in, her gaze locked on his, "I could role-play if that's your thing."

"Oh, you would just love to 'role-play,' wouldn't you?"

"Actually," Ruby said, her voice a soft whisper, "submissive is not my thing. I like to be chased, not caught."

Jason was clearly entertained by her spirited response. "A woman who likes to be chased, not caught? So, you're saying you enjoy it when a man has to work for you? You revel in the power you hold over men?"

Ruby said, "Admit it. You want to be caught in my web."

His grin widened. "In your web? You're trying to lure me in, aren't you."

With theatrical flair, Ruby recited, "'Will you walk into my parlor?' said a spider to a fly. ''Tis the prettiest little parlor that ever you did spy.'"

Amusement crossed Jason's features. "So, I'm the little fly in this scenario, and you're the pretty spider?"

"The next line is yours," she encouraged, a spark of delight in her eyes.

Grinning, he played along. "Oh, I see. You want me to be the naive little fly, oblivious to the danger I'm walking into? Fine, if you insist. 'Oh no, no! To ask me is in vain, for who goes up your winding stair can ne'er come down again.'"

Ruby enjoyed their poetic exchange. "'I'm sure you must be weary, with soaring up so high. Will you rest upon my little bed?' said the spider to the fly. 'There are pretty curtains drawn around. The sheets are fine and thin; and if you like to rest awhile, I'll snugly tuck you in.'" She looked at him expectantly.

He continued, "'Oh no, no! For I've often heard it said, they never, never wake again, who sleep upon your bed!'"

Ruby grinned, impressed with his recitation. "I've always loved that poem."

"You just enjoy talking about how the poor fly gets lured into the spider's trap, huh?"

"Is that how it ends?" she asked, feigning innocence.

"Yeah, that's how it ends. You don't think the fly got a happy ending, do you?"

Ruby pondered his question. "It could. She only wanted to tuck him in, after all. Maybe she's a sweet spider."

"Oh, you sweet innocent thing ... Do you really think the spider was just 'tucking in' the fly?"

"Okay, maybe she meant to eat him all along, but I would never devour you. Scout's honor," Ruby said.

Jason smiled warmly. "Oh yeah? You promise you won't devour me? You're not going to try to ensnare me in your trap?"

"You're far too wise to fall for that," she said.

"You think I'm not just going to walk right into your parlor and get caught like a naive little fly? Or do you think I'm going to be too tempted and fall into your trap anyway, despite my intelligence?"

"I'm not sure yet. You're an unknown quantity still. That's what makes you so fun," Ruby said, her eyes gleaming with intrigue.

Jason leaned forward, interested. "An unknown quantity? I see." He paused, letting the words linger between them, before continuing, "Well, I can say for certain that I find your feisty, attention-seeking nature quite fun, too."

"It's like a thrilling novel," she said. "Will he succumb to her charms? Will he be able to resist? We've got to read to the end to find out what happens."

Jason asked, "Oh, we're writing a story, are we? One where you, the spider, try to ensnare me but struggle because I'm too smart. I take it I end up winning in the end, though, right?"

Ruby watched him with a curious expression. "Is that how you say it ended?"

He leaned in, his grin broadening. "I thought you wanted a fun, fictional happy ending. So, I said that I win in the end—despite your best efforts to entice me. That's how I end the story: Jason wins, and Ruby loses."

"Ruby never loses," she said, defiance sparking in her gaze. She leaned in a fraction more, her voice playful. "Think about it. Are you truly going to feel victorious bragging to your friends that a beautiful, enticing woman tried to seduce you, but you managed to fight her off?"

Jason considered her words. "That's true. Bragging to my friends that I turned you down would sound kind of hollow. And I would have technically lost because I'd be admitting that I was fighting temptation."

"Ruby always wins," she declared, her tone dripping with confidence.

"You're very cocky. You think it's a foregone conclusion that you'll succeed in seducing me? Well, I'll have you know that I am incredibly strong-willed, lady."

"That only makes it more fun," she whispered. "The more you fight, the bolder I can be," she added, leaning in closer.

"Oh yeah? So, as I become more and more resistant to your advances, you become more and more determined to seduce me?" Jason asked, obviously enjoying the closeness.

"Maybe. Or perhaps I'll get bored and give up. It's like a game of blackjack. You have to push it, but not too far," she said. "You push your luck by resisting me. But you have to give in before I lose interest."

"Oh, I see. What makes you say I have to give in to you before you lose interest?"

"Because you want me," she said, her gaze unwavering.

He grinned, unable to deny it. "That's true. I do want you. But that doesn't mean I can't continue to resist you. I have a lot of willpower."

Ruby stretched and let out a yawn. "It's probably time for you to head home and consider how far you want to push your luck," she said. "But call me tomorrow if you want to play some more. Or you can call one of those submissive girls you mentioned trying to find and celebrate your victory of resisting me."

"So, you'd be totally okay with it if I went home and called up some nice, quiet girl to celebrate with?"

Ruby dropped her voice to a sultry whisper. "Honey, if that's what you like, then you're not my type after all. Think of it as a compatibility test," she explained. "You want feisty, you choose me. You want submissive, we go our separate ways."

"So, you're saying that if a guy likes your demanding and attention-seeking personality, then he's your ideal match?" he asked, clearly intrigued.

"No," Ruby corrected him. "I'm saying don't order fajitas if you want a white bread sandwich."

He laughed at her clever analogy. "Ah, so, if I want a 'white bread sandwich'—an ordinary, quiet girl—then I should steer clear of you because you're obviously not that kind of person?"

"Yes," she affirmed.

"So, tell me, how high-strung and demanding, are we talking here? I want to know what I'm getting into if I decide I like your attention-seeking personality."

Ruby opted not to respond to his probing question. The conversation was veering too close to personal territory. Glancing at her phone, she feigned a sigh. "I apologize, but our time for today has concluded. Please feel free to return tomorrow if you wish to continue this exchange."

Ruby watched Jason's reaction to her announcing the evening's end. "Our time is up?" he asked, disbelief mingling with a touch of irritation in his voice.

Ruby extended her hand, her warmth undiminished. "It was a wonderful evening, Jason. Thanks for stopping by. Hope to do it again sometime," she said, her tone sincere yet firm.

She could see the moment he understood her polite but clear announcement. His smile returned, albeit with a hint of resignation. "Fine, I can tell I'm being dismissed. I guess that's my cue to leave, huh?" he said.

"Yeah, but you've got my number. Don't be a stranger," Ruby responded, her voice light but inviting, hoping to soften the parting.

"Okay, fine. Goodnight, Ruby," he said, his spirits seeming to lift at the prospect of future conversations. "Thanks for the conversation. Have a good rest of your night. I'm sure we'll talk again soon."

"Bye-bye," Ruby called out as she walked him to the door. She watched him step outside, her smile lingering as she closed the door behind him. Alone now, she wondered if he would indeed call her the next day, a mix of hope and curiosity playing through her mind.

From her perspective, the evening had been a delightful dance of words and laughter. As the door clicked shut, a sense of exhilaration enveloped her from their exchange, her mind already replaying bits of their conversation. Ruby sensed a blend of amusement and anticipation, curious about what the future held with Jason.

# 5 Compatibility

Tabby waited at Franco's Diner, where she had arranged to meet Jason for lunch. The small diner buzzed with life, its brightly lit interior casting a warm glow. Red-vinyl booths lined the walls, while the counter was framed by a row of chrome stools. The comforting smell of fries wafted through the air, mingling with the sound of clinking dishes and laughter. Large windows at the front offered a view of the bustling street outside, where the sun filtered through.

A few minutes later, she spotted Jason as he arrived, scanning the room until his eyes landed on her in the booth. He walked over, his face lighting up as he greeted her and took a seat across from her.

Tabby's eyes were full of curiosity as she asked Jason, "So, tell me, did you end up going to Ruby's last night?"

He let out a light laugh. "Yeah, I did actually. It was ... interesting. She's definitely a unique character, huh?"

"Did you behave yourself?" Tabby asked.

He smiled. "Of course, I behaved myself. I was a perfect gentleman. As always," he said, his tone light but with a suggestion of defiance.

"Good," she said. "You know how Jack is about his sister."

"Yeah, I know Jack," Jason said, rolling his eyes.

"And did she beat you at *Mario Kart*?"

Jason's grin widened even further, and she could see the memory of their playful competition flicker in his gaze. "Ha, no. Of course not. I'm always the champ."

"I wonder if she would corroborate that if I asked her."

Jason, clearly realizing he was cornered in their playful exchange, said, "She would probably say that she went easy on me because I'm a weakling. I'm sure that's how she would tell the story."

Tabby leaned closer, dropping her voice as she asked, "Did you kiss her yet? Don't worry. I won't say anything to Jack."

Jason leaned in, his voice also dropping to a whisper. "No, I haven't kissed her yet. We did a lot of flirting, but we didn't actually kiss."

Tabby experienced a blend of amusement and intrigue. "She's quite the flirt, isn't she?"

Jason nodded. "Oh, she's a major flirt, that's for sure. She's very attention-seeking, you know? She loves getting attention, both from guys and I bet even from other girls. She's used to being the center of attention in any room she's in."

Tabby nodded, a thoughtful expression settling on her face. "I guess that's true. Well, she's so pretty. I'm not surprised."

"Yeah, she's definitely pretty, no doubt about that," Jason said. "But I think it's more than just her looks she uses to get attention. It's also her personality and the way she talks. She's very charming, but also very feisty."

"I warned you she was sassy before I introduced you," Tabby said.

"Yeah, you told me she was sassy, but I didn't realize she was such a firecracker. She's not just sassy; she's pretty demanding, too. It's a dangerous combo," Jason declared.

Tabby chimed in, "Yeah, but she's actually extremely sweet."

"Oh, she's sweet, all right. She can definitely put on that sweet little innocent girl act when the situation calls for it, but I can tell that, most of the time, she's a demanding little firecracker. You know?"

Curiosity flickered in Tabby's eyes. "What exactly did you two do last night?"

Tabby watched Jason's face light up as he reminisced about his evening. "It was just a typical evening hangout. We had dinner, played *Mario Kart* on her old Nintendo 64, and then spent about an hour just talking and getting to know each other. You know, regular stuff like that."

"That sounds nice," she said, her heart lifting at the thought of him enjoying himself. "Well, I had a great night, too. Jack is so charming. A proper gentleman."

Jason reclined, amusement in his eyes. "You had a nice night with the ol' Casanova himself, huh?"

Tabby nodded, her excitement increasing. "He's going to teach me how to shoot a handgun."

Jason erupted into laughter. "Oh wow, he's already taken you under his wing?"

"Yeah, I'm a little nervous, to be honest," she admitted. The thought of handling a gun sent a flutter of anxiety through her. "You know how uncoordinated I am. I probably shouldn't be anywhere near a handgun. But he made it sound exciting."

"Don't worry, Tabby," Jason said. "I'm sure Jack will take good care of you. And hey, there's something inherently badass about shooting a gun."

"So, are you going to see Ruby again?"

Jason's grin broadened, and she could tell the wheels were spinning in his mind. "Yeah, I probably will. She's obviously very eager to spend time with me. She keeps texting, and I'm not one to deny a pretty girl some attention."

"That's good," Tabby said, her tone shifting as she thought about Ruby's situation. "She needs more trustworthy friends to keep her out of trouble."

Jason nodded. "Does she get into a lot of trouble without having friends like me to keep her in line?"

Tabby sighed, her concern clear. "Her friends are mostly the party type," she said, glancing sideways at Jason. "You know, the kind that can be a bad influence. I'm not her keeper, but she's such a nice girl. I like to see her hanging out with a good guy like you."

"Aw, thanks for the compliment, Tabby," Jason said, his voice light. But Tabby could see the flicker of uncertainty. "Though I'm not sure if I would describe myself as the good guy in the group. Jack's the good one. I'm the one with the questionable morals."

Tabby grinned. "True," she said.

Jason relaxed, a cunning grin slowly spreading across his face. "Yes, it's true," he said, his charm oozing from every word. "I'm the morally questionable one. The player. The suave, witty guy who has all the girls swooning. Meanwhile, Jack is the all-American type."

She rolled her eyes. "Please, don't be a suave player with Ruby," she cautioned.

His grin expanded. "Why not? Are you worried I'll break her little heart or something?"

"No," Tabby said, shaking her head. "I'm worried that Jack will break your pretty face. You don't want anything to happen to those perfect teeth, right?"

Jason leaned back, clearly amused by the compliment. "Yes, my perfect teeth. Can't forget about those pearly whites, right?" He flashed a smile that could charm anyone.

Suddenly, an idea sparked in Tabby's mind. "Why don't we meet Ruby and Jack at Fitzgerald's later? The weekend's not over. We can still have a little fun, right?" she said, thinking about the four of them together that night.

Jason's grin returned, seemingly excited at the prospect of seeing Ruby and Jack again. "Yeah sure, that sounds like fun. I'm always up for a night on the town. Sounds like a brilliant plan."

As soon as Tabby finished her burger, she stood up, ready to leave. "I'm gonna head out. You pay the bill," she said, throwing a playful hug around him as she passed.

Jason feigned indignation. "Oh, so you're just going to skip out and leave me to pick up the tab?"

"I'll make it up to you!" Tabby called over her shoulder as she walked toward the door.

Jason's voice followed her, teasingly curious. "Oh yeah? And how exactly are you going to make this up to me? Should I expect something special in return?"

Tabby chuckled to herself as she stepped outside.

Later that evening, Tabby pulled out her phone and started a group message with Jack and Ruby, extending an invitation to join her at the pub.

Once she finished, she changed into something more suitable for a night out, grabbed her coat and made her way to the pub, anticipation guiding her steps.

Jason arrived first at the pub. He spotted Tabby enter soon after. "Let's get a table," she said, her voice light and inviting.

He followed her to a cozy table tucked away in the back by the pool tables. "Alright, after you, milady," he said, trying to sound suave.

"Oh, so charming," she said, settling into her seat.

Jason leaned against the table. "What, I'm not allowed to be charming? How about I'm just a polite Midwestern boy from Wisconsin who was taught good manners?"

Tabby said, "Yes, you're very charming. Maybe too charming."

Her warning amused him. "Too charming, eh? Is there such a thing? I thought you women enjoyed charming men or something."

"There's a range," she said. "Too charming can come off as lecherous," she added, crossing her arms with a seriousness that made Jason laugh.

"Whoa, 'lecherous' is a pretty strong word to use. Can't a guy just be charming without being accused of being lecherous?"

"Of course, a guy can," Tabby confirmed, her eyes filled with playful mischief. "Especially if he can keep his hands to himself and control his roving eyes. That's the part you sometimes struggle with."

"Sounds like you're implying that I have a history of misbehaving whenever I'm around attractive women," Jason said.

"Now's your chance to prove to me you can behave yourself," she challenged, as Ruby and Jack entered and approached the table. Jason was eager to demonstrate his ability to step up to the task.

As he shifted his focus, he spotted the familiar figures of Jack and Ruby approaching. "Oh, look who's here," he called out, his voice light with amusement. "Mr. and Miss Wonderful."

As Tabby stood up to greet them, Jack leaned in, planting a gentle kiss on her cheek before pulling out her chair, a gesture of old-school chivalry that made Jason chuckle.

"Ah, so chivalry is alive and well in the great state of New Jersey, I see," he remarked with amusement.

Jack smiled, as if it were completely natural. "Of course," he said.

Clearing her throat, Ruby tried to catch Jason's attention.

He turned to her, his grin widening at her sassy demeanor. "Ah, there's my little firecracker," he said.

"Where's *my* kiss on the cheek?" Ruby demanded.

Jason leaned in to oblige. "There, I kissed your cheek, you little troublemaker. Happy?"

She feigned a swoon, placing a hand over her heart. "Such passion! I'm swooning here."

"Hey, I'm a Midwestern boy. We don't know anything about passion. I was raised on good ol' boring Midwestern wholesome values," he joked.

Ruby shot him a playful glare. "Yeah, wholesome, like me. No need to pull out my chair for me, Jason. I've got it under control."

Jason's grin widened as he reveled in Ruby's feistiness. "Oh, the infamous Ruby sass has come out to play again, I see. So, I take it you don't want any special treatment from me? No pulled-out chairs and no chivalry whatsoever. Got it."

Jack, who had been listening with an amused expression, asked, "So Jason, Ruby tells me you two had fun last night. Did she behave herself?"

"Oh yeah, we had a good time last night," Jason said. "As for your question about her behavior, well, she was fairly well behaved. Though there were a handful of moments where she showed her inner sass."

Jason could sense the fondness in Jack's expression as he said, "I'm sure she did. She can be quite difficult if she's feeling mischievous. Even as a kid, she was like that."

He watched as Ruby turned to Jack. "You'll be glad to hear Jason was a perfect gentleman," she announced.

Jason beamed at the compliment, his heart swelling with pride at Ruby's favorable report. "Did you hear that, Jack? Your little sister just said that I was a 'perfect gentleman' with her last night."

"I wouldn't have expected anything less from you, Jason,"Jack said.

Jason felt a rush of gratitude at Jack's trust. "I'm so glad you have a modicum of trust in me when it comes to hanging out with your sister," he said.

Jack excused himself from the table and headed to the bar. As he disappeared into the crowd, Jason turned his attention back to Ruby. "So, will you behave yourself tonight, or are you going to cause trouble like you usually do?"

"Oh, I'll behave, without a doubt."

Jason's tone was laced with skepticism. "Oh yeah? So, does that mean the sassy Ruby will be taking the night off?"

Jack returned, sliding into the seat next to Tabby and taking her hand in his. He turned to Ruby. "Don't worry, Ruby. I ordered you a margarita. I know how you feel about wine."

Amused, Jason observed the interaction, then turned back to Ruby. She extended her hand toward him. "You can hold my hand if you want to," she offered.

"How gracious of you," he said, taking her hand.

Tabby's expression was curious. "You two have a bit of an interesting dynamic going on here, huh?"

Jason glanced at Tabby. "Oh yeah, Ruby and I definitely have an interesting dynamic. It's a classic 'opposites attract' situation."

"Jason's trying to play it cool for your sake, but he totally wants me. He told me so last night," Ruby said.

Jason erupted into laughter, shaking his head in astonishment. "Oh wow, way to throw me under the bus there! You weren't supposed to let them know I admitted to wanting you. That was supposed to be our little secret, remember?"

Jack said, turning to Jason, "Probably best not to trust this one with your secrets. She has a way of getting attention one way or another."

"Oh yeah, that's for sure," Jason agreed.

Ruby's eyes gleamed mischievously. "We played a fun game last night, right Jason?"

A grin spread over his face. "Oh yeah, we had a fun game, all right. A nice little question-and-answer game, if I remember correctly. I can still vividly recall some of your more ... interesting answers."

"Let me guess," Jack said. "You tortured the guy while he did his best to be a gentleman with you. Is that about right, Jason?"

With a resigned laugh, Jason sighed, feigning defeat. "Yeah, that's about spot on. She certainly knew how to work me over and test my gentlemanly nature."

Ruby shot him a teasing look, her playful demeanor infectious. "You loved every minute of it."

Jason smiled at her banter. "I mean, you're not wrong. I'll admit it. You definitely know how to test me. And yes, I do thoroughly enjoy our time together, even if sometimes I want to strangle you."

Jack turned to Ruby, concern in his voice. "Maybe you should go easy on the guy."

Ruby glanced between Jack and Jason. "It's fine," she said.

Tabby was observing the exchange with a trace of amusement on her face. "Interesting. I don't think I've ever seen Jason completely out of his depth before. It's kind of entertaining."

Jason laughed, realizing that everyone around him was reveling in his discomfort. "Oh yeah? So, you find it entertaining when you see me out of my comfort zone and getting worked over by a sassy firecracker like Ruby, huh?" he asked.

"Don't let her fool you, Jason," Jack said. "She actually is really sweet. Although she has an interesting way of showing it."

Intrigued, Jason asked, "Oh yeah? So, beneath all that sass, Ruby is actually really sweet? That's definitely surprising. And I'm pretty sure it must be a rare occurrence, too." He glanced at Ruby, curious about the truth behind Jack's words.

"Aw, Jack, don't tell him my secrets. I'm having fun with him."

Jack turned to Ruby, his expression shifting to one of genuine concern. "This is exactly why I worry about you so much. If you keep playing these games, you're going to get hurt."

Ruby waved her hand dismissively. "This guy is totally safe. Trust me. I was all over him, and he never even touched me once."

Jack nodded, clearly relieved. "Good. How about you repay him by being honest with him."

After a sigh Ruby relented and turned to Jason. "Alright. I actually really like that you were a gentleman. I guess I was testing you to see if it was legit or only an act. I really do like you."

Jason's eyes widened in surprise, touched by Ruby's candidness. "Oh wow, that's pretty unexpected," he said.

Tabby chimed in, bringing reassurance to the moment. "Don't worry, Ruby. We all know you're genuinely very sweet." She then turned her serious gaze toward Jason. "Right, Jason?"

He grinned, wondering if this was a trick question. "Yeah, of course. Ruby is genuinely sweet. Super sweet but also feisty. A perfect combination for a little firecracker like herself."

Jack clapped his hands together, breaking the moment. "Alright, everybody up to speed now? Ruby's not a tart, just a shameless flirt, and Jason is a genuinely nice guy."

Jason nodded in agreement. "Yeah, I think that basically covers it. Ruby's not easy, and I can exercise self-control around attractive women."

Tabby raised her glass, visibly relieved. "Happy we sorted that out."

Jason sipped his beer. "Yeah, me too. So, now that's cleared up, here's to a nice, relaxing, drama-free night with no surprises or further testing." The words hung in the air, a hopeful promise for the evening. As they continued to chat lightheartedly, Jason was completely at ease, reveling in the banter and laughter shared among friends.

Tabby finished her drink and glanced at the clock, with regret. "Well, it looks like our weekend has ended. We should call it a night. We all have to work tomorrow, right?"

Jason nodded, draining his glass. "Yeah, you're right." The thought of work loomed, but he pushed it aside for now.

Ruby turned to Jack. "Go ahead and walk Tabby home," she said. "Jason will make sure I get home safely." She turned to him. "Right?"

Jason felt a sense of responsibility. "Oh yeah, don't worry. I'll make sure Ruby here gets home safe." It felt good to be trusted.

Jack shrugged. "Okay then." He turned to Tabby, extending his arm. "Walk you home?"

She nodded, taking his arm, and the two of them stood up, ready to leave.

Jason watched as Jack and Tabby headed toward the exit. A soft smile appeared on his face, and he turned to Ruby, sensing the mood shift into something more intimate. "So, it's just the two of us now," he said, the words laced with warmth.

Ruby extended her hand toward him. He took it in his, his grip firm yet gentle as he rose to his feet. "Alright then, Miss Firecracker, let's get you home," he said, excitement in his voice.

Stepping out into the cool air, he experienced a sense of anticipation. Ruby broke the silence, sharing a thought that had clearly been on her mind. "I knew Jack was torn between walking me home and walking Tabby home. That's why I volunteered you," she confessed.

"Of course he was torn," he said, draping his arm around her shoulder as they strolled down the street.

"He must trust you if he's willing to share his chaperone duties," she remarked.

With a squeeze of her shoulder, he said, "I'm glad. It gives me a chance to talk to you alone."

"Oh yeah? What secrets do you not want my brother to hear?" Ruby asked.

Jason paused mid-step, turning to face her. "Maybe I just want to flirt with you in private," he said, his voice hushed and teasing.

"Oh, you're going to flirt with me, are you?" she asked, her tone suggestive. "Not afraid of bringing out my inner temptress?"

"Not afraid of your inner temptress in the slightest," he said. "I've seen it come out plenty before."

"Yes, but it's always been me teasing you. We've yet to see what happens when you flirt back," she countered, her voice light and challenging.

Jason sensed a spark of mischief in his own heart. "You think you're the only one with a tease in you?" he asked.

"So we're going to tease each other now?" Ruby asked, excitement in her voice.

Jason said, "That's exactly what I'm going to do. I'm going to tease you. And you're going to flirt with me." The night seemed full of possibilities, and he couldn't wait to explore them with her.

Ruby feigned innocence, her eyes wide as she looked at him. "You're going to tease a shy little girl like me? That's so wicked of you."

Jason eyed her with suspicion, unconvinced by her performance. A shy little girl? He knew better. "Don't play coy with me. I know what you're like when it's just the two of us. You're anything but shy."

"I'm a delicate maiden," she insisted, with a look of innocence that Jason found unconvincing.

He shook his head. "Since when are you delicate? You're like a hurricane—wild and chaotic. You're the furthest thing from delicate." As he pulled her a little closer, he could feel the warmth between them. "God, you're beautiful when you smile. I can't get enough of it," Jason said, his fingers sliding down to her hips, caressing her.

"You like my smile, do you?" she asked, her voice softening.

"I love that smile. It's just so ... infectious. I can't help but smile back whenever I see it on your face," he admitted.

"The more you please me, the more I smile," she teased, her voice low and inviting.

Jason let his hands wander from her hips to the small of her back, pulling her against him. He leaned in closer, their breath mingling in the intimate space between them. "So, I just have to keep pleasing you? Is that all it takes?"

"I'm difficult to please. I can be very ... demanding," Ruby said.

"I don't mind if you're demanding. I like it when you demand things. I like ... how bossy you can be."

"And I like how eager you are to please me," she said, as the playful dance between them continued beneath the starry night sky.

"How can I resist?" he murmured, his gaze locked on hers. "You're too damn beautiful and tempting."

Ruby was clearly contemplating her next move. "Hmm ... What should I do with you now that I have you in my web?"

Jason said, "Well, I'm all yours. You can do whatever you want with me."

"I like the sound of that," Ruby said.

Unable to help himself, Jason nuzzled her neck, intoxicated by her closeness. "Good. Because you can have me. All of me. Whenever you want me. For as long as you want me."

There was a challenge in Ruby's eyes as she said, "Since I caught you, that means you're 'it.' Now it's your turn to chase me."

He hesitated, amusement flickering across his face. Then, in a sudden move, he pulled away, causing her to stumble. "That's your game, is it? You tease me, flirt with me, and then run off expecting me to chase you?"

"Like I told you," Ruby said with a grin, "Tag was my favorite game as a kid. I love being chased."

Jason shook his head in disbelief. Only she would tease him and then run away, expecting him to pursue her. "Do you like being caught once I catch up to you?" he asked.

"Oh no, no, no. *I* do the catching," Ruby declared with confidence. "But don't make it too easy for me. I like a challenge."

Jason said, "Don't worry, I'll make you work hard enough. But I'm not a complete fool. I'm not going to let you pin me down too easily, either."

Ruby pulled him in closer, her fingers tangled in his hair. "Pin you down, huh? Now you've got my imagination going to naughty places."

A shiver ran through Jason at her touch. "How naughty are we talking?" Jason asked, trying to maintain his composure.

Ruby's voice was low and sultry. "How naughty do you like it?"

Jason swallowed, the tension thickening between them. "You have no idea just how naughty I like it."

"Remember," she said, a lilt in her voice, "you're supposed to be walking me home safe and sound. I think the fox has been left in charge of the henhouse."

Jason appreciated Ruby's playful jab. She was right, of course—he was supposed to ensure she got home safely. But her teasing nature made it difficult for him to keep his hands to himself.

"Hasn't anyone told you? I'm a handful," Ruby said.

He shook his head, a soft laugh escaping him.

With a sudden burst of energy, Ruby grabbed Jason's hand and pulled him along. "C'mon, protector. Big brother will be calling soon to make sure I made it home safely. You don't want to end up in his crosshairs, do you?"

Jason allowed her to lead. "Oh, definitely not. Jack would literally rip me apart if he thought I hadn't gotten you home okay."

Jason continued to walk with Ruby into the night, enchanted by the moment. "It's a beautiful night," he said, tilting his head back to admire the celestial display. "Look at all the stars."

Ruby searched the sky, her exhilaration clear. "I can see Ursa Major."

Jason squinted, searching the vastness of the sky but unable to locate it. "Can you? I can't see it. You'll have to point it out to me."

"See the Big Dipper? It's part of that," Ruby said, her voice brimming with enthusiasm.

Jason craned his neck, spotting the familiar shape streaking across the night sky. "Ah, I think I see it now. I just need you to guide me to the rest."

"It's supposed to be a bear shape," Ruby continued, her finger tracing the constellation's outline. "Hera got pissed at Zeus and turned his mistress into a bear. And she ended up in the heavens. I forget the details."

He listened, nodding along to her words. "See, this is why I keep you around. You're so damn smart and you know about everything."

He noticed Ruby's cheeks flush, surprise crossing her face. "You think I'm smart?"

"Of course," he said, his gaze softening as he watched her. "You're extremely smart. Even if you're a little devilish. I still think you're one of the smartest people I know."

"Yeah, right," she said, shooting him a sideways glance.

He rolled his eyes and drew her a little nearer, sensing the warmth emanating from her. "What? You don't believe me? I'm offended. I'm completely genuine right now. Are you saying you don't believe that I find you intelligent?"

"Most guys don't even listen when I talk. I could be dumb as a post for all they care," Ruby said, her smile fading as the words slipped from her lips.

Jason frowned at her response, a protective instinct rising within him. "Most guys are idiots then. It's not your fault that they're not interested in what you have to say. They're morons for not wanting to listen to you talk. I'm more than happy to listen to you, even if it's just you listing the stars."

He watched as her smile returned, brighter this time, and it warmed him to see her spirits lift again. He grinned back, leaning over to plant a gentle kiss on her forehead. "And as if your intelligence wasn't enough, you're also funny, bold and absolutely gorgeous. I wouldn't be surprised if someone tried to make a deal with the devil to have you as their own."

Jason watched Ruby laugh, shaking her head as she teased him. "You're disarming me with your sweetness again."

"It's part of my strategy," he said. "Disarm, then seduce."

As they approached her apartment building, Ruby turned to him. "And here we are. You got me here without being assaulted."

He grinned and tugged her closer. "Of course I was able to get you here safely. I promised Jack, after all."

He noticed the sparkle in her gaze as she said, "I think you deserve a kiss for that."

His heartbeat quickened at her words. "Oh yeah? Just one kiss?"

"Just one. Our first official kiss. This is exciting, don't you think?"

"Definitely exciting. Can't wait," he said, anticipation in his voice.

"Lay it on me," she urged.

Jason pulled her by the hips until she was flush against him. His hands wrapped around her waist, holding her firmly as he looked down into her eyes, a wide grin spreading across his face. He loved how perfectly her frame fit against his.

"Are you sure? Once I start, I won't be able to stop myself," he said, his voice low.

"Are you going to talk or kiss me?" Ruby challenged, her gaze locked on to his.

"I'm done talking." He moved his hands along her neck. Their lips hovered a breath apart. He closed his eyes as his mouth pressed against hers. After days of waiting, he was finally tasting her. He deepened the kiss as he pulled her closer, one hand cradling the back of her head.

After a few moments, Ruby broke the kiss, her voice slightly breathless. "Thank you for walking me home."

Reluctantly, Jason pulled away, his heart still racing as he savored the softness he had experienced. He understood he had to keep things in check. "It was my pleasure," he said, his voice low.

"Goodnight," Ruby said.

He gave her one last gentle kiss on the forehead. "Goodnight, Ruby."

As she walked into her apartment, Jason stood there for a moment, watching her go, his heart still beating abnormally fast. The thrill of their first kiss lingered in the air. Finally, Jason turned to walk home, mulling over the time they spent together. As he replayed their conversations in his mind, a mixture of amusement and bewilderment overwhelmed him.

# 6 Passion

Jack strolled alongside Tabby, the evening air wrapping around them as he walked her home. The laughter and chatter from their night out still echoed in his mind.

"So, I see Jason's earned your trust," Tabby said. "You were totally cool with him walking Ruby home."

Jack nodded. "He seems like a nice kid, I suppose. And he really cares for Ruby." He hoped his words sounded more confident than he felt—Jason was still a bit of a wildcard in Jack's eyes.

Tabby chuckled, and Jack found himself enjoying the sound.

"He is," she said. "They make quite the interesting pair. I don't think Jason's used to being outfoxed by his date. It's fun to watch."

Jack grinned, a warmth spreading through him. "I'll admit, it's a little funny seeing him constantly try to get the upper hand with her and fail."

As they walked, Tabby reached for his hand. Jack savored the warmth of her touch, the simple connection between them bringing a sense of comfort that made the night even more special. They fell into a comfortable silence for a few minutes, enjoying each other's company, the rhythm of their footsteps creating a gentle backdrop to their thoughts. Jack stole glances at Tabby, captivated by her presence.

"Are you trying to peer into my soul again?" Tabby asked, glancing sideways at him.

Jack feigned innocence, tearing his gaze away with a grin.

She said, "I can never tell what you're thinking, but I feel like you can read my every thought."

He directed his attention toward her. In that moment, he took the time to appreciate her features, the way the soft glow of the streetlight caught the flecks of gold in her hazel eyes. "Sometimes I wish I really could read your mind. I think it'd be easier to know what you're thinking than trying to guess."

"Maybe I should go ahead and tell you then."

"I won't try to stop you," he said jokingly, but eagerness flickered in his eyes.

After a brief hesitation, she spoke. "I think I might be falling for you."

Jack studied her face. "Is that so? Why do you think that?"

Her response was filled with genuine sincerity. "I love the way you're a perfect gentleman. I love the way you protect and care for others. I love your kindness and generosity. You're kind of easy to fall for."

Jack half-teased, "Is that all you see in me?" He stopped in the middle of the sidewalk, fully focused on her. He took her other hand in his, caressing her knuckles with his thumb.

"Honestly? Being tall, dark and handsome doesn't hurt your appeal any," she said.

"Mmm, so you admit you think I'm handsome."

"Actually, I think you're absolutely captivating," she said, her tone suddenly serious.

Jack smiled. "Captivating? I've never thought of myself as captivating. Handsome, yes. Darkly charming, yes. But captivating is new." With a gentle tug on her arm, Jack pulled her closer until their bodies were nearly touching. "I can think of a few other things I'd like you to call me," he said, his voice teasing.

Curiosity sparked in her eyes as she asked, "Like what?"

Jack lowered his voice to a whisper. His lips brushed against her ear. "*Darling*. *Lover*. *Sweetheart*. Those work for me."

"You want to be my sweetheart?" she asked.

Jack didn't hesitate. "I wouldn't mind it." He wrapped his arms around her waist, pulling her against him. The thrill of her closeness sent a rush through him.

"Are you asking me to be your girlfriend?" she asked.

He pulled back enough to meet her gaze. "Maybe. Would you give me the honor?"

"I'd be delighted," she said. "Too bad we're not teenagers. I could wear your class ring."

Jack ran his fingers affectionately through her hair. "A shame. You could've made all the other girls jealous."

"As they should be. I feel like the luckiest girl alive right now," she said, her gaze steady and sincere.

He cupped her cheek, tilting her face up to meet his. The way she looked at him made his heart race. "And I feel like the luckiest guy for having you."

As she leaned into him, her eyes locked onto his. He felt a magnetic pull drawing them closer.

Jack said, "There's something I've been wanting to do all night." He leaned in further, their faces inches apart. He could see the anticipation in her eyes as he let his gaze flicker from her eyes to her lips and back again.

"Yes?" she breathed.

With a gentle touch, Jack traced Tabby's bottom lip with his thumb. "May I ..." he whispered, leaning in closer until their noses almost touched. Heat radiated from her skin as his breath brushed against her face, Jack filled with an undeniable desire as he awaited her permission to do the one thing that had consumed his thoughts all night.

"Please do," Tabby said.

That was all the encouragement Jack needed. He closed the distance between them, their lips meeting in a tender kiss that sent sparks flying through him.

Jack felt Tabby surrender to his kiss, as if the world vanished, leaving only them. Jack held her tightly, drawing her nearer. He couldn't get enough of her. As the seconds stretched on, the kiss deepened, transforming from sweet and soft to a passionate embrace of longing and desire.

After several long moments, Tabby finally broke the kiss, breathless. "Yeah, I'm definitely falling for you."

Jack smiled, reluctantly releasing her. He gazed down at her, his eyes heavy with desire. "Good. That was my plan all along."

Tabby turned to Jack and said, "Now that you're my boyfriend, it's totally appropriate for me to invite you up to my apartment for coffee."

"Is coffee all you're going to offer me?" he asked with a rush of excitement.

"Depends. Are you planning to work your charms on me?" she asked, her tone light and flirtatious.

Jack leaned closer, his whisper soft and intimate. "Is that really necessary? Are my charms not already working on you?"

"So you're saying I shouldn't invite you up for coffee if I want to keep my virtue intact?" Tabby asked.

"I don't think I said that," he said, his lips brushing against the sensitive skin of her neck.

She sighed at his touch. "I'm willing to risk it," she declared with determination, taking his hand and leading him up the stairs, toward her apartment door.

As Jack followed her, his heart pounded wildly in his chest. Anticipation and desire surged through him. Tabby unlocked the door, and he felt this was the beginning of something unforgettable.

Jack stepped into Tabby's apartment, following her as she hung her coat by the door. He took a moment to survey his surroundings, his eyes tracing the cozy décor that felt distinctly like her. The warmth of the space enveloped him, but it was Tabby who truly captured his attention. She radiated an enchanting beauty.

"I'll go make the coffee," she said, breaking the moment as she headed into the kitchen. Jack watched her leave, his gaze lingering until she was out of sight. As he meandered through the living room, he found himself drawn to her bookshelves. The titles blurred together in his mind, a mere backdrop to his thoughts of her.

Among some philosophy and *feng shui* books, a *kintsugi* pot caught his eye. It had a gentle, muted color, with fine lines of gold highlighting its cracks and imperfections. He absentmindedly traced his fingers along the spines of the books before finally tearing himself away from a well-loved copy of *The Great Gatsby* to settle on the couch.

Moments later, Tabby returned and sat beside him, handing him a steaming mug. His gaze shifted from the coffee to her. Jack sensed that this night was different, filled with unspoken possibilities.

"How's the coffee? Do you need cream and sugar?" she asked, her voice light.

Jack took a sip, his gaze darting between the steaming mug and her face. "No, I take my coffee black. This is good." He set the mug down on the coffee table and turned to face her fully.

Tabby removed her glasses, setting them on the table. "You're so close. I don't need these to see you."

Jack's heart raced at that simple gesture. He let his fingers drift to her cheek, tracing gentle patterns with his thumb. Tabby inched closer, her fingers brushing against his face, lightly grazing his eyebrow.

"I like your eyebrows."

A small laugh escaped him at the unexpected compliment. "You do? What are you, a connoisseur of fine eyebrow structure?"

"They're so perfect. Not a single hair out of place. How do you manage that?" she asked.

He fought against a shiver. "I didn't know you could make a whole art out of making sure your eyebrows are in order."

Tabby's gaze made it hard for him to focus on anything else. "I guess it comes naturally to you."

With her hands on him, he found it increasingly difficult to concentrate. The atmosphere between them was charged. Tabby's voice was low and teasing as she spoke. "I feel a bit of sexual tension between us. What should we do about that?"

Jack's grip on her tightened instinctively. "I don't know. What do *you* think we should do about it?"

She flashed him a playful grin. "Maybe we should break that tension."

Jack pulled her closer, their bodies aligning as she settled into his lap. He reached up, his fingers brushing through her hair, the strands slipping through his fingers like silk.

"Is it time for you to sweep me off my feet and carry me through the threshold?" she asked. In one swift motion, he stood, lifting her into his arms, gauging her reaction as he looked down.

"That way to the bedroom." She pointed to a door to the right of the kitchen.

"As you wish." He carried her to the bedroom, her weight like nothing in his arms. He gently deposited her onto the bed. As he stood up to remove his shoes, he glanced back at her, noticing how her eyes had darkened with anticipation. Jack stood at the edge of the bed, his heart pounding as he unbuttoned his shirt. With a deliberate, gentle motion, he climbed onto the bed. As he crawled over her, the warmth of her body enveloped him.

"Darling, look at me," he said softly. Jack's eyes locked onto Tabby's, and for a fleeting moment, he felt as if he were drowning in the depths of her gaze. He reached out, gently cupping her face, his thumbs grazing her cheeks. "I want you. All of you. Right now," he murmured. A surge of desire overcame him.

In that charged moment, they undressed one another, every movement steeped in intimacy. The world around them faded into oblivion; it was only the two of them, entwined in a passionate embrace. As they moved together, their bodies found an instinctual rhythm, each sigh and gasp resonating with pleasure. Jack watched Tabby's breath quicken. The intimacy enveloped him, and he surrendered to the experience.

Afterward, as they lay intertwined in blissful warmth, she turned to him. "I can't begin to tell you how good I feel right now."

Jack tightened his embrace, his arms wrapping around her possessively. He buried his face in her hair. He placed a few more kisses on her neck, relishing the way she felt against him. "I could hold you like this forever," he murmured, with a surge of affection for her.

As Tabby closed her eyes and rested her head on his chest, he ran his fingers gently through her hair, sensing her relax further into him he pulled her even closer.

In his arms he felt her breathing even out, a sign that she was drifting off to sleep. He continued to stroke her hair and placed a soft kiss on the top of her head.

"Sleep, darling," he said. "I'll be right here when you wake up."

As dawn broke, Jack lay awake, Tabby nestled comfortably in his arms. The warmth of her body against his was soothing as he brushed his thumb against her cheek. "I'm sorry to have to wake you, but it's almost time for me to go," he said.

He noticed the sigh that escaped her lips, a reminder of the reality awaiting them both. "Oh yeah, work. I suppose you should go home and shower. Maybe put on some clean clothes," she said.

"What's wrong with my current state of dress?"

Her teasing smile lit up the dim morning light. "It's perfect for me," she said, "but something tells me you'd be underdressed if you went to work completely naked."

"True," he conceded, glancing down at his bare torso. "As amazing as that would be, I don't think I'd be working for very long if I went in naked."

A rush of warmth enveloped him as she leaned in and kissed him, a fleeting moment that left him wanting more. When she pulled away, he watched as she slipped out of bed, wrapping herself in a soft robe. His gaze lingered on her, captivated by the way the fabric clung to her form, finding her both adorable and alluring. In that quiet morning light, he couldn't shake the feeling of how lucky he was to share this moment with her.

"C'mon, sexy," Tabby said, playfully climbing back onto the bed and tugging at his hand. "Time to put on last night's clothes and do the walk of shame back to your place."

Jack shook his head. "You make it sound so scandalous."

"Well, you certainly bring out my sinful side. We only just met, after all," she said. Jack admired how her eyes sparkled with delight.

"I love your bad girl side," he said, a sly smile forming as he dressed. She was such a prim and proper lady, but he had discovered a devilish nature lurking beneath the surface.

"Only for you," Tabby said, and a warmth spread through him at her words.

Jack stepped closer, standing before her, and lifted her chin gently to meet his gaze. "You have no idea what that does to my ego. Hearing you say that I'm the only one who gets to see this side of you."

In a playful gesture, she covered his eyes with her hands. "I need to get you some sunglasses. Those eyes of yours cast quite the spell on me."

He grinned, pulling her hands away and leaning in closer, their faces inches apart. "My eyes casting a spell on you? Darling, you're the one who has bewitched me."

She reached for his shirt, her fingers working to button it up. "Let's cover you up. Your pecs are a bit distracting," she teased.

"A bit distracting?" Jack asked. "I think you like them."

"A little too much," she admitted, and he saw the blush creeping into her cheeks.

He whispered in her ear, "So you're telling me you're going to have a hard time concentrating today because of a particular, distracting part of my body?"

He watched as her flush deepened. "You have ... nice parts," she murmured, her voice barely audible.

"So do you," he said, his gaze sliding down to her bare legs peeking out from under the robe.

Suddenly, Tabby stood up. "I'll go make coffee," she said, almost rushing out of the room. Jack could see that she was flustered by her desire and was making an effort to distract herself. The magnetic pull between them was only growing stronger, and he relished the thrill it brought him.

When he entered the kitchen, he caught her gaze.

"Oh good, you're dressed," she said as she handed him a steaming mug of coffee.

Jack accepted the mug, warmth radiating from it and from his smile. "Did you think I'd come out here naked?" he teased, unable to resist the urge to provoke a reaction. Sipping his coffee, he maintained eye contact with her over the rim of the mug.

It was evident she was still flustered, attempting to divert her attention by picking up her phone and aimlessly scrolling. "I should check my messages," she muttered, but he saw she was struggling to focus.

Jack savored the moment, enjoying the tension between them, and he found himself drawn in deeper. He stepped closer, his hand resting on the small of Tabby's back, their bodies almost touching. He glanced over her shoulder. "Any messages from any other men? Or am I the only one who's been lucky enough to talk to you since we met?"

"Just Jason, but he doesn't count," she said.

"Of course, that doesn't count. What's he saying? Anything interesting?"

"He says, 'What's the Dewey decimal number for *Mario Kart*?'"

"Sounds about right," Jack said, taking a sip of coffee. "Have you answered him yet?"

"Yeah—794.85," Tabby said, her fingers still scrolling through her messages.

"Of course. How could I not know that?" he said, feigning a serious tone. "Remind me how you two are friends again?"

"He's always in the library. I sort of adopted him—kinda like a lost puppy," she explained.

The image of Jason as a lost puppy in the library made Jack grin. "You're well aware that you're too nice for your own good, aren't you?"

"Don't worry. He's mostly harmless," Tabby reassured him.

Jack placed his mug on the counter and held her, pulling her close. "I'm more worried about the 'too nice' part. What if some charming guy tries to sweet talk you and take you away from me?"

Tabby's arms instinctively went around his neck. "I don't think anyone could be sweeter than you."

Jack's smile widened, his hands sliding down to her hips, pulling her even closer. "Are you sure? Because you're a very attractive woman. I know there are probably tons of men out there who would love a chance with you."

"Well then, they missed their chance," she said confidently, and he admired her self-assuredness.

Jack's hands slid lower, gently gripping her thighs. He knew he should leave soon, but the moment was too enthralling to break. "Are you sure about that? What if a man were to walk in here right now, right this moment, and try to kiss you?"

"You'd defend my honor and show him the door," Tabby said.

Jack's fingers slipped under her robe, brushing lightly against her bare skin. He felt warmth at her words, but he couldn't help teasing her. "Now, you're giving me too much credit—defending your honor is not exactly what I had in mind."

"What do you mean?" she asked, her curiosity clear in her bright eyes.

He looked down at her, meeting her gaze. "What I mean is, if a man walked in here right now and tried to take you away from me, I'd make sure to leave no doubt in his mind that you are very much taken. I'd leave no room for interpretation."

Tabby held his gaze, her expression softening in a way that made his heart skip. "I believe you would."

Suddenly aware of the time slipping away, Jack glanced at the clock, a reluctant sigh escaping him as he pulled his hands from under her robe. He hated to break the moment. "As much as I'd love to keep standing here in the kitchen with you, I can't keep putting off the inevitable. I have to go to work."

He saw the flicker of disappointment cross her face as she nodded. "And I have to get ready, too. Call me later?"

He forced a smile, though his chest felt heavy as he let her go. "I'll call you as soon as I can get away. Now, go get yourself dressed before I'm tempted to keep you in that robe all day."

She pulled him in for a quick kiss, then turned and walked toward her bedroom. Jack's heart raced as he watched her go, his gaze lingering on the way her bare legs peeked from beneath the hem of her robe. Finally, he turned and left, still feeling the warmth of the moment.

# 7 Restraint

It was a typical Monday morning at the library, and Tabby felt boredom pressing down on her. Surrounded by stacks of books and papers, she struggled to focus on her tasks, the slow pace of the day stretching on endlessly. She was interrupted by the chime of her phone. Glancing down, she saw Jason's name flash up on the screen.

His text read: "I'm thinking of taking a long lunch. Want to meet at Franco's?"

"Yeah, I could do lunch," she responded

"Great! Meet me there in about ten minutes?"

"See you then." As she set down her phone, the tedium of the morning lifted. Tabby gathered her things and made her way to the diner after waiting out the clock on several unproductive minutes.

The familiar scent of grilled sandwiches and simmering soups welcomed her as she stepped inside the diner. Her eyes scanned the room until they landed on Jason, who was already walking through the restaurant searching for her. He was headed toward a booth by the window, where sunlight poured in, casting a warm glow around them.

"Long lunch, huh? Having a rough Monday morning?" she greeted.

Jason let out a sigh. "You could say that. My brain is fried from working on this report, and I hate everything about it. I needed to get out of there. What about you? Slow morning?"

Tabby nodded. "Yeah, there's never anyone at the library on Mondays. I've got a volunteer keeping an eye on things, so I can take as long as I want."

"Good. That's perfect. Gives us plenty of time to talk," Jason said, leaning back in the booth, visibly relaxing as the tension of the morning began to fade.

"I can tell you're dying to tell me something. So, spill it," Tabby urged, leaning in closer, eager for the revelation.

Jason took a deep breath. "So, you're never going to guess what happened last night."

"Well, I know you walked Ruby home. I'm assuming you got her there in one piece?"

"Of course I got her home. I told Jack I'd walk her back safely, and I'm not about to piss him off," Jason said. "But my night didn't end there."

"Oh yeah?" Tabby asked, leaning even closer as she awaited his story.

Jason's grin grew as he recounted the evening. "Once I walked Ruby to her apartment building and said goodnight, a very interesting conversation happened." Jason's smile turned sly as he recalled her words. "I was walking away, getting ready to leave, and then she said—and I quote—'You know, I think you deserve a kiss for getting me home safely.'"

Tabby's eyes widened. "Did she, now? And did you oblige?"

Jason said, "Without hesitation. It was quite a struggle, but I did my duty as her protector and accepted the kiss. Because, like she said, I got her home safely, so I earned it."

Tabby laughed, shaking her head. "Yes, you were a good boy. A well-deserved kiss indeed."

Jason leaned back in the booth, a playful laugh escaping his lips as he shook his head at Tabby. "You know, I *was* a good boy last night. A perfect gentleman, really. I didn't even try anything more. I was the epitome of restraint and chivalry. I think I deserve some kind of award for it."

Tabby, recalling her own behavior last night, quickly changed the subject. She redirected her gaze to the menu, her fingers tracing the printed words as she muttered, "So, what to order?"

Jason narrowed his eyes at her. "Not so fast. Don't even try to change the topic. You're distracting me. Did something happen with you two last night, too?"

"What? What do you mean?" Tabby asked, feigning innocence.

His grin widened as he watched her intently. "When I mentioned restraint and chivalry, you suddenly changed the subject to the menu. That means there's something you don't want to talk about. Spill it."

Tabby paused, reluctant to reveal her complete lack of restraint. "I ... had a good night too."

Jason's amusement deepened. "A 'good night,' huh? Now that's suspicious. Define 'good night.'"

"Well, you know Jack walked me home. We had a ... nice time," she admitted, her voice trailing off as she avoided his gaze.

"I see. A 'nice time.' I feel like that's an understatement. Were you a good girl, or did you misbehave a little?" Jason asked.

Tabby paused, inhaling deeply, her eyes still averted. "Well, if you must know, Jack asked me to be his girlfriend, and I said yes ... and I ... invited him up for coffee ... and he ... uh ... ended up spending the night."

Jason's expression was one of surprise. "And how exactly did he end up spending the night? Come on, give me the details."

With a smile, Tabby said, "You know ... he swept me off my feet ... literally."

"So, Jack literally swept you off your feet and took you upstairs? Sounds like a typical move from him."

Her gaze turned dreamy. "He's so charming," she said, her voice soft and wistful, lost in the evening's memory.

"Oh yeah? You fell prey to his devilish ways?" he asked.

"He is a perfect gentleman," she said, looking guilty.

"Of course he was. Jack would be nothing less than perfectly charming, especially when he's trying to woo you," Jason said.

Tabby shot back playfully, "You're the one with the roguish reputation, not him."

Jason gasped dramatically, pretending to be offended. "What are you implying, Miss Delaney? That I'm not a gentleman?"

"You *can* be a gentleman. But it doesn't come naturally to you," Tabby said.

"Touché," he laughed, a sound that always seemed to brighten her day. "I'm a little rough around the edges, I admit it, but I'm not a lost cause. I know how to behave myself."

"And we're all very proud of you for that," Tabby said, sincerity behind her words.

"Yeah, yeah, I'm a good boy. I was a complete and total gentleman. No wild, impulsive moves. Even though I wanted a lot more," he added with exaggerated emphasis, laughter spilling from him once more.

As Tabby mulled over his words, her expression turned to one of concern. She laid the menu on the table and met Jason's eyes with a steady, searching look. "Are you going to be exclusive with her?" she asked.

Jason looked at her, surprise flickering in his eyes at her directness. "Ruby, you mean? Why are you asking?"

Her expression turned thoughtful as she considered her words. "I'm wondering how this is going to play out. If Ruby gets her heart broken, that would be ... messy."

"It's going to be fine," he reassured her, a sense of conviction in his voice. "Ruby won't get her heart broken. I plan on being completely exclusive with her for as long as she'll have me as hers."

Tabby felt a rush of relief.

"You were concerned about her, weren't you?" Jason teased.

Tabby admitted, "I was more concerned about Jack's reaction and what that would mean for you."

"Oh yeah, good point—if I ever hurt Ruby, Jack will probably kill me. I've got a feeling Ruby's heart is very precious, and Jack's not going to let anyone break it."

As Tabby placed her order for a sandwich and soda, Jason focused on her, resuming his earlier probing. "So, aside from Jack's charming manners, how was the rest of last night?" He leaned forward with an inquisitive smile. "I'm assuming it was eventful."

Tabby's tone turned playful. "What exactly are you asking?"

With a grin, Jason shot Tabby a knowing look. "Well, I'm just saying that if Jack spent the night with you, things must have escalated a little further than coffee. Or am I wrong?"

Tabby paused, her mind drifting back to the night she had spent with Jack. A rush of warmth enveloped her as she recalled the moments they shared. She tried to appear nonchalant. But she could tell Jason wasn't fooled for a second. It was obviously written all over her face that she had thoroughly enjoyed herself.

"Interested in learning the private details of my love life, are you?" she asked.

"Of course I'm curious," he laughed, leaning back in the booth with a satisfied smirk. "I can see from your reaction that something happened with Jack. You're trying to be coy, but I know you that well. You enjoyed yourself last night, didn't you?"

"Alright, alright. Do you really want to know?" Tabby finally relented.

"Yes, I do. I want the details. Come on, tell me," Jason urged, anticipation clear in his voice.

Tabby's eyes sparkled as she recalled the night. "It was the best sex of my life," she admitted, her voice a blend of awe and excitement. "I'm talking, I didn't even know sex could be that good."

Jason smiled broadly. "Oh yeah? I take it Jack was the perfect gentleman and treated you right then? Or was he a little rough with you?"

A far-off look appeared in Tabby's eyes. "He was extremely considerate," she said, the memory vivid in her mind.

Jason nodded. "Of course, Jack would never be anything less than perfect. He's a smooth-as-hell bastard. He was obviously sweet to you the whole time, yeah?"

"Yes, and he held me all night long. Jason, I think I'm really falling for this guy," she confessed, her voice softening with the weight of her feelings.

His smile widened at her admission. "I can see that. You have that dreamy look on your face. You're falling hard for him, huh?"

"To be honest, I liked him from the moment we met. I liked the way he showed up at Fitzgerald's to meet us, making sure we were respectable enough to be hanging out with his little sister."

Jason said, "Yeah, It was his 'meet the family' night. He wanted to be sure you girls were proper ladies, and we weren't going to corrupt her."

"I don't really blame him," Tabby said. "Some of her other friends are troublemakers. You'll see what I mean if you meet them."

"Oh, I've heard stories. Like that guy Brad. Sounds like he's a bit of a douche," Jason said with amusement.

"More than a bit. But don't worry about him. He's not around anymore," Tabby reassured him.

"Oh? He's moved? Or did Jack strangle him and bury his body in the backyard?"

Tabby laughed at Jason's dark humor. "No, he's in jail."

"For what? Tax evasion?" Jason asked. "Or being a douche?"

"For being a douche," she said.

"That's a crime?" Jason feigned shock. "Damn! I owe some fines."

Tabby and Jason shared a laugh, the warmth of their friendship surrounding her. But as the laughter faded, a serious expression crossed Tabby's face. She looked at Jason, with concern. "We're still going to be besties, right? Even though we're both in relationships now?"

Jason's surprise was evident as he met her gaze. "Of course we are, Tabby. You think we're going to stop hanging out just because we've got relationships now? That's never going to happen."

She grinned. "Good. Because someone needs to keep you in line. Especially now that you have an unpredictable fiery girlfriend to tempt you into trouble," she said.

Jason nodded. "That's true. I'll probably need you and Jack to keep me on the right path. Ruby will no doubt lead me astray."

"We should make it a thing. The four of us at Fitzgerald's on Friday nights, so we can check-in and make sure we're all behaving ourselves."

"Yeah, that's actually a damn good idea. That way we can keep any impulses and urges in check."

As they finished their lunch, Tabby announced, "My treat this time." She grabbed the bill and made her way toward the register.

Jason laughed and shouted after her, "You didn't have to do that. I was going to pay for lunch today, you know?"

Tabby turned her head, a grin across her face. "I know, but I stuck you with the bill the last two times."

"Yeah, you did," Jason admitted. "I can't argue with that."

With the bill settled, Tabby glanced at her watch. "It's after two. Are you going back to work or are you calling it a day?"

He paused, considering. "I think I'm calling it a day. I'll probably get more work done at home than I will in the office."

"Walk me back to the library, then? I can't call it a day yet. I'm the one with the keys," she said.

"Okay, I'll accompany you back to the library. I'm a perfect gentleman now, after all," Jason said, rising to follow her.

"That's what I hear. If you get me there safely, I'll even give you a hug. No kiss, though."

Jason feigned disappointment. "No kiss? I go through all the trouble of being a perfect gentleman and walking you back to work, and I just get a hug?"

"Yes, a nice platonic hug. I'll let Ruby take care of your kissing needs," she said.

"Fine, a nice platonic hug it is. I can behave myself," he said with resignation.

As they walked together toward the library, there was a warmth in Tabby's chest. She appreciated the easy companionship she and Jason shared. When they reached the steps, she turned and wrapped her arms around him, giving him a friendly hug goodbye.

Jason's eyes were full of affection. "Have a good day, Tabby. Be good," he said, his voice carrying a hint of sincerity as she began walking up the steps.

"Always," she said, flashing him a bright smile that lingered in his mind long after she disappeared inside the building.

# 8 Uncertainty

Jack drove into the parking lot of the garden center and parked his car. He watched as the shop's front door swung open, and his spirits brightened at the sight of Ruby stepping out, looking weary and a bit disheveled after a long day at work. With a grin, he rolled down the window just as she approached.

"Come to give your little sister a ride home?" she asked.

"Of course," he said. "What kind of big brother would I be if I didn't?"

She opened the door and hopped into the car. "Good, because I'm exhausted."

As he pulled out of the parking lot, Jack glanced over at Ruby. "I can tell. You look like you've been wrangling wild monkeys."

Ruby rolled her eyes but couldn't hide her smile. "I work hard, ya know. Do you think I'm spritzing plants with water all day?"

"Actually, yes," he said, anticipating the playful smack that always followed his jabs.

True to form, she hit his arm with a laugh. "Do you know how much a bag of soil weighs? Forty pounds!"

Jack exaggerated his reaction, rubbing the spot where she had smacked him. "Ow! Yes, I'm absolutely aware of how much a bag of soil weighs."

Jack glanced at Ruby as she shifted the conversation. "So, how was your day?" she asked, her tone light as he navigated the familiar streets.

The memories of the morning rushed back. "Busy. I did a pruning job on a few trees and spent the rest of the day catching up on paperwork in the office."

Ruby shook her head, a trace of sympathy in her voice. "God, they make you do everything. Don't you have interns for that?"

"You mean the college kids? They do some of the grunt work, but they can also be a major pain. Some of them I wouldn't trust to water my houseplants without killing them."

"Well, you work too hard," she said, concern in her eyes.

"I could say the same thing about you." A thought lingered in his mind, urging him to speak up. "Can I ask you something?"

"Sure, what's up?"

He hesitated, grappling with how to broach the subject. "Have you ever thought about your future?" he began. "Dating and marriage and all that?"

Her eyes brightened at the question. "Well, I've been hanging out with Jason. I kinda like him, you know."

Jack shot her a quick glance, then returned his gaze to the road, a knot of emotions tightening in his stomach. "I had a feeling that was the case. It's obvious he's interested in you too."

"And you said you like him more than my other friends, right?"

Jack sighed, searching for the right words. "Well, he's definitely more tolerable compared to the other guys you've dated. Especially that Nick idiot."

Ruby's expression was one of exasperation. "Yes, yes. I know you didn't like Nick. Or Alex, or Liam, or Ryan."

"You must admit, you've dated some real winners. Alex was a pothead, Liam was a lazy jerk, and Ryan broke up with you over text. They're not exactly prize-winning men," Jack said.

"Jason's not a loser, though," Ruby defended, her tone earnest. "He has a good job, and he's best friends with Tabby. I know you like Tabby." She nudged him.

Jack rolled his eyes. "That's true. Jason's not a total loser. I'm only concerned, that's all."

"How about I interrogate you about your love life instead? So, you walked Tabby home last night. How'd it go? Don't bother lying, because you know she's gonna tell me."

Jack sighed, realizing he couldn't evade the question. "It went well. More than well, actually ... I like her a lot. She's not like any woman I've ever met."

"I knew you'd like her. She's exactly your type—sweet and innocent."

Jack grinned, recalling their first meeting. "Oh, she's so much more than sweet and innocent. She just doesn't advertise it as much as some women do."

"Well, I know she's holding out for her Prince Charming, so if you want to keep seeing her, be sure to treat her like a princess."

"Trust me, I will. I've never treated a woman the way I've been treating her. I've never had the urge to be so damn nice to someone until I met her. She ... makes me want to be better, somehow."

"Jack, are you already in love?"

Ruby's question took him by surprise, leaving him momentarily speechless as he pondered the significance of her words. He hadn't considered *love* and *Tabby* together until this moment.

"Damn. Maybe I am," he finally admitted, with a rush of unexpected clarity.

"Aw ... I'm jealous. I want to be in love," Ruby said, her voice tinged with longing.

As Jack drove up the hill toward their apartment building, he said, "Don't be. Being in love isn't all rainbows and butterflies. It can be brutal."

"Yeah, I remember how in sixth grade Tommy Miller told me he loved me, then I caught him kissing Isabella Lopez in the bleachers at the soccer field," she recounted with bitterness.

"Sixth-grade crushes don't count," Jack said, pulling into their driveway. "But what Tommy did to you was a dick move. He clearly didn't know what love was, anyways."

Ruby leaned over and planted a kiss on his cheek. "Thanks for the ride, bro."

"Anything for my baby sis," he said, reaching across to ruffle her hair. "Now, go get some rest. I know you've had a long day."

As Ruby climbed the stairs to her apartment and Jack headed to his own, her question lingered in his mind. Was he in love with Tabby? The thought made him uneasy. He dropped his keys on the table and collapsed onto the couch with a heavy sigh. He suddenly felt drained, from both the day and the new realization weighing on his heart.

# 9 Recklessness

There was excitement in the air Friday night as Jason waited at Fitzgerald's Pub, his heart light with anticipation. He sat in an empty booth, his eyes scanning for familiar faces. He brightened as he spotted Tabby entering.

"You're the first one here," he said. "Not a surprise—you're the very picture of punctuality."

Tabby slid into the seat across from him. "Jack's on his way. He texted me he's waiting for Ruby and will walk over with her."

Jason nodded. "Yeah, that tracks."

Moments later, Jack and Ruby arrived. Jason watched as Jack greeted Tabby, leaning over to plant a quick kiss on her cheek before settling into the seat beside her.

Ruby gave Jason a shove.

"Okay, okay! I'm making room, sheesh," he said, feigning indignation as he dramatically shifted over.

The mood was light as Jason leaned back in his seat, wrapping an arm around Ruby. He missed her presence, and it was good to have her close again. Jack's voice broke through his thoughts.

"How's your week been, Jason?" he asked.

Jason contemplated the question. "It's been busy. Same old, same old, you know? There's always a mountain of paperwork on my desk that never seems to disappear. Other than that, it's been just fine."

Jack said, "I hear that you and Ruby have been spending a lot of time together."

Jason glanced at Ruby, the warmth of their shared moments evident in his expression. "Yeah, we have. We've definitely been keeping each other entertained." He noticed Jack's shift in demeanor and braced himself, anticipating a lecture. He respected Jack for looking out for his sister, even if it meant enduring "the talk."

"I know Ruby likes you a lot," Jack began, his tone serious but not unkind. "And you're not a bad guy. So, I'm okay with you dating my sister. Just don't hurt her. I don't want to have to harm you."

Jason smiled at the standard brotherly speech. He appreciated Jack's protective nature. "Don't worry, I have no intention of hurting Ruby. I like her a lot and plan on taking excellent care of her."

Ruby said, "Wow Jack, you went easy on him." She turned to Jason. "Usually, he's armed when he has 'the talk' with my dates."

Jason's laughter burst forth. "What? He didn't bring his gun with him today? Did he forget it at home?"

"No," Ruby said, shaking her head. "He invites them to the shooting range to talk. I'm serious."

Jason laughed again, imagining the scenario. "He takes them to the shooting range to threaten them? That must be intimidating as hell."

Jack took the banter in stride. "I'd be happy to give you a lesson at the range if you're interested."

Ruby quickly chimed in, "No!"

Jack laughed at her swift response, and Jason pondered the offer. He was aware of Jack's expertise with firearms, and while it was all in good fun, the idea was both thrilling and terrifying.

"I don't know," Jason said. "It might be kind of awesome. Good thing Ruby vetoed it, though. Otherwise, I might have said yes."

Jack pushed himself up from the booth. "I'll get us a round of drinks," he announced before heading toward the bar.

Jason settled back into the seat. After the exchange he and Jack had just had, he could use a drink. He turned his gaze to Ruby. He was ready for a relaxed evening with her.

Moments later, Jack returned, a server trailing behind, balancing a tray. "Thanks," Jason said, nodding in appreciation as the server set down their drinks.

Ruby squeezed a lime, juice splattering as she licked her fingers with a playful grin. "I'm so glad the weekend is here!" she said.

Jason smiled at her antics, the sight of her licking the lime juice off her fingers stirring something within him—a tension that was both exciting and teasing. Jason glanced at Jack, aware that he might be tempted to criticize Ruby for her manners.

Tabby took Jack's hand and asked sweetly, "How was work, sweetheart?"

Jason took another sip of his beer. He appreciated Tabby's effort to maintain harmony—Ruby had a knack for becoming crabby when someone tried to correct her. The last thing he wanted was for her to clash with her brother and ruin the evening's vibe.

"Work was great," Jack responded with a smile. "I finally had that meeting with the Parks Department I've been dreading. It turned out to be very productive."

Jason nodded, recognizing Tabby's intent to steer the conversation in a positive direction. "That's great. Good to know you had a productive week."

"Isn't anybody going to ask me how my day was?" Ruby asked.

Jason smiled at her sudden outburst. Leave it to Ruby to make everything about her—it was part of her charm. "How was your day, angel?" he asked, feigning innocence.

"It sucked," Ruby said. "We got a huge shipment of marigolds in, so I had to work in the baking hot sun all day."

Jack said, "Stop fishing for sympathy. I know you love your job. Otherwise, you'd have come to work for me when I offered."

Ruby said, "You only want me to work for you because you want to monitor me. I'm on to you."

Tabby turned to Ruby, adding, "I'm pretty sure Jack's right. You've told me more than once how much you love working outdoors."

Ruby looked at Jason, her eyes wide with dismay. "Aren't you going to defend me?"

Jason chuckled at her plea for defense. The pout on her face reminded him of a child seeking attention. "I don't know ... Why should I defend you?"

"Because they're ganging up on me, and you're supposed to be my date!" she said.

He enjoyed the lighthearted exchange. "Just because I'm your date doesn't mean I have to defend your honor. You're capable of defending yourself."

"No goodnight kiss for you tonight, then," she said, crossing her arms and turning away with a frown.

"Oh yeah? You gonna be that mean to me? No goodnight kiss?"

Tabby said, "I'll defend you, Ruby. Even though you love your job, I know you work really hard. I sympathize with you."

Jack looked at Tabby with a soft smile. "I think everyone's checked in but you, darling. How was the library today?"

"Oh, very exciting," Tabby said. "It's book club night, and they'll be reading *The Pact* next. We ran out of copies so I had to call around to all the other libraries to get more. Quite thrilling."

Jason tried to decipher whether she was serious or just being playful. He found it amusing that a seemingly mundane task could be considered an exciting day for her.

Jack smiled warmly at Tabby. "Sounds like you were the hero of book club night."

"So, what are everyone's plans for the weekend, now that it's here?" Tabby asked.

Jason grinned. "I've got a surprise for my girl planned this weekend," he announced, unable to contain his excitement. "It's going to be good."

Ruby perked up. "A surprise? What is it?" she asked, eagerness in her voice.

Jason enjoyed the suspense he was building. "I can't tell you, angel. It'll ruin the surprise," he teased. "I promise you're gonna love it, though."

Ruby pouted, her curiosity clearly unsatisfied. "At least give me a hint," she pressed.

With a playful sigh, Jason gave in to her persistence. "Alright, I'll give you a hint. It'll be fun, you'll love it and you won't have to lift a finger."

Ruby frowned, clearly unimpressed by his vague clue. "That's the shittiest hint ever. Give me a real one."

"All I'm going to say is: it'll be very relaxing," he said. He wanted to keep the details minimal to tease her further.

He caught Jack eyeing him suspiciously. Tabby glanced around the group. She seemed eager to redirect the conversation.

"Anybody else?" Tabby said.

Jack said, "I promised Tabby a picnic and to teach her how to shoot. How about tomorrow? The weather is supposed to be beautiful again."

Tabby's face lit up in response. "Yes, tomorrow is perfect. With summer ending, we probably won't have many more beautiful days," she said, clearly excited. Jason noted how easily her joy seemed to flow around Jack.

As the conversation shifted, Tabby turned her attention to Ruby. "How about you, Ruby? Any plans for the weekend—besides Jason's big surprise, of course," she asked.

Ruby, obviously still harboring some resentment toward Jason for his evasiveness, answered with a hint of drama. "Well, Shannon did invite me to go to the beach. I was going to say no, but since I don't have any set plans, I don't know. Maybe I should," she said, her gaze locking on to Jason, challenging him to divulge more about his plans.

Jason sighed. The thought of Ruby spending time at the beach gnawed at him. He could picture the attention she might attract, and it made his stomach churn. The tension was thick enough to cut as Jack weighed in on the situation.

"You may as well tell her what you've got planned, man. She's not going to let you off the hook," he said.

Jason could feel the pressure mounting. Jack was right—Ruby wouldn't drop it until she got the answer she was looking for. With a resigned grin, Jason spoke. "Fine, I'll spill. How can I say no to my girl?"

He took a small sip of his beer, bracing himself for Ruby's expected reaction.

"This weekend, I'm planning to take you on a weekend trip to Miami. I've booked us a room at a nice hotel, with a rooftop pool. You can relax in the pool all day, and we'll go for some nice meals at night. It's going to be a fun weekend."

Ruby's eyes sparkled with excitement. She was the picture of joy, her happiness a vivid contrast to Jack's stern expression. Jason grinned as he looked at her. Ruby had mentioned more than once her desire to travel and bask in the sun—an adventurous spirit wrapped in a cheerful demeanor. However, he was acutely aware of Jack's discontent simmering beneath the surface.

"Wow, that's a really big surprise, Jason," Tabby exclaimed, her eyes wide with astonishment as she took in the news.

Jason took a sip of his beer while stealing a glance at Jack, trying to gauge his response.

Jack drummed his fingers rhythmically on the table. "That's very ... impetuous," he remarked, his tone heavy with disapproval.

Jason was fully aware that Jack's concerns stemmed from the fact that he was whisking Ruby away for a weekend of adventure. This wasn't just a quick trip—it was an opportunity for them to explore their budding relationship in a more intimate setting. Jason couldn't deny that this was part of the allure of the surprise.

Ruby, blissfully unaware of the brewing storm around them, hugged Jason's arm tightly. "I've never been to Miami before! I've always wanted to go!" she said, her enthusiasm radiating off her like sunshine.

Jason felt a swell of warmth in his chest as he basked in her affection. "I know, angel. That's exactly why I chose it for our weekend trip," he said, savoring her reaction.

Yet, it was clear that not everyone was caught up in the moment's joy. It was as if he could see the gears turning in Jack's mind, plotting his next move. Unspoken tension hovered in the air.

Just then, Jack's phone buzzed insistently on the table, shattering the tension. "Excuse me," he said, glancing at the screen before stepping away to take the call.

Tabby turned to Jason. "Are you out of your mind? Jack is going to tear you apart!"

Jason couldn't suppress a smile, finding amusement in the drama unfolding around him. "I think I can handle Jack," he said, unbothered by the prospect of Jack trying to persuade Ruby to back out. She could be incredibly stubborn.

"Oh my god, why did I introduce you two? Do you realize how much pleading I'm going to have to do to save your sorry ass?" Tabby said, shaking her head in exasperation.

Jason's confidence was unwavering. "Relax. Everything's going to be fine."

"I could strangle you myself," she shot back, frustration etched on her face.

"You're cute when you're angry," Jason said.

Jack returned to the table with an apologetic expression. "Sorry about that. Work emergency." Seeming to notice the tension, he asked, "Everything okay?"

Jason took a leisurely sip of his beer, grinning as he feigned nonchalance. "Everything is great. Was it a big emergency with work?" he asked, enjoying the momentary distraction from the brewing tension.

Jack shrugged and sat down. "Nah, all taken care of."

Tabby broke the fragile atmosphere, saying to Ruby, "Come to the ladies' room with me, okay?"

Jason watched as Jack stood up to let Tabby out of the booth, Ruby following closely behind. The moment they left, the weight of the conversation settled between him and Jack. Jason braced himself for what was to follow, taking another sip of his beer.

After a few long, drawn-out moments, Jack leaned in. His voice was steady as he said, "Jason, do you remember me telling you that Ruby has an impulse control problem?"

Jason nodded, a flicker of amusement crossing his face. He was ready to defend himself.

"Well," Jack continued, leaning closer, "what Ruby needs is someone levelheaded to keep her from making bad choices. Know what I mean?"

Jason felt annoyance surface at Jack's words. "Are you saying that I can't keep her from making bad choices? Because that's exactly what it sounds like you're saying."

Jack shrugged. "I don't know what you're capable of. That's kind of the problem."

Jason's glare deepened, the uncertainty in Jack's voice grating on his nerves. "You don't think I'm responsible enough for her? Is that it?"

Without missing a beat, Jack said, "A weekend getaway after only knowing her for a week seems more impulsive than levelheaded, you have to admit."

Jason's defenses rose. The trip to Miami had been last minute, and he understood why Jack viewed it as reckless, but he wasn't about to back down. "So, you think I'm just some bad influence on her?"

"I've known Ruby her whole life," Jack said, seriousness etched in his features. "You've known her a week. Maybe if you got to know her a little better, you'd understand why she needs more stability in her life and less recklessness."

Jason's irritation flared. "Are you implying that I don't know Ruby well enough to be dating her? Or that I'm too reckless to take care of her?" His voice came out sharper than he intended, but he could feel the challenge in the air all the same.

"I'm giving you advice," Jack said, appearing calm yet resolute. "And my advice is: take it slow with Ruby."

Frustration surged within Jason. His patience was wearing thin with Jack's condescending tone. "Take it slow? That's your advice?"

Jack leaned back, his expression unwavering. "That's my advice," he reiterated, his tone firm.

Jason leaned forward, his patience nearly exhausted. "How slow do you want me to take things with her, exactly? Months? Years? Decades?" He stared Jack down, ready for what came next.

At that moment, Tabby and Ruby returned from the restroom.

"Ah, good—you're still alive," Tabby said to Jason.

He forced a charming grin at Tabby's teasing, but inside he was still grappling with Jack's comments.

"I'm so tired," Tabby announced, turning to Jack. "Would you walk me home?"

Jason watched as Jack hesitated, glancing between Ruby and him before finally nodding. "Of course," he said, his voice softer now, as he bid goodnight to both Ruby and Jason.

As Jack and Tabby left, a sense of ease swept over Jason, grateful for the break from Jack's presence.

He turned to Ruby, his mood brightening now that he was alone with her. "Ready to go pack?" he asked her.

But Ruby's smile faltered, and Jason's heart sank at the sight. "Jason, I don't think I can go to Miami with you this weekend."

"Why not? What's wrong with going on a trip to Miami?" he asked, trying to keep his voice steady.

"I do want to go," Ruby said. "It's only ... remember when I told you I wanted a guy that my brother would approve of? I want that guy to be you. I like you, and I don't want Jack to hate my boyfriend."

Frustration crept in, and he sighed. He hated that she needed to seek her brother's approval. "What? You really want to give in to Jack's control-freak tendencies just because he doesn't like my plan? What about what *you* want?"

"As much of a control freak as he is," Ruby said, her eyes earnest, "I know he always has my best interests at heart. He's always been there for me, and I love him."

Irritation flared within Jason at the mention of Ruby's love for her brother. He resented the idea of Jack exerting control over her. "I'm well aware that he's always been there for you. But you don't always have to do exactly what he tells you to do. You don't have to get his approval for everything."

"Trust me, I don't," she said. "But he's a good guy. And so are you. You should try to get along with him. Not just for my sake, but for Tabby's."

Jason sighed, knowing he should probably try to be nicer to Jack. For Tabby's sake, and for Ruby's too—he didn't want to come between any of them. "I know, I know. I'll make an effort to get along with him. I just don't appreciate him questioning my ability to take care of you."

Ruby hugged him, and he felt the tension dissolve in her embrace. "I knew you would understand. Maybe I'll let you have that goodnight kiss after all."

Jason wrapped his arms around her, pulling her close. "So, I get that goodnight kiss after all, then?"

Ruby laughed. "Oh, so you want to make out right here in the booth? How about you walk me home first."

Unable to resist, he pulled her closer, kissing her neck. "You think you can wait that long?"

Ruby climbed out of the booth, taking his hand in hers. "C'mon, you're my protector tonight. Let's go."

Jason stood, holding Ruby's hand as they made their way out of the bar. He wrapped his arm around her shoulders as they strolled down the sidewalk, feeling a rush of happiness having her next to him.

# 10 Trepidation

Jack walked alongside Tabby as they made their way home from the pub. The evening had been tense, filled with unspoken worries and the tension surrounding Ruby and Jason's situation. A sour mood clung to him. He stole a quick glance at Tabby, considering how furious she would be if he arranged for Jason to have a sudden "accident."

Tabby, seeing the frustration etched on Jack's face, took his hand in hers. "Don't worry," she said. "I had a talk with Ruby in the ladies' room. I'm sure she's going to turn down Jason's Miami weekend."

"You think so?" Doubt laced Jack's voice, and the heaviness in his chest refused to lift.

"Yeah," Tabby said with determination. "She doesn't want her brother murdering her boyfriend. And I don't want my boyfriend to murder my best friend."

Jack felt a flicker of warmth at her joke, a hint of a smile breaking through his troubled expression. As they continued walking, he squeezed Tabby's hand, grateful for her presence amid the tension.

"You know how stubborn Ruby can be," Jack said, his voice softening. "She might defy me to ... prove a point."

Tabby pressed, "So, I take it you weren't able to get through to him while we were in the ladies' room?"

Jack shook his head, frustration heavy on his shoulders. "No, he made it abundantly clear that my opinion is of no consequence to him. He's going to do whatever the hell he wants with my sister, and I'm powerless to stop it."

Jack could see the earnestness in Tabby's eyes as she said, "Someone needs to explain to Jason about her mania. He thinks she's just impulsive. He doesn't understand anything about what might trigger a manic episode."

Jack nodded, the frustration boiling within him. "You're right ... he needs to understand that it's not only impulsivity. It's a serious mental illness that can lead to very dangerous situations ... especially for a vulnerable, naive girl like Ruby."

Tabby frowned. Jack could tell she was weighing her next words carefully. "I didn't think it was my place to tell him, but I also didn't think he'd be so foolish as to suddenly whisk her away after knowing her for a week."

Frustration again seeped through Jack's words. "It's not only foolish—it's reckless, too. He doesn't care about the potential consequences at all, as long as he gets what he wants. Classic behavior of someone who's used to getting their way all the time."

"Don't be too hard on Jason," Tabby said, as if trying to soothe him. "Once he gets to know you better and gets to know Ruby better, he'll be as protective of her as you are. Trust me."

Jack looked unconvinced. "I don't know, Tabby. It's not about him being protective. It's about him being respectful ... and responsible. And I haven't really seen that from him so far."

Tabby looked thoughtful. "Yeah, but from what Ruby tells me, you don't like *any* of her boyfriends."

Jack let a bashful grin escape. "That's fair. But you have to admit, she doesn't exactly have the best taste in men."

Tabby chuckled, her laughter pulling him out of his worries. "It's like you said, 'A magnet for trouble, but with a good heart.' A recipe for disaster."

Jack nodded, the gravity of the situation returning to him. "Exactly. She's attracted to the worst kind of guys ... the flashy, charming ones who can sweet talk her into anything. It's like she doesn't realize how dangerous they are."

"Yeah, but Jason's not dangerous, I swear," Tabby insisted, her voice firm. "He's just ... really, really shortsighted."

Jack scoffed. "Shortsighted is an understatement. He might not be dangerous, but he's definitely reckless. And that's almost as bad."

Tabby let out a sigh. "How about we stop talking about them and talk about us instead?"

A smile returned to Jack's face as he stopped and turned to her, taking both her hands in his. Looking deeply into her eyes, he felt the weight of the world lift for a moment. "Sounds like a good idea, darling. What should we talk about?"

Tabby's face lit up, her excitement infectious. "It's finally the weekend. You can stay the night and not have to get up and go to work the next morning."

Jack pulled her closer. "That's true. And I can think of a few things I'd like to do with all that extra time ..."

As they continued their walk, Jack's worries of the evening faded. They headed up to Tabby's apartment together, ready to focus on each other instead.

# 11 Understanding

There was a comforting hum of conversation and clinking of dishes the following Sunday afternoon at Franco's Diner. Tabby sat at a booth, her fingers tapping her glass as she waited for Jason. She glanced at the door with anticipation.

Then, as if summoned by her thoughts, Jason walked in. His gaze swept across the room until it landed on her. "Hey," he said, as he slid into the seat across from her. "Thanks for agreeing to meet me for lunch."

"Yeah—and you're welcome, by the way."

"Yeah, I owe you one. Thanks for trying to talk sense into that overprotective bastard."

She crossed her arms with annoyance. "No—you're lucky I talked Ruby out of going to Miami with you. What were you thinking?"

"I just wanted to do something cool for her, give her an enjoyable weekend away. I didn't realize Jack would disapprove."

"Are you insane?" Tabby asked, her eyes wide with disbelief.

"No, I'm not insane," he said. "I think I'm just a guy trying to impress a beautiful girl."

"You're supposed to be a mature, responsible adult trying to keep a beautiful girl out of trouble," she countered.

He nodded, acknowledging her point. "Yeah, yeah ... I know. That's what Jack was saying—more restraint."

Tabby paused, pondering her words. She had something important to share. "We need to talk about Ruby. I didn't think it was my business, but you need to know."

Jason sipped his water, suddenly attentive. "Okay, I'm all ears. Hit me with it."

"Ruby's not just impulsive, Jason. She's manic. And she struggles with her treatment plan. That's why Jack wants her supervised when she drinks. It's why there's no alcohol in her apartment and why he feels the need to vet her friends."

As she spoke, she felt the gravity of her words settle between them. It was a lot to take in, but it was necessary. She watched the realization dawning on Jason, and she hoped he would understand the importance of what she was saying.

Tabby saw Jason's eyes widen in shock, a flicker of realization crossing his face. He'd had no idea Ruby was bipolar.

"Manic? Is she taking any medication for it?" he asked, concern etched in his features.

"She's supposed to be," Tabby said. "But who knows? I know she doesn't like taking her pills."

"So, she's supposed to be taking medication but isn't? Isn't that dangerous?"

Tabby could sense Jason's frustration. As she witnessed his mind at work, she sympathized with him. "I think she relies on Jack a lot to keep her safe—maybe too much. And you're not helping matters."

She watched Jason bury his head in his hands, the revelation pressing down on him.

"Why didn't she tell me about this?" he muttered, his voice muffled.

"My guess? She likes you and doesn't want you to judge her," Tabby said.

Jason nodded, understanding dawning on him. "Well ... yeah, that makes sense."

"This is a disaster," Tabby said. "I thought you'd be a responsible friend to her, not encourage her reckless behavior."

"I'm only encouraging her to have fun," he argued, though doubt crept into his voice. "Is having fun inherently a bad thing with her condition?"

"What if she had a bad episode in Miami? What if she took off or disappeared? Jack would rip you limb from limb," she shot back.

Jason groaned. "I wouldn't be surprised if he tried to kill me if anything happened to her," he admitted.

"Neither would I. He was very intense at the gun range yesterday ... Like he was imagining the target was your head."

"I wouldn't put it past him to fantasize about shooting me."

Tabby watched Jason's expression soften, sensing the weight of the conversation they were having. "So, what are you going to do about Ruby? Are you going to keep seeing her?" she asked.

Jason took a deep breath, his look resolute, as he said, "Of course I'll keep seeing her. I really like her. I'm not going to just drop her because she's mentally ill."

"Good. Because that would hurt her."

"I have no intention of hurting her. I care about her. I'll admit, though, I'm feeling a little in over my head right now. This is a lot to take in, especially after Jack acted like such a control freak on Friday."

Tabby nodded. "Well, it wasn't his place to tell you about her health condition. It wasn't mine either, but I feel responsible for damage control, since I'm the one who introduced you."

Despite the awkwardness, there was gratitude in Jason's eyes. "Yeah, I know. It wasn't on either of you to tell me, but I'm glad you did. I had no idea about her bipolar disorder. And now I understand why Jack was treating me like a criminal on Friday."

"Trust me," Tabby said. "He was very restrained compared to what he wanted to say to you."

Jason grinned, lightening the mood. "Ah, so it was a miracle that Jack didn't knock me out?"

Tabby sighed, exasperated. "You would have deserved it. I could tell you were trying to get under his skin."

Jason laughed. "Guilty as charged. I was definitely provoking him on purpose."

"Could you please not do that in the future?" Tabby pleaded, exasperation creeping into her tone. "He's your girlfriend's brother and your best friend's boyfriend. It makes our lives miserable when you piss him off."

Tabby listened as Jason nodded, the serious expression on his face catching her attention.

"I'll do my best not to be a smartass. But can you also do me a favor to make *my* life a bit easier?" he asked.

"What's that?"

"I can deal with the fact that Jack is protective, to a certain degree. But I don't want him acting like a dictator regarding my relationship with Ruby. Can you help convince him to cut me some slack?"

"If you promise not to bait him."

Jason's grin widened, and she could see the realization dawn on him that his own antics had only added to the tension.

"Okay, okay. I won't bait him. Happy?"

"Yes," she sighed, a flicker of hope igniting within her. Maybe things would settle down now.

"I'll try to be less irritating, and Jack will try to be less obnoxious. Win-win situation, right?" he continued.

"I actually find his protectiveness sweet."

Jason let out a laugh, rolling his eyes. "I realize you're head over heels for the guy. You think everything he does is sweet."

Her thoughts drifted to Jack, and a warmth spread through her chest.

Watching her, Jason's sly smile returned. "You've got it bad for him. Is the honeymoon phase still going strong?"

"No thanks to you!" she snapped. "He was not in a great mood this weekend. But I managed to get him to forget about you for a while."

"Oh, yeah? I find that hard to believe considering how pissed off your boyfriend was on Friday," Jason said. "How did you distract him from his intense desire to knock me out?"

Tabby averted her gaze. "I encouraged him to focus his attention on me instead."

Jason burst into laughter. "By 'attention,' do you mean ... physical attention?"

"I managed to put him back in a good mood, and that's all you need to know."

"Oh yeah, I think I know exactly how you 'improved' his mood," Jason teased. He took a sip of water, then shifted the conversation in a new direction. "I spent Saturday with Ruby. It was a nice day."

"So, she didn't ditch you to go to the beach after Miami fell through? That's good."

"We had a nice time," Jason continued. "We just hung around her apartment. Watched some television, napped, had dinner. It was simple, but it was nice. Just being with her."

Tabby's expression turned questioning. "*Napped?*"

Jason chuckled. "Yeah, we napped, cuddled up together in her bed. We didn't get up to anything frisky. I swear."

"That's a weird date. I'm not gonna lie," she said, laughing.

"Sure, it was a weird date. But I liked it. It was nice being together like that. It was nice falling asleep with her in my arms."

Tabby's expression softened, a dreamy smile spreading across her face. "Yeah."

Jason watched her. "Aw, you're getting that sappy look on your face again. I bet you've got some nice memories of being in lover boy's arms."

"What can I say? You told me Prince Charming doesn't exist, but maybe you were wrong."

"Ah, so you're saying Jack is your Prince Charming? It's a bit nauseating to hear you gush about the guy, but I can't deny that he makes you ridiculously happy. You really are crazy about him, aren't you."

"I am," she admitted, sincerity in her eyes. "He's different from any other guy I've dated. In the past, it always kind of felt like I was the protector in the relationship. I mean, I'm okay with that, but it's not really a turn-on. Know what I mean?"

Jason nodded, understanding in his expression. "You've been with some pretty wimpy dudes in the past. Jack is definitely not a wimpy guy. I bet his dominant, take-charge personality got you worked up."

Tabby's eyes lit up. "And his eyes. That piercing dark gaze. Oh my god." A wistful look crossed her face, and Jason smiled at her infatuation.

"I should've known you'd be one of those women who gets weak in the knees around a pair of pretty dark eyes," he teased. "He's definitely got the whole tall, dark and handsome thing going for him."

"Anyway," Tabby said, shaking herself out of her reverie, "it sure has been an eventful week, huh?"

Jason nodded in agreement. "Yeah, stressful, eventful week. That's how I'd describe it," he said.

"Ha. The workweek will seem relaxing in comparison," Tabby joked.

"True. Work seems like a vacation compared to dealing with my girlfriend's overprotective big brother," Jason said, chuckling at the absurdity of it all.

"Are you going to tell her what we talked about?" Tabby asked.

Jason pondered for a moment. "I think I should. I'll have to break it to her gently, though. I don't want to make her feel bad about her mental illness."

"Hopefully she's not mad at me for telling you. But as long as you're willing to stand by her, I'm sure she'll forgive me," Tabby said.

Jason nodded, reassuring himself. "I think she'll realize that I'm not going to run away just because she's bipolar. But she might be embarrassed that I know."

"I'm sure you'll work it out," Tabby said. She stood up, grabbing a French fry from Jason's plate as she prepared to leave. "I think I'm going to head over to my boyfriend's place and try to convince him to cut you some slack. Take care of the check, okay?"

Jason watched as Tabby stole another fry. "Yeah, yeah, yeah. I'll take care of the check. Try to keep lover boy from being pissed at me."

Tabby waved goodbye and headed out of the restaurant, leaving Jason to contemplate the conversation he would soon have with Ruby.

# 12 Hope

Later that night, as Jason lounged in his apartment, he felt excitement when his phone rang. The familiar name on the screen brought an immediate smile to his face.

"Hey angel," he greeted.

His grin widened at the sound of Ruby's voice. "Are you busy?" she asked, with a hopeful tone.

"Currently, no. I'm just sitting here sorting laundry. Why?" he asked, intrigued by what she might have in mind.

"Wanna come over and hang out?"

"Sure, I'll be right over." His heart raced at the thought of spending time with her.

After hanging up, he grabbed his keys and stepped out the door. A deep breath filled his lungs, but a twinge of nervousness accompanied it. The conversation about Ruby's bipolar illness loomed in his mind—a discussion he and she would have to tackle. It was better to get it over with, he thought. But the idea still made him uneasy.

When he arrived at her door and knocked, his heartbeat quickened. The moment she opened the door, her smile illuminated the evening. She looked cozy in her T-shirt and sleep shorts, and he felt a flutter of affection.

"Hey angel," he said as he stepped inside, the familiar comfort of her presence wrapping around him.

"Hey, hon. Look, I cleaned for you," she said, pride evident in her voice as she gestured around her tidied apartment.

Jason glanced over the space, taking in the neatness. "Ah, I see. Looking to impress me?" he asked, affection in his eyes.

"I always impress you," she said.

"That's true. You're always impressive to me. That's why I love spending time with you so much," he said.

"Want a soda?" Ruby asked, heading to the fridge.

Jason thanked her with a fond expression as she returned with two cans. He watched Ruby as she plopped down in a kitchen chair, her feet resting on the one next to her, soda in hand. She looked sleepy, and he smiled at her relaxed demeanor. It was utterly adorable.

"You're sure you're not worn out from cleaning up?" he asked, genuinely concerned.

"Nah, but I'm ready to relax," she said, taking a sip of her drink.

"Have a seat," she said, gesturing to the chair across from her.

"So, you're all relaxed and ready for some quality time together?" he continued, hoping to keep the mood light.

"I don't really want to do anything except chat," she said, her voice casual yet inviting.

His heart warmed at her words. "That sounds fine to me. I love talking to you."

"So, you had lunch with Tabby today. How'd that go?" Ruby asked.

Jason felt a flicker of surprise that she knew about his lunch with Tabby, but he composed himself. "Yeah, I had lunch with her earlier today. It was ... interesting," he admitted, with a hint of discomfort.

"She's an interesting girl," Ruby said, and he could sense a tension in the air, the way her words hung between them.

Jason hesitated, unsure of how to navigate the conversation. He decided to be straightforward. "I found out some interesting information from her. She had some ... informative things to tell me about your mental health."

Ruby nodded, her expression shifting to one of understanding. "I figured. She wanted me to tell you myself, but I guess because I didn't, she did," Ruby explained, her voice tinged with both guilt and relief. She looked down, her fingers fidgeting. "I would have told you, eventually. But things moved too fast."

He reached across the table to take her hand in his. "It's alright. I understand you weren't sure where our relationship was headed, so why tell me?"

A moment of silence settled between them, and he could see the discomfort in her expression. "I realize now that I should have told you sooner. Tabby and Jack have been worried sick about me. I feel bad," she admitted.

Her vulnerability was striking a chord within him. He could see the seriousness in her eyes as she spoke about Jack.

"I completely believe that Jack has driven himself insane worrying about you," he said. "The guy is ridiculously overprotective."

Ruby's voice cut through his musings. "Well, he has good reason to be," she said, her tone grave. "As bad as the mania is, the depression is worse. Much worse. And Jack has always been there for me. No matter what."

Jason considered her words. He hadn't realized how deep the bond between them ran, how much Jack truly cared for her. "I'm starting to see just how protective of you he can be," he said, trying to convey understanding.

"I have a lot of guilt, actually. I feel like he's been too busy worrying about me to find his own happiness."

Reaching across the table, Jason gave her hand a gentle pat, wanting to provide some comfort. "You clearly care a great deal about him. But I don't think you're giving him enough credit. The guy probably worries about you a ton, but I think he can handle it. He's still capable of finding his own happiness."

Ruby said, "I'm not so sure. Tabby is the first girl he's dated since my last bad episode. And that was years ago."

Jason could see the guilt and worry etched on Ruby's face. It was clear that her mental health loomed large over her thoughts, and that she cared a lot about Jack's happiness. Her words had him intrigued, too. "What do you mean by 'last bad episode'?" he asked, wanting to understand more.

Jason watched as Ruby hesitated, her gaze fixed on the floor, avoiding his eyes. He could sense her struggle, the suffocating pressure of the truth she seemed reluctant to share. He held his breath, hoping she would find the courage to speak.

"Suicide attempt," she finally whispered, the words barely escaping her lips.

As her confession hung in the air, his heart dropped. A heaviness pressed down on him. "You attempted suicide? Why?" he asked, his voice tinged with heartache. He squeezed her hand, desperate to bridge the chasm of vulnerability that lay between them.

He watched helplessly as a tear slipped down her cheek, her voice quaking as she spoke. "I had a bad manic episode. I was really reckless. Stupid. Too flirty, I guess, with the wrong guy and he ..." She faltered, the memory clearly haunting her. "He forced me." She wiped away tears.

Jason's heart clenched at her words. "I'm so sorry you had to go through that. It wasn't your fault," he reassured her, tightening his grip around her hand. "You weren't stupid or reckless. That guy was just an evil, disgusting piece of trash. I'm so sorry. So, so sorry."

"After that, Jack moved to the city to be closer," she explained.

"So, you have these bad manic episodes that make you completely reckless and dangerous to yourself," Jason said, trying to piece together the fragments of her reality. "And Jack moved here to make sure you were safe."

Ruby nodded, still wiping tears from her eyes. "Yeah."

He took a deep breath, the full weight of her mental health struggles settling in for him. "So, you have to worry about depressive episodes and reckless manic episodes that can be dangerous. When was your last episode?"

Her frown deepened as she searched her memory. "Not sure. When I'm manic, I usually don't even realize I am, because I feel great. Until the crash, of course."

Jason nodded, the depth of her condition becoming clearer. "So, you have no idea when you're going through an episode. Is it just Jack who knows that you're bipolar?"

"Well, Tabby, of course. And my parents, but they don't live nearby."

He processed this, sensing her isolation. "So, there are only four people who know you're bipolar. Well, five now that I know."

Ruby added, "And my doctor, of course."

"Of course," he echoed, his mind racing with questions about her treatment. "How do you treat this? There must be something you take to prevent these episodes?"

"My doctor wants me to take mood stabilizers, but they mess with my brain. And not in a good way," she admitted.

Jason fell silent, absorbing the weight of Ruby's situation. Thoughts raced through his mind—should he really encourage her to go back to the treatment that had caused her so much pain? The fear of losing her to another episode gnawed at him, a relentless ache in his chest.

He noticed the discomfort etched across Ruby's face. "I'm sorry for asking all these questions. I know it's probably hard just to talk about it," he said, trying to ease the tension.

"For sure," she said with unease.

The urgency of the moment pressed in on him. "I'm sorry for making this a difficult conversation. I didn't mean to ask so many questions—I just want to understand," he said, reaching across the table to cradle her hand in his.

"Well, now you know everything," Ruby said, attempting a lighter tone, though her eyes sparkled with unshed tears.

"Yeah, I know everything." The gravity of her reality loomed over them, filling him with a profound concern.

"You probably don't want to be my boyfriend anymore, huh?" she asked, uncertainty lacing her voice.

His eyes widened in disbelief. Did she think he would walk away because of her mental illness? "No, I don't want to break up with you."

"Really?" she asked, a flicker of hope lighting up her face.

"Really. I have no plans to break up with you," Jason assured her.

At that moment, Ruby stood up and wrapped her arms around him, pulling him into a tight embrace. The warmth of her affection melted his heart. As he rose to his feet, his arms instinctively found their way around her, returning her embrace, stroking her back, and he nuzzled his cheek against her hair. They held each other tightly.

Jason watched as Ruby pulled back, her expression a mixture of relief and lingering tension. "That was kind of torturous," she sighed, meeting his gaze.

Jason appreciated her ability to voice her feelings. "Yeah, but I'm glad it's done. It was definitely time for me to fully understand everything about your illness and how it impacts you. I really care about you."

Her teasing smile returned, a small light breaking through the clouds of her earlier distress. "There you go, disarming me with your sweetness again."

"Did you expect anything less from me?" he said, finding a sense of triumph in the lightness that had returned to their conversation.

"Actually, I totally expected you to cut and run, if I'm being honest," she said, and he caught the hint of vulnerability in her voice. "I didn't think you'd want a girlfriend you had to worry about."

He gently tilted her chin up, locking eyes with her, wanting her to see the sincerity in his. "Of course I'm going to worry about you—you're the most important person in the world to me."

Her eyes widened in astonishment. "I am?"

"I can't imagine a single thing in this world that I care about more than you."

As she hugged him again, Jason returned her embrace, stroking her back, comforted by their closeness. In that moment, amid the weight of their conversation, he felt a deep connection to her, their bond strengthened by understanding.

The ringing of Ruby's phone sliced through the intimacy. He watched her glance at the screen, the name "Jack" flashing there.

"I should answer it," she murmured, and he nodded.

"Yeah, you should answer it. I'm sure he's been worried about you," he encouraged, pulling away to give her space.

Ruby walked into the bedroom as she picked up the call. Jason sighed, unable to escape the thought of Jack's potential reaction to the recent turn of events.

Moments later, Ruby returned, announcing, "Jack and Tabby are going to Fitzgerald's. Do you want to go?"

Jason perked up at the suggestion, and nodded. "That sounds good."

Jason watched her move to the hallway, slipping into her outerwear. He ran a hand through his hair, feeling the evening's emotional toll. The stressful night made him wonder if every night with Ruby would be as emotionally intense.

When they arrived at the pub, the lively environment was filled with chatter. Jason followed Ruby inside, scanning the room for Jack and Tabby. Almost immediately, he spotted them seated at a booth across the way.

Ruby approached their table, hugging each of them in turn. Jason trailed beside her, feeling the lingering tension in the air.

Once Tabby and Jack settled into the booth, Ruby slid in across from them, Jason taking a seat beside her. The air was charged, and Tabby wasted no time in breaking the silence.

"Did you two talk?" she asked, her gaze flitting between Jason and Ruby.

Unease crept into Jason's voice as he glanced at Tabby. "Yeah, we talked." His heart pounded at the weight of their conversation.

Ruby's voice was earnest as she added, "Yeah, he knows everything now. And I do mean everything." Her words hung in the air, heavy with meaning.

Jack nodded, his expression serious as he absorbed the implications. "That's good," he affirmed, seeming to understanding the gravity of the situation. "He should know."

Jason returned Jack's nod, appreciating the depth of concern Jack had for Ruby and her struggles. Jack then shifted his focus back to Ruby. "Are you two good?" he asked.

Jason's heart raced as he turned to Ruby, anticipation hanging between them. He held his breath, waiting for her response.

"Yeah, real good," Ruby said. Gratitude swelled within him—she still wanted to be with him, even with the complexities of her illness now laid bare.

Jack then turned his attention to Jason. "Sorry for being so hard on you," he said.

Surprised by both the apology and the admission, Jason said, "You don't have to apologize for being protective of her. I get it. I understand why you have to watch out for her." He had a newfound respect for Jack's unwavering support of Ruby.

In that moment, the tension faded. Jason knew that the honesty they shared that night would bond them together in friendship.

Tabby chimed in, her voice lightening the mood. "Oh good, we're all friends again. Thank Christ! I was a little worried for a while there."

Jason chuckled at Tabby's lighthearted remark, the weight of earlier moments replaced by a refreshing sense of ease. He glanced over at her. "Yeah, we're all friends again, don't worry," he said, his voice light.

"Good, I like this little quadrangle of friendship we've developed here," said Ruby.

Jason laughed as he turned to his girlfriend. "'Quadrangle of friendship'? Did you just make that up?"

"Seemed more appropriate than 'foursome,'" she said, her tone teasing.

He burst into laughter, appreciating her cleverness. "Yeah, 'quadrangle of friendship' is definitely a less suggestive term than 'foursome,' that's for sure."

Ruby added jokingly, "Yeah, that would be taboo in more ways than one."

Jack looked at Ruby. "Charming, as ever," he declared, obviously aware of her penchant for inappropriate humor.

Jason smiled at her audacity, finding the playful banter that flowed effortlessly between the siblings both entertaining and heartwarming. Ruby laughed, clearly relishing the opportunity to tease her brother.

"Ruby," Tabby said with envy, "You're so lucky. I wish I had a big brother like Jack. He cares for you so much."

Jack turned his gaze toward Tabby with a warm smile, his eyes softening with a protective love. "You don't need a big brother," he said gently. "You have me now."

Jason grinned at Jack's words, amused by the swift transition from tough protector to caring friend.

Ruby's eyes softened as she looked at Jack. "Aw ... It's so nice to see you happy."

"I owe it all to my interfering matchmaking sister," Jack said, rolling his eyes.

"Interfering? That's rich coming from you," Ruby accused. "But, secretly, I love knowing you're watching out for me."

"I'll always watch out for you," Jack promised. Then he glanced at Jason. "But maybe I can share that responsibility a little. What do you say, Jason? Willing to help me keep this one safe?"

Had Jack just asked him to help protect Ruby? He hadn't expected that. Yet, a protective urge surged within him, and he nodded without hesitation. "Yeah, completely. I'll absolutely watch out for her."

Ruby's eyes lit up with appreciation, obviously impressed by the trust her brother placed in Jason.

As the evening drew to a close, Jack wrapped Ruby in a warm hug and clapped Jason on the shoulder before taking Tabby's hand and leading her out the door. Jason watched them go, then turned to Ruby, who was gazing after her brother and Tabby. He took her hand in his.

"Ready to go home, angel?" he asked. Ruby nodded.

As they walked outside, the mood was transformed from the tension earlier in the evening. It had been an emotional rollercoaster, but now everything seemed brighter.

Ruby smiled at Jason as they strolled home. He glanced down at her, captivated. He squeezed her hand, unable to suppress his own grin. "What are you smiling about?"

"You and Jack," she said. "He's definitely warming up to you."

Jason found her observation amusing. It was true: he hadn't expected Jack to trust him enough to ask for his help. "Yeah, I think he's starting to trust me a bit more now. It sounds like he never really trusted anyone around you before."

He noticed Ruby frown and squeezed her hand. "What's the frown for?"

She shook her head, her voice soft. "I was thinking about all I've put him through."

Understanding dawned on Jason, and he felt a surge of guilt for bringing it up. He squeezed her hand again. "I'm sure he'd do all of it again just to make sure you're safe and well."

Ruby nodded, the determination in her eyes unmistakable. "I'm sure he would," she said. "But I'm going to do my best to make sure he doesn't have to."

# PART 2 SPIRALING

# 13 Plans

Jason leaned against the cool brick wall of the library, glancing at his watch as he waited for Tabby to finish her shift. The late afternoon sun cast warm rays over the bustling street, but his mind was only half on the world around him; he was eager to see her.

As Tabby emerged, a teasing smile spread across her face. "Still stalking me?" she asked.

Jason grinned back. "Hey, that's a strong word. 'Stalking' makes it sound so creepy."

She laughed. "It's an endearing sort of stalking."

"That's more like it." He placed his arm around her shoulders as they began walking down the street. "How was work today?"

"Long," she said, her voice tinged with a hint of longing. "I wore Jack's shirt today so I could smell him while I was at work, but it made me miss him all the more." She pulled up the collar of the oversized shirt, giving it a sniff.

"Yeah, that was probably a mistake. You're just torturing yourself."

"Want to smell?" Tabby offered, holding the collar out to him.

"Oh hell, why not." He leaned in and inhaled, catching a faint scent of fabric softener mixed with something more familiar.

"Does it smell like Jack? I think maybe it wore off and smells like the library now," she said, looking a little disappointed.

"It does smell a little like the library, sorry." He patted her shoulder as they continued walking. "When does he get back from the trip?"

"Tomorrow, I hope. I don't understand why a tree warden needs to go on a work trip. The trees are all here."

"I don't know—maybe it's some sort of arborist convention. Either way, at least it'll be over soon, and you can stop torturing yourself with the shirt."

Tabby sighed. "I should have asked him for a key to his apartment. Then I could get another one of his shirts out of his closet."

A teasing grin formed on his lips. "He doesn't trust you enough to give you a key? Are you sure he's really your boyfriend?"

"Of course he trusts me! It's just ... I never thought of it. We've only known each other a couple of weeks." She paused before shooting him a curious glance. "Have you and Ruby exchanged keys already?"

"Nah, same thing—it's only been a couple weeks, so we're not there yet. But I feel like we're about to take that next step. I feel really good about this one, y'know?"

"You probably should have a key to her place. You're supposed to be helping Jack look out for her after all. Is she still not taking her medication?"

"Nope," Jason said. "She refuses. Says she doesn't need it anymore because she's feeling good and whatever." He sighed, shaking his head in frustration. "I'm worried about her. She just won't listen to anyone."

"She should ask her doctor to change her script," Tabby suggested. "I understand why she doesn't want to take the same meds that made her suicidal."

"I've been trying to give her that advice, but she's so stubborn. She told me that it's none of my business." He frowned, as concern settled in his chest. "I was just trying to help."

"Ruby? Stubborn? I never noticed," Tabby joked, her voice lightening the mood.

"Tell me about it. It's a good thing she's cute as hell, or she'd drive me completely nuts."

Tabby nudged him. "I think she does drive you completely nuts. And I think that's what you like about her."

He let out a huff of laughter, not denying it. "Oh yeah. Yeah, totally. She's so damn infuriating, and I totally dig it."

"You do, don't you? You're totally smitten," she teased.

"Yeah, I am." Jason felt a warmth spread through him as he thought about Ruby. "I think I *will* ask her to exchange keys. Then we'll be official."

"Good," Tabby said. "As long as Ruby is safe and happy, then Jack doesn't have to worry about his little sister 24/7."

Jason paused, his mind buzzing with thoughts of his girlfriend. "I'm completely gone for this girl," he confessed with a wistful grin.

"She really likes you a lot too," Tabby said. "Who knew you were relationship material all along?"

"I know, it's a surprise to everyone, me included. But you have to admit, I'm pretty charming once you get to know me."

Tabby laughed. "Oh, you've got a lock on charming, that's for sure. It was the casual flings with the bimbos that got you scratched off my list."

Jason winced at the reminder of his less commendable past. "Will I never live down my playboy phase? I'm sorry, okay? I was young and stupid. Now I'm reformed."

"A whole new man at the wise old age of twenty-six?" Tabby asked.

"I said reformed, not perfect," Jason said. "I'm still me, after all. I'm still gonna mess up from time to time. But I think I've changed. I'm definitely not looking to start any flings."

Tabby said, "Oh, you better not. If Ruby gets hurt, Jack will go back to being the overprotective brother, and neither of us wants that."

"Don't worry, I'll continue to be on my best behavior. I'm serious about Ruby. I don't want to do anything to screw this relationship up."

"I'm surprised you're not with her tonight," Tabby remarked.

"I've been with her every night this week. I told her I'd give her a night off," Jason said, chuckling. "Can I ask you a personal question?"

"What's on your mind?" Tabby responded, her voice open and inviting.

Jason hesitated, searching for the right words. "It's about you and Jack. I don't want to overstep, I'm just curious ... You've also only known him for a couple of weeks, right? How can you be sure that he's the one for you?"

Tabby considered his question. "I guess because I fell in love with his values. How family is so important to him. How protective he is. How genuine. I mean, I definitely find him physically attractive, but it's kinda like a bonus."

"So, you really think he's your perfect match? You think that in this big, wide world, he's the one person out there that you're supposed to be with?" Jason probed, genuinely curious about her certainty.

"I don't care if he's the one I'm *meant* to be with. Jack is the only one I *want*. If my soulmate is some other guy, then that guy will have to find someone else."

"That's a beautiful way of looking at it," Jason admitted. "I wish I could have your level of certainty about these things."

"Well, nobody expects you to propose after two weeks," Tabby said.

"Yeah, I'll definitely not be moving that fast. But I really like Ruby. I don't know about soulmates or any of that stuff, but she's the first girl that I've ever been crazy about. It's actually kind of terrifying," Jason confessed.

"I have to admit, I'm enjoying seeing you in love. It's so cute," Tabby said.

"Yeah, yeah, make fun of me. I don't care. I'm all about it. Completely head over heels."

"I'm not making fun of you. I'm genuinely happy for you," Tabby reassured him.

"Yeah, yeah, you're too nice," Jason teased back, glancing at her sidelong. Even if she was poking fun a little, deep down, he appreciated her support more than words could say.

"Let's stop at the taco truck and eat in the park," Tabby suggested.

Jason said, "You know me too well."

They strolled together to the nearby taco truck where Jason ordered carnitas with extra everything. The scent of grilled meat and fresh cilantro filled the air, mingling with the sounds of the surrounding city. After receiving their order, they found a shady bench in the park.

Handing Tabby a bag, Jason boasted, "Man, I swear, these are the best tacos in town."

"Yeah," Tabby agreed, taking a bite. "Food from a truck has no right to be so tasty."

"When you think about it, they're probably unsanitary as hell, but it's worth the risk." Jason unwrapped his own taco, reflecting. "I have to admit, I'm gonna miss not being able to see you as much in the future. Who's gonna sit with me and eat in the park when you're off with Jack all the time?"

"Ruby, I guess," Tabby suggested.

"Yeah, I guess so." Jason finished his food and started on the second. "But it just won't be the same, will it?"

"Then we'll come together. All four of us," Tabby proposed.

"We'll do double-dates," Jason said, his grin returning. He imagined the future gatherings. "We'll go to sporting events and concerts. We'll barbecue together. And we'll all sit on the front porch and drink beer and watch the sun go down on warm summer nights."

"And we'll build a duplex. And our kids will play together in the front yard with a golden retriever named Scout," Tabby added, her voice playful yet wistful.

"A golden? Why not a German shepherd?" Jason asked.

"Why not both?"

"You'll spoil the crap outta those kids, I'm sure of it." Jason opened another taco. "They'll be running you ragged, and you'll love it."

"That sounds perfect."

"And I'll be your kids' cool uncle," Jason declared. "I'll teach them to swear and sneak them snacks when their mommy isn't looking."

"And I'll be your kids' nice aunt who walks them to the library for story time and gives them banned books to read," Tabby responded, matching his tone.

Jason laughed. "Oh god, we're gonna raise a family of delinquents together."

"Yes, but happy, well-loved delinquents."

"Well, that's what matters. As long as our kids are happy," Jason said. "I mean, what's a little bit of swearing and reading banned books? They're just words and paper. They can't do any lasting damage."

Tabby's look was introspective. "Have you thought about it? Your future, I mean?" Tabby asked.

"I guess I have," Jason admitted, his voice softening. "I've always wanted kids someday. I never really had much of a family life, y'know? My folks weren't around much, always off on one business venture or another. I had nannies who took care of me. I always thought that when I had kids, I wanted to be a dad that was there for them. That they could count on. I don't know, maybe those kinds of dreams are naive, but I guess that's what I've always wanted."

"Same. I also want to be there for my kids. Not that we had nannies or anything—we were dirt poor. But my dad left when I was little, and my mom had ... addiction issues. So we were never close."

Jason nodded, understanding her desire for a do-over with her own kids. "So, you definitely want kids someday?"

"Absolutely. A boy and a girl."

"Yeah?" Jason felt a connection in their shared aspirations. "That sounds perfect. Two little hellions wreaking havoc and driving their parents crazy."

As they lounged on the park bench, Tabby turned to Jason. "Does Ruby want kids?"

"I think she does, but she's never been very specific. Honestly, we haven't talked about any of the long-term stuff yet. We're just enjoying the moment right now. The passion." His eyes sparkled as he spoke.

"Passion can *lead* to kids, you know?" Tabby countered.

Jason dropped his head into his hands. "Don't remind me, please." The thought of a surprise baby sent anxiety through him. "I'm trying to be careful, but she's not on birth control or anything, so I don't know how serious she is about that. I just don't really wanna think about the possibilities right now, if I'm honest."

Tabby nodded. "I suppose the birth control talk should come before sex, but Jack and I never actually talked about it."

Jason asked, "You never had 'the talk' beforehand?"

"Did you?" she asked.

He paused, a sheepish grin creeping onto his face. "Can't say that I did. Turns out my willpower isn't as robust as I believed."

"So, you didn't use anything?" Tabby asked.

He shook his head. "You got a point there. Guess we should have been more careful. You didn't get lucky, right?"

"What?" she said, confusion etched on her face.

He sighed, realizing he probably shouldn't be prying. "I mean, you're not knocked up, are you?"

"We've only been together a couple of weeks. I wouldn't know for several more weeks at least. Do you not understand how periods work?"

Jason felt a flush of embarrassment. "I'm not completely ignorant. I'm aware the math doesn't add up yet. But you never know, right? Some girls just miss their periods for random reasons once in a while."

Tabby rolled her eyes. "Well, I'm not due for a couple more weeks anyway."

"You're awfully ... I guess the word I'm looking for is 'laid-back' about this," Jason said. "Shouldn't you be a little bit worried?"

"What about you? You're not worried?" she countered.

He sighed. "Of course, I am. But I keep reminding myself how unlikely it is. I try not to let my imagination run away with all the possibilities."

Tabby shook her head in disbelief. "What the hell is wrong with us? Are we actually this stupid?"

He let out a nervous laugh. "I mean, not stupid ... just ... kinda living in an imaginary world where we're not completely responsible. Because it just feels so good, and we get caught up in the moment."

As they sat in the shade, their conversation hung in the air, mingling with the laughter and chatter of other park-goers. Jason relaxed, watching the leaves flutter in the gentle breeze. Beside him, Tabby seemed lost in her own world of dilemmas.

Breaking the silence, she said, "Before Jack, I never had sex without protection."

Jason turned to her, nodding. "Before Ruby, I never really did either. I used to make fun of the guys who did. Always thought they were careless idiots."

Tabby sighed. "I think I need to have a talk with Jack."

Jason looked at her. "Not to be rude, but why didn't that talk happen before you guys hooked up?"

"It wasn't a hookup," Tabby said.

"Oh, sorry. I didn't mean to say that. I understand. I'm just saying ... protection probably should have been the first thing on your minds. I'm surprised Jack didn't bring it up."

"Well, you said you didn't bring it up with Ruby earlier, right?" Tabby pointed out.

Jason acknowledged her point. "True. We're both a couple of idiots."

The conversation took a sudden turn as Tabby asked, "Jason, are you Catholic?"

"Why? You think we've all got a one-way ticket to hell now or something?"

"No, but a priest once told me that without the willingness and openness to have a child, sex can't be 'all it can be.'"

"Did he really say that?" Jason looked at her incredulously, his eyes twinkling with laughter.

"Yeah. If you're Catholic, you're not supposed to use birth control."

"I don't think I've ever met a Catholic who listened to that. Even my family, which was 'crazy religious' as my sister likes to call it. I just think it's kinda crazy to have a kid before you get married. That's a lesson I learned from my parents, ironically enough."

"So, you *are* Catholic?" Tabby probed.

"I mean, technically. I was baptized and went to church every Sunday for a while when I was a kid. But I haven't really considered myself a real practicing Catholic since high school."

"Same with me," Tabby said, nodding in agreement.

"I can't say I really follow all that doctrine anymore. I probably wouldn't even if I did go to church regularly." Jason snorted lightly, his face showing a trace of disdain. "That guilt bullshit isn't healthy."

"Yeah, I was just wondering. Kinda thinking out loud," Tabby said, her tone reflective.

Jason nudged her shoulder affectionately, lowering his voice slightly. "So, hypothetically ... if worse comes to worst and you and Ruby did accidentally get knocked up ... what would you do, do you think?"

"Stop drinking for one," Tabby responded, matter-of-factly.

Jason nodded in agreement. "Smart. And after that?"

"Find an obstetrician, I guess."

Jason was surprised by her demeanor. "You're awfully casual about this, considering the implications."

"Well, what would you do?" she said, turning the question back to him.

He pondered it for a moment, his gaze drifting off into the distance. "I don't know. Like I said, it's a lot easier to think about when it's hypothetical. I mean, I love Ruby, but it's only been two weeks! And I'm not sure how Ruby would react to unexpectedly getting pregnant."

"That's quite the non-answer," Tabby laughed.

Jason joined in the laughter. "It's just a complex problem, y'know? There's no easy answers, hypothetically. But if I'm being entirely honest, if I got her pregnant, I think I'd want to keep it."

Next to him, Tabby was deep in thought. "Since we've both had unprotected sex and we don't know what we'd do about the consequences, we probably really should talk to our partners about it."

"Yeah, we probably should. It's just a talk I really don't want to have." The idea of confronting that subject filled him with unease.

Tabby's gaze was serious as she continued. "Personally, I'd like to know what Jack thinks about it."

Jason nodded, considering her words. "I think Ruby would want to know what I think about it too. It's hard to bring up, though. You know, the 'What do we do if you get pregnant? What do we do then?' question sounds so abrupt and kinda cold and clinical."

"Exactly," Tabby said. "That must be why it was easy to talk about with past boyfriends. Everything about the sex was cold and clinical. Protection was just another aspect of it."

Jason was surprised by her candor. "Cold and clinical? Doesn't sound like a lot of fun."

"I never got caught up in the moment like I do with Jack. It was all planned out and ... I don't know. Just not spontaneous."

Jason remembered his own experiences. "A little spontaneity can go a long way, I'm learning."

Tabby declared, "I think I'm going to go home and call Jack. When we talk in person I always fall under his spell. So, it's probably better if we talk about this stuff while he's out of town."

Jason nodded in agreement. "Calling is better. Less distraction. A good plan."

She gave him a hug, the warmth of her gesture lingering in the air. As she walked away, heading toward her apartment building, he waved after her.

Watching her leave, Jason sensed this conversation marked the start of something significant.

Tabby paced around her living room, her fingers twirling a strand of hair. She glanced at her phone, hesitating before finally picking it up to call Jack. He was out of town and this conversation would be better over the phone, without the distraction of his immediate presence.

Jack answered from his hotel room, his voice a comforting balm to her anxious thoughts. "Hey, darling."

"Hey sweetheart. How's the conference?" she asked, trying to ease into the conversation.

He sighed, his exhaustion evident. "Boring. I don't know why I ever agreed to go to this City Summit in the first place. It's like a never-ending stream of political bullshit."

"That sucks. Are you coming back tomorrow?" Tabby shifted her weight from one foot to the other, her heart racing at the thought of the impending topic.

"Yes, I'm flying back tomorrow morning. Can't wait to sleep in my own bed again and not in this hotel room," Jack said.

"With your scratchy sheets?" she asked.

He laughed. "Yes, even with my scratchy sheets."

There was a pause, and then Tabby said, "Are you free to talk? There's something that's been on my mind."

Jack turned serious. "Alright, you've got my attention. What is it?"

Her heart pounded as she started. "We should have talked about this sooner, but ... We need to talk about birth control, right?"

"You're right. We should have talked about it earlier. So, what are you thinking?"

"You should probably know that I was single for a while before we met, and everything was so spontaneous with us that ... I'm not on the pill, so the past two weeks have been ... well ... risky."

Jack was silent for a moment, absorbing the news. "I see what you're saying. We definitely should have had this conversation earlier. But you're right, everything just happened so quickly that we never really thought about it. So, what do you think we should do?"

"Well, my period is due in two weeks. So if I get it, then I can go back on the pill. It should take a month to be effective. And if I don't, well ... we should probably talk about what to do if I don't," Tabby said.

"Right. So, we'll wait two weeks and see. Then you can start the pill, and a month after that we'll be protected. Is that what you have in mind?" Jack asked, his voice calm and reassuring.

"Yeah," Tabby said, relieved at his reaction.

"And if you're late? Then what?" Jack's voice was gentle, probing.

"Then I take a trip to the drugstore and take a test," she said, the reality of the situation settling in.

Jack paused, then said, "That makes sense. What do you think will happen if you are?"

Tabby's voice was soft, vulnerable. "What do you want to happen if I am?"

Jack's reply came after a heartfelt pause. "I don't know ... I mean, I never really thought about it until now. But ... if you are, I'd want to be there for you. I want to support you and take care of you, no matter what happens."

"If I am, then I want us to be a family together," Tabby said, her decision clear.

"That's what I want too. If you are, then I want to be there with you every step of the way. We'll be a family together, no matter what," Jack responded, his voice filled with emotion.

"I love you so much."

"I love you too, darling. More than you know," Jack said, his voice warm and comforting.

"I should let you get some sleep since you're flying home tomorrow. Call me when you get home, okay?" They had much to think about, but for now, she knew they needed rest.

"You're right. I should get some rest before my flight tomorrow. Of course, I'll call you as soon as I get home. Hearing your voice makes me miss you even more," Jack said, his tone tender.

"Goodnight," Tabby said.

"Goodnight. Sweet dreams," Jack said, and with that, they ended the call, each lost in their thoughts of the future that might be unfolding before them.

# 14 Mistakes

As Jack's cab from the airport pulled up to Tabby's apartment building, he paid the driver and stepped out. With a determined stride, he climbed the stairs and approached her door and knocked, waiting eagerly for her to answer.

Upon seeing Jack at the threshold, Tabby's face brightened with joy. Without hesitation, she wrapped her arms around him, enveloping him in a tight embrace, her lips finding his in a passionate kiss. Jack dropped his luggage and held her, pulling her close, the familiar scent and warmth of her presence flooding him with a sense of home.

"Welcome back," Tabby said, her voice muffled against his shoulder.

"Thanks. I missed you so much," Jack said, his voice thick with emotion as he hugged her even tighter, burying his face in her shoulder to breathe in her scent, overwhelmed by his feelings.

"I missed you too. So much that I need a key to your apartment so I can be there when I'm missing you," Tabby said.

Jack was amused and touched by her forwardness. He pulled back slightly, his eyes twinkling with affection. "Is that your subtle way of asking to move in with me?"

"Maybe we should wait until we've known each other, say, a month before we move in together," Tabby suggested.

Jack grinned, feeling a twinge of disappointment mingled with admiration for her sensibility. "Fine, fine. I can wait a little longer for you to move in with me. But you're still getting a key to my place so you can come over whenever you miss me."

She responded with a kiss, pulling him close once again. Jack returned her kiss fervently, his hands exploring her back, his desire intensifying. He reluctantly broke the kiss, mindful of their public display. "Darling, we should probably go inside before I do something to you right here in the hallway," he murmured, his voice tinged with longing.

Tabby backed into the apartment, still holding him. Jack followed her in and shut the door behind them, his heart pounding with excitement. He pressed her against the wall, his hands roaming over her body as his lips found the tender skin of her neck, kissing her gently.

Whispering into her ear, his voice rough with desire, Jack confessed, "I've been thinking about you nonstop since I left. I couldn't stop thinking about your body, your lips, the way you feel when you're pressed against me like this." He looked into her eyes. "I can't get enough of you. I need you right now."

Jack lifted Tabby, wrapping her legs around his waist as he carried her to the couch. He sank down onto the cushions, her body straddling his lap, and kissed her hungrily. His hands roamed over her, exploring every inch of her skin as they both hurriedly shed their clothes, the air thick with anticipation.

With a gentle motion, he laid her back against the couch, his hands continuing their exploration. Positioning himself between her legs, he pressed against her, his desire for her almost overwhelming. Lost in the moment, he moved against her, hands roaming freely as they made love, the world outside fading into nothingness.

He kissed her neck deeply, hands cupping her face as he gazed into her eyes, utterly consumed by her presence. "Tabby," he whispered, a blend of love and desire lacing his voice as he lost himself in her. Overwhelmed by the intensity, he buried his face in her shoulder, savoring every second.

Eventually, he collapsed against her, breathless and filled with warmth. He buried his face in her shoulder, inhaling her scent as he tried to regain his composure. Tabby's contentment radiated from her, a comforting presence against him.

Jack pulled her closer, snuggling her against his chest. "I could stay like this forever," he murmured, wishing to hold her in this perfect moment with her body against his.

"Jack?" Tabby's voice broke the tranquility, and he looked down, curious about her thoughts.

"Yes, darling?"

"We had sex again without protection," she said, her tone shifting the mood from intimate to serious.

Jack froze for a moment, her words sinking in. He met her gaze with concern. "You're right. We did."

"Are we going to keep doing this?" she asked, her eyes searching his.

He sighed, a conflict brewing within him. "I don't know. I want to be with you, but I don't want to keep putting you at risk like this. We should probably be more responsible about it."

"You're right. We probably should," she agreed, her voice softening.

Jack nodded, disappointment creeping in. "It's hard when we're alone like this, and I want to touch you and be close to you."

"I know," she said, understanding in her voice. "I get you in my arms, and I lose my mind."

Jack pulled her closer, his hands gliding over her bare skin, a blend of possessiveness and affection. "And as much as I want to keep touching you and holding you like this ... we should probably get dressed."

Tabby stood and headed to her bedroom, emerging moments later in a pair of pink flannel pajamas adorned with bunny rabbits. "How's this. Too sexy?"

Jack smiled, his fondness for her choice evident. He rose from the couch and walked over, embracing her. "Not at all. In fact, I think you look downright adorable."

"Perfect," she beamed.

He kissed her on the top of her head before pulling back, grinning. "You're cute as a button, darling. Those pajamas make you look so soft and cute, like a little bunny rabbit."

"Problem is, though, that *you* look sexy as hell. Please dig through your luggage and cover yourself," she said.

Jack laughed, delighted by her request. "You think I'm too sexy? Well, I'm glad to hear it. But okay, I'll see if I can find something to wear. Anything specific you'd like me to cover up?"

"This whole area here." She gestured toward his torso. "And please wear something cute and adorable and not sexy," she said, crossing her arms.

"Are you saying that I'm too sexy for you? Because I can definitely tone it down for you."

Jack slipped back into his boxers and retrieved his luggage from the hallway. He rummaged through it and pulled out a pair of loose-fitting sweatpants and a plain T-shirt. "How's this? Cute and adorable enough for you?"

Tabby nodded. "Yes. Perfect cuddling attire."

Jack changed into the T-shirt and pants, amused by the contrast between his casual attire and her colorful pajamas. He walked over to her, pulling her into his arms once more. "Cuddling attire procured. Now, where were we?"

With a playful spark in her eyes, Tabby took his hand and led him to the bed, ready to continue their evening together. She nestled her head against his chest. "I love the sound of your heartbeat," she said.

As Jack ran his fingers through her hair, deep contentment settled over him. He nuzzled his face into the top of her head, taking a deep breath to inhale her scent. "And I love having you close against me," he said, his tone soft and intimate.

As they lay there, Tabby's hand wandered over his arm, tracing the line of a scar with a gentle touch. "Did you get these scars from work?" she asked, curiosity coloring her voice.

He glanced down at the scars that marked his body. "Yeah, there's a few of them. Occupational hazards, you could say."

"I guess that's what happens when you play with chainsaws for a living,"

"It's not all sunshine and rainbows, that's for sure. But I can't imagine doing anything else. I love it too much. I've been doing it since I was fifteen, I think. Dad taught me everything I know."

"Your dad taught you a lot. How to shoot, how to work on cars, how to play with chainsaws, and to never let a lady pay for a date," Tabby recounted.

"That's my dad alright. I love him dearly. He taught me so much—what it means to be a man, how to stand up for myself, how to care for those I love. He's the best father a man could ask for," Jack said, his voice filled with admiration and gratitude.

"Ruby says you're like him. And she's like your mom,"

Jack nodded. "A lot of people say I'm like my dad. I guess it comes through. And yes, Ruby is very much like my mom."

"I'm guessing you inherit both your looks and personality from them, given that you two don't resemble each other at all. Her, a blue-eyed blonde, and you with your black hair and ... what color are your eyes anyway? They're so dark they seem black."

Jack was amused by her observation. "They're brown, but they come off as black most of the time. And yes, you're right. We look nothing alike—but I think we share the same stubbornness."

"That's very true," Tabby agreed.

"Ruby and I can both be exceptionally stubborn. It drives my father insane when we start butting heads," Jack admitted with a laugh.

"I'll bet," she said.

Jack nodded. "My father was beside himself when Ruby told him she wanted to move out on her own. He was afraid she would push herself too much or get upset and have an episode with nobody there to help her. But she'd had enough of all the babying, and she finally told him off. Told him she needed to live her own life, and he had to back off. He didn't want to hear that, obviously. He can be a bit of a stubborn bastard."

"Stubborn bastard? I think I've heard Jason call you that a few times. Before you made peace with him dating Ruby," Tabby pointed out with a grin.

Jack laughed quietly. "That does sound like me. But can you blame me? I'm older than Ruby. I've always looked after her, and she's still my baby sister, no matter how old she gets. So, I got a bit protective when Jason started dating her."

"Ruby also told me you stopped dating after she was hospitalized after her last episode. She blames herself for you not having a life of your own," Tabby said gently.

Jack's smile faded. "She probably does blame herself. But I made that choice on my own. I wasn't about to focus on my own life and leave her to deal with everything going on. I had to make sure she was safe. And if part of that meant me putting my life on hold for a bit, I was fine with that. I would do it again, in a heartbeat."

"I understand. But things are better now that Jason knows all about her condition and he wants to help, right?" Tabby asked, seeking reassurance.

He nodded. "It's a huge relief, honestly. I mean, I was afraid she would never find anyone who could handle it."

"Aren't you glad you didn't kill him now?" she teased, lightening the mood.

"Ah hell, if I killed every man who tried to date my sister, there would be a bunch of bodies in a ditch somewhere. He stuck it out despite my behavior. So, kudos to him."

"Tell me more about your life," said Tabby. "I want to know everything."

Jack shifted to lie on his back, gently pulling Tabby along with him. He settled her comfortably against his chest, her head nestled under his chin. He held her close, the warmth of their connection enveloping them. "Well, what do you want to know?" he asked, openness in his tone.

"Tell me about where you lived before you moved to New Jersey," Tabby said, her voice eager with curiosity.

Jack hesitated for a moment, his mind drifting to his past. When he began speaking, his voice quiet but steady. "Grew up in rural Pennsylvania. We had a farm. A good bit of land, surrounded by trees and mountains. Dad made a decent enough living to support my mom, Ruby, and me. There was always meat on the table and a roof over our heads."

"I never would have guessed that. You and Ruby don't seem like the farmer type," Tabby remarked, looking up at him with surprise.

"We both wandered pretty far from that path," he admitted, his mind tracing the contours of a long-forgotten landscape. "But that's where we started. It's funny how life takes you places you'd never expect."

Jack paused briefly, a playful smile appearing as a thought struck him. "You want to know something about my parents?" he asked, looking down at Tabby.

"Yes," she said, nodding eagerly.

"When I was younger, I would hear them sometimes from my room. Making love," he said, a laugh escaping him as he recalled the memory. "Mom would scream my dad's name, loud." He shook his head. "I was never sure if they didn't care or if they forgot how thin the walls were. God, I would have done anything to not have to hear all that when I was a kid."

Tabby laughed, her voice light and teasing. "That's so disturbingly sweet."

Jack shook his head, still chuckling. "There was nothing sweet about it back then. All I wanted to do was go to sleep. I'd have to stuff my pillow over my head just to drown it out. Drove me crazy."

"Yeah, but still, it's good to have parents who are in love," she said.

He grinned and nodded. "They were good to have, even if it involved hearing way more noise than any kid should have to deal with. I didn't get it when I was younger, but now I see how special they are. My mom is tough as hell, and my dad would do anything for his family. I couldn't ask for better parents."

"You're very lucky," Tabby said.

Jack looked down at her, a shadow crossing his features. "I know I am. I always have been. But I had to sacrifice a lot to keep everything going when Ruby was in the hospital. I pretty much stopped my life for a good while to keep things together."

He turned his gaze away, uncertainty flickering in his eyes. After a moment, he continued. "I'm not complaining. Like I said, I'd do it all again if I had to. I was there for Ruby when she needed me, and I would never change that. But I quickly realized I wasn't going to date anyone until I was sure Ruby was okay. I didn't have a choice about that. All my time went to looking after her. No one would put up with that in a relationship, so I gave up the concept of one."

"Did something happen with a previous relationship?" Tabby asked gently.

He hesitated, weighing whether to share the pain of his past. Deciding there was no point in hiding it, he said, "I was in a relationship a long time ago. My first one, actually. My last one, too."

He paused before continuing. "I loved her more than I'd loved anyone before. I thought we were going to be together for a long time."

"What happened?" Tabby prompted.

Jack hesitated again. "She ... cheated on me. I found her with one of my friends. While I was busy taking care of Ruby, she'd been seeing him behind my back for months, even after we'd been together for a year. Broke my heart."

"Sounds like a bitch," Tabby said. "Wait a minute. That's not ... your type, is it?" she asked, worry creeping into her tone.

He laughed, the sound bittersweet. "No, it's not. She was the only woman I've ever been with, and she turned out to be exactly the opposite of what I'm attracted to. She was very ... abrasive, let's say, with an attitude that was like a knife stabbing me in the back." He sighed. "You, on the other hand, are exactly what I'm into. You're perfect."

"Aw." Tabby kissed him on the cheek.

He grinned, enveloping her in his embrace and pulling her closer. "God, you're a little sweetheart, darling."

"Yes, I am. And you don't have to worry about getting your heart broken anymore because I'm going to keep you forever," she declared confidently.

Jack pulled her tighter against him. "And I'm never letting you go. You're stuck with me. Even if you get sick of my sarcastic ass, you're stuck with me. There's no going back now."

"I'm exactly where I want to be," Tabby said.

"Exactly where you belong," he echoed, nuzzling his face against the top of her head, breathing in the scent of her hair and the warmth of her skin. He finally relaxed, her body against his, her steady breathing filling the air.

Tabby snuggled up to him, closing her eyes, settling comfortably against his chest. Jack ran his hand through her hair, feeling the softness of the strands. He took a deep, steady breath, utterly relaxed with her in his arms.

The rhythmic sound of her breathing was like soothing music, and he could feel the steady beat of her heart against him.

As the night deepened, Jack's eyelids grew heavy. With Tabby's comforting weight against him and her warmth beside him, he drifted off to sleep, his arms wrapped securely around her, his face buried in her hair.

# 15 Foreboding

Jason approached Ruby's apartment with a sense of excitement. He balanced a large pizza and two large Cokes in his arms, the savory aroma wafting up to tease his senses. As he knocked on the door, a wide grin spread across his face, anticipation thrumming through him.

When Ruby opened the door, her eyes lit up.

"Guess who's got pizzaaaa?" he said, his voice playful.

"Yay, pizza! Extra cheese?" she asked, stepping aside to let him in.

"Extra everything," he confirmed, stepping into the cozy space, the smell of her home mixing with the scent of the pizza. He made his way to the living room, setting the pizza and drinks down on the table before plopping onto the couch and patting the seat next to him. "C'mon, have a slice."

Ruby took a slice, and Jason followed suit, savoring the first bite. "Now that's a good pizza. Just the right amount of grease, cheese and sauce. We should definitely order from them again," he said, his mouth full.

"Mmhmm," Ruby agreed.

After a few moments of comfortable silence punctuated only by the sounds of their munching, Jason paused, a thoughtful look crossing his face. "There's ... something I kinda wanted to talk to you about, if you've got a minute."

"What's up?" Ruby asked.

Jason struggled to find the right words. "I'm not sure the best way to talk about this. But since I want to be open and honest with you, I figure I'll just be blunt."

"Yeah, don't beat around the bush. What do you want to talk about?" Ruby encouraged.

He set his pizza slice down, the playful mood suddenly heavy. "Okay, here goes. Have you ever thought about what would happen if you get pregnant?"

Ruby put down her slice. "Umm ... maybe. A bit."

Jason was surprised by her response. "Honestly, I didn't think you'd think much about it at all. I've thought about it a couple of times, which is why I kinda want to know what you would do if the worst happens, and we have an accident."

She looked down, her fingers tracing the edge of her plate. "Sometimes I wonder if I should have kids. I mean, I *want* kids, but my kids would be genetically predisposed to bipolar disorder, so maybe that would be irresponsible. But maybe if I got pregnant without trying, maybe that would mean I'm meant to be a mom. It's a lot of maybes."

Jason felt a rush of surprise at how deeply she'd considered being a parent, especially given her spontaneous nature. "That's exactly what I'm wondering, though. Even if it's not on purpose—would you keep it?"

After a long pause, Ruby met his gaze. "Yeah, I would."

He had not expected her confident reply. "You wouldn't want to terminate?"

"Is that what you would want?" she asked, her voice probing.

He was caught off guard. "I mean, on the one hand, I worry it's a terrible idea, for a multitude of reasons. On the other hand, I can't help but think that starting a family with you would be amazing."

There was a light in her eyes as Ruby said, "Our kids would be adorable."

Jason imagined the possibility. "They would be, wouldn't they? Miniature versions of you." As they shared a moment of laughter, the importance of the conversation lingered, making Jason acutely aware that their relationship had taken a significant turn.

Ruby retrieved a photo album from the shelf in her living room and flipped it open. Jason's eyes were immediately drawn to the images of her past. She pointed to a picture of a blond baby held by a dark-haired boy. "I was a super cute baby," she declared, her finger resting on the image of her infant self.

"Wow, you were," Jason agreed, leaning closer to examine the photo. "Look at those baby blues."

His gaze shifted to the boy holding her. "Is that Jack?"

"Yeah, that's him," Ruby confirmed with a smile.

She continued flipping through the album, pausing at another picture of Jack.

"And he was a handsome kid, too," said Jason. "Jack's always been good looking, huh?"

"Yeah, in school, my friends were always crushing on him. But he was too studious to notice attention from girls," Ruby said.

"You sure he wasn't just playing hard to get?"

"In high school, the only dates he ever went on were study dates. And I'm pretty sure they actually studied," Ruby said, her tone amused.

"That does sound like something he'd do. No spring flings for your brother, then?" Jason imagined the serious young man Ruby described.

"Nah, too busy being my protector. That's why I encouraged him to ask Tabby out. He deserves to be happy. I know they've only been together a couple of weeks, like us, but he's never been happier," Ruby said, her voice softening with affection for her brother.

Jason's attention was then captured by a picture of Ruby's parents, a young couple radiating happiness. "These your parents? They look very much in love here."

"Yup, they are," Ruby responded.

"They've been together a long time, haven't they? They must've gotten married young."

"Early twenties," she confirmed.

Jason observed several other pictures, all depicting a family full of joy. "You had a pretty ideal childhood, huh?"

"Things weren't perfect, but we were pretty happy."

He then noticed a picture of Ruby as an awkward preteen standing next to her tall, handsome brother. "I bet you two were really close."

"I all but followed him around, pestering him incessantly," Ruby admitted with a laugh.

Jason was absorbed by the images. "I bet you got a lot of special privileges growing up, being the baby sister and all."

"He always spoiled me. Made it tough for anybody else to measure up," she said, pride in her voice.

"Well, you were an adorable little kid. I definitely see how it would be hard to say no to you," Jason said, and laughed.

"You don't talk about your family much," said Ruby. "Do they live close by?"

Jason grew contemplative at this shift in conversation. He closed the photo album, his expression turning sober. "Nah, there's a reason for that. My parents live about three hours away, but I don't talk to them much. They're pretty conservative Catholics, and I just don't see eye to eye with them on a lot. I'm the black sheep, the lost one, in their eyes."

"What about your little sister?" Ruby asked.

He thought about his sister. "Well, I talk to her every now and then, but we're pretty different, too. She's a successful businesswoman now, and even growing up, she was a lot like my parents too. Very career driven, very focused on money and success. She basically married a carbon copy of my dad. I'm still hoping she'll realize she wasted her life on the wrong guy eventually. I think at heart she'd be much happier with someone who's a bit more passionate and spontaneous."

Ruby gave Jason a sympathetic look. "So, your brother-in-law doesn't like you, huh?"

Jason chuckled, a sound that came easily to him after years of navigating the family dynamics. "No—he thinks I'm a complete screwup. Can't blame him, honestly. From his perspective, I've spent my twenties jumping from one dead-end job to the next, getting into debt and screwing around on my girlfriends without a thought about the future."

Ruby tilted her head, a playful challenge in her gaze. "And what about now? Are you still in a dead-end job, in debt and screwing around on your girlfriend?"

He laughed at her bluntness. "I hope not. I mean, I certainly don't think so. I've got a real job now, I'm making decent money and I'm definitely not screwing around on you."

With a sudden movement, Ruby climbed onto his lap, facing him. She took his face in her hands, her expression serious. "You better not."

Jason felt a thrill. "Don't worry," he said, grinning, "I don't have eyes for anyone but you."

She kissed him then, a soft yet demanding press of lips that sent warmth through him. Jason kissed her back passionately, pulling her firmly against him, relishing the feeling of the connection between them deepening.

"What did I do to deserve you?" he said between kisses, his hands resting on her hips, drawing her closer.

"You were a very good boy."

He laughed, shaking his head. "I'm not sure if I necessarily qualify for the 'good boy' category. But you make me want to be one, that's for sure."

Ruby wrapped her arms around him in a warm hug, and he rested his head against her shoulder, savoring the moment.

"So ... you want to know the truth?" he asked, his voice suddenly serious.

"Always," she said.

Jason continued, "I've spent the past two weeks like I'm walking on a tightrope. I have the time of my life with you when we're together. You're beautiful and charming, and you drive me crazy and make me so happy ... but part of me is waiting for the other shoe to drop. I feel like I'm just waiting for the second it all goes to hell."

"Just enjoy it," Ruby said, her lips brushing against his as she spoke. She kissed him again, and he felt the tension ease, if only for a moment. In her embrace, the worries of the world seemed to fade away.

Jason kissed Ruby again. He ran his hands down her back, pulling her body firmly against him. "I am," he said, as the warmth radiated from her. "It's hard to worry when I've got you like this."

"That's more like it."

"Oh, you like that, huh?" Jason asked.

"I don't *dislike* it."

"Good answer." He slid his hands up her thighs and then slipped them under her dress. Her body responded to him, and it sent a thrill through him.

He pressed his lips against the delicate area under her ear, savoring the way she reacted. "I love everything about you, the way you taste, the way you smell ..." he murmured against her skin. As he kissed her collarbone, he traced her ribs beneath the edge of her bra with his fingers. "I can't keep my hands off you when you're close to me."

"Naughty, naughty," she teased, her voice playful.

He moved one hand up to her shoulder while the other slid down to her hip. "I'm not gonna be able to resist much longer."

"Why are you resisting at all?" she asked.

He kissed her neck, his lips moving up and down the sensitive area under her ear. "I'm trying to be a gentleman here. I don't want you to think I only want one thing."

She laughed, the sound light and playful. "You're trying to be a gentleman? You're failing miserably."

"Is it that obvious?" he asked.

"Most definitely," she said, a wicked grin on her face.

"I do find myself wishing there was somewhere a little more comfortable than this to have you all to myself," he continued, nipping at her shoulder while his hands roamed over her thighs.

"I have the perfect place. I want to ensnare you in my web. But you have to come willingly into my bed," she said, her voice sultry and inviting.

"Like I need to be enticed. Lead the way," Jason said.

With a playful tug, Ruby took his hand and led him to her bedroom. As they walked, Jason's eyes roamed over her body, still slightly amazed at her boldness. They made love, lost in each other, before falling asleep entwined in her bed.

Morning light filtered through the curtains, and Jason was still asleep next to Ruby, his expression content. A small smile played on his lips even in his dreams, one arm wrapped around her while the other lay flung above his head.

Unable to resist, Ruby poked him. “Hey, sleepyhead.”

His eyes flickered open, and he glanced over at her with a sheepish grin. “How long have you been watching me?”

“A while. What were you dreaming about? You looked happy.”

He gave her a sleepy smile, pulling her closer. “I was dreaming about you.”

“Of course you were,” she said, amusement in her eyes.

Jason kissed her, clearly still only half-awake. “Of course I was. I always dream about you. You’re always in my subconscious.”

“Yes,” she said, “I’ve burrowed my way in there, and you’ll never be rid of me.”

He pretended to shudder, taking her in his arms and rolling so she was on top of him. “Oh no, I’m doomed.”

“I’ve got to get up,” she announced. “My brother is back from his trip, and he’s taking me out to breakfast.”

Jason tightened his grip around her waist. “Are you sure you have to get up? I have a better idea.”

“I think I know what your better idea is.”

His hands slid up her sides. “Oh, I’m sure you do.”

“Seriously,” she insisted, trying to break free from his embrace. “I need to go shower and get dressed.”

With a reluctant sigh, Jason let her go, sitting up and running a hand through his disheveled hair. He looked half-asleep still, his eyes unfocused. “I was having such a nice dream,” he said, watching Ruby as she got up, gathered some clothes and headed for the shower.

Propping his head up on one hand, he called after her, “You’re so cruel, making me wait.”

Several minutes later, Ruby came back to the bedroom, dressed and ready to leave. “You’re still in bed?” she asked.

“Yes, I’m still in bed,” he said, still propped up and looking thoroughly debauched. “The view is much nicer from the bed. Come back over here.”

She picked up her keychain, removed a key and tossed it to him. “Lock up before you leave.” Then she walked over and gave him a quick kiss.

Jason caught the key in one hand while gently grabbing her wrist with the other, pulling her back onto the bed. “Hold on just a second.”

“What now?” Ruby asked.

“I just need one more kiss.” He grinned, rolling, so that she was pinned beneath him, his legs trapping hers.

“Jack is waiting for me. If I don’t go meet him, he’ll come looking for me.”

“Tell him you’ll be a few minutes late,” Jason said.

“Are you completely incapable of behaving yourself?” she asked, trying to sound stern.

“No, *absolutely* incapable.” He kissed her again. “And you’re the only one to blame.”

A knock interrupted them at that moment. Jason groaned, burying his head in Ruby’s neck. “Dammit, your brother has impeccable timing.”

“Great. This is going to be awkward.” Ruby pushed him off and threw his pants at him. “Get dressed.”

He scrambled out of bed, tripping as he tried to pull his pants on as fast as possible. “Do I have any time to run a comb through my hair?”

“Finger comb it,” she said, already moving toward the door.

“Fantastic,” he muttered, running his fingers through his messy blond locks, which only seemed to stick up more.

Ruby sighed and opened the door. Jason stood awkwardly behind her, trying not to look suspicious as Jack stepped inside. Jack smiled at Ruby, giving her a kiss on the cheek. “Hey, sis.” Then he glanced over at Jason, clearly not surprised to find him there. “Jason.”

Ruby frowned at Jason. He was a sight—rumpled hair and dressed only in a pair of jeans. To top it off, Ruby had a very visible love bite on her neck, which she had spotted in the mirror the second she stepped into the bathroom.

Jason forced a casual smile. “Hey, Jack. How was the trip?”

“Boring as hell,” Jack said.

Jason ran a hand through his hair, desperate to appear nonchalant. “Oh yeah? Not a fan of the business trip, huh?”

“I’m taking Ruby out for breakfast,” Jack announced, his tone polite but his expression less than welcoming. “You’re welcome to join us.”

Jason glanced at Ruby, who looked equally unenthusiastic about the idea. "Nah, you guys enjoy yourselves," he said. "I've got some stuff I need to do at home anyway."

Jack looked relieved. "Okay then. Ready?" he said to Ruby.

Jason hurriedly grabbed his jacket from where it had landed on the floor the night before. He pulled his sneakers onto his bare feet without tying them and slipped out of the apartment.

Jack leaned against the kitchen counter, watching as Jason slipped out the door. A knowing look passed between him and Ruby.

"So, Jason stayed here last night?" he remarked.

Ruby straightened up, crossing her arms defensively. "It's okay for me to have my boyfriend over."

Jack held up his hands in a placating gesture. "Easy. I'm not saying you can't have him over. It's an observation. That's all."

"Yeah, yeah," Ruby said with a playful roll of her eyes. "You can interrogate me about my sex life over breakfast. I'm hungry." With that, she headed out the door.

"Alright, alright. I'll leave your sex life alone. For now," he said, following her.

Ruby locked the door behind them, and they began walking toward the diner. As they strolled, Jack couldn't resist the urge to tease her. "So, how was your night with Jason? Anything exciting happen?"

"He brought pizza."

Jack grinned, amused by her evasive answer. "That's it? No wild and crazy adventures?"

"Nope. We hung out at home. Maybe I'm turning into a homebody," she said, seriousness creeping into her voice.

Jack feigned shock, placing a hand over his heart. "A homebody? You? I never thought I'd see the day. The free-spirited Ruby, settling down and staying home. What has this world come to?"

Ruby laughed, shaking her head. "Whatever will you do with your time if you no longer need to police my every move?"

He stroked his chin. "Hmm ... I'll probably take up a new hobby. Something like bird watching, or stamp collecting. Or maybe I'll finally have some peace and quiet knowing that you're not out there causing trouble."

"Very funny," Ruby said.

Jack nudged her with his shoulder, his grin widening. "But seriously, if you're really settling down and becoming a homebody, that's not necessarily a bad thing. It's actually kind of cute."

Ruby pretended to contemplate the idea, placing a finger on her chin. "Hmm. Do I want to be responsible and boring like Jack? Or do I want to be fun? It's a tough decision."

Jack rolled his eyes. "Okay, okay. You don't have to rub it in. I get it, you think I'm boring and responsible. But someone has to be the mature one in this family—and it's clearly not going to be you."

"Oh, I can definitely play the nagging sibling. You've taught me well. Now, where were you last night, mister? Certainly not at home," Ruby said, her tone playful but pointed.

Jack feigned innocence, trying to deflect the question. "Me? What do you mean? I was home, of course. Where else would I be?"

"You know I know exactly where you were. You slept at Tabby's last night, didn't you?"

Jack knew he couldn't fool Ruby—she was too observant for her own good. "You're right. I did spend the night at Tabby's. Is that such a crime?"

"No," Ruby said, crossing her arms. "I know you and Tabby have been sleeping together this whole time. You think girls don't talk?"

"It's true," he admitted, "but it's more than that. We care about each other. We're happy together. It's not only about sex."

"Yeah, she's head over heels for you," Ruby said.

Jack felt pride and concern at her words. "She is," he said, his voice softening. "And it's mutual. It's scary how much I care about her. I've never felt this way about anyone before."

"I'm glad to hear that," Ruby said, pausing for a moment before continuing. "Because you know what else Tabby told me?"

Jack glanced at her with curiosity and trepidation. "No, what did she tell you?"

"She told me she could be pregnant. Has my oh-so-responsible brother been throwing caution to the wind?"

His heart sank at her words, reality crashing down on him. "Yes, we've been ... somewhat careless. And it's possible she could be pregnant. I don't know what to do."

Ruby shook her head. "All that time working on old cars with Dad, did he never give you the condom talk?"

"No, he didn't. And I know we should have been more careful. But ... sometimes when you're in the moment, you don't always think about it."

"That's true," Ruby conceded. "How's it feel to be the reckless one in the sibling duo?"

He scoffed. "It feels ... strange. I've always been the responsible one, the one who did everything right. And now here I am, possibly having a baby with a woman I met a few weeks ago. I never would have imagined this."

Ruby laughed, her voice brightening the heavy mood. "Don't worry. Responsible Auntie Ruby doesn't judge."

"I appreciate that. But I still feel like an idiot. I never thought I'd be the one to get a girl pregnant so quickly."

"Well, maybe she's not pregnant. How many times are we talking here?" Ruby asked.

He paused, recalling the whirlwind of their recent weeks. "Honestly, I've lost count. Probably at least a dozen times, if not more."

Ruby shook her head, a mixture of disbelief and sympathy crossing her features. "Yeah, you're screwed."

Jack sighed. "I know it was careless. And if she is pregnant ... well, I don't know what to do. I care about her a lot. But I don't know if I'm ready to be a father."

As they arrived at the restaurant, the familiar jingle of the bell above the door greeted them. The sound once felt welcoming, but now it seemed to echo Jack's anxiety. He and Ruby slid into a cozy booth, the warmth of the space momentarily distracting him from his thoughts. The comforting scent of coffee and breakfast foods enveloped them, but Jack barely registered it. He grabbed the menu, his eyes scanning the options while his mind remained elsewhere, lost in thoughts of his potential fatherhood. The reality of it gnawed at him, making it hard to focus on anything else.

Ruby, sensing his distraction, reached across the table and placed a reassuring hand on his. "You'll figure it out. You're not alone in this. You have people who care about you," she said, her voice comforting.

Jack looked up, meeting her gaze. There was a sincerity in her eyes that lifted his mood slightly, but the anxiety still clung to him. "I don't want to screw this up," he admitted.

"You won't," Ruby said. "You're a good guy, Jack. Take it one step at a time."

He nodded, appreciating her support even as the uncertainty loomed large before him. He tried to push the thoughts aside, if only for a moment.

"Alright, let's order some food," he said, attempting to shift gears, hoping that the warmth of the meal would provide a temporary distraction.

As Jason walked into his apartment he was greeted by the sight of chaos: dirty dishes piled high in the sink and clothes everywhere. A sigh escaped him as he surveyed the mess, and he resigned himself to cleaning up.

As he began to tackle the clutter, his phone rang. He answered, still focused on the dishes. "Hey Tabs, what's up?"

"Wanna hang out?"

Jason glanced around at the disarray and sighed again. "Sure. I could use a distraction. What do you want to do?"

"Whatever. Jack is taking Ruby out for breakfast, so I've got no plans."

He looked back at the mess. "Why don't you come over here? I need to clean up a bit anyway."

"Alright, see you in a bit," Tabby said before hanging up.

Jason continued with his cleaning, tossing stray clothes into the laundry hamper and loading the dishwasher with dirty dishes. He made it through the kitchen and started tidying the living room when a knock interrupted him. He wiped his hands on his jeans and opened the door.

"Hey you," Tabby greeted.

"Hey yourself," he said, grinning back at her, though he still looked a bit tired from the previous night. "Come on in."

"Have you made coffee?" she asked, stepping inside.

"I live on coffee. Of course I made some. You want a cup?"

"Yes, please." She took a seat at the kitchen table.

Jason poured two mugfuls, handing one to her. "Cream and sugar, right?"

"Yeah."

Jason retrieved the cream and sugar. "You're a girl of few words today, huh?"

"I have a lot on my mind," Tabby admitted, stirring her coffee absent-mindedly.

Jason sat down across from her with his own cup. "Anything you want to talk about? You seem extra thoughtful today."

"Well, I called Jack like I said I would, and we had the birth control talk," Tabby said, her eyes focused on her drink.

Jason eyed her, surprised and amused. "Oh jeez. And how did that go?"

"Great. We decided to be careful."

Jason chuckled into his coffee cup. "Oh yeah? Careful?"

"Yeah," she confirmed.

He let out an exasperated sigh. "You're killing me, Tabby. Define for me exactly what you mean by 'careful.'"

"We're not going to have sex until I'm on the pill and it's effective. So, six weeks."

"Six weeks? Wow, I hope you've got a lot of distractions planned, because you're going to need them."

"I can go six weeks, right? I mean, I went six months before I met him."

He gave her an incredulous look. "I'm not saying you can't do it, but you'll have to distract yourself. It's a lot like giving up chocolate or something. You've got a craving, and suddenly you aren't allowed to have it."

"Actually, we already failed at it," Tabby admitted, her tone deflated.

His eyes widened as he burst into laughter. "You've already failed? So much for 'careful.'"

"I'm so screwed," Tabby said, burying her face in her hands.

Jason grinned, shaking his head. "At this rate, yeah. I give you maybe a day or two until you cave in."

"Thanks for the pep talk," she said sarcastically, peeking through her fingers.

"That's just my honest assessment. You two couldn't even manage a week. What are you going to do for six whole weeks?" he asked, unable to hide his amusement.

"What about you? Did you and Ruby talk about it?" she asked.

Jason hesitated, taking a sip of his coffee to buy himself a moment. "We did," he said, choosing his words carefully. "Although, I think our timeline's a bit shorter than yours."

"What do you mean?" Tabby asked.

Jason rubbed the back of his neck, a guilty gesture that made him feel even more vulnerable. "We ... also kind of already failed at being careful."

Tabby shook her head. "Well, I suppose you won't have to worry about it after Jack murders you."

Jason chuckled, the sound tinged with embarrassment. "Yeah, I'm honestly kind of surprised he was so chill about it. He seemed relatively okay with the whole thing this morning."

"What? He knows?" Tabby's eyes widened, and Jason immediately realized he had overshared.

"Well, yeah," he admitted, wincing as he prepared for her reaction. "He came over this morning and kind of ... saw us."

"What do you mean by 'saw us'?" Tabby asked.

Jason winced again, knowing he was about to make things worse. "I, uh ... I wasn't entirely clothed."

Tabby's laughter rang out, a bright sound in the otherwise tense atmosphere. "Wow, you have a way of winning him over, don't you?"

"I *do* have a way of putting my foot in it, don't I?"

"Yeah. Seems like we're *both* screwed," Tabby said.

Jason laughed again, though it was laced with trepidation. "So it would seem. Do you think Jack might actually kill me?"

"If you get his baby sister pregnant? Hope you're prepared for a shotgun wedding."

With a dramatic sigh, Jason buried his head in his hands, the reality of his situation crashing down on him. "I am so, so screwed. How am I supposed to even look the guy in the eye anymore?"

"Just don't get her pregnant. You said he was pretty chill about the rest of it, right?" Tabby encouraged.

Jason considered her words. "He seemed a bit resigned about the whole thing. Like he didn't have a choice but to get used to the idea."

"Well, that's good. Right?" Tabby said.

"Better than him actually murdering me, at least."

Tabby nodded. "He's a really nice guy. You should try to be friends with him."

Jason shook his head, amused. "I think that ship has sailed, Tabs. He's either going to kill me or try to scare me off by being a terrifying brother-in-law or something. Can't say I blame him, though."

"No, that's not true. He likes you. Sort of."

Jason scoffed, shaking his head. "What makes you say that? Pretty sure he's wanted to wring my neck since the first time he met me."

"Because he never would have left on that work trip if he didn't trust you to take care of his sister." Tabby's logic was flawless, and Jason paused, contemplating her words.

"Huh, I suppose you're right. Didn't think of it that way," he admitted, a flicker of hope igniting within him.

"And he trusts *my* judgment. Since *I* think you're a good guy, that gives you credibility," she added.

Jason let out a laugh, self-consciously running a hand through his hair. "Wow, thanks for the glowing endorsement. I'm a nice guy? Even after Jack found me half-naked in his sister's bed?"

"I can't be held responsible for your self-sabotage."

"It's not my fault," he protested, laughing. "She's the most tempting woman I've ever met."

"Shifting the blame onto poor innocent Ruby? How noble," Tabby teased.

Jason grinned. "Not my fault," he said. "She's all sweet and charming and gorgeous. She's the one who made me fall head over heels in love."

"How about the four of us get together tonight?" Tabby suggested. "It'll give you a chance to win back Jack's approval."

"Win him back over? You really think that's an achievable goal?"

"Like you said—he didn't murder you, and that's a good sign."

"That's true," Jason conceded, his mind whirring as he contemplated the idea. "Are you sure it's a good plan? I mean, a couple's night tonight? You and Jack, and me and Ruby?"

"Yeah," Tabby insisted. "We always have a good time when the four of us get together. Except for that one night, of course."

The memory of that particular Friday night flooded back with vivid clarity. "Yeah, let's not relive that anytime soon."

"So, where should we go?" Tabby asked.

He pondered for a moment. Then inspiration struck, his eyes lighting up. "Oh, I know."

# 16 Secrets

The chill air held a thrill of excitement as the four of them looked around the indoor skating rink. Jason inhaled deeply.

"This is great," he said. "Nighttime skating? Haven't done this since I was a kid."

"Yeah," Tabby said, her voice laced with playful sarcasm as she laced up her skates. "Nothing quite as fun as wearing a stranger's footwear and falling on my ass."

Jason let out a laugh, his own skates clinking as he tightened the laces. "Come on, it's not so bad. At least you have Jack here to catch you before you hit the ground."

Jack, standing nearby, held out his hand to Tabby. She took it, and he glided her smoothly out onto the ice.

With a grin, Jason turned his attention to Ruby, who was struggling to find her balance. He wrapped a steadying arm around her waist as she stepped into the rink. "Here, I've got you."

"I'm okay," she said, determination in her voice. "You can hold my hand, though."

Jason took her hand and guided her along the rink. "See? Isn't that better?"

Ruby's face lit up. "It's kind of magical."

Jason glanced around, taking in the scene: the other skaters, the laughter and the bright neon lights decorating the rink. "Yeah," he said, a sense of wonder in his voice. "This place is pretty cool. Like, it's right out of a movie."

They skated in comfortable silence for a few moments, passing other couples and families.

Ruby broke the quiet, her voice thoughtful. "When I was a kid, we used to skate on a pond at our farm. I remember shoveling the snow off the ice. Well, actually, watching Jack shovel the snow, so I could skate."

Jason squeezed her hand. "Yeah? Jack's always been a caretaker, hasn't he."

Ruby nodded, a distant look settling over her.

Jason pulled her in close, a soft grin on his face. "I wish I could've known you back then. I don't think I would've been able to get anything done. I'd just follow you around all day, pining like an idiot, hopelessly smitten."

"I bet you charmed all the girls in elementary school."

Jason laughed. "Me, charming? I was a complete dork. I'd have been way too shy to approach a pretty girl." Jason wrapped his arm around her waist, pulling her closer. "I didn't know how to talk to girls I liked. Spent most of school just staring at the ones I thought were pretty. I was hopeless."

"But then somewhere along the line, you became extremely confident and egotistical," Ruby said.

With a playful grin, he pulled her in tighter. "What can I say? I grew out of the awkward stage and figured out that I'm pretty damn charming."

Ruby laughed, the sound bright and genuine. "Yeah, you are."

Jason glanced over at Jack and Tabby, who were skating a short distance away. "Look at that. Jack's skating backward. Showoff," he said, chuckling.

"He used to play ice hockey," Ruby said, her eyes lighting up with fondness.

Jason was impressed. "Oh yeah? He was probably the type to get into fights on the ice, right?"

Ruby shook her head, smiling. "No, he didn't need to get into fights. He finessed his way past everyone. He was really good on skates. Still is, I guess."

Jason watched as Jack helped Tabby spin gracefully on the ice. "I see that. What happened—he quit hockey? How come? Seems like a waste to give that up."

"When I got hospitalized," Ruby explained, her gaze dropping to the ice. "He kinda put everything on hold."

Jason felt a swell of emotion at her words. He glanced back at Jack, who was still watching over Ruby, even from a distance. "He's always been a good brother to you, huh? He's looking out for you right now," Jason said, nodding toward Jack, who was still gliding backward, casting a watchful eye over them. "He's making sure you don't fall."

"Yes, it's endearing, yet unnerving," Ruby admitted.

Jason grinned, taking her hand as they made their way around the rink. "He's definitely a protective older brother. I should know—I've been on the receiving end of that protectiveness a few times already."

"You've been a good sport about it," Ruby said, her voice warm.

Jason laughed, the sound echoing in the crisp air. "I'd be an idiot not to be. The guy's been giving me the death glare since I first met him. Last thing I want to do is piss him off."

"Don't worry. He hasn't killed any of my boyfriends yet," Ruby said.

"That's very reassuring," Jason said, grinning.

"He likes you."

Jason laughed, still guiding her around the rink. "Yeah, right. If Jack likes me, he's terrible at showing it."

"Well, I can tell," Ruby insisted.

"How can you tell? I'm not exactly picking up on any warm, fuzzy feelings, especially now that he basically saw me in bed with you."

"Remember when he gave you the 'older brother' talk?" Ruby said. "He said he 'didn't want to have to harm you.' But usually it's 'I will harm you if you hurt her.'"

"Oh, you noticed that about his threat, huh? I gotta be honest, it didn't exactly come across that clear to me, given the fact he was clenching his fists and seemed about two seconds away from snapping my neck."

"Well, I didn't say he *wouldn't* harm you. Only that he doesn't *want to*," Ruby clarified, her tone light.

Jason sighed. "That's very comforting."

"Glad I could make you feel better," Ruby said, her laughter blending with the sounds of the rink.

Jason kissed her on the forehead. "See, this is exactly why I'm in love with you. Your calming presence and reassuring disposition really seal the deal."

Ruby suddenly let go of Jason's hand and skated over to Jack, deliberately crashing into him. He caught her effortlessly, a playful grin on his face.

"Causing trouble again?" he teased.

Jason skated up to them, shaking his head and laughing. "She's got it out for you tonight. Better be careful—you know the kind of damage she can cause when she's being a pain in the ass."

"Jack, Jason doesn't believe me that you like him. Tell him you like him," Ruby said.

Jack rolled his eyes but couldn't suppress a small smile. "I suppose Jason and I don't have the worst relationship ever."

Ruby turned back to Jason, triumphant. "See? I told you he likes you."

Jason laughed, eyeing Jack for a moment. "Really? That's your idea of a resounding declaration of mutual likability?"

Tabby, who had been skating nearby, said, "Well, in order to be mutual, you have to tell Jack how much you like him, too."

Jason sighed, glancing at Jack. He rubbed the back of his neck self-consciously. "Oh right. Well, okay. Jack, I would just like to let you know that I have a mutual sense of ... um ... like ... ness toward you."

Tabby clapped her hands together. "I now declare you friends. It's official."

Jason laughed, shaking his head. "There, it's official. You and I are now mutual friends, Jack."

Jack looked at Jason. "I have a feeling these two ladies won't have it any other way."

Nodding in agreement, Jason said, "I think you're right."

Ruby grabbed Tabby's hand and skated off with her, leaving Jason and Jack behind. Jason watched them glide away with amusement and relief. Turning to Jack, he said, "Looks like they ditched us. Probably a smart choice, honestly. No offense, but we're not the best conversationalists with each other."

Jack said, "Not true. We've had several riveting conversations."

"Riveting?" Jason scoffed, shaking his head. "If anything, we've had a couple of very awkward conversations involving a lot of grunting and uncomfortable silences."

"If I recall correctly, I gave you some very wise advice."

"You mean when you threatened to harm me if I ever hurt your sister?" Jason laughed. "Yes, I remember that vividly."

Jack shrugged. "If it makes you feel better, I never thought about killing you. We're talking temporary injury, at most."

Jason shook his head, still laughing. "You know just how to make me feel better. The guy whose sister I've been sleeping with only wants to temporarily hurt me if I mess things up with her—what more could I ask for?"

Jack turned serious. "We're friends now, right?"

Jason paused, sensing the genuine vulnerability in Jack's eyes. "Yeah, we're friends."

Jack placed a hand on Jason's shoulder, locking eyes with him. "You know the guy who raped my sister is in prison, right?"

Jason's heart sank, and his eyes widened. Suddenly, this conversation seemed incredibly important. "Yeah, I do know that."

"He got five years," Jack continued, his voice low and intense. "He'll be out soon. I'm going to kill him."

Without hesitation, Jason said, "Do you need help?"

Jack laughed, appreciation in his tone. "I *definitely* like you."

"Good. So, you won't object if I help you beat that guy to a pulp, then."

Jack gestured toward the girls, who were twirling on the ice. "They might not approve," he said.

"You're probably right. They would never approve of us resorting to violence."

Jack leaned in. "Which is why I don't plan on telling them."

"Yeah, we keep this between us." Jason nodded.

Jack clapped Jason on the shoulder, a satisfied look on his face. "Good talk," he said, then skated away to catch up with Ruby and Tabby.

As Jason watched Jack speed off, he muttered to no one in particular, "Huh, who knew I could get that guy's approval so easily?"

Moments later, Ruby skated back to him, her face bright with happiness. "It makes me so happy to see you getting along with Jack."

Jason grinned, pulling her close. "I've been attempting to not be a complete jackass to the guy. But yeah, your brother and I are cool."

Ruby beamed. "I told you he was a good guy."

Jason drew her even closer on the ice. "You've been saying that the whole time. I guess you were right."

Jack skated alongside Tabby, trying to maintain a casual demeanor despite his earlier conversation with Jason lingering in his mind. He cast a sideways glance at Tabby. "You're pretty good at skating. You must come here often."

"That's nice of you to say. I'm obviously struggling." Tabby glanced down at her skates with an air of self-deprecation. "And you're obviously an expert."

Jack was amused by her modesty. "I'm not an expert. I have a little experience, that's all. And you're doing fine. You just need to relax and trust yourself."

As they glided across the rink, Tabby turned the conversation back to Jason. "Did you manage to reassure Jason that you don't hate him?"

Jack nodded. "We talked. We're cool now. He knows I don't have anything against him," he said, carefully omitting the details of their conversation. He smiled, but a flicker of guilt twisted in his stomach. He wrapped an arm around Tabby as they skated, trying to keep his thoughts hidden.

"I was sure if you two spent some more time together you'd get along," Tabby said.

Jack nodded, forcing a smile that didn't quite reach his eyes. "You were right. We're getting along fine now."

"As wonderful as this has been, I'm exhausted and hungry. Let's go ask Ruby and Jason if they want to get some dinner."

He tried to sound casual. "Let's do that. I'm hungry too."

Tabby skated over to where Ruby and Jason stood, and Jack followed behind, his gaze flicking to Jason, watching for any signs of awkwardness. He hoped Jason could act normal, not give anything away.

"You guys want to go get something to eat?" Tabby asked, her voice bright.

"Sure, let's go," Ruby said with enthusiasm.

Jack nodded, trying to appear unfazed, though his heart raced. "Great. Anywhere in particular you guys want to eat?"

"There's a Chinese place across the street. How about there?" Tabby suggested.

"Chinese food sounds good to me. Let's go," Jack said, his stomach growling in agreement. Yet his anxiety continued to linger beneath the surface as the four of them made their way toward the exit.

Jason glanced down at the menu. "I'm getting the double order of crab rangoons. I hope you all like your tables greasy as hell," he declared, growing excited as the server approached to take their order. "Yup, a double order of crab rangoons, egg rolls and a pot of tea. Can't beat that. That's a goddamn perfect order," he added.

After they had all had a chance to dig into their meals, Tabby paused for a moment, setting down her chopsticks beside her half-eaten plate of sweet and sour chicken. She gave Jason a thoughtful glance. "You know, at first I didn't want to go ice skating. But it was a good idea."

Jason beamed at her. "You think so? I thought it couldn't hurt to try something a little different. But you and Ruby seemed to have a good time skating around the rink together while Jack and I awkwardly attempted to bond."

"Not awkward at all," Jack said. "I've decided I really like this guy."

Jason's heart swelled with humor and relief. "And there you have it. The official Jack seal of approval. I've finally won him over."

Tabby looked at them suspiciously. "What exactly did you two talk about?"

Jason tried to play it cool, taking a sip of his water. "Nothing specific, just man stuff. You know ... sports, cars, women. All the guy-friendly topics."

Jack nodded in agreement. "Yeah, man stuff."

Jason grinned at Ruby. "Yup, just man stuff. Very ... manly. There was probably a bit of grunting involved, too. A few fist bumps."

Ruby rolled her eyes. "You know what? You two are being uber suspicious, but I'm not going to question it. I'm just happy you're getting along."

Jason grabbed the teapot to refill his cup. "I can't deny that I might be a little curious about your brother's willingness to like me, but who am I to question progress when I see it? We're getting along really well tonight, and I count that as a major win."

Tabby eyed him incredulously. "Yeah, grunts and fist bumps. You and Jack. Sure. Something is going on. Spill, you two."

Jason held up his hands. "Nothing is going on. Really, we did not make some secret plan to do something fishy and nefarious behind your backs."

Jack said, "I thought you wanted me to like him."

Jason added, "See? We're just good bros now. I can't explain it, but we bonded tonight. No need for you two mistrustful ladies to question our genuine male friendship."

Tabby turned to Ruby, glancing at Jason with skepticism. "You're not buying this, are you?"

"No, I'm not buying it. But I'm not going to look a gift horse in the mouth," Ruby said, biting into an egg roll.

Jason sank back into his seat, rolling his eyes. "Really? I can't believe you two don't trust we're sincere. I can't believe how little faith you two have in our brotherly bond. You're unbelievable."

Jack said, "Wasn't it you two that officiated our friendship ceremony? You should be more supportive."

Jason huffed, shaking his head. "That's right. Show a little bit of respect and acceptance for the fact I've managed to win over your overprotective brother."

Tabby shook her head in exasperation, her eyes narrowing. She could see they were hiding something, but it was clear she wasn't going to pry it out of them tonight.

Jason shot Tabby a sly smile, fully aware that she was on to him and Jack. "Maybe you should just let the boys have their secrets. I can't blame you for being skeptical, but Jack and I do have a legitimate brotherhood bond forming here. It's a real thing."

Across the table, Jack turned to Ruby. "Yeah, I want to get to know your boyfriend better." He then turned to Jason. "Feel like joining me at the gun range tomorrow?"

Jason's eyes widened in surprise. He was starting to believe that Jack's approval of him was, in fact, genuine. "You want me to go to the gun range with you? Seriously?"

"Sure. Do you own a weapon?" Jack asked, his tone casual.

Leaning back in his chair, Jason felt excitement and apprehension. "Well, I've never owned one before, but I've played with the idea of getting a gun to keep in the house a couple of times. I've even done a bit of shooting in the past. It was a while ago, though."

"Great! You can just rent something at the range until you get your own," Jack said.

Jason grinned, though a hint of nervousness lingered. "Okay then, I mean, sure, I'm kind of intimidated to hang out with you and your weapons, but I'm always up for shooting a target."

Jack laughed. "I promise I'm not threatening you. Target shooting only."

Reassured, Jason said, "Nah, I know you're not threatening me. I'm just being honest about the fact that you have guns and I'm a little intimidated. But I'm down to shoot targets with you, no problem. Sounds like a good time."

Tabby and Ruby exchanged incredulous looks, and Jason laughed nervously when he noticed. "You ladies better stop being so suspicious. I can sense your disbelief."

"I feel like I'm in the Twilight Zone," Tabby said, shaking her head.

Jason reached for another egg roll, still grinning. "Why, because Jack and I are getting along so well? Come on, ladies, that's not so crazy. We're just bonding as friends."

Ruby turned to Jack. "Not that I don't trust you, big brother, but … pinky promise you'll bring my boyfriend back alive and well?" She held out her pinky.

Jason shook his head in affection and disbelief. "Jesus, she's treating me like some little kid that's about to go on his first school field trip."

Jack held out his pinky to Ruby. "Of course. Pinky promise. Jason and I are friends now. Nothing will happen to him."

Suddenly, the server arrived with the bill. Jack took it, handing over his credit card without hesitation.

Jason looked up in surprise. "Wait, I'm sorry—are you paying for everyone?"

"Yes, if that's okay. You can get the next one," Jack said casually.

"I'll get the next one for sure. I don't have any problem contributing to this bill, though. You don't need to pay for all of us."

Tabby said, "He's got a thing about paying. You'll get used to it now that you two are *bros*."

Jason watched Jack pay the bill. "Oh, he's got a gentleman thing about paying for food? I'm so jealous—he's making me look bad."

"Are you going to start grunting again?" Tabby teased.

Rolling his eyes, Jason grinned at her. "No, no more grunting. My manliness has reached acceptable levels for now."

"Let's go," Tabby said, leading the way as they all left the restaurant and headed toward Jack's car, parked near the rink.

Jason settled into the backseat, unexpectedly content. "Thanks for the ride, dude. I appreciate it," he said, glancing up at Jack.

"No problem."

Jason felt a warmth spread through him. "I have to admit, this evening went a lot better than I expected."

Ruby turned to him, curious. "How were you expecting it to go?"

He thought back to all his prior interactions with Jack. "I don't know, I guess it was just hard to picture this night ending without some sort of physical violence on Jack's part."

Jack scoffed. "I think you're exaggerating. I haven't killed anyone yet, after all."

Jason nodded his head. "You're right. You haven't harmed me yet. And now we're officially friends."

Jack dropped Jason off first, and Jason waved goodbye to Tabby and Ruby as all three drove away. "Goodnight, ladies. See you two again soon."

Jack arrived at Tabby's apartment after spending the day at the shooting range with Jason. The moment he crossed the threshold, he spotted Tabby pacing, her steps quick and restless. He was aware she had been uneasy about his sudden and inexplicable friendship with Jason.

"Oh, you're back," Tabby said, relief and concern in her voice.

Jack nodded, trying to sound casual, despite his worry. As he clicked the door shut behind him, he turned his attention back to Tabby, who wore a frown of concern.

"So, you had a good time?" she asked, her eyes narrowing.

Jack took a seat on the couch, adopting a nonchalant demeanor. "It was great. Jason's actually a cool guy. We really hit it off." He hoped his casual tone would put her at ease.

"I guess that's good," she said, though her voice didn't carry the enthusiasm he had hoped for.

"Why do you seem so worried? You look like you've seen a ghost," he asked.

"It's kind of weird. You barely tolerated Jason, and after a ten-minute conversation at the ice rink, you're suddenly best bros?" Her skepticism hung in the air between them.

Jack sighed. He needed to come up with a believable excuse. "It wasn't just a ten-minute conversation. We talked for a while. And we just realized we have a lot in common, that's all."

"Oh yeah? Like what?" Tabby crossed her arms.

"Sports, cars, beer, women ... that kind of thing." He tried to sound convincing, but he could feel the cracks forming in his facade.

"You don't even drink beer," she pointed out, her tone incredulous.

Caught in his own lie, Jack cringed. "I might have exaggerated a little. But we do have some things in common. We both like cars, for starters."

"Does Jason like cars? I've known him a lot longer than you, and I didn't know that," she challenged, her skepticism unmoved.

Jack frowned, feeling foolish. "Well, actually ... I might have exaggerated that a little too. But it doesn't matter, does it? The point is, we got along well. Why are you so suspicious anyway?"

"I just don't understand why you two are pretending to be such good friends all of a sudden," she said, her voice tinged with frustration.

"We're not pretending. We really did get along. Maybe we don't have a ton in common, but can't we be friends anyway?" Jack's voice rose slightly.

"Of course. I want you to be friends. It's ... I don't know—something's off," she said, her eyes searching his for reassurance.

Jack sighed, feeling trapped in his own web of half-truths. "You're being paranoid. Everything's fine. Can we drop it?" He hoped to change the subject, to ease the tension in the room.

"Alright, fine," Tabby said, though the worry still lingered in her expression.

He took her hands in his, looking intently into her eyes. "Look at me. I'm serious. Everything is fine. You don't need to worry about me."

Tabby pulled him into a warm embrace. "Are you staying over tonight?" she asked, her voice muffled against his shoulder.

"I'm staying. Is that okay?" he said, holding her tightly.

"Yeah, I want you to stay," she said, a hint of a smile breaking through her earlier worry.

Jack ran his fingers through a lock of her hair. "Good, because I want to be here with you tonight."

Later, as they settled into bed, they drifted off to sleep in each other's arms, a comforting calm settling over them.

# 17 Complications

As the weeks continued to clip by, Jack's anxiety grew. He wondered how long he could keep Tabby in the dark.

Jack had never anticipated that he and Jason would grow so close. Their shared plan had forged an unexpected bond, and they were spending more time together, strategizing in secret. He was haunted by a lingering sense of guilt that he couldn't shake.

One morning, as Jack entered the kitchen, he had spotted Tabby sipping orange juice, her demeanor tense. He walked over and kissed her gently on the head. "Hey darling, you're up early."

"Yeah," she said, biting her fingernail, a habit he recognized as a sign of her nerves.

In noticing her anxiety, he felt another twinge of guilt. "You seem a little tense."

"I expected to get my period by now. But I haven't gotten it yet," she admitted, her voice tinged with worry.

Jack froze for a moment. He tried to sound calm and reassuring. "Could it just be late? It happens sometimes, right?"

"Yeah, that totally happens," she said, though the uncertainty lingered in her tone.

He placed a hand on her shoulder, trying to offer comfort. "So, don't worry. It's probably just late. Nothing to freak out over, right?"

"I'll probably get a test today, just to see how it comes out. But false negatives can happen this early, so I'm not sure how reassuring that will be."

Jack nodded, a knot of anxiety tightening in his stomach. He knew he should come clean about Jason, but the words wouldn't come. "A test is a good idea. But, like you said, it might not be accurate right now anyway. So don't freak out."

"Okay. I'm going to get dressed," she said, her voice steadier.

As she got dressed and prepared to head to the drugstore, Jack paced the apartment, his mind racing with worry and guilt. He was torn between his feelings for Tabby and the secret he was keeping from her. The minutes seemed like hours until she finally returned, a small bag clutched in her hand.

"Got it. I'll go take it right now," she said, heading straight to the bathroom.

Jack's heart raced as he waited, pacing the living room, anxiety gnawing at him. He could only imagine what the test result might mean for their future.

After what felt like an eternity, Tabby emerged from the bathroom, the test in her hand. "We have to wait two minutes," she said, her eyes darting to the clock rather than the test.

Jack stopped pacing and stood beside her, his heart pounding in his chest. He didn't want to look directly at the test either, but he couldn't help himself. He squinted at it, dread pooling in his stomach. "Hmm ... there's two lines."

"Two?" Tabby turned to him, her expression shifting from anxious to shocked as she grabbed the test.

"Two. What does that mean?" Jack asked.

She looked up at him, her eyes wide. "I'm pregnant."

Conflicting emotions crashed over him. Shock, joy and guilt twisted inside him, rendering him momentarily speechless. "You ... you're sure?" he stammered, eventually.

She nodded, and in that moment, Jack's heart swelled with happiness, even as guilt clawed at him for the secret he was still hiding. He embraced Tabby, holding her tightly as she clung to him.

In that embrace, he felt a bittersweet mixture of emotions—joy at the thought of a child and guilt at his deception. He kissed the top of her head gently, cherishing the moment while grappling with the uncertainty of what lay ahead. Tabby held him just as tightly, and for a moment, everything else faded away.

"I'm so happy. I'm so happy for us. For our baby," he said.

Her eyes widened in surprise. "You are?"

He pulled her even closer, overwhelmed by a surge of love and tenderness. "Of course, I am. I'm terrified, but yes—I'm happy. This will change everything, but it will be good."

Tabby let out a deep sigh. "Well, at least the uncertainty is over now."

Jack nodded, both relieved and anxious. He pulled back slightly to look at her face, noticing the worry lingering in her eyes. "Are you ... are *you* happy about it?"

She nodded, as tears began streaming down her cheeks. "I am. I don't know why I'm crying. I'm really happy."

Gently, he wiped away her tears, his heart swelling with tenderness. "It's okay. These are happy tears, aren't they?"

She smiled through her tears and nodded. Jack smiled back, as his heart swelled with love.

"I'm so happy," he said. "I can't believe we're going to have a baby. We'll be a family—you, me and our kid."

"Yeah. I love you," she said, her voice thick with emotion.

He hugged her tightly, feeling an overwhelming rush of love for her. "I love you too, darling. So much."

"What do we do now?" she asked.

Jack pulled back, his mind racing with possibilities. "Well, for now, we need to focus on you and the baby. We have to take care of you, make sure you're feeling well and eating right. I'll take care of you." He looked at her, concern etched in his features. "Is there anything you need right now? Water, tea, something to eat? I can get you anything you want."

She said, "No, but I need to sit down."

"Okay, let's go sit down." He took her hand and led her to the couch, where they settled in, Jack wrapping his arm around her and pulling her close.

Tabby's phone chimed, breaking the moment. She reached for it, glancing at the screen. "It's a text from Ruby."

He gently squeezed her shoulder, striving to keep his voice calm. "Are you going to tell her the test is positive?"

"Yeah, I mean—unless you want to tell her."

He shook his head. "No, you can tell her. I'm sure she'll be excited for us."

Tabby rose and walked to the bedroom to make the call.

Jack sat on the couch, his heart racing as he waited for her to return. He was nervous about what Ruby was going to think, but right now he was just glad he got to avoid her gut reaction. After a while, Tabby stepped back out of the bedroom. "Ruby says congratulations. Oh, and she hopes she can be there when you tell your parents."

Jack nodded, relief flooding through him at Ruby's genuine happiness for them. Typical Ruby, he thought. Always ready for a dramatic moment. "I'm guessing they won't be expecting this sort of thing from you," Tabby said, worry creeping into her voice.

"You could say that. They'll be shocked, no doubt. I mean, I'm their baby boy, and here I am, knocking up my girlfriend. They're going to lose their minds."

Tabby sighed, her expression turning pensive. "I suppose that's the downside of being perfect. Disappointing people when it turns out you're not *actually* perfect."

Jack felt a twinge of guilt at her words. He knew he hadn't been perfect lately—far from it. He squeezed her hand gently, trying to reassure her. "I've messed up plenty of times before, and I'll probably mess up plenty of times in the future too."

"Well I think you're perfect," she said with sincerity.

Warmth spread through him at her words. "Thanks, but I'm definitely not. I have my flaws, like everyone else." He looked at her intently. "But you—*you* are pretty damn perfect."

She laughed, and the sound filled the room with lightness. "I'm glad you think so. Does that mean I get to look forward to disappointing you in the future?"

Jack smiled. "I'm sure you'll find a way to disappoint me eventually. But it won't matter, because I'll still love you anyway."

With that, she leaned in and kissed him. He kissed her back, feeling a rush of love and tenderness as he pulled her closer, wrapping his arms tightly around her.

"Are you going to the shooting range with Jason today?" she asked, breaking the moment.

Jack nodded, the guilt creeping back in as he remembered their plans. "Yes, I have plans to meet him there."

"Are you going to tell him?" she asked, her voice laced with concern.

He looked at Tabby, conflicted. "I should probably tell him ... right?"

"If we don't tell him, Ruby definitely will. Maybe she already has," Tabby pointed out.

Jack nodded, realizing she was probably right. "You're right. I'll tell him. I'll text him right now." Jack pulled out his phone, tapping Jason's contact.

"Hey, Jay. I need to talk to you about something. I'm OMW to the range now," Jack typed, pocketing his phone as he turned back to Tabby.

"I'm going to head over there now. I'll talk to him and tell him about the baby," he said.

"That's better. He won't lecture *you*," she said, gratitude in her voice.

He nodded and stood up from the couch. "No problem. I'll be back soon." With that, he stepped out, ready to face whatever awaited him at the shooting range.

Jack stepped into the gun range, the sharp echo of gunfire filling the air. His heart raced as he scanned the room, searching for Jason. He spotted him at a shooting station, focusing on the target. Jack approached, a burden heavy on his chest.

He patted Jason on the arm to get his attention.

Jason turned, his gaze shifting from the target to Jack. He removed his hearing protection and placed his weapon down. "Hey. What's going on?"

Jack braced himself for the conversation. "I've got something important I need to talk to you about. It's ... about Tabby."

"What about Tabby? Is everything okay?"

Jack nodded, forcing himself to remain composed. "We found out that she's pregnant."

Surprise flared in Jason's eyes, and a small smile broke through his initial concern. "Pregnant? That's great news. Congratulations! I'm happy for you both."

"Thanks," Jack said. "But it's making me have second thoughts about Brad."

The smile faded from Jason's face as realization dawned. "Brad? The guy who ... ?"

"Yeah. You didn't know his name?" Jack asked, a sense of disbelief in his voice.

"I didn't. But now I do ... and I understand your second thoughts, given that you're about to become a father. It's a big responsibility, and it brings new perspectives, especially when it comes to ... something like that."

Jack rubbed his forehead in frustration. "I don't know if I can deal with that bastard walking around free. But now ... I don't know."

"I get it. It's a tough situation. But you have to think about your child now. And about what kind of legacy you want to leave behind for them."

"I should have done it before he went in," Jack said, bitterness lacing his words. "But he turned himself in. So, I never got the chance. He lives in the neighborhood, you know. Well, he used to. So I assume he'll be coming back here."

Jason's eyes widened at the revelation. "He lives in the neighborhood? That's ... concerning." He paused, collecting his thoughts before continuing. "Have you talked to Ruby about this?"

"Ruby pretty much wants to forget it ever happened," Jack said, frustration in his voice. "Hard to do with him living down the street."

Jason sighed. "It's tough. I get it. But do you really think your original plan is the right solution? Think about what it would do to you, your child and the future you're building with Tabby. It's a path that's difficult to come back from."

"That's the problem," Jack said, his voice heavy with uncertainty. "It's not only me anymore."

"Exactly," Jason said. "It's not just about you or Tabby, or even Ruby, anymore. It's about your child as well. And they deserve a future that's free from violence. Are you willing to risk that future for momentary satisfaction?"

"It's not about satisfaction," Jack insisted, frustration boiling over. "It's about Ruby feeling safe. Afterwards, she was terrified of being alone. And that was when he was locked up. How's she going to feel when she has to deal with him just walking down the street?"

Jason crossed his arms, considering Jack's words carefully. "I understand your concern for Ruby, and it's completely valid. Her safety and well-being matter, especially given her past trauma. But there have to be better ways to ensure her safety than resorting to violence. Have you considered talking to her about it?"

"I thought you were on board with this?" Jack shot back, frustration evident in his tone.

Jason sighed. "I was, to an extent. But that was before you told me about Tabby and the baby. My priorities have shifted a bit. If your child ever found out what you did ... think about the psychological damage that could cause."

Jack fell silent, Jason's words settling over him. He was torn between his protective instincts and the reality of the life he was about to create.

"I've been thinking about that," Jack said. "This morning, Tabby told me I was perfect. I wonder if she would still think that if I went ahead with my plans for Brad."

"And that's something you need to really think about. Because once it's done, there's no going back. You won't be just a husband or a father-to-be," he said, then, in a whisper, "You'll be a killer." He stared hard at Jack. "And that changes you. Fundamentally. Maybe irrevocably. You don't want your child to grow up wondering if they can trust you to make the right decisions, do you?"

Jack let out a laugh. "You should meet the guy. Maybe he'd be someone you'd like to kill."

"I'll pass on that, thanks. But, hey, I get it. This guy is a scumbag, and he deserves to pay for what he did to Ruby. But the question is, are you willing to sacrifice your own future and that of your child? I mean, what kind of life would your child have if"—Jason lowered his voice again—"you spent the next three decades in prison?"

"Two tops. I can afford a good lawyer," Jack said, attempting to brush off the gravity of the situation.

"I'm serious. This isn't a joke. Two decades behind bars, without seeing your child grow up. That's a lifetime worth of memories and moments that you'd miss out on. Plus, even if you go free, are you ready to explain it all to your kid? How would that conversation go, exactly?"

Jack shrugged, shaking his head. "I don't know."

Frustration and concern flickered across Jason's face as he looked at Jack. "I'm not trying to lecture you. I'm just trying to make you think about all the implications. This isn't some action movie where the hero kills the villain and rides off into the sunset with the girl. Real life has consequences, and not just for the bad guy, but for you too. For everyone involved. Are you sure you're ready to deal with those consequences?"

"I'll think about it," Jack said. Eager to shift the conversation away from the heavy topic, he turned his attention to Jason's target. "How's your aim coming along?"

"My aim's coming along just fine, thanks for asking. But you know what I really need to work on? My patience. Especially with friends who are contemplating murder."

"What good is a friend who won't help you hide a body, right?" Jack asked with a shrug.

"Oh, now you're just testing me. I'm not saying I don't get where you're coming from. I do. If I were in your shoes, I might be thinking the same thing. But remember: you're not just thinking about yourself anymore. You've got Tabby and the baby to think about too. They're counting on you now. So, take some time to think about what they need, too, alright?"

"Yeah, man. Take care," Jack said.

Jason nodded, giving Jack a reassuring pat on the shoulder. "You too. And congratulations again about Tabby. I mean that. Just think about what we talked about."

As Jack walked away, the echoes of gunfire faded into the background, but the gravity of their discussion remained, swirling in his mind like the smoke from a freshly fired shot. He knew he had a decision to make, and it wouldn't be easy.

Jason stepped into his apartment, the door clicking shut behind him as he sank onto the couch. He sat there, motionless, his earlier conversation with Jack still on his mind. With a sigh, he closed his eyes and pinched the bridge of his nose, trying to stave off the headache that was already beginning to throb at his temples.

As he gathered his thoughts, his phone rang, breaking the silence. It was Tabby calling. "What's up?"

"Hey, you," she said, her voice brightening the otherwise somber atmosphere. "I haven't seen you in a while. I think my boyfriend stole my best friend."

"Oh jeez, don't tell me you're feeling neglected."

"I'm used to having you guys around. Now you're off doing secret stuff together," she said, playful accusation in her voice.

He sighed, knowing she had a point but reluctant to admit it. "We're not doing anything secret. We're just doing guy stuff. Don't worry. I thought you girls were happy we were getting along."

"We are," she said, her voice softening. "But I miss our talks."

He had been so wrapped up in his own life that he hadn't even considered how Tabby might feel about his growing bond with Jack. "I miss our talks, too. I'm definitely not replacing you, I swear."

"Can I come over? Or are you too tired from hanging out at the gun range?" she asked.

Jason rose from the couch. "No, you can come over, of course. I'd love to hang out with you."

"Alright, see you soon," she said.

A short while later, a knock echoed through the apartment. Jason opened the door, his mood lifting as he took in Tabby's familiar features. "Hey, princess. I'm glad you're here."

"Thanks," she said, stepping inside and settling at the kitchen table. "Jack said he was going to tell you the news. So, did he tell you?"

Jason nodded, resting his chin on his hand. "Yeah, he told me. Congrats!"

"Thanks. You're not even going to tease me about being irresponsible? Man, you've changed. What has my boyfriend done to you?" she said, feigning shock.

He smiled, the tension in his chest easing. "Believe me, there is a sarcastic comment on the tip of my tongue about you being irresponsible and all that. But I'm going to play the mature card for once and refrain from saying anything. You and Jack are clearly happy and excited, so I'm happy for you."

"Thanks. I *am* happy. And I'm impressed. Maturity, huh? Are we becoming real adults, finally?"

Jason grinned and shook his head. "Don't get used to it. I haven't completely dropped my sarcastic tendencies. I'm just attempting to be more mature on this one occasion."

"So, I've barely seen you the past few of weeks. How have you been?" she asked.

Jason momentarily looked away as fatigue settled over him. "I've had a lot on my mind lately. There's been nothing major going on. Just a lot of thinking about stuff ... I'm fine, though. Don't worry about me."

"What's on your mind?" she asked. "You used to unload on me all the time."

Jason looked into Tabby's eyes, trying to convey a sense of reassurance. "Oh, don't worry about it. Like I said, it's nothing major. I'm just trying to sort out the facts of my life."

Tabby's voice was laced with frustration. "I'm not going to lie. I'm kinda feeling shut out. By you, and by Jack too. Something's on his mind, but he won't talk about it."

Concern flickered across Jason's face. "Seriously? Has he been secretive about something? He's actually been open about some stuff with me lately."

"Like what? What has he been open about with you?" she asked, her curiosity evident.

Jason hesitated, knowing he couldn't divulge the private conversations he'd had with Jack. "Just guy stuff. Jack shared some concerns we both have, so we've been getting along."

"I've noticed," Tabby said. "I'm starting to regret my wish that you two would get along."

Jason said, "Oh, come on. You and Ruby were totally on my case about Jack and I becoming friends. Now that you're getting what you wanted, you're saying you regret it? You can't even make up your mind."

"Ruby says the same thing. Still, I can't seem to let go of the feeling that you guys are hiding something," she insisted.

He grinned. "What, you think Jack and I are having a secret affair or something?"

Tabby laughed. "No, that didn't cross my mind, but thanks for that image."

"You're ridiculous. There's nothing going on—it's just two men bonding as friends."

"Sure—it's not suspicious at all that two guys who were practically enemies became instant best friends and hang out constantly talking about 'man stuff,'" she said.

He rested his elbows on the table. "It's not that crazy, I swear. Jack and I have things on our minds that are specific to the male experience. That's why we're talking. Like we've been saying: It's guy stuff. You wouldn't understand."

"So, you're giving me the brush-off, again?" she asked, disappointment in her voice.

Jason studied her for a moment, then sighed, relenting. "Fine. You want the truth?"

"Yes," she said, leaning in, eager for more information.

He glanced down at the table, lowering his voice. "We've been talking about one specific issue that has been ... bothering both of us. But it's not my secret to tell you. You're going to have to talk to him about it. All I can say is that Jack is going through an important time in his life right now, and he's ... well, he's got a hard decision to make."

Tabby frowned, instantly deep in thought. "It was pretty obvious something's been bothering him, but he refuses to talk about it. It can't be about the baby, because we just found out, and he's been acting strange for weeks. Besides, he told me he was happy about the baby."

Jason sighed, wishing he could share more, but his promise to Jack lingered in his mind. "Yeah, he's happy about the baby, but he's struggling with ... other stuff. I can't give you any details. I really want to, but I promised him I'd keep his secret. But I can at least say that he's definitely got a lot on his mind."

"Alright, thanks for being honest with me. I'll have to talk to Jack," she said.

He nodded, warmth in his gaze. "Anytime, princess. Just ... try to be gentle with Jack right now. He's got a lot going through his mind. Don't push him too hard to talk."

"So, Jack is going through something difficult, and *you're* his confidant? Not very reassuring."

Jason looked at her, confusion clouding his features. "What do you mean? Why is that not reassuring?"

"Because you're reckless," she answered.

"Excuse me? What do you mean, 'I'm reckless'? I'm a very responsible guy!"

"Ha!" Tabby said, clearly amused.

Jason grinned, leaning back in his chair and crossing his arms. "Don't get a smug attitude with me. I'm offended. Go ahead, tell me how I'm reckless. Give me examples."

"Miami?"

"Are we ever going to let that go? It was a one-time mistake!"

Tabby's expression softened somewhat, but she continued. "Not so long ago, you asked me to convince Jack to cut you some slack. And I did. Can you return the favor and convince him to be honest with me?"

Jason looked down at the table, mulling it over. After a moment, he sighed. "Yeah, I'll try my best, Tabby. I can't make any promises, but I'll talk to him again. Maybe I can get him to open up to you."

"Thank you," she said with relief. "Alright, I'm going to head home. You should go to bed—you look exhausted."

He yawned, nodding his head in agreement. "Yeah, I'm tired after our time at the gun range today. Jack's been focused on being physical lately—he's been doing all this running and bodybuilding stuff. It's been tough to keep up with him."

"You don't have to keep up with him," Tabby pointed out.

"Yeah, but I kind of want to. I'd like to be able to kick the ass of anyone who tries to hurt someone I care about. Especially you."

"Don't worry. I don't need your ass-kicking services. So, get some rest."

Jason stood up from the table, still grinning. "Okay, okay. I'll get some sleep. You make sure you rest up too, since you've got a baby in there."

Tabby waved goodbye as she headed out the door, her figure disappearing into the evening light. Jason waved back, then yawned again, suddenly fatigued. "I really am tired ..." he said to himself. "That does it for my social life. Time to turn into a hermit all week."

# 18 Guilt

Jack walked into the apartment, his heart sinking slightly as he spotted Tabby sitting on the couch, her expression thoughtful and distant. He could sense something heavy on her mind. The guilt of his secret was becoming increasingly burdensome with each passing day.

"Hey darling. You okay?" he asked, trying to sound lighthearted.

"Yeah, great. You?" she responded, but the way her smile faltered told him everything he needed to know.

He nodded, relieved that she seemed fine on the surface, but the guilt gnawed at him. "I'm good. Just got back from the gym." He sat down next to her, the tension in the air thick.

"Ah, the gym. Was Jason there?" she asked, her curiosity evident.

"Yeah, he was. We got a good workout in," he said, forcing a smile.

"Hmm ... He used to follow me around like a puppy. Now he seems to be your puppy."

Jack laughed, but her words struck a nerve. He felt another surge of guilt. How could he respond without giving anything away? "Yes, he's my gym buddy now. Guess he's taken a liking to me."

She studied him for a moment. "You told me you're happy about the baby. But is there anything else that's been bothering you?"

He hesitated, torn between the urge to confess everything and the instinct to protect his secret. "No ... no, everything's fine. Why do you ask?"

"I'm getting a worried vibe from you," she said.

Jack forced a smile, trying to maintain the facade. "Nah, I'm fine. I have a lot on my mind, that's all. The gym kind of helps clear my mind."

"What's on your mind? Maybe I can help," she offered, reaching out for his hand.

He searched for a diversion, his heart weighed down by the truth. "It's nothing. Work stuff. The usual."

Tabby nodded, but he could see the frustration brewing beneath her calm exterior.

"What's wrong? You seem annoyed or something," he said.

"If you're going through something, I want to be there for you. You can be honest with me," she pressed, her eyes searching his.

Jack's heart sank further. She deserved the truth, but he wasn't ready to confess yet. "I'm fine. I would tell you if something was wrong. You're my girlfriend—I trust you."

"It's not about work. Am I right?" she challenged, her intuition sharp.

He hesitated, wrestling with his thoughts. He didn't want to lie to her, but the secret loomed large. "I ... I've been thinking a lot, that's all. About the future."

Tabby squeezed his hand, her touch grounding him. "You're worried about your future?"

He nodded. "A little. In the past, my thoughts about the future seemed distant and hypothetical. But now that I have you, I want to make sure I'm being responsible and making the right decisions."

"You're very responsible. I'm sure you'll make the right decisions," she reassured him, and he felt a flicker of relief.

"Thanks, I appreciate that. I want to make sure I'm doing everything right for you, for us and now for the baby too."

"I'm a little worried that Jason is your sounding board for your worries about the future. You know how shortsighted he can be," she said.

"He can be a bit of an idiot sometimes. But he's a good friend. I know not to take his advice too seriously," Jack said.

"Good, because I trust your judgment."

He nodded, appreciating her unwavering trust. "Thanks, that means a lot to me. I'll always do what's best for us."

Her voice broke the silence, laced with concern. "So, you're worried about making the right decisions for your future. Is there any particular decision that's especially weighing on you?"

He nodded. This was a delicate dance, and he was unsure how to navigate it. "There is something I've been considering ... but I'm not sure if I'm ready to make a decision about it yet."

"Maybe we could talk about it," she offered, her tone encouraging.

Jack hesitated, torn between the urge to confess and the instinct to protect her from his turmoil. "Maybe ... It's kind of a big decision, and I don't want to worry you or anything."

"I know you want to protect me, but you don't have to," Tabby said, her sincerity cutting through his defenses.

He looked at her. "I know. But it's ... complicated. I don't want to burden you with my worries."

"Of course you don't. You're incredibly stubborn. But not telling me won't keep me from worrying," she said, frustration creeping into her voice.

Jack sighed, realizing she had a point. "I get it. But promise me you won't freak out when I tell you what it is?"

"I promise," she said, her eyes steady and unwavering.

"Well ... the thing is, I've been thinking about something pretty ... extreme. And I'm not sure if I should do it or not."

"Okay," she said, a look of concentration on her face.

Jack struggled to find the right words. "It's something ... violent. And I'm not sure if it's the right thing to do, but I can't stop thinking about it."

Tabby's eyes widened, and he could see the wheels turning in her mind, but she remained silent, allowing him to continue.

Jack could feel uncertainty as he gathered his thoughts. He sensed Tabby's curiosity, her eyes searching his face for answers. He plunged into the depths of his worries. "I've been thinking about ... what if I took matters into my own hands to make sure everyone we care about is safe? Specifically, what if I did something to ensure that the man who hurt Ruby never comes near her or anyone we care about ever again?"

Tabby absorbed the gravity of his words. She nodded, understanding and compassion in her eyes.

Jack's anxiety spiked as he registered the realization dawning on her. "It does sound extreme, and maybe even crazy. But I've been thinking about it nonstop for days now. I can't shake the idea from my mind."

"Just so we're clear," Tabby said carefully, "we're talking about a permanent solution here. Am I understanding it correctly?"

He nodded. "That's what I'm talking about."

"Okay." Tabby's voice was steady, but Jack could sense the turmoil beneath her calm exterior.

He tried to convey the urgency of his thoughts. "I can't stop thinking about it. I can't sleep, I can't eat. I'm constantly on edge, wondering if that guy will come back and hurt you or Ruby or ... our baby."

"I get that," she said. "And this is what you and Jason have been bonding over?"

"Yes. Jason's been helping me work through the details. He's on board with the idea, and he's willing to help me make it happen."

"This is a lot," Tabby said, looking a bit overwhelmed.

"I know, and I'm sorry I've been keeping it from you," Jack said, his heart heavy. "You have enough to be concerned about already, with the baby and everything else."

"Yeah, I get it now." She exhaled, disbelief creeping into her tone. "Plotting a murder is not exactly casual conversation."

Jack nodded. "It's not exactly watercooler material. But the more I think about it, the more I feel like it's something I need to do. For everyone's safety."

She took both of his hands in hers, grounding them in the moment. "I'm not really sure how to react to this."

"It's fine," he said. "It's a lot to process, and I don't expect you to feel a certain way. I only needed to tell you what I've been thinking about."

"Right. I'm having trouble wrapping my head around this." She stood up suddenly. "So, you just asked Jason if he wanted to help you murder someone, and he was like 'sure'?"

Jack nodded. "Pretty much. I was kind of surprised he was so on board with it, but he was unusually supportive."

Tabby started biting her fingernail, clearly extremely agitated. "How do I talk you both out of this?"

Jack's voice was low and earnest. "Listen to me. I need you to trust me. I've thought this through a million times, and I believe it's the best thing to do."

"Are you listening to yourself right now?" Tabby's voice trembled with disbelief. "Murdering someone? The best thing to do?"

Jack was frustrated as he watched Tabby struggle to understand his perspective. "Trust me, I don't want to hurt anyone. But I can't shake the feeling that this is the only way to keep you and the baby safe."

Tabby's voice was sharp as she said, "And what about you? Who's going to protect us when you're in prison for murder?"

Her question hung heavy in the air. "I have it all planned out. Nobody will find out. I'm not going to get caught."

"Well, at least you've thought things through, and you've got a solid plan," she said, her sarcasm obvious. "Have you completely lost it? You can't just commit murder like you're going out for ice cream. This is batshit crazy, and I can't believe Jason is encouraging this! What the hell is he thinking?"

Jack said, "This is about safety, about protecting us. I've put a lot of thought into it. I'm not some psycho who's out for blood."

"Jack," she said, her voice softer now, almost pleading. "You said you haven't made a decision yet, right? That you're not sure if it's the right thing or not?"

He nodded, his words hesitant. "That's right. I mean, it's a huge decision. And I'm not sure if I'm even capable of doing what needs to be done. But the idea of potentially losing you is unbearable, and I can't shake it off."

"Jack, promise me you won't make a decision yet. I'll figure something out."

He hesitated a few moments, then finally nodded.

Tabby moved closer and wrapped her arms around him in a reassuring embrace. Jack hugged her back, comforted by her touch, even as the tension lingered.

"I'm sorry for putting you through this."

"I'm glad you told me," she said. "We'll figure something out. I promise."

Jason arrived at the library to see Tabby that Thursday evening.

"Hey, princess," Jason said as he approached Tabby, who sat behind the circulation desk.

Tabby glanced at her phone and saw that it was lunchtime. She turned to her co-worker and announced she was stepping out for a break. Grabbing Jason by the arm, she practically pulled him out of the library.

"Whoa, are we in a hurry or something?" Jason laughed, surprised by her intensity.

"We need to talk," she said, her voice low but insistent. "Jack told me what you two have been bonding over. Have you lost your fucking mind?"

Jason stopped in his tracks, confusion flickering across his face. "No, I haven't lost my mind. Why are you asking?"

"Oh, I don't know," she snapped. "Maybe because my boyfriend and my best friend are planning a fucking murder together! Has that slipped your mind?"

He fought to maintain his composure. "Relax. I promised him I wouldn't tell you this, but Jack and I have talked about it extensively. We're not planning a murder together ... we're just discussing options."

"Discussing options? Options like murder?" Tabby asked, her voice full of incredulity.

Jason glanced around, suddenly aware of the people milling about them. He lowered his voice, trying to keep the conversation private. "We've discussed that as a possibility, yes. But like I told you, we're just talking. We haven't done anything."

"Thank god!" she exclaimed. "What the fuck, Jason? I had to pretend to be okay with this. The more upset I got, the more defensive he became. I had to act cool about it, so he'd agree not to do anything rash. But I am very not cool with this. I'm pregnant, and the baby's father is pretty sure he wants to kill someone. And I can't seem to convince him that it's not a good idea."

Jason sighed, running a hand through his hair. "I get it, alright? You're upset, I understand. This isn't ideal, believe me ... but you have to understand where Jack is coming from. He's got a right to kill Brad."

"No, Jason. Actually, he doesn't. You think the cops are gonna be like, 'Dude, we totally get it. No worries'?" Tabby shot back, her voice rising again.

He ran a hand over his face, a headache developing. "You think Jack and I haven't already talked about the possible consequences? We've spent hours discussing every possibility. Yeah, it's risky. We both know it's dangerous. I'm not even saying it's the right thing to do; we recognize the downsides. We're not ignorant to them."

"Downsides? *Downsides*? I can't believe my fucking ears right now," she snapped.

Frustrated, he grabbed her shoulders, his grip firm but not aggressive. "What do you want me to say? That I don't want Jack to kill Brad? That I don't think it's the right choice? Well guess what: of course I don't want Jack to do this! I don't think it's right! But I also understand where he's coming from. So, I'm going to support him, no matter what."

"Support him? Jason, he is serious about killing Brad. If we don't stop him, this is going to happen," Tabby insisted, her eyes wide with fear.

Jason met her gaze, suddenly exhausted and frustrated. "I know he's serious. I've seen how determined he is. I know how far he's willing to go. Do you think I haven't tried to dissuade him from this? Don't you think I've said the same thing you're saying now? But Jack is hellbent on doing this. It's going to happen one way or another."

"Jack says you're totally on board. According to him, he invited you to help him kill someone, and you were like, 'Yeah sure. Sounds like fun,'" she accused, her voice trembling with anger and desperation.

Annoyed by her accusations, Jason said, "Oh, I get it. Jack told you I was on board with this. So now you're angry with me, thinking I'd just carelessly agree to help kill someone. Is that it?"

"Well, did you?" she asked, her eyes searching his for the truth.

"No, of course not!" he said, sighing. "Jesus, what do you take me for? I'm not a goddamn criminal. I was against it at first. I told Jack he was crazy for wanting to do this. I was just as appalled by the whole situation as you are."

"Really? Tell me honestly—what did you two say to each other at the skating rink?" Tabby demanded, her voice firm.

He hesitated, weighing whether to reveal the truth. "Alright, I'll tell you the truth. But you have to promise me that you'll remain calm and open-minded. Can you do that for me, please?"

Tabby nodded and Jason continued. "Okay, here it is. Jack asked me if I wanted to help him kill Brad. I was surprised, of course. I didn't know what to think. So, I did what any good friend would do. I made sure he was completely serious about it and told him I'd support him no matter what his final decision was. I was still against the killing, but ultimately he's a grown man, and I trust his judgment. So, I told him I'd watch out for him. Does that answer your question? Now you know exactly what happened at the skating rink," he said, his voice steady despite the tension.

"Oh, my god." Tabby shook her head in disbelief, the shock clear on her face.

A tightness formed in Jason's chest as he watched her reaction. "What was I supposed to say? Jack has made up his mind about killing Brad, and nothing can change it. I really don't like it. I wish Jack wouldn't do this, but I feel like I have to be there for him. I'm his friend. Friends help friends when they're at their lowest points."

"You didn't even like him a month ago! Now you're besties because he invited you to a murder?" Tabby's voice was sharp, her frustration evident.

"Listen, don't just assume we became friends overnight. It was a slow process, alright? We started talking more, opening up to each other. We found out we actually have a lot in common. Our situation is odd, but the bond Jack and I developed is real. We really are friends now."

"Fine! Then as his friend and as my friend, you need to help me talk him out of this," Tabby insisted, her determination unwavering.

He sighed, running a hand over his face in frustration. "You think I haven't been trying that? I've already told you—I've tried so goddamn hard to convince him to drop it, and I've failed. Jack isn't some stubborn kid who's easily discouraged. You can't just talk him into changing his mind."

"He hasn't made up his mind. He just wants to protect everyone. If we can figure out a way to make sure everyone is safe, we can talk him out of it. He doesn't want to hurt anyone. I'm sure of it," she countered, her eyes shining with sincere hope.

Jason met her gaze, the determination radiating from her softening his frustration. "You seriously think we can talk him out of this, don't you?"

"We have to. We can't let him do this. It'll ruin his life," she said, her voice resolute.

He nodded, the truth of her words settling in. Deep down, he agreed. He didn't want Jack to be burdened with this decision either. "Alright, I'm with you. I want to convince Jack out of this just as much as you do. What do you suggest we do?"

Tabby paused. "I don't know. I'm a librarian—I'm not exactly skilled at neutralizing threats of violence."

They stood in silence for a moment, both grappling with the situation. But despite the uncertainty, Jason felt a flicker of determination.

# 19 Trust

The next evening, Jason was waiting outside Jack's apartment building when Jack pulled into the driveway. He felt the burden of his promise to Tabby compelling him to confront Jack about his dangerous plan, and to talk him out of it, if he could.

"Hey, Jason. Visiting Ruby?" Jack called out casually as he stepped out of the car.

Jason shook his head, the gravity of his mission settling in. "Not exactly. I actually came here to see you. There's something important we need to talk about."

"Okay." Jack nodded, leading the way to his apartment. He unlocked the door and stepped inside, gesturing for Jason to follow.

Once inside, Jason closed the door behind him and took a deep breath. "Listen, we need to talk about this plan to kill Brad ... You can't go through with it."

Jack moved to the fridge, retrieving a couple of cans of soda. He tossed one to Jason, who caught it and cracked it open, leaning back against the kitchen counter.

"That guy's a real scumbag for what he did to Ruby," said Jason. "But you've got too much at stake now."

Listening, Jack opened his soda and took a sip. Finally, he spoke. "Did Tabby tell you to tell me that?"

Jason nodded. "She's worried about you. We both are. I get it—you want to protect Ruby, and you want her safe. But there's got to be a better way than, you know, murder. You've got a kid on the way. A kid who's going to turn to you for guidance and love. You want them to grow up knowing their dad's a killer?"

"Things are pretty complicated now," Jack admitted, his voice laced with uncertainty.

Jason nodded, empathetic. "Yeah, they are. But that's life. It throws curveballs at us when we least expect them. The question is: How do you deal with them? You can either let yourself be consumed by anger, or you can focus on the good in your life. Like Tabby and the baby. Doesn't that mean anything to you?"

"Of course. They mean everything to me. And it's not about anger. It's about eliminating a threat. As far as the law is concerned, he's done his time. He's no threat anymore. But you and I know that's bullshit," Jack said, his voice rising with frustration.

Jason sighed, knowing Jack had a point. "I get it. I do. But you can't just take the law into your own hands. This ain't the Wild West. Besides, have you thought about what it would do to Ruby? Or your kid? Can you tell me you want your child's first memories to be about violence and murder?"

Jack smiled wryly, shaking his head. "I don't know, man. Like I said, I'm having doubts. This whole fatherhood thing has got me wanting to do the right thing, but at the same time, more protective than ever."

Jason felt a flicker of hope at Jack's admission. "That's good. It means you're thinking about this from all angles. And yeah, I get what you mean. I can only imagine how much more protective I'll be when I have kids. But being protective doesn't have to mean being violent. There are other ways to protect the people you love. Ways that don't involve taking a life."

Jack looked doubtful. "What did you have in mind? Ask him politely to stop raping people?"

Jason was aware how absurd that sounded. "I'm not saying you need to be nice to the guy. I'm just saying that there's got to be a way to ensure

Ruby's safety without resorting to murder. Killing Brad isn't going to undo what happened to her."

"But it will undo what happens to the next girl," Jack countered, his resoluteness seeming to return.

Jason sighed, frustrated. "I know. Believe me, I do. But you're not Batman, alright? Do you think Ruby wants you to get blood on your hands for her?"

Jack laughed, the tension breaking slightly. "Not Batman? Now, you're hurting my ego."

Jason rolled his eyes. "Yeah, I'm sorry to burst your bubble, buddy. Batman's got more gadgets and a better car. And you?"

"What? You don't like my Lexus?" Jack asked.

"Oh, the Lexus is cool. But let's face it, a nice car is about the only thing you've got in common with the Bat."

Jack shrugged, a flicker of uncertainty crossing his face. "You've got a point. I know Ruby won't like it. That's why I planned on never telling her. But now Tabby knows, and she's not happy about it. Which is why I planned on never telling her either ... But I couldn't take the guilt of lying to her."

"And that's the thing—when you keep secrets, they have a way of biting you in the ass. You can't maintain a lie forever. Sooner or later, the truth always comes out. Especially when you're married—or about to be, in your case. You really want to start your marriage with secrets and lies?"

Jack took a sip of his soda, contemplating Jason's words. "I guess not, since I ended up telling her."

Jason nodded, relieved. "Good. It's a crappy situation all around. But being honest and open with Tabby is the right move, even if it's hard. Trust me, a marriage built on lies and secrets will crumble faster than you can say 'I do.'"

There was a hint of defiance in Jack's eyes as he said, "If I wanted a relationship coach, which I do not, you're the last person I would call. Sorry, man, but it's the truth."

"Oh, come on. I'm not trying to be a relationship coach, alright? I'm just trying to talk some sense into your stubborn head."

Jack's expression was unreadable. "You have to admit, it's the solution with the best guarantee."

Jason sighed, knowing Jack had a point. "Maybe. But that doesn't make it the right one. Is it worth it? I mean, once you cross that line, there's no going back. You'll never be the same person again. Is that what you want?"

Jack's eyes darkened, and Jason could see the anger simmering beneath the surface.

"You've got a little sister, right? Now, imagine someone hurts her. Hurts her so bad she tries to take her own life. Would you sit back and hope it doesn't happen again? And worse, if it does, that this time you might lose her forever?"

Jason flinched at the thought, his heart clenching as he imagined his sister in pain. "You think I haven't thought about that? Hell, my first instinct would probably be to do the same thing you're planning to do. But what I've learned over the years is that the best protection for the people we care about is love and support."

Jack's expression turned to anger. "When your sister tries to overdose on pills and you have to watch her get her stomach pumped and wait to hear from the doctor if there will be permanent liver damage, then you can tell me what you would do in my shoes. Until then, I don't want to hear it."

Jason's voice softened, sensing the raw pain behind Jack's anger. "Hey, listen. I'm not trying to belittle your pain or your feelings. I know what happened to Ruby was horrifying. And I can't even imagine the anger and helplessness watching her go through that. But you have to understand—taking a life is a line that cannot be uncrossed. You do this, and it'll haunt you for the rest of your life."

Jack regarded him for a moment before saying, "You worry too much. Everything's going to be fine. Now go tell Tabby you convinced me to let it go. I know she's waiting to hear it."

"Damn it, you're really not going to listen, are you?" A familiar knot of frustration tightened in his stomach. "I get that you think I'm worrying too much. And maybe I am. But I just worry about you, alright? About you, and Tabby, and the baby. You think you're going to get rid of Brad and, poof, everything goes back to normal? Life doesn't work that way. You make this choice, and you have no idea what the consequences are going to be."

Jack shrugged, nonchalant. "Thanks for the advice."

Jason sighed as helplessness settled over him. He realized there was nothing more he could say to change Jack's mind, at least not right now. "Just think about what I said. Really think about it. And for Christ's sake, don't do anything stupid. Promise me that much, at least."

Jack waved a dismissive hand. "You've got nothing to worry about. I'm the responsible one, remember?"

Jason chuckled dryly. "Yeah, right. The responsible one. The one who's planning a murder. That checks out."

Jack said, "Thanks for the visit. Tell Tabby I'll call her later."

Jason nodded as the familiar sense of defeat washed over him. He knew he had lost this battle for now. "Yeah, I'll tell her. Have a good night. And try not to do anything I wouldn't do, alright?"

As he turned to leave, a sense of foreboding lingered in the air, Jack's choices heavy on his mind.

Jason knocked on the door of Tabby's apartment, anxiety gripping him as he anticipated the conversation ahead. Moments later, the door swung open, revealing Tabby's expectant face.

"Hey, I need to talk to you," he said, stepping into the apartment.

"Yeah, yeah. Come in," she said, her tone casual but her eyes searching.

He moved into the living room. He stood there awkwardly, his hands shoved deep into his pockets. "So, um, I just talked to Jack."

"How'd it go?" Tabby asked.

Jason avoided her gaze, rubbing the back of his neck. "Um, he said he's thought about it and he's ... decided to drop the whole thing."

Tabby's expression turned from curiosity to confusion. "Really?"

He chanced a glance at her, trying to appear confident. "Yeah ... yeah, absolutely. He's decided he's going to move on and let it go. He told me to tell you that everything is going to be fine. That he's done thinking about this."

"So, what's the plan then? For when Brad gets out of prison?"

Her question caught him off guard, and he panicked as his mind scrambled for a response.

"The plan?" he stammered. "Well, I told him we should just ... watch Brad. Make sure he stays away from us. If he tries to come near any of us, we'll deal with it then."

Tabby's tone was skeptical. "And Jack agreed to that?"

"Yes, he agreed!" Jason snapped, irritation in his voice. "Why are you looking at me like that? Like you don't believe me?"

"Why are you avoiding looking at me? You're a terrible liar. Why are you lying? Tell me what he really said."

With a sigh, Jason ran a hand over his face, feeling her scrutiny. "First of all, I'm pretty sure I'm not a terrible liar. Second of all, if I was lying, which I'm not, I'd be doing it to try and protect you. You're a pregnant woman, and you shouldn't have to worry about stressful things like this."

"Unbelievable! You didn't convince him at all, did you? Did you encourage him again?"

"It's not that simple!" he said with frustration. "Despite having some doubts, it's clear that Jack is ultimately hellbent on doing this, and nothing you or I say is going to change his mind. We've both tried talking him out of it, remember?"

"Oh, Jesus Christ. Thanks for nothing," Tabby said, her voice laced with disappointment.

Jason felt a surge of indignation. "Thanks for nothing? I tried my best here, alright? You're the one who asked me to talk to him. I did exactly what you wanted me to do!"

"You were supposed to talk him out of it. How difficult can it be to convince someone that murder is wrong?"

He looked at her in disbelief. "Do you seriously think it's that simple? You say, 'Murder is wrong, so don't do it,' and he's supposed to just listen? You think it's that cut and dry?"

"Yeah. Yeah, I do. It's not really up for dispute, I would think."

Jason was amazed at her naivety. "You're being so goddamn obtuse. Let me explain something about Jack. When Jack makes up his mind about something, he's not going to change it. He's stubborn as a mule, and the more you argue with his choice, the more stubborn he becomes."

Tabby sighed, accepting the truth in his words. "Well, you're right about that."

"So you can understand why he isn't going to change his mind. And trust me, I did try to dissuade him, but he is dead set on murdering Brad, okay?"

"No, that is very much not okay!" she said, her voice rising.

Jason's frustration reached a boiling point. "It's not? Well, it's going to happen, whether we like it or not. I don't like the idea of Jack going through with this. I'm worried about him getting in trouble. I care about him, and I'd never want to see him get arrested. But at this point, the die has been cast. There's nothing we can do to change it."

Tabby shook her head, determination in her eyes. "No, I'm certain he's really still not made up his mind. There has to be a way."

"What way? What do you suggest we do? We already tried talking to him, and it didn't work. Do you want to try locking him in a room until he comes to his senses?"

"And what are you going to say to the cops when they interrogate you? 'Oh yeah, I definitely knew Jack was going to murder Brad. I told him not to. What else could I have done?'"

He shook his head, annoyed by the thought. "Of course I'm not going to say that. Jesus, have some faith in me. Look, Jack is stubborn, but he's not going to get himself into trouble. He's already thought of every possible outcome for this. He's got it planned to a T. He's not going to get caught, and you and I aren't going to get in trouble either. Just trust him and trust me."

"Trust you? You treat lying like it's a sport. I'm supposed to trust you?"

Jason's anger flared, offense taking over. "*Lying a sport*, really? You think I do it just for fun, is that it? When are you going to realize I'm doing this for your own damn good? I'm trying to prevent you from worrying and stressing over this! I'm trying to keep you and the baby safe and sane."

Tabby covered her face with her hands. "You're doing a terrible job."

His patience was wearing thin. "Jesus, you're so damn frustrating. I'm not doing a terrible job. I'm doing exactly what you need. You're pregnant, and you shouldn't be stressing over this. I don't want you to, okay?"

"Oh yeah, I'll just be like, 'My future husband is going to prison for murder. No point stressing about it. Gotta stay calm. Teehee.'"

The sarcasm in her voice cut deep, and despair settled over him. How had it come to this? Jason stared at Tabby with disbelief. "God, you're acting like a goddamn child," he burst out, frustrated. "You're not listening to anything I'm saying. You don't trust me, you don't trust Jack and you don't want to believe anything I tell you. What the hell do you expect me to do?"

Tabby shook her head. "I can't believe this is happening."

He sighed, the heat of his temper cooling. "Come on now. I get it's hard to deal with, trust me. But you have to relax. Just let it go. Let Jack handle this his way. I assure you he knows what he's doing."

"You're a lunatic," Tabby said, her voice rising. "Let Jack murder this person. That's actually what you're suggesting."

Irritation crept back into Jason's voice. "Don't be so damn dramatic. It's not 'letting him murder.' It's more like letting him handle the problem on his own. I'm going to ask you a question, and I want an honest answer. Do you trust Jack?"

Tabby hesitated, her expression thoughtful. She met his gaze, uncertainty flickering in her eyes.

Jason looked at her, hoping this would click. "So, it comes down to this. If you trust Jack, then you also need to trust his decision. You trust that he's a reliable, good person. You can't have it both ways. Either you trust him, or you don't. Which is it?"

"I trust him," she said, the words finally tumbling out.

He nodded. "Then let him handle this. He's making the call, and he knows what he's doing, so just let him do his thing. I'm sure everything will be fine."

Tabby sighed, her shoulders slumping. "I guess I have no choice. The more I push him, the more stubborn he'll get. I have to trust him, like you said. Trust that he'll make the right choice for us."

Jason felt a sense of confidence return. "That's it, exactly. You're getting it. Jack is going to handle this alright. You just don't need to worry about it."

She nodded, and he could see the tension in her face fade.

"Sorry if I sounded annoyed before," he said. "Truth is, I really do care about you. I don't want you to be upset and stressed. I want you to have faith in Jack and trust him to do the right thing."

"Aren't you worried that Ruby is going to be mad that you kept this from her?" Tabby asked, a note of concern creeping into her voice.

Jason rubbed the back of his neck, anxiety creeping back in. "Yeah, that's something I've been trying not to think about. But if Ruby finds out, I'll just talk to her and try to explain. Hopefully, she'll understand and not be too pissed off."

Tabby scoffed. "Good luck with that."

He sighed. "Yeah, I'll need it. She's going to be mad, isn't she? She's really not going to like this."

"And she knows something is up," Tabby added. "She's willing to overlook it because you and Jack are getting along, but I'm pretty sure that'll change once her brother is in prison for murder."

Jason ran a hand over his face. "You're right about that. I'm so screwed. And she always seems to know when I'm lying to her. I don't know how she does it."

"I need a muffin. Do you want a muffin?" Tabby moved to the kitchen counter and opened a package of blueberry muffins.

He blinked, surprised by the sudden shift in topic. "Um, sure. I'll have a muffin," he said following her.

"Here," she said, handing him one.

Tabby sat down at the kitchen table pulling out blueberries, eating them one by one. Jason watched her, a little amused despite the gravity of the conversation. How was she still able to focus on something as trivial as blueberry muffins? He took a seat across from her.

"Look," he said, trying to regain control of the conversation, "I just need to know you won't do anything stupid. Just let him deal with this. Trust him."

"I won't push him anymore," Tabby said. "I realize he needs to come to the realization on his own that this is a terrible idea. But I still think you should try to convince Brad to skip town. Just in case. He can't kill him if he can't find him, right?"

Jason considered her suggestion, nodding. "That's not a bad idea. I'll go talk to him. Maybe Brad needs a little push to get the hell out of town for a little while, so Jack won't have the chance to murder him."

"You mean, you're actually going to visit him in jail? What makes you think he'll even talk to you?" Tabby asked, skepticism etched across her face.

Jason said, "I don't think he'll have a problem with me. Plus, it can't hurt to try, right?"

As Tabby looked at Jason from across the table, a sense of urgency filled the air. "Alright, do you know when he's due to get out?" she asked, concern apparent in her face. "I'm sure Jack knows the date exactly. But I have no idea."

Jason pondered the question for a moment, trying to recall the details. "I'm pretty sure he gets out soon," he said. "He's only got about a month left. But I'm not quite sure of the exact date."

"Okay," Tabby said. "That gives us a month for Jack to come to his senses and for you to convince Brad to get the hell out of Dodge."

Jason nodded. "I think that's the best we can do right now. I'll talk to Brad, and you just hang tight. Keep supporting Jack and act like everything is normal."

"Oh, yeah. Of course. Easy peasy," Tabby said, her sarcasm cutting through the tension.

He offered her a weak smile, sensing her underlying frustration. "Yeah, it's not necessarily 'easy peasy.' But just do the best you can, alright?"

Tabby nodded, her resolve firm as she met his gaze.

"Thanks," Jason said, appreciating her cooperation. "Just don't get too stressed about this. Things will work out."

"Okay. Thanks for keeping me in the loop," she said.

He nodded. "You're welcome. I'm sorry I had to keep this from you in the first place, but I didn't want to stress you out even more. Plus, Jack basically made me swear to secrecy."

Tabby sighed. "Fine, but no more secrets, alright? And you might want to consider coming clean with your girlfriend while you're at it."

The thought of revealing the truth to Ruby filled him with dread. "I was hoping you wouldn't bring that up."

"I'm going to trust you to do the right thing. See? I can trust," she said, a challenge in her voice.

He appreciated her trust and admired her stubbornness. "Ha ha, thanks, Tabby. Real nice of you to throw my own words back at me."

"Alright, call me tomorrow?"

"I will. I'll let you know how things go with Brad. But hang in there in the meantime," Jason said, standing up to leave. "And keep your anxiety in check, alright? Don't stress too much, or you'll hurt the baby."

"Yes, yes," she said playfully, as she walked him to the door.

He gave her a quick side hug. "Good. That's what I like to hear. And if you have any questions or need anything, call me, alright?"

"I will," she assured him.

"Alright, talk to you later," Jason said, stepping through the door and into the uncertain world outside.

That night, Jack felt both relief and anxiety as he picked up his phone to call Tabby. He needed to hear her voice, to make sure she was safe, but he also couldn't shake the worry about how she would react to his call.

"Hello, my love," came her voice, warm and familiar, instantly easing some of his tension.

"Hey, darling," he said. "I wanted to hear your voice."

"I miss you," she said, and Jack nodded, his heart aching with longing.

"I miss you too. I wish you were here with me right now," he admitted.

"Maybe one of us should give up our apartment so we can be together all the time," she suggested, her tone playful yet serious.

The idea sparked excitement within him. He had been thinking about it for a while but had hesitated to bring it up. "Mmm ... that sounds great. Can you imagine what life would be like if we had a place of our own? Somewhere we could relax and be together?"

"Maybe we could both give up our apartments and buy a house," she proposed, her voice filled with enthusiasm.

Jack's heart raced at the thought. A house together sounded perfect—a sanctuary where they could build a life. "A house ... that sounds amazing.

Somewhere we could make our own, with a big yard and plenty of room for the baby to grow up in."

"That sounds perfect," Tabby agreed.

"It does. And you know what else would make it perfect? You. You make everything better."

"I love you."

His heart swelled with emotion. "I love you too. More than anything."

For a moment, silence wrapped around them.

"Did you by any chance talk to Jason today?" asked Jack.

"He came here after your place. He told me I should trust you. And not to worry. He told me you asked him to come over to reassure me," she explained.

Jack nodded, relief flooding through him. "I did. I thought you'd be worried, and I wanted to make sure you weren't panicking."

"He did. And I do trust you. I know I can rely and depend on you."

Jack felt a tenderness surge inside him. "You can always count on me. No matter what. I'll always be there for you." He contemplated whether to share something that had been on his mind. "Don't freak out when I say this. But ... I've been thinking about something."

Tabby sighed. "It seems like every conversation I have lately involves someone asking me to not freak out."

Jack realized the truth in her words. "I guess you're right about that. But this time I really need you to not freak out."

"Okay," she agreed.

"So, I've been giving some serious thought to this whole situation with you being pregnant, and ... well, the truth is, when you first told me you were pregnant, I wasn't exactly excited. I mean, don't get me wrong, I was happy. But also, I was freaked out. I wasn't sure what to expect, and I didn't know if I was ready for the responsibility of being a father."

"I understand," Tabby said, her voice soothing.

"I was pretty overwhelmed," he continued, relieved at her understanding. "But over time ... things started to change. I began to imagine what it would be like to have this little life growing inside of you, a little piece of us that we created together. And the more I thought about it, the more I realized how much I wanted to be a father to this baby."

"I'm so happy you feel that way. You're going to be a great father. I'm sure of it."

Pride swelled in Jack at her words and filled him with warmth. "I hope so. But, honestly, it's all about you right now. You're the one who's going to be pregnant for the next nine months. I want to be there to support you through it all."

"Let's make plans to go house shopping. I want to start building our life together. I want you to be there in the middle of the night when I have blueberry muffin cravings."

He grinned at the thought. "Sure, I'll be your midnight blueberry muffin supplier. And when you want ice cream at three a.m., I'll get it for you. I won't complain once."

"Jack, I'm so happy."

"Me too. I'm the happiest I've ever been. And it's all because of you and this baby."

As their conversation continued, Jack could sense Tabby yawning on the other end of the line. "Seems like it's about time for you to get some sleep," he said.

"I'll see you tomorrow?" she asked, her voice softening.

"Yes, I'll be over tomorrow. Get some rest. I love you," he said, already anticipating their time together.

"I love you too," she echoed, and Jack felt a warmth spread through him.

He wanted to say more, to express everything in his heart, but she needed to rest. "Sweet dreams. I can't wait to see you tomorrow."

# 20 Anger

Jason arrived at Tabby's apartment on the Friday evening before Columbus Day, the air crisp with the promise of the long weekend ahead. "Come on in," she said as she swung the door open.

As he stepped inside and closed the door behind him, he asked, "Hey, how are you today?"

"Great—I'm house shopping," Tabby said, excited.

"Really? I knew you liked buying clothes, but now you're looking at houses, too?"

"Yeah, Jason. A one-bedroom apartment isn't big enough for a baby," she said matter-of-factly as she walked toward the kitchen. Jason trailed behind her.

He nodded. "I guess that makes sense. Find anything good?"

"Never mind that. Did you visit Brad in jail?" she asked.

Jason sighed, recalling the uncomfortable visit. "I was just over there, and, yeah, I talked to him."

"Tell me everything, word for word," she demanded, her eyes wide with anticipation.

He groaned, already annoyed at having to retell the entire story. "Can I just give you a basic summary instead?"

"No—your 'summaries' tend to leave out the most important parts," she insisted, crossing her arms.

Jason sat down, exasperated. "Jesus, fine. Don't get your panties in a twist. I went to see him this afternoon. It wasn't exactly comfortable walking into the prison and asking the guard to let me talk to Brad. They escorted me to the visiting room and left me there for a few minutes. Brad showed up after that." He paused, gathering his thoughts, unsure how much of the conversation he wanted to share. "He wasn't exactly happy to see me, by the way. He more or less just sat down and wouldn't look at me."

"Well, he has no idea who the hell you are, obviously. I told you I'd be surprised if he even agreed to talk to you," Tabby said, her tone condescending.

"Yeah, yeah, you don't need to remind me. I kind of figured that one out by the way he practically ignored me the whole time."

"Go on," she urged, with impatience.

"Relax, I'm getting there," he said, trying to keep his cool. "Basically, after a few minutes, he finally broke the ice and asked me what I wanted ... He just leaned back in the chair and looked up at the ceiling, like he couldn't be bothered to even make eye contact with me." Jason sighed, remembering the rudeness. "Anyways, I told him I wanted to talk to him about something important. He just looked at me and laughed, like the whole thing was a joke. When I told him it was serious, he just stared at me, like he was waiting for me to get to the point and didn't care what I had to say."

"Did you expect him to be pleasant? I've never met the guy, but it seems pretty clear to me that he must be a total asshole. Were you not expecting that?" Tabby asked.

"No, I didn't expect him to be overly 'pleasant.' But I expected him to at least be mildly polite and pretend to listen to what I had to say. Instead, he acted like a defiant teenager."

"Whatever, go on," she urged.

He sighed again, knowing he had already shared the best parts, but he was compelled to continue. "Fine, I'll keep going if you're going to be so impatient ... So, I basically just got right to the point and told him that Jack is still really mad about what happened and is planning to go after him. Brad sort of just laughed at that, like it was a big joke. That's when he sat up and actually looked me in the eye, but only to tell me that I'm full of crap. He said Jack's full of crap, too."

"Wow. Well ... we tried," Tabby said, her voice laced with disappointment.

Jason nodded. "Yeah, we did. Brad didn't seem to care. He said Jack can do whatever he wants and that he doesn't scare him. He claims that, after he's out, Jack won't be able to find him. So, basically, the conversation went nowhere."

Tabby frowned, considering his words. "He said Jack won't be able to find him? So, he's not coming back to the neighborhood?"

Jason pursed his lips, mulling over what Brad had said. "Yeah, that's what he claims. You know, 'Jack won't be able to find me because I'll be gone.' He didn't mention where he's planning to go, but I definitely got the sense he's not coming back here."

"Well, that's good. Problem solved, right?" Tabby said.

Jason frowned, skepticism creeping in. "I'm not sure how solved the problem actually is, but, yeah, maybe. I'm not sure Jack will see it that way, though."

Tabby sighed with relief and moved to the fridge, pulling out a container of blueberries. "Blueberry?" she offered.

He smiled, already accustomed to her new obsession. "Sure."

"I feel a lot better now. Don't you?" she asked, her eyes brightening.

Jason took a blueberry from the container and popped it in his mouth, considering her question. "I don't like to count my chickens before they hatch, but ... I guess I'm feeling a tiny bit better about the whole thing.

"Come check out this house I found!" Tabby said, moving toward the desk where her laptop sat. "It's so cute, and it's got a separate in-law house in the back." Tabby pointed to the screen. "It'd be great for guests or kidnap victims or whatever."

He scoffed, shaking his head at her twisted sense of humor. "Ha ha, you're so cute, princess."

"Do you think Jack will like it?" she asked.

Jason played along with her banter. "Yeah, absolutely. It's a two-in-one deal. The in-law suite can be used for guests *or* it can be used to hold prisoners. Who can argue with that? It's a win-win."

"I'm going to call the real estate agent to see when we can view it," Tabby said.

Jason nodded. "Sounds like a plan."

Tabby turned her attention back to him. "So, how have things been with you? Have you gotten to spend any time with Ruby, or have you been too busy with your murder plot?"

He rolled his eyes, already weary of her sarcasm. "Don't start. And yeah, yeah, before you make the inevitable comment—I'm still planning on coming clean to Ruby at some point. I just haven't had a chance to do it yet."

"I wasn't going to say anything," she said, feigning innocence.

"Bullshit. You were going to ask me why I haven't come clean yet. Admit it."

"To be honest, I get why you haven't told her. I certainly have no desire to drag her into this mess. And I'm sure Jack doesn't want her to hear about it. But none of that is going to save you if she finds out you've been lying to her about something so important that has to do with her and Jack."

Jason scowled, knowing she was right. "Damn it, why do you have to be so logical about everything? You're right. I'm going to have to come clean eventually. I just need to figure out how and when."

"Good luck with that," she said, her tone sympathetic. "I don't envy you."

He managed a weak smile, already dreading the conversation ahead. "It's not going to be a fun talk, but I'm not one to shy away from confrontation. I've just been feeling a little guilty lately, but that's my own damn fault. I should have come clean sooner."

"If you're headed over there, I'll walk with you. I want to talk to Jack about the house," Tabby offered, determination in her voice.

Jason thought a distraction might be just what he needed. "Sure, why not? Let's go."

After locking up, they walked side by side toward Jack and Ruby's apartment building. As they strolled, Jason asked, "Hey, Tabs, can I ask a personal question?"

"Sure," she said, glancing up at him with curiosity.

"Have you given any thought to baby names yet?"

"What do you think of Simon?"

He grinned, already amused by her choice. "Simon? Why Simon?"

"Do I need a reason? Can't I like the name?" Tabby asked.

"No, you don't need a reason. I'm just curious as to why you'd pick such a plain name like Simon."

"Maybe I have a secret crush on Simon Baker."

"You have a crush on Simon Baker, the actor?" Jason asked.

"Well, he does have that dazzling smile. Just like you," she said, poking him playfully in the cheek.

He rolled his eyes, swatting her hand away. "Shut up—no one has a smile as dazzling as me."

"Who is *your* celebrity crush?" she asked.

He paused, pretending to ponder her question. "I don't know. You're going to have to give me a few moments to come up with a valid answer."

"Bullshit. Everybody knows who their celebrity crush is. You're trying to play it cool," she challenged.

"No, that's not it. I'm seriously trying to think about who gets my vote as the hottest celeb. It's a hard choice. There are so many to choose from."

When they arrived at the apartment building, Tabby said, "You're off the hook for now. Tell Ruby I said hi," Tabby said, before approaching Jack's apartment.

Jason climbed the stairs that led to Ruby's apartment and knocked on her door. "Hey Ruby, it's me. Can I come in?"

The door swung open. "Hey stranger, come on in," Ruby said.

He stepped inside, closing the door behind him. "How are you?"

"Good. I was watching TV," she said, gesturing toward the couch.

Jason walked over and they sat down together. "I can see that. What are you watching?"

"Some romance movie."

He rolled his eyes. "Oh, come on, you're seriously watching one of those sappy movies?"

"There was nothing else on."

He reached for the remote. "Well then, you weren't looking hard enough. We are not watching this. We're finding something more entertaining." He began clicking through the channels.

"Oh, I can hardly wait to see what you pick," she said, her tone dripping with sarcasm.

Jason grinned. "Trust me, I can find something way better than any of these lame-ass sappy movies."

He continued flipping through channels, pausing when he stumbled upon *The Godfather*. "Wait, hold on ..." He stared at the screen. "You know, I've always been quite partial to Marlon Brando."

"Yeah, I love this movie. But I've seen it like a hundred times."

Jason said, "Yeah, but c'mon, how could you resist watching a young Al Pacino be a reluctant mafia boss? This movie is way more enjoyable than some mushy-gushy flick."

"Fine," Ruby said pouting, but he could see the glimmer of excitement in her eyes.

He grinned, sensing victory. "I knew you'd cave."

"I've hardly seen you lately. Since you started going to the shooting range with my brother ... and the gym ... and jogging. Should I be jealous of Jack?"

"You, be jealous of Jack? I think you're safe on that one. I just want to stay in shape and learn something new. You're still the only one for me," Jason said.

"I told you he liked you," Ruby said, a note of satisfaction in her voice.

He scoffed, shaking his head. "I always thought he tolerated me rather than liked me. But I actually think we're becoming good friends."

"Does that mean you're going to stop referring to him as 'that overprotective bastard?'" she asked.

He grinned. "Oh, well, I don't know about that. I kind of like referring to him that way. But only in a friendly joking sort of way, of course."

"Of course. You would never be rude about my brother," she said, her tone mocking.

Jason put a hand on his heart, feigning innocence. "Of course not. I'm not capable of rudeness. I'm sweet as pie, remember?"

"Oh, that's right. Why do I always forget that?" Ruby asked.

He smiled, trying to look charming. "I really don't know. You don't seem to have a very good memory ... I've told you multiple times how sweet and lovable I am."

"That's why we make such a cute couple. We're just a couple of cherubs," she said, her voice light.

Jason draped an arm around her shoulders. "Exactly. Together, we're basically a sickening display of cuteness overload."

"Do you really want to watch this movie? I've got it on Blu-ray. We can watch it anytime you want," Ruby offered.

He pulled her close. "Nah. I think I have something better in mind."

"What's that?" she asked.

With a playful grin, he leaned in and nibbled at her neck. "What do you think?"

The playful tension in the air shifted, and her laughter turn into a soft sigh, the teasing atmosphere settling into something deeper and more intimate.

Saturday morning Jason stirred in the cozy warmth of Ruby's apartment, the soft light filtering in through the curtains. He had been lost in a dream when the shrill ring of his phone sliced through the tranquility, pulling him back to reality. Groggy and disoriented, he fumbled for the phone, squinting at the screen. He answered, his voice thick with sleep. "Hello?"

"Hey, it's Tabby. Are you still sleeping?" came the voice on the other end.

Jason sighed, irritated. He had never been a morning person, and being jolted from a deep sleep didn't help. "Yes, I'm still sleeping. And if you have any love for me whatsoever, you'll know it's too damn early to be calling me yet."

"You do realize it's after 11, right?" Tabby said.

Jason glanced at the time on his phone and blinked in surprise. "Oh ... really? Damn. Maybe it's not so early. You're still an evil wench for waking me up, though."

"Rough night?" Tabby asked.

Jason grinned as he recalled the previous evening. "You can say that. Ruby's been keeping me up, what can I say?"

"Wait, are you at Ruby's apartment?" Tabby asked.

"Yeah, I'm at Ruby's. So what?"

"I'm downstairs at Jack's. I'll come up there." With that, Tabby hung up.

The prospect of an impending visit only added to his morning grumpiness. He rolled out of bed, the remnants of sleep still tugging at him. He looked around for Ruby, but apparently she had gone out somewhere. "Hold your damn horses, I'm coming!" he called out as he heard a knock on the door.

After a moment, he opened the door, grumbling, "This better be important or I'm going to be pissed."

Tabby stood there, arms crossed, a bemused expression on her face. "What the hell? Why are you so grouchy?"

Jason sighed, running a hand through his messy hair. "I don't know. Just waking up on a Saturday is bad enough, but you woke me up even earlier than usual. What the hell do you even want?"

"11:30? Earlier than usual? How do you manage to function as a human being," she asked.

He glared at her. "I function perfectly fine. I just like sleeping as late as possible on Saturdays. Waking up around noon would be much more acceptable to my taste."

"Rawrr. You're in a mood. Did you not get laid last night?" Tabby asked.

Jason couldn't suppress a smile at her boldness. "It's none of your business if I got laid last night or not."

"Anyway," she continued, entering the apartment and taking a seat at the table, "I have great news. Jack and I looked at the house and he loves it. He wants to make an offer."

Jason perked up, his earlier irritation fading. "That's great! He wants to make an offer already?" he said as he shut the door and joined Tabby at the table.

"Yes! I hope we get this house. I really love it," Tabby said, with excitement.

"If Jack loves it, then I'm sure you'll get it. I know I wouldn't want to get between you two when you're both determined to get something."

"Are you calling us stubborn?" Tabby challenged, her eyes narrowing playfully.

"Oh hell yes I am. You're both pretty damn stubborn when you want something. I just feel sorry for the poor agent who has to deal with you," Jason said.

"With any luck, a month from now Jack will be too busy moving into our new home to worry about Brad getting out of prison. Either that or he'll turn the in-law suite into a kill room. I'm not sure which," Tabby mused, her expression thoughtful.

Jason pictured the absurdity. "Probably a kill room, knowing Jack. And I'm guessing you're going to turn a blind eye to it?"

"Speaking of turning a blind eye, I see you didn't come clean with Ruby. She and Jack went out to brunch, and she seemed very chipper."

"Fine, you got me. I still haven't told her everything. I've been thinking about it! I just haven't found a good opportunity."

"Just be like, 'Sorry Ruby, I can't come over today. Your brother and I have plans to orchestrate a murder.' I'm sure she'll understand," Tabby suggested, her voice dripping with sarcasm.

He shot her an unimpressed look. "Very funny. You're not being the least bit helpful right now.

"That's essentially how it was presented to me. Oh, I forgot: first, you have to say, 'Promise you won't freak out,'" she added.

"Right, that's obviously how I should start a conversation about a murder plot. I can totally see myself saying that to her," Jason said, shaking his head.

Tabby asked, "So, what are you *actually* going to say?"

"I'm going to have to tell her the truth. Soon. Preferably before Jack actually kills Brad." The thought gnawed at him. He knew it would upset her, but it was a conversation that had to happen. Complications were inevitable, and he hated he was about to add another layer to this already messy situation.

"Well, you kinda put yourself in this situation when you promised Jack you would lie to me and Ruby," Tabby pointed out.

Jason scowled. "Oh wow, thanks for that. I know I put myself in this stupid situation by promising Jack I would lie to you and Ruby. I don't need the reminder."

"Sorry. Jeez, you're so sensitive," she said, amusement flickering in her eyes.

He scoffed, exasperated. "I'm not sensitive. I'm just not in the mood for any of your smartass comments."

"Hanging out with Jack has made you less fun. His brooding demeanor is rubbing off on you. It works for him—not so much for you."

Jason scoffed, dismissing her accusation. "It has not! I'm as fun as ever. Jack's just rubbing off on me a *tiny* bit. I mean, the guy is planning somebody's murder. Not exactly cheerful, lighthearted stuff on a daily basis, ya know?"

Tabby scoffed. "So, you're blaming your bad mood on your new hobby of killing people? You need to learn to compartmentalize."

Amused by her casual tone, Jason said, "Yes, I'm blaming my bad mood on the fact that my new hobby of plotting a murder isn't very cheerful. You know, the usual thing. And I *am* learning to compartmentalize. I can be cheerful. Now, will you stop being such a smartass?"

She feigned innocence. "I don't know if I can promise that. You taught me everything I know about being a smartass."

"I take offense to that. You've always been a smartass, long before I came along. It's just unfortunate that we both happen to be such master smartasses. You and I make a great team of assholery," he said with a grin.

"Finally, a smile," Tabby said. "I should have known that teasing me would cheer you up."

Jason chuckled, warmth spreading through him. "I have to admit, you're absolutely right about that. Teasing you is the gift that keeps on giving."

"Anything else going on?" she asked, leaning in with a curious expression.

"Not really, other than getting ready to tell Ruby about the whole Brad situation. That should be a fun conversation ..."

The front door creaked open, and Ruby stepped inside, her presence instantly shifting the atmosphere.

"Hey Ruby," Tabby greeted, standing up. "I'm going to head home now. Have a good chat." She shot Jason a knowing look before slipping past Ruby and out the door.

Jason took a deep breath. He forced a smile for Ruby, even though, inside, he was anything but cheerful. He let out a heavy sigh as he watched Tabby walk away. "Bye, Tabby ..." he said, knowing he had to face Ruby next.

"What was that all about?" Ruby asked, closing the door.

He turned to her, a sense of apprehension creeping in. "We have something to talk about. Something important."

"What is it?" she asked, with eagerness.

Jason's heart raced as he realized the moment had arrived. "Before I start, I need you to promise me one thing. Promise you won't freak out or get upset."

She let out a laugh, rolling her eyes. "C'mon. Don't be dramatic. Just tell me."

He grumbled under his breath, knowing Ruby's reaction would be anything but positive. "Fine, but I'm just warning you. This is going to piss you off."

"Nothing could piss me off. I'm in a great mood. So, shoot," she challenged, her confidence unyielding.

Jason braced himself for the storm he was about to unleash. "Remember to not freak out. Just please try to stay calm. Just listen to what I have to say and don't interrupt."

Ruby rolled her eyes again. "Do you have something to say or not?"

He took a deep breath, knowing this was going to suck. "Okay, okay. So, basically, Jack and I have been working on a plan to murder Brad."

Ruby stared at him, her expression frozen in disbelief. "Come again?"

He inhaled deeply, preparing for the inevitable anger and indignation. "Jack and I have been planning out how to kill Brad. Before you go insane, just listen to why we're doing that."

But before he could finish, Ruby shot up from her seat and stormed out the door.

"Wait a second! Hold on!" Jason called after her, panic rising in his chest as he rushed to follow her. "Where do you think you're going?"

She raced down the stairs, her determination clear as she pounded on Jack's door, leaving Jason in a whirlwind of anxiety and regret.

As Ruby continued to bang on Jack's door, her voice cut through the hallway. "Open the door, Jack! I need to talk to you!"

Just as the door swung open, Jason caught up to her, sensing the tension emanating from her. He stood a few steps behind, feeling the charged atmosphere.

"Hey, sis. Long time no see," Jack greeted.

"Ruby, will you just calm down and listen?" Jason said, trying to keep the peace.

"Come inside, you two. Let's not do this out in the hallway," Jack said, stepping aside to let them in.

Jason sighed, resigned to the conversation he had hoped to avoid. He followed Ruby and Jack into the apartment, the door closing behind them with a soft thud.

"What the fuck, Jack?" Ruby's voice sliced through the air, sharp and accusing.

Jason leaned against the wall, grimacing in anticipation of the confrontation. He had tried to warn her to remain calm, but at heart he knew how this would go.

"Let me guess—he told you," Jack said, glancing at Jason. Ruby shot Jason a glare. "This is exactly why I didn't want you to know, Ruby. I didn't want to upset you," Jack said.

"I tried telling her not to freak out, but she wouldn't listen," Jason said.

Jack turned to Jason, sarcasm dripping from his words. "Yeah, thanks. Brilliant plan."

"What was I supposed to do? She was going to find out sooner or later," Jason grumbled, feeling the pressure of being in the middle.

Ruby's voice rose. "Are you absolutely determined to ruin your life, and mine?"

"Ruby, you need to trust me. I'm only looking out for you," Jack insisted.

Jason watched the siblings carefully. "Jack has a point, Ruby," he said, trying to mediate.

She turned on him, disbelief flashing in her eyes. "I would expect this from him, but I can't believe you went along with it!"

"It's not my fault. It's kind of hard to say no to a plan like that coming from Jack."

"Ruby, listen. If you don't want me to do it, I won't," Jack offered.

"Liar! You're trying to placate me. Do you think I won't know what happened when Brad winds up dead?" Ruby snapped, her voice filled with anger.

"He's not going to wind up dead. I'll convince him to leave town. You don't have a problem with that, right?" Jack said, his confidence unwavering.

"And how exactly are you going to do that, Jack? Give him an offer he can't refuse?" Ruby challenged, crossing her arms.

Jack shrugged, an infuriatingly casual gesture. "Something like that. What does it matter? As long as he's gone."

Jason said, "Good luck with that. You don't have anything that Brad wants enough that would convince him to actually leave."

"Trust me. I can convince him," Jack insisted, his tone steady.

Jason shook his head, skepticism etched on his face. "Sure, you just keep telling yourself that, buddy."

Jack pointed at Jason. "You're not helping."

"I'm not trying to help. I'm just pointing out that your plan is ridiculous and will never work," Jason said.

"Stop fighting!" Ruby yelled, her voice echoing in the small apartment.

Jason scoffed. "We're not fighting. We're having a debate."

"This is not up for debate!" Ruby yelled, turning to Jack. "You are not going anywhere near Brad!" Then she turned to Jason, her eyes blazing. "And neither are you!"

"Whatever you say," Jack muttered as Ruby stormed out, slamming the door behind her.

Jason sighed, knowing the situation was far from over. "Well, that was a disaster."

Jack turned to him, his exasperation clear. "Why do you think I told you not to tell her?"

"I know! But I just thought it would be worse if we tried to keep it from her," Jason grumbled, still upset that Ruby had yelled at him.

"Anyone else you plan on telling?" Jack asked, his tone dripping with sarcasm.

Jason scowled, irritation flaring. "Of course I'm not going to tell anyone else! Why the hell would I do that?"

"Just making sure. I didn't think I had to explain that the fewer people who know about this, the better," Jack said.

Jason shot Jack a glare. "Yeah, I'm not an idiot. I realize the fewer people who know, the better."

"Okay then, go up there and calm down your girlfriend. Would you please?" Jack said.

Jason grumbled but went anyway. "Yeah, yeah, I'm already going."

As he walked toward the door, he braced himself for the battle ahead. Jason ascended the stairs to Ruby's apartment, a heaviness settling in his chest as he anticipated her reaction. When he stepped inside, he found her pacing back and forth, her expression furious.

"So, I take it you're still pissed at me?" he ventured, trying to break the tense silence.

Ruby shot him a glare that could have burned a hole through steel.

Jason slumped into a chair. "Are you going to give me the silent treatment? I've haven't seen your infamous glare of death for some time now. I almost forgot what that looks like."

"What do you have to say for yourself?" she demanded, her voice sharp.

He sighed, knowing he was likely to say the wrong thing. "I don't know. What do you want me to say?"

"So, this is the reason you and Jack have been getting along?"

Jason hated himself for lying to her. "Yeah, we bonded over planning out a murder. Who knew that plotting a killing spree would bring two guys closer together?"

"Heartwarming, really," she snapped, her voice full of anger.

"I'm sorry," he said, desperation in his voice. "I'm sorry I lied to you about it, but what did you want me to do? You know how determined Jack can be."

"So, you do everything Jack tells you now, including murder?" Ruby's words cut deep, and Jason winced at the harshness.

"No, I don't do everything Jack says. He just got me roped into this thing in the heat of the moment. I didn't exactly say no to his plan."

"Why not?"

Jason tried to articulate his thought process. "I didn't say no because, for once, I agreed with Jack about something. I am just as pissed off as he is about what Brad did to you."

"How nice for you. And did it occur to you that you and Jack would be taking Brad's place in prison?"

"We've both been worked up about the situation. We haven't exactly been thinking rationally at all times."

"This is actually none of your business," Ruby said, crossing her arms.

Jason scowled, feeling insulted. "What do you mean it's none of my business?"

"It was years ago, and you weren't even around. What do you know about it?"

He glared at her, frustrated. "I know enough to want the guy dead. I don't need to hear all the gory details to hate Brad's guts for what he did to you."

"Yeah—to me. Not to you. Let me deal with it."

"That's not how a relationship works, damn it," he said. "We're a couple. Partners. I'm not just going to stand by and watch you deal with this on your own."

"Partners? You were plotting a murder behind my back. Is that what 'partners' do?"

"You have a point there. But I didn't say anything to you about the murder plot because, one, I promised Jack I wouldn't. Two, even if I didn't promise him, I wouldn't tell you. I knew you'd freak out like you are right now. Which just kinda proves why I shouldn't have told you."

"You are unbelievable," Ruby said, her voice dripping with disbelief.

"You're the one being unreasonable here. I know you're angry with me, and you have a right to be, I guess. But you can't just expect me to be okay with Brad walking around a free man after what he did to you. He's done some unforgivable things, and he doesn't feel any remorse from what I can tell. Why should he get to go on living a normal life?"

"And how exactly would you know that he doesn't feel any remorse?" Ruby challenged.

He looked at her, feeling guilt creep across his face. "I may have gone to the prison to talk to him, just to see what his demeanor is like. And also to see if I could convince him to leave your life of his own free will."

"Oh, my god! You are not serious. Are you saying you visited Brad in jail?"

Jason winced, knowing this revelation would upset her even more. "Yes. I tried to be civil with the guy at first, just to see if I got any remorseful responses or any indication that he regrets what he did to you."

"Jesus fucking Christ. Do you have absolutely no boundaries whatsoever? Any other past trauma you want to dig up and rub in my face?"

Jason realized he should have kept this information to himself. "I didn't mean to dig up more bad memories or rub anything traumatic in your face. I only wanted to learn more about Brad, alright? After how hurt you ended up being because of him, I had to see with my own eyes the guy that caused you so much pain."

"Well, I'm sure you have a lot in common. Maybe you and Brad can plot some violent crimes together as well!" Ruby said, her voice full of scorn.

"Damn it, Ruby. I did not go in there just to rub salt in the wound of your trauma. I already told you I was trying to see if the guy had any remorse."

"I need to get out of here." With that, Ruby walked out the door, slamming it behind her.

Jason sighed and followed her, mumbling to himself as he closed and locked her door. "This is exactly why I didn't want to tell her. Dammit."

He watched as Ruby stormed out of the apartment building. Jack must have spotted her stomping across the sidewalk, because he rushed out after her, calling out, "Ruby, wait!"

Jason felt a knot tighten in his stomach as he watched the two of them outside, hoping desperately that they wouldn't fall into another screaming match.

"I don't want to talk to you, Jack," Ruby said, her voice cold.

But Jack wouldn't let it go. "Wait a minute. I have to say something." He placed a hand gently on her shoulder. "Ruby, I'm sorry I got Jason involved in this. He's a good guy. I don't want to cause problems for you two."

"Really, Jack? If you're not threatening to murder my boyfriend, then you're recruiting him to murder someone else. Can you please stop worrying about me so much?" Ruby said, her frustration clear, though her anger was clearly beginning to diminish.

"No," Jack said, his voice firm. "I can't stop worrying about you so much. But I'll stay out of your relationship. How's that?"

As Jason observed the exchange, he was uncertain whether it would lead to a peaceful resolution or another blowup.

Ruby sighed, her expression softening. "I'll take what I can get. Don't worry, I'm not running off somewhere. I'm only going to go see Tabby."

Jason let out a sigh, glad that the conversation wasn't escalating.

Jack kissed Ruby gently on the top of her head. "Okay. Be safe." He watched her as she walked away, concern etched on his face.

Jason approached with a grin as Jack turned to head back to his apartment. "So, a peaceful conversation for once? That's a good sign, right?"

"She's just upset. She'll calm down," Jack said.

Jason laughed, amused by the whole exchange. "I've seen her upset before, but I've never seen her *that* pissed off. She was furious with both of us."

Jack nodded, a hint of guilt crossing his features. "I guess we deserved it."

Jason agreed, recalling Jack's overly elaborate plan to deal with Brad. "I mean, what were you thinking? How did you figure I wasn't going to eventually tell Ruby what you were planning?"

"In my defense, you did promise not to say anything," Jack countered. "You didn't tell me your word didn't mean shit."

"Yeah, fair enough. You got me there."

Jack's expression turned serious. "You're not involved in this anymore. I promised Ruby."

Jason sighed. "I know. She already made it very clear that I'm not allowed to have anything to do with this.

"Take care, man," Jack said heading back to his apartment.

"Yeah, see ya," Jason said, watching as Jack walked away.

With a heavy heart, Jason trudged back to his own apartment, guilt gnawing at him for the role he had played in all of this.

# 21 Promises

Jason spent Saturday night pacing the confines of his apartment, guilt dominating his thoughts. Ruby's anger still lingered in his mind, and he couldn't shake the feeling that he had disappointed her. With a sigh, he snatched up his phone, hoping that a quick call would ease his conscience, even if she was still upset.

When Ruby answered, her voice was sharp and clipped. "What do you want?"

Jason winced at the irritation in her tone. "Hey, I just wanted to call and make sure you're okay. I know I probably wasn't your favorite person today."

"So, I talked to Tabby," Ruby said, her voice still frosty. "I was surprised to hear that you and Jack told her everything."

"Yeah, I told her, alright? It was a stupid idea, and I probably should've kept my mouth shut ..."

"Anyone ever tell you you're terrible at murder?" Ruby accused.

He sighed, irritation flaring. "I don't have much experience in planning kills."

"That's a good thing," she said.

"I really am sorry for upsetting you. I should've just said no to Jack's plan when he first suggested it. But the more we talked about it, the more I hated Brad for what he did to you. I just wanted him dead if it meant you'd never have to face him again."

"Promise me you'll drop this. No murdering, no threatening, no over-protectiveness." Ruby's voice softened slightly, but the firmness remained.

He sighed. He knew he had messed up and was now on his last chance. "I won't do anything that involves Brad anymore. No threats, no plots, no violence, and no visits whatsoever."

"Let's forget this ever happened, alright?" Ruby said, her exhaustion evident.

Jason cringed, fully aware that he wouldn't ever forget about it. But he also recognized that he had to respect her wishes. "If that's what you want, I won't bring it up again."

"Alright, I'm going to bed. I'm exhausted," Ruby said, her voice fading.

"Yeah, alright. Go get some sleep. You need it," he said, wishing the call had ended on a better note.

After Ruby ended the call, Jason let out a frustrated groan and hung up as well. He tossed the phone, watching it land with a soft thump on the couch. He sank down into the cushions, the reality of his mistake crashing over him. He had been an idiot to go along with Jack's reckless idea, and now he was left with the aftermath—his relationship with Ruby hanging by a thread.

The next day, as the noon sun filtered through the diner's windows, Tabby was already seated at a table, her fingers tapping on her water glass when Jason arrived.

"Hey," he said, sliding into the seat across from her.

Tabby said, "Nice to see you alive and well. Between Ruby finding out about your plans for Brad and Jack finding out you told her about them in the first place, I was a little worried for your safety."

"I don't think I need to worry about Jack. He was more preoccupied with calming Ruby down than plotting my demise."

"Good. So, Jack managed to smooth things over?"

Jason rolled his eyes. "If by 'smooth things over' you mean convincing Ruby to not dump my ass, then yeah, sure, he smoothed things over."

Tabby sighed, relieved.

"I'm never getting involved in murder plots with Jack ever again."

Tabby shook her head. "So, is your bromance with Jack over, or are you two still going to hang out?"

"Our broship isn't quite over, but, right now, we're definitely on rocky waters. Ruby's forbidden me from being involved in the whole Brad thing, and Jack promised to respect her wishes."

"Good. What about Jack? Is he done too?" Tabby asked.

Jason rolled his eyes, still irritated. "Who the hell knows. Last night he said he'd respect Ruby's wishes, but today he'll probably be back to plotting a whole new plan, just without me involved in it."

"So that's how he managed to calm her down? He agreed to drop it?"

"Seemed like more of a temporary agreement than a permanent one. He told her he wasn't going to actively do anything about Brad, just to appease her for now. That's about as good as it's gonna get with Jack."

"Right," Tabby said, her earlier relief replaced with concern.

Jason groaned, his forehead resting against the cool surface of the diner table "I just don't understand how I let myself get involved in the first place. What the hell was I thinking?"

"That's a rhetorical question, right? Or should I answer?" Tabby asked.

"No, actually, you should answer the question. How stupid was I to even agree to Jack's ridiculous idea?" He lifted his head slightly, looking at her with desperation and disbelief.

"I think when I asked you what the hell you were thinking, you told me something about doing what any good friend would do and supporting him no matter what."

"I remember saying that. I'm an idiot, aren't I?" Jason asked.

"Well, probably not your proudest moment. But you're loyal. I'll give you that."

Jason said, "Apparently too loyal. So loyal that I agreed to commit"—he dropped his voice—"a murder to prove a point." Then, he loudly added, "Brilliant, huh?"

"At least you didn't go through with it."

"That's something I'm thankful for at least." He ran a hand through his hair. "Imagine how much worse things would've been if I had gone ahead with it. God, Ruby would probably kill me herself if I did something that idiotic."

"You don't suppose Jack will be satisfied if I tell him Brad is leaving town, do you?"

Jason scoffed. "I doubt it. At this point, Jack won't be satisfied until Brad is six feet under."

"Do you think Brad is smart enough to get out of town before Jack ... Well, do you think Brad can disappear like he said?"

Jason groaned again, frustrated. "I want to say he's smart enough to at least realize that Jack's going to try something. But considering that Brad's an arrogant idiot, I think he'll probably underestimate the situation."

"Yeah, I'm realizing that our plan relies on Brad outsmarting Jack. And well ... let's face it—that's not going to happen."

"Exactly." Jason's head dropped into his hands. "There's no way in hell Brad can outsmart Jack."

"Now I'm worried again," Tabby said.

"Believe me, I'm worried too," he said. "Jack can be pretty determined when he wants to be. That's actually how we ended up with this ridiculous plan in the first place." He facepalmed again.

"I was kinda hoping that Ruby would talk Jack out of it. She knows him better than either of us," Tabby said.

"That would have been ideal. Unfortunately, she's been too busy yelling at me about being an idiot to talk Jack out of his own insanity."

"Even now that you've agreed to drop it?"

"Yeah." He rubbed his temples, exasperated. "I swear I will never understand how women think sometimes. We have one minor argument, and it's the end of the freaking world. Meanwhile, Jack and I have these arguments practically on a daily basis. We fight, then it's over a couple minutes later, and we're friends again."

"I guess it's going to take some time," Tabby said.

"Probably," he muttered. "I honestly hate the whole silent treatment thing. I would prefer her to just yell at me some more and get it over with already."

"Want me to yell at you?" Tabby offered.

He shot her an exasperated look. "Don't you dare. I know you're more than capable of yelling just as loudly and angrily as Ruby does. I do not need that."

"I'm only trying to make you feel better," she said.

"I appreciate that," he said, knowing she meant well. "But I really don't need an angry woman yelling at me right now, even if that woman is you."

Tabby laughed, the sound lightening the mood. "On the upside, now that you're on the outs with Ruby and you've been kicked out of the murder club, I get my best friend back."

A hint of amusement broke through Jason's frustration. "I guess that's an upside. Good ol' BFF Jason is back with no pesky girlfriend in sight."

Smiling, Tabby felt the burdens of the world momentarily eased by their friendship.

Tabby leaned back, crossing her arms. "Trust me. I talked to her. She wants to put this whole thing behind her even more than you do."

Jason's skepticism was clear. "Yeah, right. I highly doubt that she's desperate to move on from this whole 'I agreed to commit a crime on your behalf' situation."

"Honestly, I don't think it was so much about what you two were planning to do," Tabby said. "I don't think she ever dealt with the trauma of what happened to her. It's more about having to face what happened than anything else. Which is probably why Jack wanted to make sure she didn't have to."

Jason felt a familiar frustration. "Trust me, I'm well aware of how Jack is when it comes to any situation involving Ruby's well-being. I wish he wouldn't try so damn hard to 'protect' her. The guy is going to drive himself crazy with how overprotective he is."

"Well, he almost lost her, which was traumatizing for him. I get it."

Jason sighed. "You're right. I actually forgot that he probably dealt with a lot of trauma because of that, too. Even if he didn't have to actually go through what she went through, it still had to be rough on him."

"They're dealing with this the best they can," Tabby said. "Maybe it's good that this is all coming to a head. Or maybe it will end in disaster. Hard to say at this point."

Jason put his head in his hands again. "That's what I'm worried about—disaster. At this point, my main goal is to get out of this whole shitstorm without any of us getting hurt."

"I should probably try to talk to Jack again," Tabby said, her voice tinged with reluctance. "But part of me wants to ignore it, like Ruby. I sympathize with her."

"I get it," Jason said, understanding her hesitation. "This whole situation is a pain in the ass. Trust me, I've considered just saying to hell with it and letting Jack and Ruby deal with their own business. But the idiot inside of me keeps telling me that I should stay involved for some reason."

"That's exactly how I feel."

"I know, right? I feel like I should help deal with this bullshit somehow. Not doing anything feels just as bad as helping Jack with his plan."

"What should we do?" Tabby asked, her voice laced with uncertainty.

"I don't know," he admitted. "What are our options? Do we support Ruby? Do we support Jack? Do we try to go in the middle? Honestly, at this point, I have no idea what the hell I'm supposed to do."

"Have you tried googling how to stop a friend from committing murder?" Tabby suggested, a glimmer of humor in her eyes.

Jason shook his head in disbelief. "No, I haven't. Do you honestly think someone will have written a step-by-step guide for that on some website somewhere?"

"We can't be the first people to have this problem, right?"

"Hey," he said, his irritation rising. "I'm going to tell you right now that if we get ourselves into an even more ridiculous situation after reading some bullshit online, I'm going to be even more pissed."

Tabby laughed, her lightheartedness a welcome distraction. "Maybe the internet is not the right resource. But there's got to be something we can do."

"I don't know," Jason said, frowning. "How the hell are we supposed to know what to do when a good friend of ours is hellbent on doing something like this?"

"Tell his mom?" Tabby suggested.

He laughed at the absurdity of it. "Sure, that'll work. 'Oh, Mrs. West! Your son is planning on committing murder, and I thought you'd like to know!'"

"Well, I would want to know if it was my kid," Tabby countered.

"Okay, we should go tell Mrs. West. Let's see what she thinks of her precious little boy being a psychopath."

"He's not a psychopath," Tabby said.

"Oh, he's not?" Jason shot back, frustration returning. "The guy just casually talks about murder like he's discussing the weather. In my book, that qualifies Jack as a psychopath."

"A week ago, you were doing the same thing," Tabby reminded him, her eyes narrowing.

Jason groaned, not wanting to acknowledge his own idiocy. "Point taken. You're right. A week ago, I was part of Jack's little murder club, and I fully admit to being a complete idiot."

Tabby paused, a spark of inspiration lighting up her eyes. "Wait a minute. That gives me an idea."

"Oh? Let's hear it."

"You were on board with Jack's plan until you thought Ruby might leave you over it. What if I threaten to leave Jack unless he lets it go?"

"Yeah, I'm sure he's going to take that extremely well, and it will totally not backfire at all."

Tabby was unfazed. "It worked with you and Ruby."

Jason argued, "You're right. It worked on me because I'm a bit of a coward about pissing off my girlfriend. But Jack is Jack. The guy might try to call your bluff."

"That's true," Tabby conceded. "I don't think I could lie convincingly. He'd see right through me."

"Exactly. He knows you way too well." Jason leaned back, the frustration mounting.

"Well, you're shooting down all my ideas. What's your genius plan?" Tabby challenged, crossing her arms.

"That's the problem—I don't have a genius plan. Believe me, I've been struggling with that problem all week."

Tabby glanced at the clock on the diner wall, realizing how much time had passed. "It's getting late. I should go see Jack."

Jason nodded, resignation settling in. "Yeah, go talk to Jack and keep me updated."

"I will. Try to relax."

Frustration wrapped around him. "Easier said than done, but I'll try."

With that, Tabby stood and walked out of the diner, her footsteps echoing behind her. Jason sat alone for a few minutes, the din of the restaurant fading into the background, but the stress remained, a constant pressure on his shoulders.

Jack opened the door to his apartment, a smile spreading across his face at the sight of Tabby. Her presence always brightened his day, but today something felt off. As she entered, he studied her expression, searching for the warmth he usually found there.

"Hey darling. How was lunch with Jason?"

"Lunch was good," she said, her voice steady but lacking its usual cheer. "Everybody's worried about you."

Jack's heart sank, anxiety gripping him as he closed the door. "Why's that?"

Tabby's eyes met his with a seriousness that made him uneasy. "Well, I heard what happened with Jason and Ruby. That Jason told Ruby about the murder plan, and how pissed she was."

Jack nodded, as the memory resurfaced. "I guess I should have expected that. But I told Jason not to tell anyone, especially Ruby."

"Well, he knows Ruby would never forgive him if he didn't tell her," Tabby said.

He sighed, frustration forming beneath the surface. "I suppose you're right. But I didn't want her to know. It will worry her too much."

"I know that," Tabby said softly.

"I want to let it rest, but it's eating away at me. I can't stop thinking about how this guy is going to walk free. I can't stop thinking about how he could come back to hurt any of you."

"I know," Tabby said, her voice softening even more.

He didn't want to disappoint Tabby, but the urge to protect his family was overpowering. "I want you to understand where I'm coming from. I've already failed to protect Ruby once. I can't let that happen again. And I'll do whatever it takes to keep you and the baby safe. Even if that means doing something not so legal."

"Maybe I feel the same way about you," she said, her eyes fierce with emotion. "Maybe I'd do whatever it takes to keep you safe."

Jack was surprised by her protectiveness. He reached for Tabby's hand, squeezing it gently. "You would?"

"Yes," she affirmed. "I don't care what happens to Brad. I'm worried about what's going to happen to *you* if you go through with it. Whether you get caught or not, I don't want you to bear that burden."

He felt love and guilt at her concern as he looked into her eyes. "I appreciate how much you care about me. But I can handle it. I can live with myself if I have to do something drastic to keep our family safe."

"Jack, you're a good person," she said, her voice filled with conviction. "You won't be able to shrug off taking someone's life. No matter what the reason."

Uncertainty clawed at Jack's insides as Tabby's words hung in the air. She was probably right. He had never been a violent person—the mere thought of taking someone's life made him sick. But the protectiveness for her and their unborn child surged within him. "I know it would change me. But I can't sit back and do nothing. I have to do something to protect you and the baby."

"I won't let you throw your life away," Tabby said, her voice firm. "I'll kill him myself before I'll let you do that."

The absurdity of her statement almost made him laugh, but when he looked into her eyes, he saw the seriousness etched on her face. She meant it. "Whoa! You would not kill someone."

"I would if it meant you didn't have to," she said, her determination unwavering.

He shook his head vehemently, overwhelmed with affection and worry. "No, absolutely not. You're not killing anyone, darling. Especially not for my sake."

"Well, you're giving me no choice," she yelled. "It's the only way to stop you from doing it."

Jack stared at her in disbelief. "You're serious? You'd be willing to kill someone to stop me from doing it?"

"Yes," she said. "You're not the only one who would stop at nothing to protect the people you love."

He felt a mixture of love and concern at her fierce determination. It touched him she cared enough to say this, but it also frightened him. "You realize murder is a felony offense, right? You would go to prison for me."

"I definitely realize that. Why do you think I'm so determined to stop you?"

He shook his head again, both moved and frustrated by her stubbornness. "Jesus, what is it about me that's worth going to prison for?"

"I love you," she said simply.

The significance of her declaration settled around them. "You're crazy, you know that?"

"No crazier than you are," she replied.

Affection and exasperation flooded his heart. He reached over, grabbing her around the waist, pulling her close. "You're the most infuriatingly stubborn woman I've ever met."

"And you're the most infuriatingly stubborn man I've ever met."

He settled her comfortably onto his lap, burying his face in her hair. He inhaled the familiar scent of jasmine. "You've got me there."

Tabby hugged him tightly, and he held her close, cherishing the warmth of their embrace. "You would really kill a man for me?"

"I would. Please don't make me though, because then we'll have to be apart," she said, her eyes serious.

He shook his head, still grappling with shock and affection. Gently cupping her face in his hands, he said, "I don't want you to ever have to do that. I can't lose you."

She kissed him, and he responded, running a hand through her hair.

"I love you," he said.

As Tabby took his hand and led him toward the bedroom, a spark of excitement ignited within him. He followed her, kicking off his shoes and unbuttoning his shirt in anticipation, grateful for this moment shared with the woman he loved.

The next day, Jason got a text from Tabby—"Call me when you wake up." It was around noon when Jason stirred from sleep and glanced at the message. With a resigned sigh, he tapped the call button.

"Seriously? You slept 'til noon?" Tabby answered, her tone one of disbelief and amusement.

Jason hated the judgment he could hear in her voice. "If I want to sleep until noon, I'm going to damn well sleep," he snapped, trying to sound more defiant than he felt.

"Grouch! Hey, I was considerate. I texted instead of calling this time," she said cheerfully.

"So considerate. What a good friend you are," he muttered.

"I *am* a good friend. You're welcome," she said.

"Wow. I'm so lucky to have a friend as kind and considerate as you. However will I repay your kindness?"

"You can buy me lunch. I have news. Meet me at Franco's."

Jason glanced at the clock, realizing it was indeed close to lunchtime. "Sure, I'll be there soon. See you in like twenty minutes."

Tabby was already at the diner when Jason arrived.

He slid into the booth across from her. "So, what news do you have?"

"I convinced Jack not to go through with his Brad plans."

Jason's eyes widened in disbelief, and he groaned, baffled yet hopeful. "You actually convinced him to drop the whole thing?"

"Yeah, I did."

"Oh, thank god. You have no idea what a load off my mind that is. So, how did you convince him to drop it?" he asked, a hint of dread in his voice.

"Well, I don't think you'll approve of my method, so we don't need to get into the 'how' of it all," she said, avoiding his gaze.

"Oh boy. Yeah, by the look on your face, I can already tell I'm not gonna like this. What did you do? Please don't tell me you did anything stupid, like threaten to break up with him."

"No, no. Not that," she assured him.

Jason waited for the punchline. "Come on, just tell me what you did to convince him."

"I um ... I told him I refused to let him throw his life away and that I would deal with Brad myself before I let that happen ... And I wasn't bluffing."

Jason facepalmed, and lowered his voice to a hiss. "You threatened to commit murder to convince him to not commit murder? Am I understanding that right? That's what you went with?"

"It was the only way," Tabby insisted.

He groaned, struggling to process this information. "Jesus, I'm not sure if that is brilliant or completely insane."

"Well, obviously he's not going to let me go to prison for him, so he had to let it go. It only worked because he knew I wasn't lying."

"Wait a minute. You're telling me that you were completely serious? Like, you actually would have done that to someone, just to prevent Jack from going through with his plan?"

"That's what I'm telling you."

Jason facepalmed again, his mind reeling. "Oh my god. I ... I don't even ... that's just ... God damn—going straight to threatening to carry out the plan yourself just doesn't seem like a sane solution to the problem."

"Well, you shot down all my sane solutions. So what was I supposed to do?"

He paused, unable to counter that. "I just didn't think you'd be willing to go that far. I thought you'd maybe get pissed at him and storm off or something."

"No, I wasn't pissed at him. I understand exactly why he felt he had no other choice to protect us, because I felt like I had no other choice to protect him."

"I suppose I get that. But what if Jack had still refused to drop his plan after that threat? What was your next move going to be?" Jason asked.

"Then, I would have done it myself—dealt with Brad—so Jack didn't have to."

For a moment, Jason sat in silence, realizing she was serious about everything she had said. "I'm not arguing that Jack would be throwing his life away if he went through with it. I'm fully on board that he would be a complete idiot if he did. Not arguing that at all. I'm just saying that you were willing to commit murder for him. You'd kill someone to save Jack. That's just ... Jesus, that's intense."

"Are you forgetting that you also agreed to kill Brad?" she countered.

He realized she had a point. "I never said I wasn't being insane. In fact, I'll readily admit that I was stupid as hell for going along with that plan."

"Well, now nobody has to kill anybody," Tabby said, relieved.

Jason nodded, starting to come down from the shock of the conversation. "Good. That's good. I'm glad nobody is going to do that, because it would have ended very badly for everybody. I mean, we have enough problems in our group already. We don't need to add a criminal investigation to the list."

"Has Ruby forgiven you yet?" Tabby asked.

He realized he was about to dive into a whole different mess. "No, she's still kinda pissed at me," he admitted, running a hand through his hair. "And honestly, she has every right to be."

"Please don't tell her how I got Jack to let it go. I don't want to be added to her shit list," Tabby said.

"Yeah right—I wouldn't dare mention your strategy. Ruby doesn't need to know your methods for dealing with Jack."

Tabby ordered a blueberry muffin, the server nodding as she scribbled down the order. Jason decided to go for another coffee, relishing the warmth of the cup in his hands.

"To be honest," he said, "I think we're all a bunch of batshit crazy fools."

"You're definitely right about that," Tabby agreed, amusement in her voice. "At least we have each other's backs, though."

"That is one positive side of being stuck in a friend group full of crazy idiots."

"Let's get together again, the four of us," Tabby suggested. "But not the skating rink this time."

He groaned at the memory. "Oh god, yeah. We all need a do-over on that one. Let's just steer clear of that disaster spot."

"How about the jazz club?" Tabby proposed, her enthusiasm infectious.

Jason perked up at the idea. "That's perfect. No disasters will happen at the jazz club. That's a much better idea."

"Great! I'll go pitch the idea to Jack and Ruby, and we'll pick you up. I'll text you when we're on our way."

He nodded. "Sounds good. I'll be ready when you text."

With that, Tabby grabbed her muffin and headed out, leaving Jason to finish his coffee in peace. He took a moment to enjoy the bustling mood of the diner before gathering himself to head home, feeling a little lighter knowing plans were in motion.

That evening after a short drive through the city, they arrived at East Side Beats. The building exuded charm, with its warm glow and inviting entrance, and Jason could hardly wait to step inside.

As they entered the club, Jason was captivated by the relaxed atmosphere and gentle hum of conversation that enveloped them. The soft glow of dim lighting and the sound of smooth jazz filled the air, creating an intimate setting that put him at ease.

"Wow, this place looks great. I like it here," he said as they made their way to a cozy table nestled in the corner.

After settling in, Jason was compelled to share his thoughts. "So, I'm just going to state that this is a much better location for a night out. This place blows the skating rink out of the water," he announced, his voice brimming with satisfaction as he leaned back in his chair, a grin plastered on his face.

"Could you please shut up about the skating rink?" Tabby snapped with exasperation.

"Fine. I'll stop. No more talk about the skating rink. Got it," he said, feigning surrender.

Jack said, "Well, we may as well talk about it, since Jason's obviously never going to shut up about it."

"Oh, I see how it is. You're gonna blame me for the fact none of us can stop talking about the skating rink, huh?" he asked, pretending to be offended.

Jack took a moment to address the group. "Anyway, everyone is obviously tense about the skating rink because that's when I recruited Jason into my plans. I admit it was somewhat ... irresponsible. But it's also when I developed a respect for him. So ... there's that."

Jason burst into laughter, shaking his head in disbelief. "Gee, thanks, Jack. It's good to know you developed respect for me only as we were hatching that absolutely insane plan," he said, still chuckling at the absurdity of it all.

"Well, it was at that moment that I realized how serious you are about protecting Ruby."

Ruby spoke up. "Maybe we should all promise not to kill anyone for Ruby's sake."

Jason nodded, considering the idea. "I would feel a lot safer going forward if we could all agree to not do anything stupid. Let's make a promise to not harm anyone for Ruby's sake." He looked around the table.

Jack held up three fingers, sincerity in his voice. "Scout's honor. I promise not to kill anybody."

Jason raised his own fingers into the Boy Scouts salute. "I promise not to harm anyone for Ruby's sake. Scout's honor," he declared.

Tabby added, "I'm not a Scout, but I promise if he does." She gestured toward Jack.

Jason said, "So, we're all agreed then. No one is going to kill anyone for Ruby's sake."

Ruby shook her head, disbelief etched on her face. "I absolutely cannot believe that was necessary," she said, her voice tinged with incredulity.

Jason said, "To be honest, neither can I. But I feel a lot better knowing we're all on the same page now, regardless." Jason was relieved to see everyone getting along again. "So, looks like the topic of murder is officially taboo, huh?" he said.

Tabby shot him a teasing look. "Why, Jason? Somebody else you'd like to kill?"

He rolled his eyes. "No, and thank god. I don't think I'd survive another murder plot after the last one. You were all out of control."

Jack said, "It didn't help that you kept telling everyone."

Jason glared at Jack. "Thanks for pointing out the obvious, jackass."

"Can we please talk about something else for once?" Tabby asked.

Jason nodded. "Gladly. I'm sick of hearing about it, to be honest."

Ruby piped up, shifting the topic. "Let's talk about the baby! Jack, have you told Mom and Dad yet?"

Jason snickered at Ruby's boldness, enjoying the discomfort it brought Jack. "Come on, Jack. Have you broken the news yet or not?"

Jack looked uneasy. "No. Didn't seem right to tell them over the phone."

"Jack, they live three hundred miles away," said Ruby. "It's not like you'll be seeing them around the neighborhood anytime soon. You have to call them."

Jason relished Ruby's relentless teasing. "I mean, you can't avoid the call forever, right?" Jack's discomfort was tangible, and Jason leaned in, ready to tease him further. "Don't want to tell your parents that you got your girlfriend pregnant, huh?"

Jack said, "To be honest, I haven't even told them Tabby and I are dating."

Jason blinked, surprised. "Wait, you haven't?"

Jack shrugged. "They never asked. I usually say: Ruby's fine, work's fine, and talk to you later."

Jason looked at him incredulously. "And you never thought to mention that you're in love with Tabby and that she's pregnant with your kid?"

Jack shrugged again. "Never came up."

"You've been dating for a while now. How the hell does that not come up? I mean, don't your parents ask about your love life?" Jason asked.

Jack scoffed. "No. Are you saying yours do?"

"Yes, my parents ask me about my love life. Is that such a weird thing?"

Ruby interjected, "You told me you don't even get along with your parents, Jason. I very much doubt you've told them we've been sleeping together."

Jason sighed, realizing she had a point. "Alright, so I don't exactly share my love life with my parents."

Tabby said, "Wait a minute. Are you saying your parents asked if you were seeing someone and you haven't told them about Ruby?"

Cornered, Jason said, "Fine—I haven't mentioned Ruby to them just yet." He sighed in aggravation, sensing the conversation was about to open up a whole new can of worms. "And okay, fine—I lied and told them I was single. Happy?" he said, his tone tinged with frustration.

"Why didn't you tell them?" Tabby asked.

Jason responded with defensiveness. "I've got a complicated relationship with my parents. They're judgmental assholes who tend to criticize every goddamn thing that goes on in my life. They'd just tell me my relationship is doomed to fail. Is that a good enough answer?"

Ruby turned to Jack. "I know—let's all go on a trip to Pennsylvania together. Then you can introduce them to Tabby and tell them you knocked her up in person."

Jason looked at Ruby. "Seriously? You want to travel three hundred miles just to witness Jack get chewed out?"

"Heck yeah. He's never been in trouble with Mom and Dad before. I can't miss this," Ruby declared.

Jason laughed, the absurdity of the situation playing out in his mind. "I'll admit that is gonna be pretty entertaining to witness."

Jack responded dryly, "Yeah, super fun. Can't wait."

Tabby tried to offer some reassurance. "I'm sure it will be fine. I've always got the impression you and your parents are really close."

Jason snorted in response. "They're real close alright. He's always been the perfect little soldier to his parents. They've never even been cross with him a day in his life."

"Pretty much," Jack agreed, his voice flat.

"Well, now you can join the rest of us in the 'Disappoint Your Parents' club," Tabby said. "Do you really think they'll be mad, though? I mean, you're twenty-eight. Weren't they much younger when they had you?"

"They were like twenty, twenty-one—something like that. But they were married. So, there's that," Jack explained.

"Maybe you should marry Tabby," Ruby suggested.

Jack's reply was firm yet gentle. "I'd really like to make that proposal without an audience, if you don't mind."

"Yeah, okay," Ruby said. "But we're all still going to Pennsylvania, right?"

Jason snickered at Ruby's unrelenting enthusiasm for witnessing Jack's impending downfall. "Oh yeah, I'm not gonna miss a single second of it," he said, a grin spreading across his face.

Jack sighed, clearly resigned to the situation. "Sure. I'll put in for some time off work and tell them we're coming for a visit. I'm sure they'll be thrilled. Tabby?"

Tabby's response was laced with sarcasm. "Of course. Meeting the future in-laws who have no clue I exist. What could go wrong? Count me in."

Jason watched Tabby, amused by the way she embraced the chaos. The whole situation felt like a bizarre game, and he was all in for the ride.

The server approached their table, and they ordered drinks.

"Now that the most important business is out of the way, we can enjoy our night out, you know, like normal people," Jason said, ready to embrace the evening ahead with his friends.

As the music played, Jason felt a warmth in his chest, grateful for the laughter and the bonds they shared.

# 22 Fractures

Jack made the long drive to their family's farmhouse in Pennsylvania, a place brimming with the echoes of their childhood. Along for the trip were Ruby, Tabby and Jason.

As they approached the familiar old house, Ruby said, "It's been so long since we've been back home. Feels weird to be here again."

Jack nodded in agreement, his gaze sweeping over the landscape that had shaped him, taking note of the subtle changes. "Yeah, it's different, but so much still feels the same," he said, his thoughts wandering through a flood of old memories.

Tabby nudged Jack. "Let's do it. Let's go meet your parents."

Jason, straightening his shirt, said with impatience, "Let's get this over with."

Ruby shot him a look, her voice tinged with annoyance. "Over with? We drove four hours to get here. You realize we'll be here for a while, right?"

Jason sighed, resigning himself to the extended stay. "Yeah, I know we're going to be here a couple days."

Jack led the group to the front door, knocking confidently. It swung open to reveal his mother, Kate, an attractive woman dressed in jeans and flannel, her hair the same shade as Ruby's, pulled back in a casual ponytail.

Her face brightened at the sight of her children. "Jack, Ruby, you're here," she said, pulling them into a warm embrace before inviting everyone inside.

"Mom, this is my girlfriend, Tabby. And that's Jason," Jack said.

"It's nice to meet you both. You want anything to drink? Eat? I made banana bread."

The mention of banana bread brought a collective smile. "Banana bread. That sounds great," Jack said as they all settled around the kitchen table.

As they snacked, Jack asked, "So, where's Dad?"

"He's working in the fields. You know your father. He'll be in as soon as he's done," Kate answered, her hands busy serving more bread.

"Right," Jack responded, hesitation in his voice.

Ruby said impatiently, "Jack's got big news, right Jack?" She nudged her brother playfully.

Kate's interest was immediately piqued. "What news, Jack?"

Jack felt a sudden twist in his stomach. "Well, Dad should be here for it," he managed to say, hoping to delay.

Kate's expression turned from curious to concerned. "Well, he won't be in for another hour. You can go ahead and tell me."

Encouraged by Jason's nudge, Jack mumbled through a mouthful of banana bread, "Tabby's pregnant."

The room seemed to pause. Kate, clearly processing the news, said, "I'm sorry. Did you say that Tabby's pregnant?"

Tabby took a bite of her bread, looking equally guilty.

Ruby added, "Yup, Jack knocked up his girlfriend. Bet you never expected that from him."

Kate, obviously still reeling from the shock, asked, "How long have you known?"

Jack, wiping crumbs from his lips, said, "A while."

"A while? You've known for a while that you're going to be parents and didn't think to mention it?" Kate's tone was one of astonishment mixed with a hint of hurt.

Jack shrugged, a defensive humor in his voice. "You didn't ask."

Turning her attention to Tabby, Kate asked, "How far along are you?"

Tabby, cornered, admitted, "Um ... like ten weeks now."

Jack quickly added, "We were trying to wait until the second trimester before we told anyone."

Kate nodded, her initial shock giving way to understanding. "That's smart. Probably for the best."

"So, you're not mad?" Ruby asked, a trace of disappointment in her voice.

"No, I'm not mad. Surprised. Caught off guard. But not mad," Kate affirmed, then turned to Tabby with genuine warmth. "Congratulations."

"Thank you," Tabby sighed, relieved.

After a moment, Kate said to Jack, "Can I speak with you alone for a moment?"

"Sure, Mom," Jack agreed, rising to follow her.

Ruby piped up, "Can I come too?"

"No," Jack said firmly, leaving Ruby to pout as he and his mom stepped away to talk privately.

Jason sensed Ruby's irritation as he awkwardly commented on the banana bread in an effort to lighten the mood. "So, uh ... what on earth is in this banana bread? It's delicious."

Tabby, sitting across the table, said with a touch of sarcasm, "So, this isn't awkward at all."

Ruby crossed her arms. "I can't believe I came all the way down here and I don't even get to see Jack get his lecture."

Seeing an opportunity to inject a bit of humor into the situation, Jason suggested, half-jokingly, "Maybe we can listen in a little."

Tabby looked at him, clearly incredulous. "What the hell is wrong with you?"

Jason said, "What? This is the best entertainment we could hope for." He then moved closer to the door of the study, trying to catch snippets of the conversation between Jack and his mother. Despite the tension, Jason found himself oddly entertained by the whole setup, his earlier reluctance giving way to a curious fascination with the family's interactions.

In the other room, Jack sat across from his mother. "So, uh. What'd you want to talk about?" he asked, trying to sound casual, despite the conversation ahead.

Kate's expression was serious. "Are you sure this is what you want? I mean, I don't know if you've thought this all the way through. Being a parent is incredibly hard. Do you know how you're going to provide for a baby? And if you're still living in the city? Where will you even put a baby in your apartment? That's a whole other question. Are you even living together? How serious is this relationship?"

Jack felt the pressure mounting as he said, "We're going to buy a house in the city. Obviously, this relationship is pretty serious. We've been together ... almost ... three months now, I guess." As he spoke, he became aware of how flimsy that timeline sounded in the context of their conversation.

Kate shook her head in disbelief, her voice rising slightly. "Jack, you've known this girl three months and you impregnated her?"

Jack shrugged. "It just kinda happened, okay?"

Kate leaned forward with a look of disbelief, searching his face. "It just kind of happened?"

Jack nodded, trying to maintain his composure. "Yup. Can we go back in there now?" He eagerly sought an escape from the heavy conversation and his mother's scrutiny.

Jason stood by the study door with Ruby, both straining to catch snippets of the conversation from the next room.

"What are they saying?" she whispered, her eyes wide with anticipation.

"Shhh," Jason said, raising a finger to his lips. "I'm trying to listen."

Ruby edged closer, tilting her head to better capture the muffled voices seeping through the door.

Jack pushed the door open, not expecting to find Jason and Ruby on the other side. The door hit them with a soft thud as it swung open.

His eyes narrowed slightly as he looked at them. "You were listening?" he asked, his voice tinged with disbelief.

Jason, glancing at Ruby's guilty expression, quickly jumped in to take the blame. "Well yeah, but ... it's not like we could really help it ... the door just ... wasn't shut ... all the way," he stammered, trying to sound casual.

Jack rolled his eyes and moved past them to take a seat next to Tabby.

Ruby, seizing the moment to shift the focus, asked her mom, "Did you lecture him?"

"Sort of," Kate said, giving Ruby a look that promised more details later. Ruby gave a thumbs up, temporarily satisfied.

Jack turned to his sister. "Enjoying yourself?" he asked.

Kate, looking uncomfortable with the direction of conversation, quickly changed the subject. "Why don't you tell us about this new house, Jack?" she prompted.

Grateful for the diversion, Jack's face lit up as he began describing the property. "It's a single-family home in a nice neighborhood. It has four bedrooms, a huge yard ... I think you'll really like it."

Jason said, "Yeah, and it's got an in-law suite that Jack is totally not going to use as a kill room."

Jack shot Jason a glare. "Shut up," he snapped, not appreciating the humor.

Kate, ignoring the comment, pressed Jack further. "Four bedrooms? That sounds like a big house. How can you afford it, Jack?"

"I make good money, Mom. It's fine," Jack said, his tone firm yet trying to remain respectful.

Unrelenting, Kate turned her inquisition toward Tabby. "And what do you do for a living?"

"I'm a librarian," Tabby answered politely.

"How much does that pay?" Kate continued, her tone indicating she was far from done.

"Mom, stop," Jack said, his annoyance growing.

Kate continued, "What? I'm curious about how my son is going to be able to afford a big, expensive house in the city. Especially with a baby to support."

At that moment, Jack's father, Scott, entered the room, dressed in well-worn work clothes. He bore a striking resemblance to his son. Tall and sturdy, he had dark hair and deep-set dark eyes. The tension was unmistakable. "Why do I suddenly feel like I've missed something big?" he asked.

Jack introduced Scott to Tabby and Jason before Kate could explain the situation.

"Jack has ... an announcement," she managed to say, looking unsure.

Scott looked puzzled. "What kind of announcement?"

Jack blurted out the news. "Tabby's pregnant and we bought a house in the city."

Scott's reaction was one of sheer astonishment. "When did this happen?"

"Like, August, September," Jack responded vaguely.

"You got a girl pregnant and bought a house in the span of three months?" Scott questioned.

"Pretty much." Jack shrugged, trying to appear nonchalant.

Scott, after a moment's hesitation, beamed. "I'm going to be a grandfather?"

Ruby, looking disappointed and confused, lamented to her dad, "You're not going to yell at him?"

"What good would it do? It's done. The baby is coming. And I'm going to be a grandfather," Scott responded, his grin widening.

Kate, still somewhat shocked, asked, "Can you all, um ... give me a moment alone with Jack? I need to talk to him in private."

"Again, Mom?" Jack grumbled. "What is it now? Just say whatever you have to say."

But Kate persisted, looking at Tabby. "Sweetheart, would it be alright if I speak to Jack alone? Just for a moment."

"Of course," Tabby said, and Jack reluctantly followed his mother out of the room, grumbling as they went.

Jason, watching the unfolding drama, whispered to Ruby, "It's like watching a car accident in slow motion."

Ruby, shaking her head, said, "I wish they'd stop leaving. Can't really eavesdrop with Dad here."

Back behind the closed door of the other room, Jack turned to his mother, anxiety and frustration etched on his face. "Now what?" he asked, bracing himself for the coming conversation.

Kate met his gaze with a seriousness that made Jack uncomfortable. "When exactly did Tabby get pregnant?" she asked, her tone direct and unyielding.

Jack hesitated, wishing she would get to the point. "Um ... right away. Soon after we started dating," he said.

Kate pressed on. "Do you think Tabby got pregnant on purpose?"

Jack felt a surge of anger rising within him. "She didn't do this on purpose. It was an accident. A stupid, stupid accident," he snapped, his frustration spilling over.

Kate's voice trembled slightly. "Tell me you've considered the possibility, at least. Do you think it could have been intentional?"

"No! I don't think it was intentional!" Jack yelled, his agitation growing with each passing second. "And I didn't consider the possibility either, if you must know. Why is it so hard to believe that this pregnancy was an accident? I'm an idiot, I screwed up and we made a baby. That's it. That's the entire story."

Kate's expression was one of disbelief. "You've only been dating this girl three months. You barely know each other. I can't fathom you not taking precautions."

Jack exploded, his voice rising to a yell. "I don't know! We were careless, if you want to know the truth. We didn't take any precautions. I was an idiot! Is that what you want to hear me say? That I was stupid? That I screwed up? Well, there—I said it! You happy now? Does that make the situation more believable?"

In the kitchen, Ruby's voice cut through the air. "Well, that was loud and clear. No eavesdropping necessary at all."

Tabby glanced at Ruby. "I don't think your mom is thrilled," she said.

Scott offered a rational take. "Maybe it's shock. This all happened so fast. I don't blame her for being caught off guard."

Tabby appreciated his attempt to defuse the situation, but the tension remained thick.

The mood shifted abruptly as Jack stormed back into the room, visibly irritated. Tabby instinctively reached out, full of concern.

"Everything okay, sweetheart?" she asked, hoping to soothe his anger. His sharp reply—"Everything's fine. Totally fine"—did little to reassure her. His irritation was unmistakable.

Kate, seated nearby, shot Jack a sideways glare as he settled down. Tabby sensed the tension escalating even further, and Scott glanced back and forth between the two, his discomfort obvious. Kate was clearly wrestling with her own emotions, knowing she had crossed a line but seemingly struggling to let it go.

Scott diverted the conversation toward Tabby, in a clear attempt to avoid the brewing storm. "So, Tabby, what do you do for a living?"

The question felt like a lifeline, and Tabby seized it. "I'm a librarian," she said, hoping he wouldn't inquire about her meager salary.

Scott's face lit up with genuine interest. "A librarian? That's wonderful. My mother was a librarian at the public library for years. Do you work at a public library, too?"

His enthusiasm was contagious, and Tabby felt a rush of pride. "Yes, I work at the Leveret Municipal Library. It's a wonderful job."

Scott gave her an admiring look. "There's something very special about working in a library. My mother absolutely loved it. She said it was like spending every day in paradise."

Ruby interjected, "Oh, so you approve of Tabby's job, huh? How come you never say nice things about me working at the garden center?"

Scott rolled his eyes, clearly exasperated. "First of all, it's a different situation. The fact that you work at a garden center isn't exactly something to write home about."

Tabby jumped to Ruby's defense. "I know Ruby works really hard and she's great at her job, too."

Scott shrugged. "I'm sure she's great at whatever it is that she does there. But being a librarian is a skilled profession. Working in a greenhouse is ... not the same."

Ruby shouted, "Dad, it's literally what you taught me to do. Look at this place. You raised me on a goddamn farm, for Christ's sake."

Scott shook his head, his disappointment evident. "I'm sorry, Ruby, but I can't figure out why you're wasting your life at the garden center. It's never made sense to me."

Tabby, sensing the tension, interjected awkwardly, "This banana bread is really delicious." She looked at Jack for help, but he still seemed to be annoyed, his thoughts no doubt lingering on the earlier conversation with his mother.

Jason leaned over to Ruby, whispering, "I can't tell if this is the most uncomfortable evening of my life or the most entertaining."

Ruby, shifting gears, said loudly, "Why don't we show Tabby and Jason around the farm."

"Great idea," Jack said, grabbing Tabby's hand and immediately leading her out the front door, with Ruby and Jason following closely behind.

Once they were outside, away from the charged atmosphere around Jack's parents, Tabby turned to him. "So, your mom's not very happy, I take it?"

Jack shook his head, frustration etched on his face. "No. I think it's fair to say that you're currently not her favorite person. She pretty much said she thinks you got pregnant on purpose to trap me."

Ruby said, "I thought it'd be Dad who'd be mad. But he already seems to really love you, Tabby."

Jack nodded. "He seems excited about the whole baby thing. It's Mom who's being the problem."

Tabby suggested, "Maybe we should tell her about the murder plot. She doesn't realize things could have gone a lot worse."

Ruby added, "It's kinda not fair, Jack. Tabby was the one who talked you out of doing something supremely stupid like committing murder, and she can't even take credit."

"Yeah, I'm sure it'll make Mom feel so much better to know how close I came to killing someone. Then she'll be totally cool with everything," Jack said.

"This is so disappointing," Ruby said. "They don't blame you at all—Dad's thrilled, and Mom blames Tabby. Typical. You're such a golden child. I bet you could tell them about the murder plot, and you still wouldn't get a lecture."

Jason added, "Yeah, your dad would probably say, 'Good job thinking it through and then not doing it. You have so much common sense.'"

"Let's let Mom cool off," Ruby suggested. "We can go to the tavern in town."

"Yeah, let's go to the tavern. I can use a drink right about now," Jack agreed.

"Me too. Even I could use a drink after that conversation," Jason said.

Tabby hesitated, then said, "Yeah, I could use a ... glass of orange juice, I guess."

Ruby patted her on the shoulder sympathetically.

Jason said, "You can't drink alcohol since you're pregnant, right, Tabby?"

Ruby snapped, "Of course she can't drink alcohol. Are you a total dumbass?"

"I was just asking! I didn't want to assume. I'm still learning all the damn rules," Jason defended himself.

Jack, clearly eager to escape the awkwardness, gestured toward his car. "Can we please get the fuck out of here?"

As they arrived at the parking lot of the One Twenty One Tavern, a sense of relief swept over Jack. "Finally, some peace and quiet," he said, stepping out of the vehicle.

However, as they walked through the entrance, he could sense Tabby's unease. Her expression spoke volumes as she surveyed the dilapidated building and the rough crowd milling about. "Charming," she remarked, her voice dripping with sarcasm.

Jack rolled his eyes at her playful jab. "It's not exactly a fancy country club. It is what it is," he said.

Jason inspected the décor, his eyebrows raised in amusement. "It's certainly ... interesting, that's for sure. Look at that mural over the bar. Is it *trying* to be depressing? I literally can't tell."

"Let's get a table," Ruby suggested, and they all sat down around one near the bar.

"I'll get our drinks," Jack announced. He made his way to the bar, ordering a round of Mike's and an orange juice for Tabby. As he waited for the drinks, he observed his friends taking in their surroundings.

Jason scanned the room shaking his head. "Yeah, I have to say, this is probably the sketchiest tavern I've ever been in."

"It's no jazz club, but they do have a jukebox," Ruby said.

"This will definitely be a memorable visit, if nothing else," Jason said.

"Welcome to the country, city boy," Ruby said.

Jack returned with drinks in hand, setting them down on the table. "What's the matter, Jason? Not classy enough for you?" He took a sip of his drink, enjoying the moment. "Were you really expecting some sort of upscale bar in the middle of the country?"

Ruby's expression shifted, her eyes darting across the room. "Oh shit! I think I see someone I know," she said, her voice suddenly tense.

Jack turned around, concerned. "It was your brilliant idea to come back here, sis. Who do you see?"

Before Ruby could answer, a man approached their table. "Ruby West, right?" he said, smirking.

Ruby's discomfort was obvious. "Yeah, Dylan. Long time no see, huh?"

Jack immediately stood up, positioning himself protectively between Ruby and Dylan. "Hey, Dylan. I'm Jack, Ruby's brother. I don't think we've met."

Dylan extended a hand, and Jack shook it, but he could sense something off about the guy.

"Hey, man. How's it going? It's nice to meet you." Dylan said.

Jack tried to wrap things up. "Yeah, man. See you around." He waited for Dylan to leave, but the other man lingered.

Dylan laughed awkwardly. "Yeah, for sure." Then he turned back to Ruby. "See you around. Take care."

As he walked away, Jack felt a knot of tension. "Who the hell was that?" Jack asked, turning back to Ruby, who looked unsettled.

"He went to our school. He was in my year. A real dirtbag," Ruby said.

Jack noticed Dylan glaring at them from across the room. "He's still looking at us. You sure there's nothing else you wanna tell me about him?"

"No," she insisted. Ruby shook her head, but her nervous demeanor told Jack that there was more to the story.

"That's not exactly convincing," he said, his protective instincts kicking in.

"He's still staring at you, Ruby," Jason said, his tone serious.

Jack made a decision. "I'll take care of this." He strode over to Dylan's table, his demeanor calm but firm. "Hey, Dylan. What's going on?"

Dylan put on a show of innocence. "What do you mean? I'm having a couple pints with the guys. That's all."

Jack nodded at Dylan's friends before turning back to him. "Want to tell me why you're staring at my sister?"

Dylan feigned surprise. "I was staring? Oh, sorry about that. I didn't even realize I was doing it. I was spacing out, sorry."

"Shit," Ruby muttered, approaching Jack. "It's okay, Jack. Let's just finish our drinks."

But as they started walking away, Dylan called out, "Hey, Ruby! You're looking good. You're even prettier than before. I didn't get a chance to say a proper hello before your brother interrupted us."

Sensing Ruby's discomfort, Jack felt a surge of protectiveness. "Back off, alright?" he warned Dylan, his voice low.

Dylan laughed, waving a dismissive hand. "No need to be hostile. I'm just being friendly. Calm down."

A few tables down, Tabby turned to Jason, her eyes wide. "Jason, you should help Ruby with Jack."

"Yeah, you're right. I'll handle it," Jason agreed, standing up and moving to Jack's side. "I just wanted to say that if you know what's best for you, you'll back off. Stop staring over here. You're making us uncomfortable."

Dylan continued to feign innocence. "Making you uncomfortable? I wasn't doing anything. I swear, I'm just having some beers with the guys. Relax."

Jack shook his head in disbelief. "Cut the crap, alright? You've been staring at Ruby since we walked in here."

Dylan stood up, looking Jack in the eye. "Alright, sure. I'm sorry if I stared at her a little too long. I swear I didn't mean anything by it. I just couldn't take my eyes off her, you know what I mean? She's looking smoking hot tonight."

Jack grabbed Dylan by the collar and shoved him hard. Dylan stumbled back, and Tabby muttered, "Oh shit."

Ruby, clearly shaken, bolted for the door.

Jack turned to Jason. "Go after Ruby, okay?" Jason nodded and took off after her.

Dylan glared at Jack, unfazed. "Come on, I just said your sister's hot. I was complimenting her. There's no need to get violent."

Tabby came over and tugged on Jack's arm. "Let's go, Jack."

As Jack took Tabby's hand and turned toward the exit, Dylan stepped in front of them. "I'm just talking here."

"Do you want to move out of my way?" Jack demanded.

Tabby suggested, "Maybe we should sit back down and finish our drinks."

"Yeah, come on," said Dylan. "You should listen to your girlfriend. Relax and finish your beer, alright?"

Jack looked between Tabby and Dylan, feeling the tension rising. "Move out of the way."

Dylan didn't budge. "I'm not moving until we shake on it. Quit being such a hothead and shake my hand before you make a scene."

Jack's voice dropped dangerously low, each word laced with tension. "I'm going to ask you one more time to get out of my way."

Tabby sensed Jack's frustration boiling over. "Can we just leave, please?" she pleaded, her eyes darting between Jack and Dylan.

Dylan finally relented, shoving his hands into his pockets. "Alright, alright, but tell your boyfriend to relax," he muttered, stepping aside.

With a swift motion, Jack grabbed the door and threw it open, his rage unmistakable as he led Tabby out of the tavern. As they stepped into the cool air, he glanced over to see Jason and Ruby leaning against the car, their expressions a mixture of concern and curiosity.

"You okay?" Jason asked, worry etched on his face.

Ruby asked, her tone cautious, "You didn't kill him, did you?"

Jack shook his head, the anger still boiling beneath the surface. "No, but I should have. The dude was asking for a beating." The words hung in the air, and a heavy tension settled on Jack's shoulders.

"Can we please go?" Tabby asked with impatience.

As they were about to get into the car, Dylan stepped through the tavern door, calling out to Jack, "Hold on a minute."

Jack turned to face him, his irritation clear.

Dylan halted, spreading his hands in a gesture of goodwill. "Listen. I'm sorry for what happened in there. I didn't mean to stare. I was just admiring your sister. I didn't mean any disrespect. I just think Ruby is hot. You can understand that, right?"

Jason took a step forward, his jaw tightening. "You're clearly not intelligent enough to know when to shut your mouth and walk away. I'm giving you one more chance. Walk away."

Dylan's grin widened, an unsettling mix of arrogance and anger flashing across his face. "Or what?"

"Or I'm going to kick your ass," Jason said, his voice firm.

Jack stepped in front of Jason, feeling the tension escalate. "Go back inside, Dylan."

"Oh yeah? Are you going to have your pal kick my ass? Or are you gonna do it yourself?" Dylan asked.

Jack shook his head, his anger rising. "I am so tired of your shit, man. And I wasn't in a good mood tonight to begin with."

Dylan feigned innocence, spreading his arms wide as if genuinely surprised. "Whoa, take it easy, alright? All I wanted to say was your sister is looking mighty fine tonight. That's all."

In an instant, Jack's patience snapped. He grabbed Dylan by the arm, spinning him around and locking him in a chokehold.

"Jack, stop it!" Jason rushed over, trying to intervene.

"Don't worry. I'm not going to kill him," Jack said, his grip unyielding.

"Jack, you need to stop right now. You're letting him get to you. You need to calm the fuck down," Jason insisted, his voice laced with urgency.

"I'm totally calm," Jack said, though he didn't loosen his hold on Dylan.

Jason looked him squarely in the eye, his expression serious. "No, you're not. You're letting anger take control. Let him go, Jack."

Jack leaned closer to Dylan, his voice low and threatening. "Dylan, I promised my sister I wouldn't kill anyone. I don't want to break that promise, so you're going to go back inside and chill out." With that, he released Dylan, who crumpled to the ground, gasping for breath.

Jason knelt beside Dylan, concern etched on his face. "You alright?"

From the ground, Dylan rubbed his throat and shot Jack a glare. "Just great," he muttered sarcastically, his bravado dimmed.

Jack turned away, marching toward the car. "Let's go."

Jason followed Jack, climbing into the back seat while stealing glances at Dylan, still sitting on the ground, visibly shaken. Once Tabby and Ruby had settled in, Jack started the engine and drove off, the air filled with tension.

"You sure went a bit overboard," Jason remarked, breaking the silence.

"Overboard? Seriously?" Jack snapped, incredulous.

"Dude, you practically strangled the guy," Jason said.

"He's lucky I promised Ruby not to kill anyone," Jack said, his frustration still simmering.

"Yeah, but you didn't need to act like a psychopath. You could've just kicked his ass and left it at that," Jason countered.

Jack shook his head, his grip on the steering wheel tightening. "He pissed me off, okay?"

Jason sighed. "I get it. You wanted to defend Ruby and your family. I respect that. But you gotta control your temper."

"Are you serious, man? I was the very picture of restraint. He was asking for it," Jack argued, his voice rising.

"I know he was asking for it, Jack. I saw what was happening. But you went way too far. We're lucky you didn't accidentally kill him," Jason said.

The rest of the drive to the farm was silent, each of them lost in their own thoughts, the events of the night lingering heavily.

# 23 Fragmentation

Jack led Tabby up the creaking stairs to his room, a space frozen in time from his teenage years. As they entered, Tabby glanced around, taking in the old trophies and band posters that still adorned the walls.

"So, this is your childhood room?" Tabby asked, a hint of amusement in her voice.

Jack was struck by a sense of nostalgia. "Yeah, it hasn't changed much since I left. Looks exactly the same as it did when I was a teenager."

Tabby nodded. "So. That was an interesting night."

Jack sighed deeply and sat down on the edge of the bed, the mattress squeaking under his weight. "You could say that. Sorry you had to see me lose it like that."

Tabby's gaze softened as she sat beside him. "Jack, I think it's time to deal with what happened to Ruby."

Jack looked at her, a flicker of surprise crossing his face. "What do you mean?"

Tabby exhaled, concern on her features. "I mean the trauma of Ruby's suicide attempt. You never dealt with it."

Jack remained silent for a moment, his eyes downcast. "I don't know what you expect me to say, Tabby. I was scared to death when Ruby tried to kill herself. I thought I was going to lose her."

"I know," Tabby said gently. "But you can't rid the world of dirtbags. They'll always be out there. And you have to learn how to deal with them without killing them."

Frustration crept into Jack's expression as he stood up and began to pace the room. "You think I don't know that? I'm trying my damned best to keep my temper under control. I am. But sometimes it gets the better of me. Like tonight."

Tabby wrapped her arms around him in a comforting embrace. Jack hugged her back, his body tense with pent-up emotions.

He buried his face in her hair, his voice muffled. "I'm trying so hard here, Tabby. I really am. But it's so damn hard. It's like I have this fire inside of me and I can't control it sometimes. Especially when I see someone I care about hurting."

After a long moment, Jack pulled away, his face set with resolve. "I'm going to check on Ruby," he said.

Tabby nodded, watching as Jack exited the room, his steps heavy with the burden of unresolved pain and a fierce protectiveness for his sister.

Jack approached Ruby's room, his heart heavy with concern. Jason stepped out, giving them the privacy they needed. As Jack entered, he found Ruby sitting on the edge of her bed, her posture tense.

"How are you?" he asked softly, hoping for a glimpse of light in her eyes. Ruby didn't answer. "Are you mad at me?" Jack ventured, sensing the distance between them.

"I'm not mad," Ruby said. "I'm sick of you worrying so much about me. Sick of you getting violent with everyone that hassles me."

Jack's frustration surged. "Sorry, I can't help it ... I care about you, and I want you to be safe."

"I know," she said, her voice softening slightly. "But I worry about you too. I worry you're actually going to kill someone one of these times."

He sighed, rubbing his forehead as if to ease the pressure building there. "I'm not trying to kill anyone. I just can't control myself sometimes."

"Jack, you could have killed Dylan. You can't choke out every guy that leers at me."

Jack let out a frustrated sigh. "You don't understand. When I see someone harassing you, I can't help but react. Sometimes, things get out of hand."

"Out of hand?" Ruby echoed. "That's what you call almost killing someone?"

He rubbed his forehead, exhaustion etched on his face. "Look, I didn't mean to go that far. But when I see someone disrespecting you, it ... it triggers something in me. Can't you understand that?"

"Jack, what would have happened to that guy if you hadn't promised me not to kill anyone?"

Jack's face hardened at her question. "Don't ask me that." He glanced away, guilt flashing across his features. "I ... I don't know. I wasn't thinking. I was only reacting." Shame made it hard to meet her gaze. "Sometimes ... sometimes I scare myself."

Ruby sighed, her voice firm yet gentle. "You need to stop."

Jack shook his head, vulnerability in his eyes. "It's not that simple. Whenever I see someone threatening you, my mind goes dark. It's like everything else disappears. All I can think about is protecting you, no matter what."

"I don't know what to say to that," Ruby admitted, her voice soft.

Frustrated, Jack stood up and left the room, closing the door behind him. But the conversation lingered in his mind.

In the hallway, Jason leaned against the wall. "Did she talk to you?"

Jack nodded. "She wants me to stop reacting violently to people who hassle her."

"Yeah, I can't say I'm surprised by that. Your reaction to people giving her a hard time is getting kind of out of control, you know?"

"I know," Jack said.

Jason's expression became more serious. "Do you? You seriously need to take it down a few notches before you do something you'll regret."

"You saw what happened. You know I did my best to walk away. That guy wouldn't let up," Jack countered, frustration rising to the surface.

"Yeah, I know. I'm not saying that guy wasn't a jerk, but you don't need to be threatening to kill every guy who so much as talks to Ruby."

Jack said, "He wasn't only talking to her. He wouldn't leave her alone. And I never threatened to kill him."

Jason snickered. "Threatening to beat him to a pulp was equally unhinged, you know?"

"You're the one who threatened to kick his ass. I only made sure you didn't have to."

"Clearly there was no need to kick his ass while you had him in a chokehold. You can kill someone doing that," Jason pointed out, annoyance in his voice.

Jack's jaw tightened. "Well, I didn't have my gun on me. What would you have preferred?"

"I would have preferred you not act like a goddamn psycho."

"I'm going to check on Tabby. Take care of Ruby," Jack said, brushing past Jason.

"Will do. Keep your psychotic behavior to a minimum from now on, alright?" Jason called after him.

Jack turned, anger flaring in his chest. "Listen. Someday, someone is going to hurt someone you love. Really hurt them. And you're going to hate yourself for not going psycho and eliminating that threat sooner."

Jason's eyes narrowed. "Sure, if someone was actively hurting someone I love, I'd probably go at them like a maniac. But that's a lot different from what you've been doing to people who are just talking to Ruby."

Jack's expression darkened. "I'm getting a little sick of your judgment. And if someone tries to hurt her, you'd better put a stop to it by any means necessary, or you'll wish you had. Understand?"

Jason scowled. "Dude, you think I'm incapable of protecting her?"

"Just do what needs to be done," Jack said, his voice low and steady as he walked away.

As Jack walked down the hallway, fragmented memories flickered through his mind uncontrollably, each one refusing to be silenced. He tried to push them away, but they persisted with relentless intensity.

In one moment, he was reaching out his hand, a moment of introduction echoing hollowly—*Jack, this is Brad. Brad, this is my brother Jack.* The grip of Brad's handshake was strong, the encounter brief. *Nice to meet you*, Jack had said.

Abruptly, the memory shifted. Ruby's worried expression flashed before him, his own words to her trying to provide comfort. *I'll talk to him. Don't worry about it.* Her response, filled with relief, came softly. *Thanks, Jack.*

Then, another sudden flash—Jack's firm declaration: *She wants you to leave her alone.*

His voice came again, this time offering reassurances to Ruby. *It's taken care of. I talked to the police. He won't bother you anymore.*

Another memory intruded, more urgent. Jack's voice commanded, *C'mon. I'm taking you to the hospital.*

Each memory, replaying in Jack's mind, was like a relentless wave of broken promises and hollow reassurances. When he reached his room, he opened the door and slipped into bed, wrapping his arms around Tabby as she slept, unable to quiet his racing thoughts.

The sun peered through the kitchen window, illuminating the breakfast table where Jason sat, half-awake and still groggy. Tabby descended the stairs, her footsteps soft against the wooden steps. Ruby and Kate were already seated, the room full of unspoken tension.

"Good morning, Tabby. Jack's already gone out to help Scott with some work. How was your night?" Kate asked, her voice a warm invitation into the day.

"Great," Tabby said, but her tone lacked conviction, barely masking the unease that lingered in the air.

Jason, sensing the mood, tried to inject some positivity into the conversation. "Good, it was good," he said, hoping to spark some real enthusiasm.

Ruby sat quietly, her fork absentmindedly poking at her pancake, her silence echoing louder than words.

Kate, attuned to the discomfort, attempted to shift the focus. "So, I made pancakes, Tabby. You hungry?"

Tabby's face brightened. "I love pancakes!" she said, although her cheerfulness looked forced.

"There's enough for everyone, so dig in," Kate encouraged.

"Ruby, you need to eat something," Kate said, her concern evident. "You can't live on coffee alone." Ruby continued to poke at her pancake, her gaze distant.

Tabby exchanged a worried glance with Jason, knowing Ruby's silence was far from her usual demeanor.

"Ruby, honey, is everything okay?" Kate asked. Ruby nodded, but her silence spoke volumes.

After they were all done eating, Kate announced, "I have a few errands to run in town. We need some things at the grocery store. Does anyone need anything while I'm out?" Everyone shook their heads, but Kate's eyes lingered on Ruby. "You look terrible. Have you had any sleep at all?"

Ruby sighed with exhaustion. "Actually, I'm really super tired. Is it okay if I go lie down?"

"Yes, of course, honey. You go rest," Kate said, her voice softening. Ruby slipped away to her room, leaving a cloud of worry hanging over the table.

Once the dishes were cleared, Kate headed to the store, leaving Tabby and Jason alone in the kitchen.

"I'm really worried about Jack," Tabby confessed, her voice low.

"I know, me too," Jason said. "He's trying really hard, but his anger seems to have a mind of its own sometimes."

Tabby hesitated before speaking again. "Jason, I need to ask you something."

"Yeah, go ahead," he said.

"Do you think that if Jack hadn't promised Ruby not to kill anyone, he would've killed Dylan last night?"

Jason let out a deep breath. "Honestly ... I think he might have."

Tabby nodded. "We talked about it last night a bit. He admitted that he's struggling to control his anger."

"It's a damn shame." Jason said, shaking his head. "He's a good person, but all that rage is eating away at him."

Tabby shifted in her seat. "How about Ruby? I'm concerned about her too."

"She's not handling things well," Jason admitted. "I can tell she's in a ton of pain, but she won't talk about it with me. It's like she's shutting me out. I'll try talking to her again."

Jason made his way to Ruby's room, where he found her lying on the bed, her face turned away.

"You mind if I sit down?" he asked.

"I don't care."

He took a seat on the edge of her bed, concerned. "So, are you going to eat anything today?"

"Leave me alone. I don't want everyone worrying about me," she snapped, her voice edged with frustration.

"No, I'm not leaving you alone," Jason insisted, his tone firm yet caring. "I'm worried about you. So, I'm going to stay here and bug you."

Ruby buried her face in her hands, and Jason could see the tears slipping through her fingers. He moved closer, his heart aching for her. "Please don't cry. You're killing me right now."

"I ruin everything. I wish I was never born. Then, everyone I care about wouldn't be hurting all the time," she said, her voice muffled.

"Ruby don't say that," Jason urged, his mind searching for the right words. "You haven't ruined anything. I get that you're upset, but don't say things like that."

"It's true," she said.

"No, it's not," Jason said, his frustration growing. "And I wish you would listen to me and stop this self-loathing bullshit."

"Go away," Ruby snapped at him.

But Jason didn't budge. "Sorry, can't do it. You're just going to have to deal with me being here," he said.

Ruby moaned and pulled the blanket over her head, but Jason wasn't deterred. He yanked the blanket off, refusing to let her hide. "Nope, that's not going to work to get rid of me, either."

"What *will* get rid of you?" she mumbled.

"Nothing. I'm going to be stuck to you for the foreseeable future, so you might as well just get used to the idea," he said, breaking through the tension with a smile.

Ruby shook her head. "Anyone ever tell you that you're a real pain in the ass?"

"Not the first time I've heard that," Jason said. "And something tells me it won't be the last. But I can't help myself. I care too much."

"If you won't leave, then hold me and shut up," Ruby said, her voice softening.

Jason moved closer, encircling her with his arms. "That, I can do." The world seemed lighter, if only briefly.

Later that night, Jack entered his room to discover Tabby sitting on his bed, engrossed in his copy of *Stranger in a Strange Land*. She set the book aside and greeted him with a kiss that ignited a rush of warmth within him.

"I should shower. I don't want to get you all filthy," Jack said, as he turned toward the bathroom.

Tabby followed, stepping into the bathroom while he washed away the remnants of the day. He turned to find her undressing. "This is a nice surprise," he said, wrapping his arms around her as she joined him under the warm spray of the shower.

Their lips met again, and Jack savored the moment, his hands gliding down her back, pulling her closer. He kissed her neck, feeling her shiver beneath his touch. With a sudden burst of boldness, he pushed her against the wall of the shower. Her warmth radiated against him, her body responding to his touch.

As Jack kissed her deeply, all his worries washed away. Everything else disappeared, leaving only their shared connection. He picked Tabby up, pinning her to the wall with an urgency that made her gasp. "I want you. Now."

Tabby's moan of pleasure echoed in the small space as they lost themselves in each other. Afterwards, he set her down gently, still holding her tightly against the wall. "I needed that. I needed you. But we should probably get dressed."

She nodded, and together they dried off. Tabby slipped into a comfortable T-shirt and sweatpants before flopping onto the bed, a look of contentment settling over her.

"You look adorable," Jack said as he climbed in beside her. "And, more importantly, you look relaxed."

"You too. If only we could live every moment in each other's arms, we'd always be perfectly happy."

Jack kissed the top of her head. "That does sound like a pretty damn good life. Unfortunately, we probably have to rejoin reality at some point."

Tabby covered her head with a pillow. "No, I don't want to."

With a playful grin, Jack pulled the pillow off her head. "You can't stay covered under a pillow for the rest of your life."

Tabby laughed, her spirit infectious. "Yes, we can." She covered both their heads with the pillow.

Jack chuckled, joining her laughter. "This is all well and good, but we do need oxygen to survive."

A knock at the door interrupted their playful banter.

Tabby groaned. "Reality is knocking."

Reluctantly, Jack climbed out of bed and threw on some clothes that were thrown over a nearby chair. He opened the door to find his father standing there, a serious expression on his face.

"Hey, son. Can I talk to you for a minute?" Scott asked, stepping back into the hallway.

Jack closed the door behind him. "Sure, is something wrong?" he said, concern in his voice.

Scott placed a hand on Jack's shoulder, his grip firm but supportive. "A friend of mine was at the bar last night. He saw what happened and knew I'd want to know, so he called me this morning."

Jack nodded. "Yeah, okay."

Scott squeezed Jack's shoulder. "I know how angry you are about what happened to Ruby, but you need to stop with the vigilante routine now and be responsible. You have a good life with a beautiful wife and a great career. Don't screw it up."

Jack remained silent, contemplating his father's words.

Finally, Scott asked, "Now ... is this over?"

Jack looked his father in the eye. "Yeah, Dad, don't worry. It's over now. I promise."

Scott nodded, looking relieved. "Alright. I love you, son. Don't forget that."

"I love you too, Dad," Jack said, watching as his father walked away, silently hoping he could keep his promise.

When he returned to his bedroom, Tabby was still sitting on the bed.

"Everything okay?" she asked.

"Everything's fine. Come here." He beckoned her over, wrapping his arms around her as she approached. "Nothing you need to worry about. I had a talk with my dad. He needed to give me the 'responsible adult' lecture."

"Oh, so your dad finally lectured you and Ruby missed it. She'll be so disappointed."

Jack grinned back at her. "I'm sure she'll be jealous that she missed what was probably the world's most boring lecture." He sighed, the previous tension easing. "I should go check on her."

"Jason's been watching her like a hawk, but I know you're probably still worried," Tabby said.

Reluctantly, Jack let her go and headed out to check on Ruby. He was leaving behind the warmth of the moment, but carrying Tabby's smile with him as he stepped back into the reality that awaited.

The morning sun cast a gentle glow on the group gathered by the car. Jack stood beside Tabby, Jason and Ruby as they prepared to depart.

Before the four of them got in the car, Kate turned to her daughter, her voice tinged with concern. "Are you sure you're ready to leave? I'm worried about you."

Jack, sensing the anxiety in his mother's voice, reassured her, "Don't worry, Mom. We'll keep her safe." He believed in his words, confident that the strong bond they all shared would ensure Ruby's protection and support.

Scott, stepping forward with open arms, enveloped Ruby in a warm hug. "I love you, sweetie. Call us if you need anything," he said, his voice soft and encouraging.

Kate wasn't done yet. She pulled Ruby into a tight embrace, her maternal instincts on full display. "I love you, honey. And don't you try to shut me out. Call whenever you want," she insisted, her eyes locking with Ruby's in a clear but silent plea for openness.

Jack placed his arm around Ruby's shoulder, a protective gesture that spoke volumes. "She'll be okay, Mom. I'll make sure of it," he promised, trying to infuse as much certainty into his voice as possible.

Jason nodded in agreement. "Yeah, we'll take care of her," he said, reinforcing the collective commitment to Ruby's well-being.

With their reassurances hanging in the morning air, Jack, Tabby, Jason and Ruby climbed into the car, heading back to New Jersey.

# 24 Reprieve

A few days had passed since Jason, Ruby, Jack and Tabby returned from Pennsylvania, and in that time, Jason had made it a point to keep Ruby company at her apartment. He sensed her heavy burden and wanted to help, even if just a little.

One afternoon, as Jason sat at the kitchen table lost in thought, Ruby walked into the room, her expression determined.

"I've been moping inside for days," she said, her voice brightening with a hint of hope. "I think I need to get out to lift my mood. Can we go back to the jazz club together? I want to go back to when the four of us were getting along."

Jason nodded, understanding the need for a change of scenery. "Probably a good idea. The four of us having fun together sounds good!" he said, trying to match her enthusiasm.

"I'm going to shower. Can you invite them?" Ruby asked as she headed off to get ready.

"I'll take care of it" Jason said, reaching for his phone. A knot of hesitation formed in his stomach, thinking about Jack. Their last conversation in Pennsylvania had been tense, and it lingered in Jason's mind.

By the time Ruby got dressed, Jason had finished making the necessary arrangements. He was settled into the couch, waiting for her to finish getting ready.

"How do I look," she asked, emerging from her room.

"You look great. All set to head out?"

"Yeah—let's go," Ruby said, her spirits noticeably lifted.

Jason walked over to the front door and opened it for her. "After you."

Outside, Jack was already waiting for them, leaning casually against his car. They made their way over, and Jason climbed in, feeling the familiar mix of camaraderie and unease that often accompanied their outings. As they drove to pick up Tabby, Jason found himself lost in thought, replaying Jack's ominous warning from their previous conversation.

When they arrived at Tabby's place, Jack parked the car and walked around to open the door for her. The mood was light, but Jason couldn't shake his apprehension. As they drove, Jason could see Tabby appraising him with a look of concern.

Soon they arrived at East Side Beats. As they entered and settled into their seats, Tabby turned to Jason. "What's on your mind? You seem distracted this evening."

Surprised by her observation, Jason sighed. "Am I always that easy to read or something?"

Ruby said, "You've been doing that thing where you rub the back of your neck when you're worried or guilty."

Jason rubbed the back of his neck at her comment. "I guess I do have a tell, huh?"

"How do you think we all know when you're lying?" Tabby said. "Remember, you agreed—no more secrets. So, what's on your mind?"

He weighed his options for a moment, debating whether to share his concerns. Finally, the truth slipped out. "Don't freak out, but Jack said something really ominous to me before and I can't shake it."

Ruby and Tabby exchanged glances, turning their attention to Jack, who shrugged as if he had no idea what Jason was talking about.

"Jack, what did you say this time?" Ruby asked.

Jason interjected before Jack could downplay it. "He told me that someday someone is going to hurt someone I love, and if I don't go psycho and end them, I'm going to hate myself for it later."

Jack nodded in understanding. "Oh, that."

"Yeah, 'Oh, that,'" Jason echoed sarcastically. "You act like it's no big deal. You honestly don't hear how unhinged that sounds?"

"Sorry. I shouldn't have said that," Jack said.

Jason studied Jack's face, unsure whether to accept the apology. "No, you really shouldn't have said it. Because what I'm gathering from what you said is that you think violence and murder is something I should be totally cool with."

"I was upset," Jack said, defending himself.

"Yeah, Jack, I know that. But the point is you were just casually telling me that I'm going to have to get used to violence and potentially murdering someone. And that's not normal."

Jack nodded, seeming to grasp the severity of his words. "You're absolutely right. We're all agreed—no more murder."

Jason couldn't shake his skepticism. "Really? That's a promise you're going to keep, right?"

"Absolutely."

Jason took a deep breath, trying to gather his thoughts. "What if someone does end up hurting someone I love and I can't protect them? What then?"

Jack frowned, and Tabby said, cutting through the tension, "Nobody's in danger. We're all perfectly safe. We don't need to worry about that."

"I know that," Jason said, his voice firm. "But I really don't like Jack's whole warning that I better be prepared to go nuts and become a killer if someone does end up threatening one of you."

Tabby said, "He misspoke. That's all."

Jason sighed again, trying to calm himself. "I know he did. That's not the point here, though. Jack is so okay with the notion of violence and killing that it actually scares me sometimes."

"Jack, apologize to Jason," Ruby said.

Jason shot her a surprised look, not realizing she would intervene. "Wait—you don't have to do that."

"Of course." Jack nodded, then continued, sincerity in his voice, "Jason, I'm sorry I upset you. Won't happen again."

Jason studied Jack for a moment, searching for any signs of dishonesty. Finally, he nodded. "Alright, apology accepted."

Tabby sighed with relief, and Jason glanced over at her, sensing her hope that everything would return to normal.

From there, the night unfolded pleasantly at the jazz club. Laughter and music filled the air, and the tension that had clouded their friendship began to dissipate. Jason was grateful as he watched his friends enjoy each other's company, the earlier heaviness lifting like a forgotten burden.

Tabby felt a flutter of nerves as she knocked on Jack's door. When he opened it, she found him surrounded by boxes, clearly deep in the packing process. Although he seemed happy to see her, there was also a trace of concern on his face.

"What's up? Everything okay?" he asked.

Her spirits lifted at the sight of him. "Yes. I've been packing too—I can't wait to move into our new house." She made an effort to sound cheerful, even though a heavier topic loomed ahead.

Jack's expression brightened in response. "I'm looking forward to that as well. How's the packing going?"

"Almost finished," Tabby replied. "Though some packing will have to be put on hold since we'll be staying at my place until we close on the house." Tabby's tone shifted, taking on a more serious note. "Can I talk to you about something?"

"Of course," Jack replied, as he settled onto the couch with her. "What's on your mind?" he asked, turning to face her fully.

Tabby hesitated, choosing her words carefully. "I was surprised you never mentioned Brad being released from prison."

Jack paused, a flicker of discomfort crossing his features. "What do you want me to say about it?" he asked, avoiding her gaze.

She continued, her voice soft yet insistent. "I thought maybe you could tell me where you were the day he was released. And why he never came back to the neighborhood."

Jack contemplated his response, letting out a heavy sigh as he rubbed his forehead in agitation. Finally, he spoke, his voice low and resolute. "I ... I took care of it. That's all you need to know."

Tabby nodded in understanding, though questions still lingered in her mind. She couldn't bring herself to voice them, not wanting to force him to revisit painful memories. Sensing the burden of his secret, she wished she could lighten it for him.

"Okay," she replied simply.

She wrapped her arms around him, resting her head on his chest, hoping the closeness would offer him some comfort. Jack relaxed into her embrace. In that moment, he conveyed a silent promise of safety amid the unspoken truths that lingered between them.

A few days later, Jason came home from work, feeling drained and ready to relax. He settled into the comforting embrace of his couch, enjoying the peacefulness of his apartment. Just as he started to unwind, his phone rang, breaking the silence. Checking the screen, he saw Jack's name. Considering recent events, he knew this call could lead to any number of conversations.

"Hello?" Jason answered, trying to mask his apprehension.

"Hey, Jason. Tabby wanted me to call you. We're moving into the new house today. We're going to order some pizzas and hang out. Ruby will be there," Jack said, his tone as serious as ever.

The mention of Ruby piqued Jason's interest, easing some of his worries. "Yeah, I guess I could come hang out. Sure."

"Alright. I'll pick you up." Jack's voice was clipped, and before Jason could respond, Jack hung up.

Left in a state of mild confusion, Jason stood up from the couch and tidied his apartment. While organizing some overdue library books, a knock interrupted him. He opened the door to find Jack standing there, his expression as serious as always.

"Hey," Jason greeted, trying to gauge Jack's mood.

"Ruby's down in the car. Ready?" Jack asked.

Surprised by the abruptness, Jason nodded. "Sure. I'm ready."

They made their way to the car, and Jack took the wheel, driving them to the new home. As they arrived, Jason took in the scene: furniture haphazardly arranged, boxes piled high, and an air of chaos that seemed to envelop the place.

"Wow, still working on the move, huh?" he remarked, shaking his head in amusement.

Tabby appeared from the kitchen, wiping her hands on a dish towel. "Sorry about the mess."

"Don't worry about it," Jason reassured her. "You just finished moving!"

Tabby opened a pizza box and said, "The internet's not hooked up yet, so we'll have to talk to each other for entertainment."

Jason glanced at the pizza and grabbed a slice. "I think we can manage that. What are we going to do for fun? Play a game or something?"

Jack said, "We don't have any games, sorry. We actually *will* have to converse."

Jason groaned in jest, taking a bite of his pizza. "Great. We're gonna have to talk to each other. This is a nightmare."

Ruby laughed from her spot on the couch. "Once upon a time, you told me that talking to me was your very favorite thing. It's how you won me over."

"Oh, that was different. Talking to you and being with you is not at all the same as talking to Jack and Tabby."

"What are you talking about?" Jack said. "I'm way more fun than she is."

Jason snickered, shaking his head. "Yeah, sure. More like I'm always scared of you flying off the handle on me."

"Exactly. I add excitement to your life," Jack said.

"You know, I've gotta say, your idea of fun, excitement and entertainment is a little messed up."

"I guess that's why you don't come to the gym with me anymore." Jack shrugged.

"That's exactly why. There's only so many times I can handle that kind of fun before your 'training' starts to make me tired and sore."

"Well, it's a good way to relieve pent-up energy," Jack said.

"I have a much better way to relieve pent-up energy that doesn't leave lasting physical pain whatsoever," responded Jason.

"Okay, keep it to yourself, please," Jack said, rolling his eyes.

Tabby interrupted their banter. "So, I got my ultrasound, and we're having a boy."

Jason's surprise was evident. "A boy? Congratulations! That's awesome!"

Jack said, "She wants to name him Simon. It doesn't really go with West."

Amused by Jack's bluntness, Jason said, "No, you're right. 'Simon West' sounds very strange."

"I could give him my last name," Tabby proposed. "'Simon Delaney' sounds great."

Jason thought about it for a moment. "Tabby, I'm gonna be completely honest. 'Simon Delaney' doesn't sound bad at all."

"It does sound good," Ruby added. "But I think you're forgetting how stubborn my brother is. I'd bet my last dollar that this baby's last name will end up being West."

Jason grinned, "Alright, I'm willing to take that bet. Twenty bucks."

"You're on."

He extended his hand to Ruby to shake on the bet. "Twenty bucks says the baby gets Tabby's last name."

Jack said, "No, because I'm going to marry her before this baby comes, and her name will be West too."

Jason threw his hands up in frustration. "How's a guy supposed to win that bet?"

Tabby mused, "Tabby West? Tabitha West? I don't know, Jack. It doesn't exactly roll off the tongue."

Jason enjoyed watching Jack's words turn against him. "Yeah, Jack, have you considered the fact that Tabby's last name actually sounds better?"

Jack asked, "Delaney? Better than West? C'mon."

Feigning disbelief, Jason said, "Of course it's better than West. Delaney is such a classic last name. West sounds so plain in comparison."

Ruby said, "Wait a minute. You don't like my last name?"

Jason was caught off guard. "I didn't say I didn't like your last name. I'm just saying Delaney is better than West. That's all."

Ruby said, "And they're both better than Michael. It's not even a proper last name. It's a first name."

"Now you're getting way too judgmental about last names here. Are you really going to make me defend the name Michael?"

"Yes! What if I want to name my future son Michael? You expect me to name him Michael Michael?"

Jason burst into laughter. "Yes, Ruby, exactly! I want you to name your kid Michael Michael. It's a unique name, and he'll be the coolest kid on the playground."

Tabby said, "It should definitely be Adam. Adam West."

Jason threw his hands up in desperation. "For the love of god, do not name your child Adam West."

"Why not?" Tabby asked, laughing.

Jason looked at her seriously. "Because it sounds absolutely ridiculous, that's why. He's going to hate you, Tabby. Do not do that to that poor child."

"Fine. What's the point in having a last name like West if you can't have a little fun with it?" Tabby countered.

Jason sighed, shaking his head in disbelief. "Oh, I don't know. So, your kid doesn't grow up to despise you, maybe?"

"Well, what the hell does go with West, then?" Tabby challenged.

Jason thought for a moment. "Off the top of my head, some solid names would be James, Christopher, Nicholas. They all sound good and work well with West."

Jack said, "Jack works with West."

"Yes, Jack, we're all aware your name would go with West, but that's kind of a biased answer on your part," Jason said.

Tabby laughed, "You seriously expect me to name this kid Jack Junior? No, we'll call him Michael. It'll be Michael West and his cousin Michael Michael."

"Now you're just trolling me," said Jason.

"Just call him Simon Delaney West," suggested Ruby.

Jason nodded. "Yes, that! I like that. That's a great name. It's simple and classic. Simon Delaney West. No confusion, no need for a nickname, just a solid name."

Jack agreed, "Sure, sounds great."

Surprised, Jason looked at Jack. "Wait a minute. I didn't expect you to agree with me that easily."

"It's the perfect compromise. She gets Simon, and I get West." Jack shrugged.

Jason ran a hand down his face. "Of course it is. So, basically, you're saying that I still lost the bet because the kid will have your last name?"

Ruby said, "Sounds like I've got twenty bucks coming to me on this kid's birthday."

"I feel taken advantage of," Jason said.

Glancing at his watch, Jack asked, "You kids want a ride home? Or do you want to stay here?"

Jason paused, looking around at the mess from the move and the boxes everywhere. "As tempting as it is to stay here, I might as well go home."

"I want to stay," said Ruby. "My apartment feels creepy now that some stranger is living below me instead of my big brother."

Jason looked at her, surprised. "You don't like your apartment anymore? It's a little too scary knowing a stranger is downstairs?"

"The new people make weird noises at night. It's creepy," Ruby admitted.

Jason frowned, concern settling over him. "What kind of noises are they making? I'm curious now."

"Like scratchy noises. You know—creepy," Ruby said, her eyes wide.

Jason gave her a skeptical look. "Creepy scratching noises?"

Jack shrugged. "Maybe they have a cat."

Ruby nodded. "Okay, yeah. Probably it's the cat, but can't I miss having my brother nearby?"

Jack reassured her, "You're welcome to stay here anytime, Ruby. You don't need to make up stories about creepy scratching noises."

"Wow, Jack," said Jason, surprised by Jack's bluntness. "There's a rare show of empathy. I'm impressed."

Jack asked, "When have I ever not been empathetic?"

Jason rolled his eyes. "Oh, don't give me that crap, Jack. You're about as empathetic as a freaking brick wall."

"C'mon, I'll drive you home," Jack said, motioning for Jason to follow.

Jason nodded and stood up, stretching a little. "Yeah, fine. I'm ready to go."

As Jack maneuvered his car through the quiet streets toward Jason's apartment, he could feel the unspoken tension between them. The night was unusually still, the silence accentuated by Jason's restless observations.

"Jeez, it's pretty dead out here tonight," Jason remarked, his gaze fixed on the darkened scenery slipping past the windows.

Jack glanced briefly at Jason, acknowledging his comment with a nod before returning his attention to the road. The air grew cooler, the atmosphere inside the car thickening when Jason added, "Everything just seems so still and cold."

Jack frowned at these words, an uneasy feeling settling in, but remained silent.

Breaking the brief silence, Jason turned to Jack with a curious expression. "I had a weird thought just now."

"What's that?" Jack asked, his voice steady.

"I wonder sometimes how the hell you and I ended up friends," Jason mused, his tone half-joking, half-probing.

Jack's mind flashed back to the dark, intricate plot they had once shared—the plan to murder Brad—an event that had inexplicably bonded them. He kept these thoughts to himself, wary of revisiting that dangerous memory aloud.

"Seriously, Jack," Jason continued. "Our personalities are so different. How the hell did you and I ever become friends?"

Jack glanced at Jason, sensing the depth behind the casual inquiry. "Ruby," he said simply.

"What about Ruby?" Jason looked puzzled.

"How we became friends. You're dating my sister," Jack clarified, though it wasn't the full story.

"Obviously that's how we met, but that doesn't really explain how the hell we actually became friends," Jason countered, his grin growing as he noticed Jack's discomfort. "What's wrong, Jack? What's got you all uncomfortable?"

"Nothing," Jack muttered, focusing intently on the road ahead.

"Yeah, right. It's totally nothing, just you avoiding eye contact and looking uncomfortable." Jason snickered, pushing for a reaction.

"Dude, I'm watching the road. I *am* driving, you know," Jack responded, a bit defensively.

Jason looked out the window again, his voice softer. "I get it, Jack. You're not ready to admit that you actually enjoy my company. It's a big pill for you to swallow."

Jack let out a small laugh, the tension easing slightly. "Nah, you're cool. I'm glad we're friends."

"You know, you're cool too, Jack. In your own deranged and weird way," Jason said, turning to look at Jack.

"Thanks, man," Jack said as he pulled up to Jason's apartment building. "Here ya go. Thanks for hanging out with us. It was fun."

Jason got out of the car, his mood light. "'Fun' is one word for it. But I'll admit, pizza with you guys wasn't a bad way to spend the evening."

"See ya, Jason," Jack called out as Jason walked toward his building.

Once alone, Jack let out a sigh of relief. Despite Jason's odd behavior and probing questions, he hadn't mentioned Brad. With another glance in the rearview mirror, Jack pulled away and drove home, their shared past lingering in his thoughts.

Jason sat at his office desk, engrossed in the latest work that had landed there. The rhythmic sound of his fingers tapping against the keyboard filled the air as he worked through pages of text. Just as he was about to lose himself in the words, his phone chimed, breaking his concentration. He reached into his pocket and pulled out the device, glancing at the screen. A smile spread across his face when he saw Ruby's name.

Opening the message, he read her simple yet heartfelt words: "Miss you." The warmth that enveloped him was instant and uplifting. "Miss you too," he typed, and hit send, feeling a rush of excitement.

Moments later, another message popped up. "I'm staying over Jack and Tabby's tonight. Want to come too?"

Jason's grin widened at the thought of spending time with Ruby. The tension that had caused him to avoid Jack had also been creating a rift between him and Ruby. In that moment, he resolved to set aside his reservations for the sake of his relationship with her.

He typed back, "Sure, sounds good. Mind if I stop by my place real quick and grab a change of clothes first?"

Her reply was swift, a thumbs-up emoji followed by, "We'll swing by your place later to pick you up."

"Looking forward to it. See ya soon," he texted back, his heart light with anticipation.

Time seemed to stretch endlessly as the workday dragged on. Jason kept checking the clock, impatient for the day to end. When the hour arrived, he sprang from his chair, a newfound energy propelling him home. He packed a change of clothes, then settled into the couch to wait for Ruby and Jack to arrive.

An hour later, he heard the familiar sound of Jack's car pulling up outside. Jason grabbed his things and rushed out to meet them.

"Hop in," Jack called from the driver's seat.

Jason climbed into the backseat, grinning. "Thanks for picking me up. I hope it's not too much trouble."

Ruby beamed at him from the front passenger seat. "It's no trouble at all. Right, Jack?"

"Right. Whatever Ruby wants, Ruby gets," Jack said. "You'll be happy to know that we're all unpacked," Jack continued as he pulled onto the road. "The house is fully furnished. The guest house even has clean sheets."

"Fully furnished means no more boxes everywhere?"

"Tabby's building her nest. Everything's all tidy. You'll see what I mean when Tabby's lecturing you for your shoes not being in the 'shoe spot,'" Jack added.

"Oh, god. The shoe spot? She has a shoe spot now?"

"Give her a break. She's preparing the nest for the new baby," Ruby said.

"I get that. But the shoe spot? It's just so specific."

Ruby laughed, shaking her head. "Just put your shoes where Tabby tells you to."

"Fine, I'll put my shoes in their precious spot. But only to make Tabby happy, not you," Jason said grinning.

"God yes. Please let's keep Tabby happy," Jack said.

Jason snickered. "What's the matter, Jack? You scared to upset the pregnant lady?"

"Yes, I am. My greatest fear is that Tabby will want something from me and Ruby will want the opposite," Jack said.

After they pulled into the driveway and Jason pulled his bag from the backseat, he stepped through the entryway to find Jack and Ruby already removing their shoes at the door. They placed them neatly on the shoe rack.

Jason shook his head as he slipped off his shoes and joined them at the rack. "Yeah, yeah. I get the hint. No more shoes in the middle of the floor."

Tabby stood nearby. "How have you been? I don't see you as much now that we don't live within walking distance."

There was nostalgia in Jason's eyes. "I'm alright. Work's the usual chaotic hell, but other than that, things are going pretty well. It sucks being farther away, though. I miss those random drop-ins."

Tabby said, "I'm surprised you don't come over more often."

Jason hesitated, feeling a twinge of embarrassment. "I don't want to be a third wheel. You guys just moved here, and I know you probably want some time alone together."

Jack said, "Actually, you'd be a fourth wheel. Ruby's here all the time."

Jason turned to Ruby, surprised. "Wait, what? You're here all the time too?"

Ruby said, "Jack's been giving me rides from work. Most of the time, he kidnaps me instead of dropping me off at my apartment, though."

Jack rolled his eyes. "Invites you, not 'kidnaps.'"

"Oh really? Does that mean you've been crashing here every night, Ruby?" Jason asked surprised.

Tabby said, "She practically lives in the guest house."

Jason's eyes widened in amusement. "Guest house? You've got your own little sanctuary on their property? Do you think you might move in permanently now?"

Ruby considered it. "It *is* kinda silly to keep paying rent on an apartment I'm not even using." She sighed. "I'd hate to move away from you, but I'm never there anyway—so I guess that's not a very good reason to keep my apartment."

"It'd be a real shame to miss out on my presence. I'd totally get it if you stayed for that alone."

Jack gave Jason a serious look. "Sounds like it's time for you to get a vehicle. Then you can come here to visit Ruby, and we can be blessed by your presence as well."

Jason nodded. "I know. I seriously need to get a car. My legs could definitely use a break every once in a while."

Tabby teased, "Or you could move into the guest house with Ruby."

Jason nearly choked at the suggestion. "What? Move in with Ruby?"

"Let's not talk crazy," said Jack. "Jason doesn't want to move out of downtown. He loves it there."

Jason nodded in agreement. "That's true. I do like my apartment downtown. Although, I'll admit it has its downsides."

Ruby shot a look at Jack. "Jack, don't pretend you care about what Jason wants. You just don't want me moving in with my boyfriend."

Jason grinned at Jack. "You'd be jealous if I moved in and took away your precious Ruby?"

Jack shrugged. "No, it's just not a good idea. What if you two break up? Then you'd have given up your apartment."

"What? Do you think our relationship is going to implode or something, Jack? And even if we did end things, I doubt either of us would be immature enough to not be able to cohabitate," Jason said.

Ruby's eyes sparkled with excitement. "So, you do want to move into the guest house with me?"

"I'm only considering it because you look so damn excited about it. But you better be real sure about living with me, 'cause once I move in, I'm never leaving."

Jack interjected, "Rent's three hundred a month."

Ruby frowned, turning to Jack. "Didn't you offer to let me stay in the guest house rent free?"

"You're my sister. He's not."

Jason feigned hurt. "So, I have to triple the standard because I'm dating your sister? How cold, Jack."

Jack merely shrugged.

"So, if I do, hypothetically, move in, there's one condition you should know."

Jack shook his head. "I can't wait to hear this."

With a devilish grin, Jason continued, "My new living situation has to have one feature: a pet. And by 'pet,' I of course mean a dog."

Ruby squealed with delight. "Yes! A dog! I want a dog!"

Jason nodded, feeling triumphant. "I knew you'd be excited. So, we're agreed? A dog is a stipulation of me moving in, right, Jack?"

Jack sighed, resigned. "Whatever Ruby wants, Ruby gets."

Jason beamed at Ruby. "You've got him wrapped around your little finger. A dog is definitely happening now."

Ruby hugged Jack, who smiled at her display of affection.

Jason said, "Aw, I see. Jack has a weakness for a show of affection? Duly noted."

Jack said, "It won't work with you. So don't bother."

Jason pretended to pout. "Damn, I can't bat my eyelashes and get you to do what I want? That's a real shame."

Ruby stood up with excitement. "C'mon! I'll show you the guest house. I've got it all cozy."

Jason grinned, following her. "I can't say no to going on a tour with an adorable guide like you."

As they walked into the guest house, Jason took in the space, noting how Ruby had truly made it her own. It was filled with her belongings and smelled distinctly of her—a comforting, pleasant scent that he couldn't quite put into words.

Ruby plopped down on the couch, grinning. Jason took a seat right beside her, his heart light. Sitting together, a warmth filled the room, giving Jason the feeling that this new chapter in his life could be something special.

Jack stood in the living room of their new home with a sense of contentment. It wasn't only the joy of moving into a fresh space that filled him with happiness; it was the thought of Ruby and Jason as neighbors, only a few feet away. The idea of having them close brought a genuine smile to his face.

Tabby, noticing his elation, turned to him with a warm gaze. "You look so happy. I love seeing you happy."

He took her hand. He lifted it to his lips and placed a gentle kiss on the back of her hand. "I am happy," he said, his voice filled with warmth. "With you, in this house, and having Ruby and Jason nearby ... It's perfect."

"I know you like having Ruby nearby, but I'm surprised you're on board with Jason moving in with her," Tabby said.

"I'll admit, I may have had some reservations at first ... but I can't deny her anything. Besides, it's not like I don't trust the guy. He's okay."

"Yeah," Tabby said, but Jack saw a hint of worry flicker across her face.

Concern crept into Jack's eyes. "Is something on your mind? You look concerned."

"I don't want to spoil the moment."

Jack took both of her hands in his, stroking his thumbs over her knuckles. "You can tell me anything. You can spoil nothing."

Tabby hesitated before speaking again. "I was thinking about Brad."

At the mention of Brad's name, Jack's expression darkened, though he fought to hide his reaction. He tried to compose himself. "Why were you thinking about him?"

"I was thinking about how well you and Jason are getting along. I don't want anything to spoil it. Jason hasn't mentioned anything about Brad, but he must be aware that he was released from prison. I feel like the subject is bound to come up, eventually."

Jack let out a slow sigh, his mind racing with thoughts he usually kept buried. He nodded, understanding Tabby's concern, and squeezed her hand. "You don't have to worry about it. If the subject comes up, we'll deal with it then." Jack sat down on the couch, suddenly lost in thought.

"Does Ruby know what you did?" Tabby asked, her voice laced with apprehension.

Jack paused, burdened by his secret, knowing he couldn't lie to her. "She ... probably suspects something. But I've never outright told her."

"We've never really talked about it either. It was obvious you wanted to keep us out of it, so I didn't ask questions, but I also don't want you to deal with this alone. It was while we were in Pennsylvania, wasn't it? The day you were out working in the fields all day with your dad. That's not actually where you were, was it?"

Unable to meet her gaze, Jack looked away, the truth hanging heavy in the air. "No, that's not where I was, love."

Tabby sat down next to him. Silence enveloped them for a moment, but, finally, Jack spoke again, his voice low. "I knew when he was getting out. I thought it would be easier if we were out of town. But then that mess at the tavern happened. When that jerk Dylan wouldn't leave Ruby alone, I ... lost it. I realized I needed to confront Brad. To put it behind me once and for all. I borrowed one of my dad's junkers and drove back to talk to him."

Tabby said nothing, she simply squeezed Jack's hand. She let him talk, giving him the space to express what had been bottled up inside for so long.

"He wasn't surprised to see me," Jack continued, his voice tinged with remembrance. "He said Jason had paid him a visit to try to convince him to leave town. So, I asked him why he didn't leave. He said *payback*." Jack's gaze drifted, lost in the memory. "He straight up told me he was going to make my family pay for the five years he spent in prison."

The silence stretched again, heavy with unspoken words. Finally, Jack concluded the story quietly. "Now he's buried on my parents' farm ... along with the gun that killed him." The finality of his words hung in the air, a burden lifted but replaced with a different heaviness.

Tabby wrapped her arms around him, pulling him close. "I'm sorry for making you talk about it. It's over now. We don't have to discuss it anymore."

Jack held her tightly, burying his face in her hair, inhaling her comforting scent. "It's okay. I'm glad I shared it with you. No more keeping secrets from each other."

In that moment, surrounded by the warmth of their new home and the strength of their bond, Jack felt a sense of relief.

# 25 Consequences

Ruby flung the ball across the yard and watched as the indifferent puppy merely glanced at it before continuing its leisurely exploration of the grass.

"C'mon Tristan, fetch the ball," she urged. She sighed in frustration, finding the simple game more difficult than she had expected.

Meanwhile, Jason approached, hands tucked in his pockets, taking in the scene.

"He won't fetch," Ruby declared, her tone one of annoyance and resignation.

Jason gave a small, understanding smile. "He's still getting the lay of the land. He'll come around," he reassured her. After a moment's pause, he shifted the topic. "So, I've been invited out to the bar for drinks. Do you have plans tonight?"

Ruby looked up as she considered her options. "No," she said.

Jason's face lit up. "Want to come with? It'll be a small group. Just a couple old friends."

"Sure," Ruby said, surprising even herself with how easily the word had slipped from her lips.

"Yeah? Cool. It'll be nice to get you out of the house," he remarked. "The people we're meeting are pretty cool. You'll have fun."

Curiosity piqued, Ruby asked, "Tell me about them."

"Well, there's Matthew and his fiancé, Rebecca. Those two are the cutest couple you'll ever meet. She's kind of a firecracker, though, so she keeps Matt in his place. They're both a lot of fun. It's never boring when those two are around."

"Matt and Rebecca? Another couple? Are they going to pick us up?" Ruby asked, wondering how the logistics would work.

"I figured we could grab an Uber," Jason suggested.

"That sounds good. I'll go take a shower."

"We'll head out in about an hour," Jason confirmed.

Ruby took her time in the shower, letting the warm water wash away any lingering doubts. After she dressed, she emerged, feeling refreshed and ready. Meanwhile, Jason checked himself in the mirror, adjusting his shirt and making himself look presentable.

"I look good, don't I?" he asked, a playful grin on his face.

"You always look good."

He beamed, flashing his perfect smile. "You're right. I can rock anything, I guess." Then, as he glanced at Ruby, he did a double take. "Damn, you look amazing."

"Thanks," Ruby said, feeling a rush of warmth at his compliment. "Is it time to go?"

Jason stared at her for a moment longer before nodding. "Yeah, we should probably get going."

They ordered an Uber and made their way to Fitzgerald's Pub. Upon entering, Jason spotted his friends seated at a table.

"There they are," he said, gesturing for Ruby to follow him.

As they approached, Jason grinned and motioned Ruby forward. "Guys, this is Ruby. Ruby, here's Matt and Rebecca."

"Nice to meet you," Ruby said, offering a faint smile.

Matthew smiled warmly at Ruby. "It's a pleasure, Ruby." Matthew was lean, dressed in designer clothes, with styled sandy hair and sharp features.

Rebecca greeted Ruby with a compliment. "I love your dress." She was tall and slender. She had long brown hair and wore a chic, elegant dress.

"Thank you," Ruby said, feeling a little more at ease as she took a seat next to Jason.

Jason scanned the drink menu. "What does everyone want? I'll grab the first round."

Ruby almost ordered a margarita but hesitated, remembering how Jack had always nagged her about drinking hard liquor. She suddenly missed him, wishing he could be there with them. "I'll have a cabernet sauvignon," she decided.

Matthew said, "I'll have a pale ale."

"A mojito for me," said Rebecca.

"I'll go grab those," Jason said, rising from the table to head to the bar.

As Jason walked away, Ruby turned to the others. "So, you're both friends of Jason?"

Matthew nodded. "We met in high school. We ran in the same social circles. We've been friends for a long time."

Rebecca's eyes glimmered with nostalgia. "He was always that good-looking guy everyone had a crush on. But he's like a brother now. It's impossible to think of him as anything other than that."

Ruby smiled politely, feeling a slight twinge of discomfort. It was strange to talk to people who were close with Jason long before she came into his life.

Ruby watched Jason return to the table, a triumphant grin on his face as he balanced a tray of drinks. He began handing them out with an exaggerated flourish, clearly enjoying the moment. "So, what did I miss? Did you three start gossiping about me?" he asked.

Matthew, leaning back in his chair, chuckled. "Why would you say such a thing?"

"Because you're a troublemaker," Jason said, laughing.

"You're one to talk," Rebecca accused.

"Hey, I am a perfect saint now. I learned my lesson. I don't start trouble anymore."

Ruby rolled her eyes. She wondered how he could make such a claim after the wild scheme he had cooked up with her brother.

Jason caught her skeptical look and tried to read her mood. "What? Yeah, I might still cause a little trouble from time to time, but nothing too reckless."

"'Nothing too reckless.' Yeah, right," Ruby said sarcastically.

"Alright," Jason conceded. "Yeah, I've done my share of reckless things in the past. But I've chilled out. I'm trying to set a good example for you, so you don't get any crazy ideas."

Matthew said, "You do realize the more you deny being trouble, the less we believe it, right?"

Jason raised his hands as if to plead. "Fine, I admit it—I'm trouble. But don't I do a good job of hiding it?"

Matthew shook his head with a grin. "Not really. But we appreciate you keeping things entertaining."

Jason lifted his beer. "Alright, guys, I propose a toast."

Matthew raised his own beer. "What are we toasting to?"

"Friendship," Jason declared, looking around the table. Ruby felt a twinge in her chest as they clinked their glasses together. It felt somehow wrong toasting to friendship without Jack and Tabby by her side. She clinked her glass halfheartedly, her thoughts drifting to the friends who were missing from this moment.

Matthew raised his voice. "Hear, hear. Good friends are hard to find."

"I've had a lot of friends come and go over the years," added Rebecca, "but I'm happy to say that I've made the right choices when it comes to true friends."

Jason took a sip of his beer, and then made a confession. "I have to admit, I was a little worried about this whole night. I haven't done much social stuff like this lately. I wasn't sure if it would be weird. But with you guys, it's easy—like no time has passed at all."

Matthew responded with a reassuring smile. "Good friends always pick up where they left off."

Rebecca nodded in agreement. "No need to worry about us, we're always good company."

Jason grinned. "I never doubted that for a second. Enough sappy friendship talk. Let's have some fun."

Matthew perked up. "Who's ready to play some pool? I'm feeling lucky tonight."

Jason's eyes lit up at the challenge. "That's what I'm talking about. I'm ready to put you in your place."

Matthew teased him, "Big talk from someone who loses every time."

Jason turned to Ruby. "You better be ready to be swooned by my mad pool skills, Ruby. I'm about to impress you."

As Ruby's phone beeped with a new message, she glanced at it and smiled. Jason noticed her expression and couldn't resist asking, "Who you texting?"

"Jack," Ruby said.

"Of course. What's he want?" Jason asked.

"He's bringing home takeout. Wants to know if we want anything?"

Jason rolled his eyes. "Sounds like Jack. He's such a mother hen. Always the uncontrollable urge to nag us about whether or not we've eaten."

Matthew laughed. "He's got that mom vibe going on, huh? Sounds like an interesting dynamic in your group."

Ruby felt a twinge of protectiveness. "He's my big brother."

"So, he's always giving you advice and looking out for you, then?" Matthew continued, seeming genuinely curious about their relationship.

Jason scoffed. "Yeah, something like that. He's got a real bossy 'I know best' attitude. It gets annoying after a while."

Matthew nodded in understanding. "I know what you mean. I'll bet he's always trying to act like he's in charge even if he isn't."

"Exactly. That's Jack. He always has to be the one in control, telling everyone what to do. He can't handle it any other way."

Ruby, growing irritated with the conversation turning into a critique of her brother, responded to Jack's text. "We're good. I'm at the pub with Jason and some friends of his."

Matthew grinned, teasing, "You two sound like the siblings who don't get along but can't live without each other."

Ruby scowled. "My brother is my best friend, okay?"

Matthew held up his hands apologetically. "I'm just a neutral party trying to feel out the family dynamic here. Don't shoot the messenger."

Jason, clearly still curious, glanced at Ruby's phone. "Did he respond? What'd he have to say about us being out and socializing?"

Ruby checked her phone and read Jack's response aloud. "Okay. Love you. Be safe."

Jason scoffed. "Be safe. Like we're not capable of looking after ourselves. See what I mean? It's like he thinks we'll get into trouble without him here to boss us around."

Matthew laughed. "I see exactly what you mean. He can't help himself. I bet he's got the whole group on a short leash, huh?"

"You got that right. He takes over and tells us all what to do for everything."

Ruby, feeling more and more exasperated, redirected the conversation. "I thought you guys were going to play pool or something."

Jason glanced over at the pool tables, shifting the focus. "You're right. We were talking about kicking some ass at pool. Who's ready for a game?"

Matthew stood up. "Let's do it. I'm going to show you who's top dog at the pool table, like I did last time."

Jason called out enthusiastically, "Come on, Ruby. Let's go get some pool cues and teach these kids a lesson."

But Ruby wasn't in the mood. "No thanks. I don't really want to play," she said.

Jason looked surprised at her response. "Come on, I thought you were up for some fun."

"Not a pool player, huh?"Matthew asked.

Ruby shook her head, feeling a bit out of place. "Nope."

"Have a seat then, and watch me kick his ass," Matthew suggested, with a grin.

Ruby grabbed her glass of wine and settled into a chair near the pool tables, deciding instead to focus on her phone. She scrolled through her messages, her attention drawn away from the friendly competition unfolding before her.

Rebecca interrupted her. "Who you texting now?" she asked.

"Nobody," Ruby said quickly, her fingers still tapping on the screen as she sent a message to Jack.

Rebecca pointed at Ruby's phone. "Texting your brother again?"

Ruby put her phone down, feeling a bit caught.

"I can't help noticing that you're on your phone a lot, messaging your brother. You seem really close," Rebecca remarked.

"Yeah. Usually when Jason and I go out, Jack and his fiancé are with us. But Jason and my brother have kind of a complicated relationship," Ruby explained.

"Really? Why is it complicated?" Rebecca asked.

Ruby hesitated. "I'd rather not talk about it."

Rebecca laughed lightly, apparently enjoying herself. "You're getting very cagey all of a sudden. I was just making conversation. I'm intrigued."

"Maybe you should ask Jason about it," Ruby suggested, trying to redirect the conversation.

Rebecca was undeterred. "I don't know if Jason is going to be as fun to gossip with as you. But now you have me curious. Maybe later I'll try to pry it out of him."

"Good luck," Ruby said, knowing all too well that Jason would keep his cards close to his chest when it came to his relationship with Jack.

"Oh, I bet I'll get him talking. I have my ways of getting people to open up," Rebecca said playfully.

Ruby ignored the comment, her focus returning to her phone.

Rebecca laughed. "You really are a tough one. I get it—you're not going to spill. I like that! You keep your friends' secrets. Very admirable."

"Thanks, I guess," Ruby muttered, unsure of what she thought about Rebecca's assessment of her.

Rebecca looked apologetic. "I wasn't trying to be rude or invasive. I'm just one of those curious types who's interested in what's going on with everyone. I wasn't meaning to offend you. I like you—you're cool. Not sure why you're spending your night texting your brother, though. You need some real, live human interaction."

Ruby placed her phone gently on the table, her eyes meeting Rebecca's with sincerity and frustration. "You seem nice. But your fiancé is a bit of a douche. But I suppose I can't fault you for it. My boyfriend's being a bit of a douche himself tonight."

Rebecca's laughter filled the air, a lighthearted acknowledgment of what was clearly a shared sentiment. "You're not the first person to say that about Matthew. But he's a good guy, really. He's just a little opinionated. He can't help himself. He says whatever is on his mind, and sometimes it comes out a little harsh. What makes you think Jason is being a douche tonight?"

Ruby's expression turned somber. "He has no right to badmouth my brother. Jason knows how much Jack has sacrificed for me."

The look on Rebecca's face shifted to one of skepticism. "From the little I've seen, Jason doesn't seem to have the best relationship with your brother. I admit, I'm being nosy, but there seems to be a story that you don't want to share."

Ruby sighed, a trace of nostalgia in her voice. "There was a time when they were really close friends, but ..." Her voice trailed off momentarily before she abruptly said, "Anyway, I miss spending time with them together."

Rebecca probed further. "So, things changed, and they drifted apart?"

"Something like that." Ruby's response was terse, signaling her discomfort with the topic.

"You don't like opening up much, do you," Rebecca said.

"I don't even know you," Ruby said.

Rebecca's laughter broke the tension slightly. "That's the point of getting to know each other, isn't it? Look, I wasn't intending on asking you personal questions. I was just trying to have a friendly conversation. Sorry for being curious. I'll stop pestering you."

Ruby felt a twinge of guilt. "Sorry. I guess I'm out of practice with the whole 'girl talk' thing. My brother's fiancé is really the only girlfriend I've had for a while now."

Rebecca shook her head. "It's alright. I think I just came on too strong. I'm a naturally curious person. I've always wanted to know what makes people tick. It's the psychologist in me. I can't seem to turn it off sometimes."

Ruby leaned forward slightly with sudden interest. "You're a psychologist?"

Rebecca nodded. "Yes. I mostly work with dangerous and volatile criminals. So, you could say that reading and analyzing people comes with the job. I apologize if I was a little too nosy and put you on the spot earlier. It's a habit."

"Are you saying you work with murderers?" Ruby asked.

"I have. I work with all sorts of violent offenders," Rebecca said, her tone unflinching.

Ruby's interest deepened. "Are you able to ... help them?"

Rebecca sighed, her gaze drifting as she contemplated her answer. "It all depends. Some respond well. Others don't. I won't lie—there are certain types of people beyond help. They're too far gone. But some respond well to treatment and are on the right track to rehabilitation. So that's what keeps me going. I like to think I've helped people start fresh."

Ruby's expression turned thoughtful. "What about someone who does a terrible thing but didn't want to? They didn't have a choice. How would you help someone like that?"

Rebecca's demeanor shifted to one of understanding. "I've met people like that. They've committed violent crimes or done unspeakable things, but they didn't have control over their actions. They've been pressured or threatened somehow, or they've suffered a psychotic break or have severe mental health issues that have skewed their mental well-being."

Ruby probed further. "So, how do you help them?"

Rebecca's demeanor shifted back to warmth. "Well, it depends how severe the mental health issues are. If it's a mental illness that a person has been born with, it's not as easy to deal with, obviously. They need to work long-term with a professional who specializes in their specific issues. If it's something like a psychotic break, which is temporary and happens when someone is pushed over their mental limit, then they can be stabilized with medication and therapy."

Ruby nodded, absorbing the information. "And what if they don't get medication and therapy? Can someone still be okay?"

Rebecca paused, considering the question. "If someone doesn't get the mental health services they need, they could be a danger to themselves or others. They might not have the emotional stability or the mental capacity to take control of their life and make healthy decisions. If they don't get the help they need, without a doubt, they will suffer for it."

"I see," Ruby said, a shadow crossing her face as she contemplated the implications of Rebecca's words.

Rebecca studied Ruby intently, seeming to sense that the conversation was touching on something deeper. "Have you known someone who's suffered from mental illness?"

Jason appeared behind Rebecca, leaning casually against the back of her chair. His goofy grin, amplified by a few too many drinks, broke the momentary seriousness. "Are you two having a girl chat? I could tell you're talking about something serious by the way you have such a thoughtful look on your pretty face."

Ruby forced a smile, her thoughts momentarily derailed. "Yeah, girl talk."

Ruby shifted uncomfortably as Jason attempted to inject humor into the moment. "Girl talk, eh? Should I give you two ladies some privacy so you can gossip and have a good old-fashioned pillow fight or something?" he joked with a wide grin.

"Ha ha," Ruby said with a dry tone. "I'm actually really tired. Are you almost ready to go?"

Jason's surprise was evident as he looked at her, the lively sparkle in his eyes contrasting sharply with her weariness. "What? No! The night is just starting. Come on, you can't seriously be ready to go, can you?"

At that moment, Matthew approached, placing a calming hand on Jason's shoulder. "Dude, you need to take it down a notch. Ruby just said she's tired. You sure you haven't had enough to drink?"

Brushing off Matthew's concern with a nonchalant grin, Jason said, "Nah, I'm fine. I've had way more than this before and still been perfectly coherent. I'm having a great night. Why would I want it to end already?"

Rebecca, observing Jason's unfocused eyes and flushed face, chimed in with a touch of firmness. "I hate to break it to you, honey, but you're not exactly 'coherent.' I think you've had enough and the night's over."

Seeing the situation escalating, Ruby said, "Yeah, let's go home." She pulled out her phone to arrange a ride.

Jason's laughter rang out. "You can't be serious. I'm not drunk and I don't wanna go yet. We're still having fun. Right guys?"

"I'm going home. Are you coming or not?" Ruby's voice held an edge of finality.

"Come on, Ruby. Why are you being such a buzzkill?" Jason asked.

Ruby walked away, tapping Jack's number as she moved toward the entrance of the pub.

Jason watched her, frustration evident on his face. "Wait, don't leave. Where are you going?"

Rebecca gently tugged Jason's arm, guiding him to sit. "She's going home. And you're going to finish off your water and get some food in you."

On the phone, Ruby's voice was calm but urgent. "Jack, can you pick me up? I'm at Fitzgerald's Pub."

Jack's voice, groggy with sleep, came through the speaker. "You're at the pub by yourself? Where's Jason?"

Ruby glanced back at Jason, who was reluctantly settling down under Rebecca's watchful eye. "Jason's here. But he doesn't want to leave, and I don't want to take an Uber by myself."

Jack sighed, the sound heavy through the phone. "Damn it. Alright, I'm getting dressed. I'll be there in fifteen minutes."

Relieved, Ruby thanked him and ended the call, ready to leave the night behind her.

Fifteen minutes later, Jack arrived at the pub, his eyes scanning the bar until they landed on Jason. It was immediately clear that his friend was in no condition to be out. "Jesus, he's wasted," Jack muttered under his breath.

Ruby stood beside Jason, her expression weary. "Let's go."

Jack shook his head and approached Jason, who was slumped at the bar. "Hey man, get up. It's time to go home."

Jason looked up, his face breaking into a wide, drunken grin. "Jack! Buddy! There you are. I haven't seen you all night. Where you been?"

Jack said, "I was home, sleeping, like normal people do at one a.m. Come on, get up. Ruby and I are taking you home."

As Jack spoke, Matthew approached, concern etched on his face. "You okay? You're not looking too steady on your feet there."

Jason waved him off with a laugh. "I'm good. I'm great! Why would you say I'm not looking too steady? I'm fine!"

Jack rolled his eyes. "You're not only drunk, you're obnoxious. Shut up and start walking."

Rebecca gave Jack an apologetic look. "Sorry. He's had way too much to drink."

Jack nodded. "I can tell. Damn it, Jason. How many drinks did you have?"

Jason's expression was carefree. "I don't know. Lots, though. That fruity tequila shot was delicious. I had a few of those."

With a resigned sigh, Jack dragged Jason out of the pub, Ruby following closely behind. He opened the back door of the car and shoved Jason inside before taking the driver's seat, Ruby sliding into the passenger seat beside him.

As they drove, Jack's grip on the steering wheel tightened, his knuckles turning white. He stole a glance at Ruby, her face a mixture of frustration and weariness. "What the hell happened?" he demanded, his voice low but edged with concern.

Ruby sighed, the sound heavy with disappointment. "Jason wanted to introduce me to some friends of his. I guess he sort of got carried away."

"Jesus Christ! He's supposed to be looking out for you," Jack said, shaking his head in disbelief. The anger simmering beneath the surface was hard to contain.

From the back seat, Jason chimed in, "I'm having a good night! Why do you have to be such a wet blanket? We're hanging out with friends and having fun. So, I had a few drinks—don't act like you've never gotten drunk before."

Jack gritted his teeth, his irritation flaring up. He shot a glare at Jason through the rearview mirror, trying to rein in his temper. "A few drinks? You're so shit-faced you couldn't even get Ruby home safely. I should kick your ass."

Jason let out a laugh, the sound brimming with bravado. "You'd try to kick my ass? You think you could take me? Come on, let's do it! We can do it right now." His tone was mocking, as if the idea of a confrontation was nothing more than a game to him.

Jack pulled into the driveway, his patience wearing thin. "Go ahead inside, Ruby. Jason and I are going to have a chat."

Ruby nodded, her expression one of resignation and understanding. She slipped out of the car, leaving Jack and Jason alone in the dim light of the night.

Jack got out, opened the back door and pulled Jason out of his seat.

"So, we're gonna fight now, huh? Bring it on. Let's see what you got," Jason said, a self-satisfied grin plastered on his face.

Jack's voice was steady, but his frustration continued to simmer beneath the surface. "You've been trying your best to piss me off ever since Pennsylvania. What is your problem, man?"

Jason leaned in closer, his body language aggressive, the playful facade slipping away. "What's my problem? My problem is that you're always treating me like I'm some worthless prick. You don't respect me, and you're always acting like Ruby can do better than me."

"No, that's not it," Jack shot back, his voice rising slightly. "You've been itching to confront me since we got back to New Jersey. Go ahead, ask your question. I know you're never going to let it go."

Jason stepped even closer, his gaze intense and unyielding. "You wanna know why I'm pissed at you? You really wanna know?"

"I know why you're pissed at me. Stop trying to provoke me into a fight and ask your question," Jack said, his voice low and even, as the tension crackled in the air between them.

"Are you going to answer? Are you going to tell the truth this time?" Jason demanded, irritation lacing his tone.

Jack met his gaze, unflinching. "You already know the truth, don't you? That's why you're so pissed off all the time."

Jason's eyes narrowed, the challenge evident in his posture. "You killed him, didn't you?"

Jack's silence spoke volumes as he stared back at Jason, the unspoken truth hanging heavily in the air between them.

"Answer me, damn it! Don't play games with me. I know you did it. I just want to hear you say it." Jason's voice was low and urgent now as he pressed for confirmation.

Finally, Jack spoke. "Yeah, I killed him."

"Why? Why'd you do it?" Jason asked, his eyes searching Jack's for answers.

Jack's frustration boiled over, emotions spilling out. "Why do you think I did it? He was going to hurt my family. He told me to my face that's what he was going to do."

"Was that the real reason? Or were you angry and wanted revenge?" Jason challenged, his voice rising as he pushed for clarity.

"Oh, fuck off! You think I'd throw away my future with Tabby for revenge?" Jack snapped, the fire in his voice undeniable.

Jason laughed bitterly. "That's a convenient answer. You're sure putting a lot of trust in her to stay with you when she finds out who you really are. Do you even deserve her?"

Jack's expression turned serious. After a long silence he said, "She already knows."

Surprise flickered across Jason's face before he laughed again, incredulous. "Bullshit! She doesn't know."

Jack's gaze hardened, unwavering. "She's known for a long time now. I'm pretty sure Ruby knows too."

"No, they don't know," Jason declared, but doubt crept into his voice. "Then tell me, why haven't they told the cops? Why haven't they ratted you out?" Jason's voice rose with intensity.

"Why haven't you?" Jack asked.

Jason paused, contemplating the question, his bravado faltering. "Touché," he muttered, the fight draining from him.

Jack pressed on. "So, tell me. Why haven't you gone to the police yet?"

Jason hesitated, his gaze drifting to the ground as if searching for answers in the gravel beneath his feet. "I don't know." He looked back at Jack, vulnerability in his voice. "It's not that I don't think you should have consequences. But ..." Jason's expression turned thoughtful. "If I were in your place, I might have done the same thing ... Maybe I'm just selfish. I want the people I care about to be safe. I don't want to lose them. Maybe that makes me an awful person."

Jack remained silent, absorbing Jason's words, feeling the impact of their shared history and the complexity of their emotions.

After a moment, Jason continued, his voice softer now, almost reflective, "And I've had a lot of time to think about this, and I've come to a realization … I've come to think that … maybe I understand you more than I'd like to admit."

Jack nodded, the tension between them easing a fraction. "Go get some sleep," he said, a sense of reluctant camaraderie settling between them.

Jason nodded, his shoulders slumping as he made his way to the guest house. The confrontation left a lingering sense of unease in the air as Jack approached the house.

Once inside, he entered the bedroom, watching Tabby sleep peacefully, the soft rise and fall of her chest a reminder of everything he had to lose. As the hours passed and the first rays of sunlight crept through the window, Jack walked over to the bed and kissed her gently on the top of the head. Silently, he turned and exited the room.

Jack walked to the office and pulled out a piece of paper and a pen from his desk. "Dear Simon …" he began, his thoughts spilling onto the page, words flowing as he tried to make sense of the turmoil inside him.

*If you are reading this letter, you are already much older than I can picture now, as I sit to write these words to you.*

*This life was never what I imagined for myself or you.*

*I am sorry I cannot be the father you need, one who guides, protects and watches over you.*

*Do not let my mistakes define your view of who you can become. You are not your father's choices. You have the potential to make your own path, one that is filled with better decisions and brighter outcomes.*

*I love you, Simon. I always will, no matter where I am. I hope one day you will understand my situation and find it in your heart to forgive me. Until then, live well, my son, and remember that despite my absence, my love will always be with you.*

*With all the love I have,*
*Dad*

After sealing the letter and placing it on the kitchen table, Jack slid behind the wheel of his car and began to drive, meandering aimlessly through the streets. The world outside blurred as he grappled with his tumultuous thoughts. In the end, his journey brought him to the police station, his heart racing with every beat. He sat in the car, contemplating the significance of his next steps, understanding that confession was the only way to free his friends and family from the burden of his secret and allow them to move forward.

After what seemed like an eternity, he mustered the courage to enter the building. Each step laden with apprehension, he approached the front desk officer. Jack's voice was steady, yet heavy with the magnitude of his admission.

"I killed a man," he declared.

The air thickened with the gravity of his words, a sense of finality enveloping him as he braced himself to face the consequences of his actions.

# Epilogue

Tabby stood in her living room, gazing thoughtfully at the abstract painting that hung above the mantle. It prompted her to reflect on the significant changes that had unfolded over the past decade since Jack's incarceration for voluntary manslaughter.

Her once intense desire for thrilling experiences had gradually given way to the responsibilities of motherhood. In her pursuit of drama and excitement, she came to realize that those fleeting moments of exhilaration didn't bring her true happiness. Instead, it was the quiet joys of family life that filled her heart.

Jason's dedication to Simon's welfare extended far beyond the role of an uncle, often stepping into the role of father figure, mirroring Tabby's deep commitment to Simon's well-being. He set aside his desires for a carefree, unattached lifestyle, choosing instead to support his friends and cultivate meaningful relationships.

Not long after Jack went away, Ruby reached out to a psychiatric nurse with expertise in mood disorders, committing herself to the treatment process. When Jack returned, he found that Ruby had embraced her independence—she was no longer reliant on his protection. Instead, she was thriving and confidently navigating her own life, bolstered by Jason's unwavering support.

After facing the consequences of his actions, Jack had begun to heal, taking responsibility for the fallout of his choices. In reconciling his previous failure to protect Ruby, he was finally able to move beyond his past, now fully devoted to his roles as a father to Simon and husband to Tabby.

Suddenly, a memory surfaced in Tabby's mind, one from years ago, Jason's words echoing in her mind: *To me, this painting represents the journey of life. The winding path through the forest is the journey we all take as we move through life, full of twists and turns and unexpected obstacles. The trees represent the challenges we face along the way, and the beauty of the forest is the beauty that we can find in life's journey, even amidst the struggles.*

# ACKNOWLEDGEMENTS

I would like to thank my friends and family who provided feedback and encouragement for this book, Jeffrey Plumadore, Noël Plumadore, Mitrian Yaeger, Tobias Trainor Austin & Emma Lauriat. Special thanks to my editor, Jaclyn Arndt, for providing exceptional professional feedback, ensuring the authenticity and readability of my story.

# About the author

Judy Smith is the pen name of Celeste Plumadore, who was raised in the countryside of Massachusetts. She uses her personal experiences to create engaging stories. This debut novel represents a noteworthy achievement in her writing path, highlighting her distinctive voice and viewpoint. Through her heartfelt storytelling, Judy encourages readers to delve into the intricacies of human experiences.

www.ingramcontent.com/pod-product-compliance
Lightning Source LLC
Chambersburg PA
CBHW020458310726
48979CB00016B/2705/J

* 9 7 9 8 9 9 1 8 5 2 5 0 0 *